KT-151-407

MOLLY'S CHRISTMAS ORPHANS

Carol Rivers, whose family comes from the Isle of Dogs, East London, now lives in Dorset. Visit www.carolrivers.com and follow her on Facebook and Twitter @carol_rivers

Also by Carol Rivers

Lizzie of Langley Street
Bella of Bow Street
Lily of Love Lane
Eve of the Isle
East End Angel
In the Bleak Midwinter
East End Jubilee (*previously* Rose of Ruby Street)
A Sister's Shame
Cockney Orphan (*previously* Connie of Kettle Street)
A Wartime Christmas
Together for Christmas
The Fight for Lizzie Flowers
A Promise Between Friends

MOLLY'S CHRISTMAS ORPHANS

Carol Rivers

**SIMON &
SCHUSTER**

London · New York · Sydney · Toronto · New Delhi

A CBS COMPANY

First published in Great Britain by Simon & Schuster UK Ltd, 2017
A CBS COMPANY

This paperback edition published 2018

Copyright © Carol Rivers, 2017

The right of Carol Rivers to be identified as author of this work has been asserted
in accordance with the Copyright, Designs and Patents Act, 1988.

1 3 5 7 9 10 8 6 4 2

Simon & Schuster UK Ltd
1st Floor
222 Gray's Inn Road
London WC1X 8HB

Simon & Schuster Australia, Sydney
Simon & Schuster India, New Delhi

www.simonandschuster.co.uk
www.simonandschuster.com.au
www.simonandschuster.co.in

A CIP catalogue record for this book
is available from the British Library

Paperback ISBN: 978-1-4711-5488-1
eBook ISBN: 978-1-4711-5489-8

Typeset in Bembo by M Rules
Printed and bound by CPI Group (UK) Ltd, Croydon, CR0 4YY

I'd like to dedicate this book to 'the Forces' Sweetheart',
Dame Vera Lynn, who celebrated her hundredth birthday in
2017, the same year in which Molly was first published.

Dame Vera was born in East Ham, a stone's throw
from the Isle of Dogs, East London, the setting of my novels.
Her remarkable and unique singing voice brought much needed
hope and consolation for our troops and their loved ones
during the turbulent days of the Second World War.

Acknowledgements

As always, I'd like to thank Jo Dickinson and the team at Simon & Schuster, and my agent Judith Murdoch for their help and advice with *Molly's Christmas Orphans*. During the writing of this saga I've listened to many people who have both sweet and sad memories of the 1940s. I marvel at the spirit, fortitude, and sacrifices of men, women and children who lived through the Second World War – which unbelievably, followed the First World War a mere twenty years later. But my deepest gratitude goes to those souls who lost their lives during the bloodshed, yet live on in our hearts and memories.

For more information on my books, newsletter and freebies, please go to www.carolrivers.com or join me on Facebook and Twitter where I love to hang out.

Prologue

London's East End, June 1940

'Molly, love, the PM's on the wireless! Come upstairs and we'll listen to what he's got to say. I've turned the shop sign to "Closed" so we won't be disturbed.'

'Someone's bound to want serving, Dad,' Molly Swift objected, narrowing her observant brown eyes at the busy street outside. 'And it's our customers who come first.'

'Even if Winnie is addressing the nation?'

'Even if it's the good Lord himself.'

Bill Keen smiled ruefully as he approached his daughter, who stood weighing out the potatoes. Very slowly he took her arm and drew her round to face him. 'I know all about our customers, ducks. Your mum and me ran this shop before you was born. So bugger the customers for an hour. Today it's our chance to find out from the horse's mouth just what's going on over the Channel. France is where Ted is, fighting his heart out on the beaches. Your husband, my son-in-law, beloved to us both. So set aside your concerns for the store and its patrons and let's go upstairs.'

Molly understood precisely what her father was saying. But it was these softly coated words she was reluctant to hear; it was far less painful to imagine Ted safe and sound instead of listening to the reports on the Home Service, or reading the upsetting headlines of the newspapers. It was bad enough the customers asking after Ted. She knew they meant well but, poor souls, many were already touched by tragedy. Sometimes they'd come in the shop to buy their ration of tea or jam or a slice of bacon if there was one available, and yet she could tell it was for another reason altogether. Women needed to share their losses. A flicker of hope would ignite in their eyes as they spoke of their soldier or sailor or airman – just as if he was standing there.

Molly had paused on many occasions since war was declared between Britain and Germany in September of last year, to listen to tales of separation and loss, some ending choked by tears, with heads bowed as the spirit of that brave departed soul faded. So she had given a kind word, a hug, a bit of discount here and there, or an extra helping out of her own ration as small compensation.

And always she'd kept the faith – her faith – that Ted, her living and breathing man, would return with his fellows of the brave British Expeditionary Force, not necessarily a hero or with the commendations that every man deserved in this bedlam of war, but alive! This was her prayer. Her hope. Her belief. And as long as she remained behind the counter, giving sympathy to others, she could go on in her world, believing in the very best possible outcome. This store was her and Ted's livelihood, an extension of their combined efforts for the past five years. Surely it could never be taken away?

'Molly, come now, ducks. It's time.' Bill Keen slipped his hard-working, capable fingers around his daughter's arm and firmly drew her towards the stairs.

'Dad, I'd rather not. I have the orders to set up.'

'Orders can wait,' her father objected as Molly racked her brains to get out of the uncomfortable request. Then, tilting his head to one side, he said softly, 'Molly, you are my lovely girl and full of spirit when it comes to running this shop. Ted's been away since November last and you've carried on valiantly. There's not a customer you don't serve with a smile and often a little bit extra. Oh yes, don't think I'm a blind old codger, ducks. I've still got me wits about me, if not me hair.'

Molly smiled, embarrassed to know she'd been caught in the act. 'It's just they've got such sad stories, Dad. With all their men away and having to manage on their own—'

'And so are you on your own,' said Bill, cutting her short.

'I've got you, Dad, don't forget.'

'Why, I'm barely able to lift a sack of spuds these days!' he returned jovially. 'When I sold you and Ted the shop five years ago, I was on me last legs.'

At this Molly laughed, her brown eyes lighting up and reflecting the colour of her thick chestnut hair coiled into a bun at the nape of her neck. 'You were nothing of the sort,' she disagreed. 'You did us the biggest favour of our lives. You knew we had to get our teeth into something after ... after

Emily.' Here she stopped and took a breath. The memories of her two-year-old daughter who had been so cruelly taken from them in the flu outbreak of 1935 were still raw, still bitter-sweet.

'Right, chin up, lovely,' Bill replied staunchly, for Molly knew he had mourned his granddaughter as keenly as she and Ted. 'We'll sit with our sandwiches and listen to Winston,' he encouraged. 'The papers say that 220 of our navy ships and 700 small craft are already sailed for the rescue. I wouldn't mind betting the BEF boys will be climbing aboard this minute. First in, first out – stands to reason, don't it?'

Molly nodded, giving in as she had known she would, before unbuttoning her gabardine overall, looping it over the peg and mounting the stairs to the large and airy flat above.

Molly's stomach clenched the minute she heard the cut-glass accent of the announcer. 'The miracle of deliverance of Allied troops' – as it was so delicately put – 'is now in prog-ress. The operation to bring back thousands of our retreating troops trapped by the German army in Dunkirk, is almost accomplished.'

Molly dared to breathe, though the word 'almost' hung like a scythe in the air, ready to fall. And then it came, the hidden facts, slowly fed to the public. The strategic oper-ations were complete, but not before the Luftwaffe had reduced the town of Dunkirk to rubble and destroyed 235 vessels and 106 aircraft, claiming, so far, at least 5,000 lives.

To add to Molly's confusion, it was revealed a further 22,000 Allied troops had been rescued from other ports: Cherbourg, St Malo, Brest and St Nazaire, including those from the battle-weary BEF units of which Ted was one. Was this the good news she had been waiting for?

'God willing, he'll be home soon,' declared Bill as he sat with his knees spread, leaning forward in his armchair, making a concerted effort to listen to every syllable coming from the walnut-encased wireless set. 'Hear that? Hundreds of boats, love – hundreds! All out there, braving the waves and the gunfire and stealing our lads from the clutches of the sea. Ted could plant his feet on English soil any time now.'

Sitting opposite in her late mother's chair, Molly anxiously clutched the crocheted covers on each stout arm. The feel of them reminded her that if her mother was present this very moment, twelve years after her passing, she'd be offering her own brand of maternal wisdom that Molly missed and needed so much.

'If only your mum was here,' Bill said, echoing Molly's thoughts as he patted his pockets, stood to search for his pipe on the mantelpiece, found it and stuffed it, unlit, into his mouth as he flopped down again. 'She'd be down at the docks this very moment. Checking every face, seeing Ted well in advance of him seeing her.' He laughed robustly, shaking his head, until slowly the smile slipped from his lips and he looked at Molly with questioning eyes. 'It's not too late for us to nip down to the water, love. Check along the wharfs. See where they're disembarking. It's said the Little Boats are bringing them back to nigh on every port in the country.'

Molly slid her hand to her neck, easing the tight muscles with her fingertips. She couldn't wait to hold Ted in her arms, nor to savour the kiss he would lay on her lips when they met. She had no words to describe the expectation of her hopes and dreams. It wouldn't be fair – it just wouldn't – to take Ted away from sharing them too.

'No, Dad. There's a chance we might miss him. I wouldn't want him walking into an empty store without the welcome he deserves.'

Molly averted her gaze and slipped back into the world she had created. A world of routine and reliability. A war might be raging, but she had her shop. Her customers depended on her and she depended on them. It was the only way she knew of existing in a world full of uncertainty.

She would be patient, listen a few minutes more to please her father, then go downstairs, put on her overall and turn the sign. Her customers would come in, one by one, or sometimes in groups, enjoying the meeting place as much as their purchases.

Then, towards teatime, her attention would be taken by a shadow. A figure. The man would come walking up Roper Street towards the shop's front door. A familiar stride; the Blakeys on his boots scuffing the crowns of the pebbles . . . and she'd run out and into Ted's arms and never – ever – let him go again!

'Listen, Molly, will you, it's him! The prime minister of England, by God!'

Molly stirred, only half listening, reluctant to emerge from her dreams. But the defiant words echoed through the speaker of the wireless and stole away her peace.

'We shall defend our island whatever the cost may be.

We shall fight on the beaches, we shall fight on the landing grounds, we shall fight in the fields and in the streets, we shall fight in the hills. We shall never surrender . . .'

'Never,' Bill Keen agreed, with clenched jaw and raised fist. 'Never!'

Suddenly an icy panic filled Molly. 'Never' was such a very long time. And how could she face this 'never' without Ted if, God forbid, Ted's life was the price she had to pay for Britain defending her soil?

BOOK ONE

Chapter One

Six months later, 29 December 1940

Molly was sitting, frozen to the bone, in the hospital corridor where some hours ago, according to the battered wall clock, a nurse had instructed her to wait. In that long eternity of time her mind had been replaying the moments after the bomb had exploded just a short way down from the shop. She could still hear the air raid warden warning her to stay perfectly still. But in her dazed state, she wasn't aware she was covered in rubble.

Her priority had been her dad, who lay prone on the floor of their general store. On top of him were rafters and plaster, leaving a gaping hole in the ceiling.

All the while the plaintive cries from the injured and distressed in the street outside had echoed in through the shattered window. A kind of smog had swirled into the atmosphere. The poisonous stink of cordite had made it almost impossible to breathe.

'Careful as you go, Molly. The ceiling above you is unstable. It could collapse any moment,' Mr Stokes, the warden, had shouted when he realized it was too late to stop Molly from stumbling over to her father's side. She'd been like an animal, burrowing away with her bare hands at the mountain of debris.

With a jolt, Molly returned to the moment and the comparative safety of the hospital. There were so many casualties here! Some managing to walk, all bandaged, bruised and bloodied. Others, the not-so-lucky ones, many suffering from shrapnel wounds and crushed limbs, were being rushed away on stretchers.

Molly shook herself determinedly.

She couldn't weaken now.

She'd suffered tragedy six months ago, losing Ted at Dunkirk, and yet somehow she'd held on to life. At first she'd lost all interest in the store, the business she and Ted had worked so hard to build up after Bill's retirement. She'd gone through the motions, giving the customers what sympathy she had left, but she felt drained dry. Emotionally she hadn't much left in reserve. And if hadn't been for her dad – well, she might very well have faded away.

'Rise and shine, lovely,' he would say every morning, attempting to fill Ted's place the best he could. 'We've work to do. Let's get the blinds up and the sign turned.'

And so, where once she had sprung from bed eager to start the day, instead she'd crawled reluctantly into her clothes, plastered a smile on her lips and pretended. Just as she had done after Emily five years before.

Shivering again, a combination of winter's cold and shock,

Molly pulled back her shoulders. It was her dad who mattered now. It was her turn to find strength for him, just as he had for her.

Why hadn't the doctor come to explain what was wrong? She understood how hard-pressed the staff were, especially as the raids were still continuing over London. But she had been sitting here long enough.

The minutes were crawling by so slowly, and with each one, new fears clamoured inside her head. *You'll lose him too. You'll have no one. This is the end, Molly . . .*

And then, through her threatening tears, she saw the child.

A little girl, no more than three, with tousled blonde curls hanging damply around a dirty face. Her tears had etched muddy tracks down her cheeks and plopped onto the cloth of her ill-fitting coat. She was trailing after a dark-haired woman who wore an expression of barely disguised annoyance at the child's presence.

Molly averted her eyes and waited for them to pass. The little girl reminded her of Emily. But she couldn't think of Emily now. She couldn't let in any more pain. And she would, if she looked at that lovely blonde hair and blue eyes – just like Emily's.

So she kept her back stiff and her gaze upon the wall opposite, noting the details; cracked seams and peeling plaster, minuscule holes where propaganda posters had been pinned and fallen away. But as much as she tried, Molly was unable to keep her attention focused. She felt the child's warmth, felt her presence. And before she knew what was happening, the woman had taken the seat beside her.

'This kid's nothing to do with me,' the stranger snapped, catching Molly's glance. 'Dunno who she belongs to. Keeps following me around. I've asked the volunteers to take her. But do you think they'll oblige? No! They just tell me to wait at the desk and register. But I've got me own troubles to sort. Me injured husband's somewhere in this bloody awful place. I ain't got time to see to her.'

'I'm sorry to hear that,' Molly said, trying not to seem unfriendly. 'Have you asked for help at the WVS? Or tried the First Aid post?'

'They just tell you to wait your turn. No special staff to help with waifs and strays.'

'But someone must be dealing with lost children!' Molly challenged.

'I told you, I've got me own troubles,' came the terse reply. 'As it is, I'm dying to go to the lav. Would you stay with her for a minute? I'm almost peeing me knickers.'

Molly wanted to say that she, too, had family injured here in the hospital. And that if she was called by the nurse she would have to go immediately. But the woman was already on her feet.

'Thanks, love. I won't be long.'

Alone with the little girl, who stood staring up at her, Molly looked around for help. All she could see was volunteer aids helping to carry the stretchers. She rose to her feet and was about to ask one of them, when an almighty explosion rocked the building. The walls seemed to shake and little whorls of dust fell down from the high ceilings.

'Quickly, take shelter in the basement!' one aid yelled at

her before making off with the wounded victim prostrate on the stretcher.

But she quickly realized there was no time to find safety. The drone of the planes above was answered by the boom-boom of the anti-aircraft batteries, and the thud of falling bombs came closer.

Instinctively, she grabbed the child and fell to the floor. The earth shook beneath them and she tightened her arms around the little body, whispering any words of comfort she could think of. Words that brought back Emily and the yawning gap of grief after she had passed away.

It was as she was whispering that Molly felt a strange calm wash over her. Even if I die, she thought, Lyn will look after Dad. And there will be someone, somewhere, to care for this little girl.

And she, Molly, would at last be reunited with her lost family, Ted and Emily.

When finally the all-clear sounded, Molly raised her head. The noise of the aircraft was now distant and she took a choked breath, prising herself gently apart from the little girl.

The lights slowly returned, one by one, flickering at first, and figures emerged like ghosts from doors and even cupboards. An acrid smell polluted the air and a fine veil of dust skittered around the old building's cavities.

She moved slowly, helping the child to her feet and dusting down her coat. 'It's all right, Curly Top,' Molly soothed. 'The planes have gone. They won't be back just yet.'

The big blue eyes, as round as saucers, just stared at her.

'We'll sit here together, shall we?' Molly coaxed, wondering what she should do next as she lifted the tiny scrap onto her lap. 'Is your mummy here in the hospital?'

In answer to the many questions Molly asked, there was no response. Just a long, baleful stare and eventually a very wide yawn.

Molly found herself stroking the unruly blonde tresses filled with all manner of tangles. And before very long, there was the soft sound of snoring against her chest.

Molly looked right and left, past the porters and patients and medical staff all going about their business once again. Would the dark-haired woman return? It seemed unlikely. After all, she'd said she had a family of her own to consider.

'Mrs Swift?' A hand landed gently on Molly's arm and she looked up to see a nurse, not the one she had spoken to previously, but a nurse all the same.

Molly nodded eagerly. 'Yes, that's me!'

'The doctor sent me to look for you. Are you all right? The last raid was very close. You should have taken shelter in the hospital's basement.'

'There wasn't time,' Molly said hurriedly. 'What's wrong with Dad, do you know?'

The nurse hesitated. 'I'm afraid he must have fallen awkwardly and fractured his leg. It's a rather nasty injury. But fortunately all his vital signs are satisfactory.'

Molly felt even more perplexed. 'Vital signs? What does that mean exactly?'

'His heartbeat, breathing rate and temperature are giving us no cause for concern,' the nurse explained with a forced smile that really didn't give Molly much comfort. 'He took a nasty knock to his head. Did you see what happened?'

Molly hesitated. 'I think he must have fallen on the counter. I run Swift's General Stores on Roper Street, you see. Dad's retired but he came in to help me with the stocktaking.'

'So it was just you and your father who were admitted? No other family?'

Molly shook her head. 'Lyn, my sister, moved out to Sidcup before the war. Dad lives with me over our general store on the Isle of Dogs.' She added quickly, 'I ran the business with my husband until he died at Dunkirk in June of this year. He was part of the British Expeditionary Force.'

'Oh dear, what bad luck.'

'So what will the treatment be for Dad, do you think?' Molly asked, eager for more information. 'When will he be able to come home?'

The nurse consulted the papers in her hand. 'Not for some time, I'm afraid. The possibility is, when he's stabilized, he'll be sent to another hospital, away from the bombing, where, after the fractures are mended, he'll go through quite a rigorous rehabilitation.'

Molly was shocked. 'Does this mean weeks, or even months he'll be away?'

'Yes, that's very likely.'

'How will I get to see him? I drive the shop van, but it's up on blocks because of the petrol rationing. I don't even know if it's roadworthy after the raids.'

'Listen, let's take one step at a time. I think the most

important thing at the moment is rest, and he'll have plenty of that in here.' The nurse glanced down at Molly's sleeping charge. 'Where was your daughter when all this happened?'

Molly looked blankly into the nurse's curious gaze. 'My daughter? Oh, you mean . . .' She gave a helpless shrug. 'She isn't mine. A woman said she found her wandering in the hospital and asked me to look after her while she went to the toilets. But she never came back.'

'It wasn't her mother?'

'I don't think so.'

'I should take her straight to the desk if I were you. Give them what information you have.'

'Yes, I will,' Molly agreed patiently, 'but first I must see me dad.'

'Come to Ward B in ten minutes,' the nurse consented. 'Third on your right down the corridor. I'll be in my office by then and you can see him, but just for a few minutes.'

When the nurse had gone, Molly wondered if she had time to go to the desk with the child. But what if there was a long queue? And she had to do something to smarten up. Her clothes looked as though they'd been dragged through a hedge backwards.

The ladies' reeked of Woodbines and strong disinfectant. A woman stood by the old washbasins and looked up when she saw Molly carrying the little girl in her arms.

'You all right, love?' she asked in a friendly manner.

'You don't have a comb I could use, do you?'

'Sorry. Everything I owned went up in smoke today.' She slipped a small flask from her pocket. 'Like a drop of the other?'

'No thanks. I'm trying to keep a clear head. This little girl is lost and I have to take her to the desk. But first I must see how my dad is and I wanted to freshen up.'

'What happened to your dad?'

'A bomb went off in the street outside our shop and blew the window in. His leg's broken and he's taken a nasty knock to the head. What about you?'

'Me and Ethel, my landlady, was under the kitchen table when the planes flew over. They pulled me out with just a few bruises. But Ethel's heart packed up in the ambulance. She was a lovely old gel, an' all. We got along famous. Once did me a very good turn.' The woman heaved a big sigh. 'Sorry to have a moan, but this war is just so flamin' unfair.' She smiled and Molly thought how the smile lit up her face under her curtain of dark, unkempt hair. 'I'm Cissy Brown, by the way.'

'Pleased to meet you, Cissy. I'm Molly Swift.'

'Sure you don't want a swig of this?'

'I don't really have time,' Molly answered politely. 'But thanks anyway.' She glanced in the mirror. 'Oh, crikey, look at the state of me!' Her auburn-coloured hair had turned to grey and her skin was streaked with soot. Only her eyes, as large and shiny as brown marbles in her small, heart-shaped face, glimmered in their white sockets to prove she was truly human. 'I can't let me dad see me like this!' she cried. 'I could be a hundred and seven. Not twenty-seven.'

'Splash your face with water, that'll do the trick. I'll hold the kid while you use the basin.'

'Would you?' Molly carefully passed the child over. 'She's not very heavy.'

Cissy nodded. 'She's a dear little thing. Wonder where her mum is?'

'That's what I thought. She's far too young to be on her own.' Molly turned on the tap. A trickle of brown water flowed out. She closed her eyes and took the plunge, shaking the surplus off and threading her wet hands through her hair to smooth it.

'Are you taking her in to see your old man?' Cissy asked.

'I was going to ask the nurse if I could leave her inside the ward.'

'They ain't very nice places, love. Full up with casualties, moaning and groaning.'

'I can't just abandon her.'

'I don't mind helping you out. She don't seem to be any trouble. I could sit with her in the passage while you was with your dad.'

'Are you sure?'

'Course.' The stranger jerked up her expressive dark eyebrows. 'We've all got to help each other in times like this. And look at her, flat out in me arms.'

Molly smiled. The little girl was as Cissy said, flat out. Where had she come from? And why was she lost? Questions that Molly put to the back of her mind, as she and Cissy went into the corridor.

Chapter Two

'Dad?' Molly asked softly as she stood at the bedside. 'Are you awake?'

Her father opened his eyes and blinked. 'Oh, hello, love.'

She bent to kiss his cheek, inhaling a big whiff of antiseptic from the bandage around his head. 'You frightened the life out of me, you know.'

'Did I? Blowed if I can remember.'

Molly nodded down to the cage under the blanket. 'You've broken your leg, and the nurse says you've got to rest.'

'Can't I get up?'

'Certainly not. Just do as you're told!'

'There's your mother talking,' he teased her, though Molly could hear the weakness in his voice.

'You've hit your head too. It must have been the blast that threw you against the counter.'

'The last I remember is the warning and then that bloody

awful explosion.' He looked at her bewilderedly. 'What's the damage back home?'

'Nothing we can't put right.'

A smile went over his lips and his cheerful expression returned. 'You're not a very good fibber!'

'Listen, I can cope, Dad. You're not indispensable.'

'I know you must miss Ted at times like this. I certainly do. He was like a son to me. If only he hadn't bloody volunteered he might be here now.'

'Ted was as stubborn as you, Dad. He reckoned it was his duty. And I never did nothing to stop him.'

'But what will you do?' her father asked anxiously. 'A woman on her own – oh, Molly, I could kick meself.'

At this Molly smiled. 'Don't try kicking anything,' she said, trying to lighten the moment. 'You've only got one good leg left.'

He chuckled weakly. 'Ask Dennis Turner to help you. He's a good all-rounder and only lives down the road. Get him to do something temporary till I get home. As for cash, there's a bit put by under the kitchen floorboard. When I'm on me feet again I'll see to everything. I know you haven't got Ted at the helm, but I'll soon be back to help out.'

Suddenly there was a loud yell and, although there were curtains around the bed affording a little privacy, nothing could disguise the pain that some poor soul was enduring. There were soft mutters and yet more screams and a rush of rubber soles over the ward's floor.

'Poor bugger,' Bill whispered. 'There but for the grace of God, go I.'

Molly placed her hand gently on the bedcover. 'Will you be able to sleep?'

'Don't worry, I've had a knockout drop. Me eyelids feel like lead weights.'

'I'll come in again on Tuesday.'

'Don't go telling your sister what's happened,' Bill said anxiously. 'Lyn will only fuss and force me out to bloody Sidcup!'

'Oscar's not so bad,' Molly said, defending her brother-in-law. 'Though he can be a bit of a know-all.'

'That's putting it mildly,' Bill huffed. 'I'll have it rammed down me throat we should have moved out from the East End when war was declared. I'll be a sitting duck with me gammy leg.'

Molly hid her smile. She knew Oscar would be the first to criticize them for not relocating, and Lyn could be just as bossy. But perhaps, after this development, they might have a point.

'Dad, Lyn won't forgive me – or you – for not telling her what's happened. You could have been killed. It's not like you tripped over in the street, something daft like that.'

'Just wait a few more days before you write,' Bill pleaded drowsily. 'I might even be home by then.'

After what the nurse had told her, Molly thought that highly unlikely. 'Is there anything you need?'

'Too bloody true there is,' he replied with a yawn. 'Me pipe and baccy. Now, love, you'd better be off. I can feel meself dozing. And I . . .'

Molly smiled as his eyes closed under the bandages. At least he didn't seem to be in pain.

She went on tiptoe from the bedside but was startled by a

loud shriek. Nurses hurried to the stricken patient as Molly made her way out to the corridor.

'Here, this bloke wants the kid,' Cissy cried as Molly approached. 'Do you know him?'

'No,' Molly replied, looking the stranger up and down. 'Who are you?'

'I'm Evie's dad. Where did you find her?'

'I didn't,' Molly answered. 'Someone else did. A woman who went off, leaving her with me.'

'Well, I'll take her now.' He stepped forward but Molly barred his way.

'What proof have we got that you're this child's father?'

'Proof!' the man exclaimed. 'I'm her dad. Ain't that enough?'

'You ain't done a very good job of looking after her so far,' Cissy said loudly as she clutched the child.

The man threw up his arms in exasperation. 'All right, if it's proof you want, then I'll get it.'

To Molly's surprise he sprinted away, a tall, agile man with long legs and broad shoulders hidden under a navy duffel coat that had clearly seen better days. His dark beard and untidy hair had made him look rather frightening.

'What was all that about?' she wondered aloud and Cissy shrugged.

'Dunno, but he looked a bit iffy to me.'

'What would he want with a child though, if he wasn't her father?'

Cissy sneered disdainfully. 'He might be a nutter. Shall we take her to the desk and let them deal with it?'

'Yes, perhaps we should.'

She was about to do just this when Molly saw him reappear. This time, a little boy of about four or five accompanied him.

'Now, Mark, tell these people who Evie is,' the man said breathlessly.

The boy looked bewildered. 'What they gonna do with her, Dad?'

'They want to know if I'm her father.'

The little boy nodded slowly. 'She's me sister an' all.'

'You see,' the man said, his voice raised in agitation. 'Now, if you're satisfied?'

'We was only looking out for her,' Cissy argued stubbornly. 'If she'd walked out of here on her own Gawd knows what would have become of her.'

'Dad, don't let them take our Evie.' The boy's eyes filled with tears and the tall man sank to his knees, winding his arms gently around the tiny frame.

'It's all right, Mark. It's all right.'

'I'm sorry,' Molly apologized immediately. 'We didn't mean any harm.'

'See, they was just doing us a good turn.' The man stood up and looked at Cissy. 'I'll take her now.'

Molly watched as Cissy, with a scowl, allowed the man to take his daughter. 'Evie, why did you run away from your old man?'

The little girl rubbed filthy knuckles in her eyes. 'I want me mum.'

'Our mum's dead,' the boy told his sister. 'Ain't she, Dad?'

'Yes, son, I'm afraid so.' The man looked at Molly. 'Stella died when our house was bombed. I came here to identify her body.'

'The name's Andy Miller. I'm sorry I lost me rag. But I was worried sick about Evie. She's only three and a half. I told them to wait outside the room where they took me to see Stella. But when I came out, Mark said she'd wandered off.'

Molly looked at the little boy, all spindly legs and short trousers, wearing a threadbare jacket several sizes too big for his body.

'I'm sorry to hear of your loss,' Molly said sadly.

'I searched the hospital looking for Evie. Couldn't find her nowhere. Till I saw you.'

'You dunno who people are these days,' Cissy said, looking the man up and down. 'What with so many bleeding warnings of enemy aliens trying to infiltrate, you end up suspecting your own mother.'

'I ain't no alien, far from it,' Andy Miller assured them. 'I'm in the merch and on leave from me ship. I've got to be back on Thursday. Meanwhile, I have to sort out a place round here for Evie and Mark to stay.'

'That's a tall order,' Cissy replied. 'They're evacuating all the kids from the East End.'

'Yeah, I know. But not mine.' His piercingly dark eyes hardened. 'How would I ever get to see them if they was out in the country somewhere?'

'You ain't got a lot of choice,' Cissy retorted impatiently.

'I'm going to try round here,' he said, ignoring her and looking at Molly. 'Go to the Salvation Army.'

'Are you a Salvationist?' asked Molly.

'No, but mates of mine are. Betty and Len Denham. Like us, they lived on the East India Dock Road. Betty looked after the kids sometimes. But they got bombed out too. All I know is they were taken to the Red Cross shelter somewhere round here.'

'Needle in a haystack,' said Cissy unsympathetically.

Just then there was a low, droning sound followed by the siren's haunting wail.

'Better get down to the shelter,' Andy Miller said, taking his son's hand.

They all joined the crowd rushing towards the basement of the hospital, as the thunder of the bombers grew louder and closer.

There was barely enough light in the basement to let them find their way over the shelter floor. Tilley lamps had been lit and at one end nurses were quietly attending to patients in wheelchairs. At the other a WVS volunteer with gas masks hanging from her shoulder directed them to the free spaces. 'There are mattresses down there,' she told them hurriedly. 'We've set up a tea urn by the wall.'

Molly and Cissy led the way between the huddled bodies of men, women and children. Most were asleep, with their gas masks and bundles of clothing piled up beside them.

Molly picked her way carefully; the smell of unwashed human bodies was overpowering.

'There!' Cissy said, clambering towards a mattress that was just being vacated.

'Here you are, love, kept the bed warm for you,' the elderly woman said, pulling on her coat and lifting her heavy bags. 'I'm off to see me son in ward nine. He wasn't doing so well when I came down here to get a bit of kip. Good luck to the lot of you.'

While Cissy went to the tea urn Molly sat on the floor, leaning her head against the wall. She watched Andy Miller make his children comfortable on the mattress, kissing them goodnight and drawing the blankets up to their chins.

'Thanks,' he said as he sat beside Molly. 'You were good to look out for Evie.'

'I would have been frantic if I'd lost my little girl in a big place like this. You must have been very worried.'

'Have you got kids?'

Molly shook her head, a sudden image of Emily flashing through her mind.

'You're lucky,' he told her bitterly. 'You don't know what it's like seeing them go through this hell.'

'Have you any relatives who can help you out?' Molly asked quietly.

'Not a soul, only the Denhams. I'm an orphanage boy and Stella's old woman died of the drink.'

'Do you think you'll find those friends of yours?'

'Don't know. But I have to try. I'm a DEMS gunner, see. And I'll be hauled over the coals if I'm absent without leave.'

'DEMS?' Molly repeated, remembering she'd read about the defensively equipped merchant ships that had been hastily, and often poorly, fitted with guns. 'That's dangerous, ain't it?'

'No choice,' Andy shrugged. 'Well, that ain't strictly true. It was DEMS or get kicked out for the regular navy. And then I'd be in a worse fix, sent off for months, perhaps years at a time. At least I can get leave at the end of each trip and see me kids.'

'Your wife must have been very worried.'

'Stella couldn't have cared less,' he replied.

'Why's that?' asked Cissy, having overhead this remark as she returned with the mugs of tea on a battered tin tray.

'Stella wasn't the worrying sort.'

'When do you go back to your ship?' asked Molly.

'Thursday.'

'That's not very long.'

Andy shrugged. 'It's all I've got.' He sipped his hot tea. 'What about you? Are you married?'

'I was,' Molly replied, feeling a twist to her stomach. 'Ted was with the British Expeditionary Force and died at Dunkirk in June.'

'Christ,' Andy said, frowning. 'He was in the middle of it too, poor sod.'

Molly nodded, then went on to explain how she and Ted, after her dad's retirement, had planned to build up the business and had even bought a van so they could travel to buy cheaper stock and make deliveries. 'Then suddenly it all came to an end. I'd known Ted since we were kids. We had so many plans in mind.'

'What're you going to do now?' asked Andy. 'Keep the shop open?'

'It depends on the damage. The bomb completely shattered the window. I didn't even get time to go upstairs to look at our flat.'

'You live on the job?' asked Cissy.

'Yes. Me and Lyn grew up there. After Mum died, Lyn got married and moved out to Sidcup—'

She stopped, as once more the ground began to tremble. 'Oh, Gawd, where's it all gonna end?' Cissy moaned.

'Let's hope we've got someone looking over us,' said Molly as she thought of the shop and flat already battered and bruised by the aerial assault. What were the chances that she, too, might not have a home to return to?

'Don't believe in that silly stuff,' said Cissy fiercely. 'Once we pop our clogs, that's the end of it.'

'Don't be too quick to judge,' Andy scolded. 'My kids were dragged out of death's jaws today. I dunno who arranged it, but whoever did, I'm grateful.'

Molly smiled. There was more to Andy Miller than met the eye.

Chapter Three

Molly woke with a start. Where was she? Slowly, yesterday's events came back to her thoughts. The explosion outside the shop, her dad trapped under all that rubble, the hospital and meeting Cissy, Andy and the children.

She gingerly stretched out her arms and legs. Her coat had been no protection from the draughts that swept over the cold floors, and every bone seemed to ache.

'Is there a lav round here?' Cissy asked a male volunteer as he passed by. Bleary-eyed and yawning, she pushed back her mop of dark hair.

'Only one's working upstairs as most of the water's off,' he answered gruffly. 'Army's been brought in to connect us up again. Poor bloody firemen can't use their hoses, so there's fires burning in nearly every street and no water to douse them.'

'Where can we get something to eat?' Andy said, jumping to his feet.

'You'll have to wait your turn,' the man replied. 'They're feeding the sick and the elderly first.'

'But me kids haven't eaten since they was dragged out of a burning building yesterday.'

'Go to the rescue centre. They'll set you up.'

'How far is that?' Andy asked grimly.

'Down the Commercial Road.'

'That's a long way for kids to walk on empty stomachs.'

'Have it your own way, son,' the man said, walking away. 'After last night, there will be hundreds if not thousands in the same boat.'

Andy drew his hands over his face and shook his head wearily. Molly knew he must be exhausted.

'I could do with a fag.' Cissy brushed down her creased coat as a large black beetle scurried across the floor. 'You ain't got one, I suppose, Molly?'

'No, sorry.'

Cissy rolled her eyes. 'So what are we gonna do now?'

'Find a toilet that works,' Molly suggested, once again threading her fingers through her hair and pulling at the tangles.

Evie sat up and rubbed her eyes. 'I'm 'ungry.'

Mark stirred beside her, pushing aside his blanket. 'What we got to eat, Dad?'

'I'll find you something,' Andy said as he lifted his daughter into his arms. 'Even if I have to carry you both up the Commercial Road.'

Molly and Cissy followed Andy and the children upstairs to the only working public toilets, then made their way to the hospital's entrance. From the hospital steps they could see fires still burning, forming clouds of grey smoke that hung heavily over the city. Those people made homeless were carrying their few possessions in prams and carts; anything they could salvage from last night's onslaught. The roads were covered in debris, bricks and shattered timbers.

'Looks like hell,' Andy said under his breath.

'You ain't wrong there,' agreed Cissy, coughing and sliding out her flask. 'I'll drink to that.'

'And I'll say goodbye,' Andy told them, lifting Evie into his arms. 'Thanks again and good luck.'

'You'll need it most with them young 'uns,' Cissy said in her forthright manner, but Molly looked anxiously at the two bedraggled children.

'You could all come back to Roper Street,' she offered suddenly. 'I've food, and water from a yard pump if the mains aren't working. But I can't promise my shop and flat above will still be there. Who knows what happened overnight?'

'How far is it?' Andy asked with a frown.

'Closer than the Commercial Road. About thirty minutes' walk.'

'That don't sound too bad.'

'Suits me,' Cissy said with a shrug.

Molly just hoped she wasn't leading them on a wild goose chase.

Molly noted the many incendiary bombs still burning as she took them towards the docks, navigating the uneven ground and obstacles as best she could. Most of the streets had deep holes and wreckage from the devastating attacks.

'You can't go no further,' an ARP warden told them at the top of Westferry Road.

'Why?' Molly asked in alarm.

'The rope factory's still on fire. An unexploded bomb's just been found—' He stopped as a loud explosion shook the half-demolished buildings around them. 'No time to jaw. Go back the other way!'

Molly held out her arms to Andy. 'Let me take Evie. Then you can carry Mark.'

Hesitating only briefly, Andy passed his daughter to Molly and they all began to run, trying to avoid the shattered glass, collapsed brickwork and clouds of dust. Very soon she'd lost sight of Andy and Cissy as another billowing black smog enfolded them.

'This way!' the warden yelled from somewhere close by and grabbed her arm.

Molly held Evie close, though even with the warden's help she began to feel tired and choked with the thick, cloying dust. By the time they reached the small wooden hut with a large red cross painted on the door, Molly was breathless and coughing. She fell onto the bench inside, gasping for air.

'You two on your own?' the warden panted as he gave Evie some water from an enamel mug.

'No, Evie's dad's out there somewhere, and her older brother. There's another woman too.'

'Sit tight. Keep the door shut and use those masks on the shelf if you have to.' He put on his own mask and disappeared.

It was a long ten minutes before the door opened again and Andy, Mark and Cissy, all coughing and spluttering, fell inside, followed by the warden.

'Bloody Norah,' Cissy gasped as she stared at Molly. 'I thought I'd had me chips.'

Andy nodded as Mark gulped down water from the mug.

'What you doing round these parts?' the sooty-faced warden demanded. 'Don't you know this area is off limits? The bomb-disposal teams are still working.'

All three shook their heads.

'Well, you know now.'

'We must get to Roper Street,' Molly said desperately. 'That's where I live.'

'You won't get there this way,' was the answer. 'Roserton and Chipka Street, Cleveland Terrace and East Ferry Road – they're all no-go areas.'

'There must be some way we can get to Roper Street,' she tried once more. 'There's an alley leading off from Westferry Road. What about that?'

'Too dangerous, love,' replied the warden. 'Specially with the kids.'

Suddenly the wooden hut shook again. All the first aid supplies rattled on the shelves. A bucket of sand toppled from a stool.

'Flamin' heck!' cried the warden. 'Another one!' He ran outside and there were raised voices. When he didn't return, Molly lifted Evie into her arms. 'Let's go before he comes back. We'll find a way somehow.'

'Not bloody likely!' swore Cissy. 'You heard what he said.'

'He didn't say the alley had been hit. He only said it was dangerous.'

'I'm with you,' said Andy, taking hold of Mark.

'You're both mad,' cried Cissy frantically. 'But I ain't staying here on my own.'

'Come on, then,' shouted Molly and Cissy shrugged.

'In for a penny, in for a pound, I suppose.'

Ten minutes later they stood huddled together on Chalk Wharf, the moss-covered bank that led down to the steel-grey waters of the Thames. Molly's heart sank as she witnessed the extent of the bombing: from the Isle of Dogs down to the city, enemy bombers had left a trail of destruction in their wake. Across the Thames, the south bank and Surrey Docks were hidden by a sickly pink smog, while the north-easterly wind fuelled the fires still burning, spilling sheets of ash across the water.

'Which way now?' said Andy. 'Is it far?'

Molly shook her head. 'But look, the alley's been sealed off!' She pointed along the road to where there were fixed barriers and men in uniform patrolling the debris. Air raid wardens and rescue parties were digging in the ruins of Howeth Street, the road next to Roper Street, where many of the houses had sustained damage.

'Fine mess we're in,' said Cissy accusingly. 'What we going to do now?'

'We'll go that way instead,' Molly decided, pointing to the houses nearest the water. 'Most of them have been evacuated. We'll cut through their yards.'

'What if we get caught?' Cissy scowled. 'I don't fancy walking all the way back again.'

Molly ignored this and hoisted Evie onto her other hip. She took a deep breath and forged on; one way or another, she was determined to get them safely back to Roper Street.

Chapter Four

At last they were there! But Molly's legs almost buckled at the sight of the gaping hole in the road where the bomb had gone off. Two of the houses beside it now stood in ruins. Molly thought of Mrs Lockyer, the frail elderly lady at number six. And Liz Howells next door. Had they escaped?

'At least those places are still standing,' Cissy observed, nodding to the jagged line of terraced houses farther down the road. To Molly's relief she saw that Dennis and Jean Turner's house was safe.

'Is that your shop?' Andy asked as he joined them.

Molly nodded eagerly. 'And someone's boarded the broken window.'

'Perhaps it was the warden,' Andy guessed. 'He'd have bolted the front door too, to stop any looters.'

They all made their way carefully around the crater, passed the disused bicycle factory and stood outside the store.

'The sign's lopsided,' Andy said, 'but not broken. A couple of nails will put that right.'

'We'll go round to the yard. I keep a spare key under the pump.'

With her breath held, Molly gave Evie to Andy and retrieved the spare key from the yard.

She cautiously opened the back door. What would they find inside?

There was a strong, sour smell when Molly walked into the room nicknamed by her father as the 'glory hole'. It was where all the stock was kept adjacent to the shop, and normally as clean as a new pin.

Today a grey veil of dust had been draped over the many shelves of tins and packets of dried food, nails, screws, tools, needles and cottons, bottles and candles.

'What's that stink?' Cissy enquired, turning up her nose.

'Pickled onions,' Molly replied as she saw the broken jars on the floor. 'What a mess!'

'Cripes, I could go down on me knees and lick all that up,' Cissy laughed. 'I could even eat the broke bottles.'

'I's 'ungry,' said Evie with a tired sob.

'So am I,' said Mark.

'Let's go upstairs to the flat,' Molly told them. 'I'll find you something nice to eat in the larder.'

'I'd better go first. See if it's safe.' Andy lowered Evie to the floor. 'Hold Molly's hand and wait till I say you can come up.'

They all watched Andy mount the steep staircase. There

was a long, tense silence. But finally he shouted down. 'All clear. Except the front room. There's a blooming great hole in the floor.'

Cissy thrust the last mouthful of bread, soggy with the juice of the pickle, into her mouth. To her, the National Loaf, a grey lump of stodgy dough, together with the spring water from the pump, tasted like manna from heaven. Her eyes almost popped out of her head when a pickled egg landed on her plate.

For once I've struck lucky, she thought to herself. Fancy finding meself in a place like this! A gaff with a kitchen and front room, and a passage leading off into three good-sized bedrooms. I must be dreaming!

Interrupting her train of thought, there was a shout from downstairs. Molly jumped up and went to see who it was.

Cissy took advantage of the moment and grabbed the last slice of bread.

Chapter Five

'Den!' Molly threw her arms around her good friend and neighbour, Dennis Turner. 'How are you? How's Jean and the twins? Is everyone all right?'

With a shy chuckle, Dennis Turner nodded. 'We're fine, Molly. Just fine. But old Stokesy, the warden, told us he'd taken you and yer dad to the hospital.'

Molly explained all that had happened, and Dennis's lean, work-worn face with its toothy smile registered shock. He pushed a hand through his thick fair hair and frowned. 'You was both lucky to come out of that lot. Have you seen across the road?'

Molly nodded. 'Do you know if Liz and Mrs Lockyer are all right?'

'Ain't sure. It was bloody chaos in the streets but I managed to board up yer window.'

'Oh, thanks, Den. I thought it might be Mr Stokes. Come upstairs. I'd like you to meet some people I met at the hospital.'

A few minutes later Molly introduced her guests. 'Dennis, meet Andy Miller and his children, Evie and Mark. And this is Cissy Brown.'

'Nice to meet you all,' Dennis said in his friendly fashion. 'Now, I saw that bloody great hole you had in yer front room, Molly. Think I've got some boards I can put over it for you.'

'Like a hand, mate?' Andy asked before Molly could reply.

'Just the job,' Dennis nodded.

'That all right with you, Molly?' Andy asked politely as he made his way round the table.

'Well, yes, of course,' she said, blushing.

'You're all welcome to use the Anderson tonight,' Dennis told Molly after he and Andy had successfully made the repair. 'Jean and the twins wouldn't mind a bit of company while I'm out with the rescue squad. Be sure to put on your warm togs, though, as it'll be freezing. Your two nippers, Andy, can kip in the bunks with Susie and Simon.' He winked at Mark and Evie and they giggled as he hurried off down the stairs.

'Well, you heard what he said.' Molly held out her hands to the children. 'Let's find you some nice warm clothes, shall we?'

A few minutes later they were peering into the depths of Molly's large wardrobe. 'Now let me see. What can I find you?'

'What's in there?' asked Evie, pointing to a small brown leather suitcase on the lower shelf.

'Just a few things.'

'Can we see?' Mark pulled on the handle.

Molly hesitated. She'd packed all Emily's things away in there and hadn't looked at them since.

Before she could answer, Mark slipped the locks.

'Whose clothes are these?' he asked as he lifted the dusty lid.

Molly took a deep breath. 'I had a little girl called Emily once.'

'Where's she gorn?'

'She's with her dad in heaven.'

'Me mum's gone to heaven too,' Evie said, pulling out a brown coat with a chocolate collar. 'Can I have this?'

'Yes, if it fits.'

'This'll do me,' said Mark, winding Emily's grey woollen scarf around his neck.

Suddenly Evie burst into tears. 'I want me mum,' she sobbed. 'I wanna go 'ome.'

Molly gathered both Evie and the brown coat into her arms. What could she tell the child?

But it was Mark who answered. 'You can't go home cos we ain't got one.' His serious brown eyes swivelled to Molly. 'We gotta find Betty and Len.'

Molly clutched the little girl tightly, smelling Emily as she did so. Why was life so cruel? Why had Emily and Ted been taken from her? Why were these children motherless? They'd done no harm to anyone.

'I'm 'ungry,' said Evie and stopped crying as quickly as she'd begun.

'She always says that,' accused her brother.

There were more tears and finally Molly looked firmly at the two squabbling children. 'Now listen, you two, your dad won't want to see you unhappy before he goes back to his ship.'

'Are we staying 'ere, then?' asked Evie, brightening.

'Well, no, your dad is hoping to find your friends. Now why don't you both run along and show your new clothes to your father?'

Molly watched them scamper off, Mark with his thick woollen scarf and Evie in Emily's brown coat. They were delightful children and very brave. Just like Emily had been.

'Are they all asleep?' Jean asked as they sat in the Turners' Anderson that night after Andy had gone with Dennis to the rescue squad's station.

Molly nodded. 'There's just enough room for the four of them on the bunks.'

'All a bit of fun for my two,' Jean said with a sad smile as they drank the warm tea from the thermos. 'But I feel sorry for Andy's kids. Losing their mother so young and him having to go to sea again, well, it's a lot to take in at their ages.'

'By rights they should be evacuated,' Cissy said sharply. 'In my opinion he ain't got a hope of finding these pals.'

'I can understand how he feels,' Jean replied thoughtfully as she tucked her short, permed fair hair under her paisley headscarf. 'For about half a day I thought about sending my two away. But the truth is no one really wants our East End kids. They're too much of a liability.'

'Yeah, but they'd be safe.'

'P'raps,' agreed Jean. 'Me head tells me you're right, Cissy, but me heart won't let me do it. And anyway, it's not the kids I'm worried about. It's Den. He failed his medical for the services, cos he's got a dicky chest. Had it from birth. I worry about him more than I do Simon and Susie.' She laughed. 'Saying that, nothing I ever say stops Dennis Turner from doing what he wants, so I—'

A faint vibration went through the shelter and all three women fell silent.

'The Luftwaffe's back,' said Cissy after a while.

'But it's not close yet,' said Jean in a whisper.

They all listened again. The brief silence was broken by the faint thud-thud of ack-ack guns.

'You from around here, Cissy?' Jean asked eventually, and Molly knew her friend was trying to distract their thoughts.

'I was in digs at Blackwall, but Ethel, me landlady, died.'

'Got any family?'

'Nah. My old man ditched me years ago. I was glad to be rid of him. He was a selfish bastard. Never knew what he was up to or who he was with.'

'That's awful,' sympathized Molly, though she could tell Cissy wasn't keen to discuss her past.

'Well, Cissy, there are mostly good apples in the barrel,' Jean said brightly. 'You've had a hard time, but don't give up on men just yet. You're still young and attractive. You'll meet someone nice one day.'

'Doubt it.' Cissy looked away.

Molly exchanged glances with Jean. Then there was a shattering explosion nearby and everyone fell to the floor.

Next morning, Molly woke with her head at an unnatural angle. She slowly opened her eyes to find a bright light shining in through the Anderson door. Andy and Dennis, with dirty black faces, were standing there.

'Rise and shine,' chuckled Dennis.

'Oh, Den, it's you,' said Jean, rousing herself next to Molly. 'Is the house still standing?'

'Not a brick loose,' announced Dennis, removing the steel helmet from his head, leaving a white rim above his eyebrows. 'A few heavy explosives went in the drink last night.'

'Yes, we heard them.'

'Sorry we couldn't get back. It was pandemonium out there. But the good news is the gas and water are on. Reckon we could rustle up breakfast indoors, don't you, love?'

Jean put a hand to her back and stretched. 'Kids, wake up. Get yourselves into the lav and empty the bucket. Then we'll have something to eat.'

Molly followed Cissy into the morning air as the children made use of the outside closet. 'I'd like to visit Dad,' Molly said to Jean as they stood on the scrubby patch of yard grass.

'You do that, ducks,' Jean told her. 'Me and Cissy will look after the little ones and cook the men a good breakfast. Now, you'd better be off.'

As everyone was occupied, Molly made her way over the rough path and through the house to the street. The crater in the road was now cordoned off. She passed the old bicycle factory and followed the footpath to the back of the shop. Taking the key from under the pump, she let herself in.

The store held an eerie silence as though it stood still in time.

Molly went up to the flat and found her dad's tobacco, then she washed her face and fixed her hair. She wanted to make a good impression at the hospital so her dad could see she was able to look after everything while he was away.

'I'm afraid your father had a disturbed night,' an unfamiliar nurse told Molly when she arrived at the hospital. 'He developed a temperature, which was a little worrying.'

Molly looked over the nurse's shoulder to the curtained cubicle. 'What brought that on?' she asked anxiously.

'Dr Neil believes it may be concussion. From time to time he gets confused, probably a result of the blow to his head.'

'Can I see him?'

'It's not visiting hours, but I'm sure we can make an exception.'

Her dad was asleep when Molly sat quietly on the chair beside his bed. The bandage on his head was very white against his flushed face. Every now and then he jumped or trembled. Molly stood his pipe and tin of tobacco on the cabinet.

As she did this he woke, screwing up his eyes. 'Molly, is that you?'

'Yes, it's me, Dad.' She took his hand. 'They tell me you had a bad night.'

'What day is it?'

'Tuesday.'

'Thought it was Sunday.' He rolled his head towards her. 'Where am I?'

'You're in hospital, after a bomb exploded outside the shop.'

He nodded slowly. 'Oh yes, I remember now.'

'Thank goodness for that.'

He gave a yelp when he saw the protective cage under the covers. 'What have they done to me leg? They ain't cut it off?'

'No, course not. Your leg's broken and you'll have to be patient while it mends.'

Just then, there was a penetrating cry. Through the curtains, Molly could hear someone crying and the nurses running.

'This is a very noisy ward,' she said.

'The way I feel at the moment Big Ben could strike in me ear and I couldn't care less. Think they're giving me jollup to shut me up. Now, before I drift off, tell me how you're managing?'

'There's no need to worry about anything. Dennis and another man called Andy have done the repairs at home.'

'Andy? Who's he?'

'Someone I met here. His wife was killed that night, leaving him with two small children. I also met a woman called Cissy who lost everything in the raid. I felt very sorry for them and—'

'Offered to help?' Bill gave a chuckle. 'I leave you for a

couple of days and look what happens! Half the bloody East End is lining up at our door!'

'Do you mind?'

'Ducks, like your mother, you'd help any soul in distress.' He squeezed her hand tightly, then looked at her intently. 'You ain't told your sister about me, have you?'

'Not yet.'

'Good. I don't want no fuss ...' Slowly his eyes began to close. A long, heavy sigh slipped from his lips and Molly sat, her mind full of confused thoughts. She would have to tell her sister soon about Dad. Lyn would be very upset to think she'd been kept in the dark.

Once outside the hospital, Molly took a deep breath. She knew the nurses and doctors were doing the best they could, but they couldn't bring about a miraculous recovery. Even if Dad managed to walk again, there was the matter of the steep flight of stairs that led from the shop up to the flat.

Hands deep in pockets, Molly made her way home. Cranes, tractors and lorries were noisily trying to clear the streets amidst the long queues of people waiting at the coach station. Under a large sign saying EVACUEES, all the children and their parents were lining up.

One little boy was lifted aboard, screaming and crying. Molly's stomach dropped as the coach moved off. The boy stared out of a window as his mother waved frantically. Who knew how long they would be separated?

Chapter Six

Although it was the first day of 1941, the celebrations were brief. After another unsettled night in the Turners' Anderson, everyone went quickly on their way. Andy left for Poplar with the children to look for the Denhams and Molly and Cissy went back to the shop.

'Well, I suppose I'd better say goodbye,' Cissy said as Molly pulled up the blinds. 'I can't put on you for much longer.'

'You could help me sweep up if you like,' Molly said. 'But perhaps you'd like to be on your way?'

'Got nowhere special to go,' Cissy shrugged and grabbed the broom. By the time the afternoon came, the shop and glory hole were spotless.

'Have you ever worked in a shop before?' Molly asked as Cissy took off the apron Molly had given her.

'Me? No!' Cissy laughed, lighting up a thinly rolled cigarette. 'I wouldn't know one spud from another.'

'Are you any good at figures?'

'I know if I'm fiddled when I get me change in the pub. But that's not the same as operating one of them things.' She nodded to the till.

'You just enter the sum with the keys and keep a record of the coupons.'

'You offering me a job?' Cissy asked in surprise.

'I need to see me dad, so you'd be alone in the shop at times. But I'd include board and lodging too.'

'What!'

'Don't underestimate the work. Serving in a shop is hard,' Molly warned. 'There's a lot of lifting to do. And we don't close till very late.'

'That don't sound too bad at all.'

Molly smiled. 'You can have me dad's room while he's away. And I can lend you a few of me clothes to tide you over until we get to market. We're about the same size, I think.'

Just then Molly heard the children, and Evie, with her blonde waves tumbling over her shoulders, ran in and wrapped herself around Molly's legs. 'Hello, Curly Top. What mischief have you been up to?'

'I tried the Sally Army Mission, but drew a blank,' Andy said as he walked in the door with Mark.

'What about the Red Cross?' Molly asked.

'No luck there either.'

'So what are you going to do?'

'I went to the evacuation office. They told me to turn up early tomorrow morning at the coach station and see the billeting officer.'

Molly's thoughts flew to the little boy staring out of the coach window.

'I don't wanna go away, Dad,' said Mark.

'I know you don't, son. But I've got to go back to sea.'

'Why can't we go to Betty's?'

'Cos I can't find her.'

Molly lifted Evie into her arms. 'Would you two like something to eat? You must be hungry.'

Evie nodded immediately, but Mark's eyes were filled with tears as he ran out of the door. His father followed and Molly heaved a sorrowful sigh. Without the Denhams to help him, Andy had no choice but to evacuate his children. And Mark seemed to sense what was in store.

Andy's thoughts were all over the place as he stood the following day, waiting to speak to the billeting officer. He felt he was failing his children. But what else could he do, other than evacuate them? He'd made Evie and Mark carry their gas masks and had filled in the informations tags he'd been given yesterday at the offices. But how could a scrap of paper give a child's complete history, especially the circumstances of Stella's death?

'Don't want to go,' Evie said, looking up at him with big blue eyes. 'Where's Molly?'

'You can eat the picnic she made you on the coach,' he said, forcing a bright smile.

'I don't wanna go neither,' said Mark, his small voice lost in the many voices around them.

'I know, son.' He knelt down and drew them towards him.

'Listen, you two, I have to go back to sea. I wish I didn't, but there's a war on. I promise to come and see you as soon as I get leave.'

'Name!' a voice shouted and he jumped to his feet. A stern-looking official was addressing him. The man, who wore a smart suit and tie, held a board in his hand.

'I'm Andy Miller,' said Andy. 'This is my son Mark and my daughter Evie.'

'Are you registered? I don't have a Miller down here on my list.'

'No, the welfare sent us.'

'Then you're in the wrong place.' The middle-aged man's thin, unsmiling face showed disapproval. 'You should have registered before coming here, to get a place on a coach.'

'I didn't know that,' said Andy, keeping his temper in check. 'I was told at the billeting office to be here early. And that was all.'

'You have no idea how difficult it is to find host families, let alone at a moment's notice,' the man complained.

Andy's annoyance surfaced. 'Listen, chum, do you think I want to pack me kids off like this?'

The man stood back, staring at him with astonished eyes. 'There's no need to take that attitude.'

'What attitude should I take?' Andy demanded as he lifted a distraught Evie into his arms. 'Just tell me which coach to put my kids on.'

The man stiffened his thin neck. 'I told you. All the seats are allocated on coaches. Transport for the unregistered is provided separately – over there.'

Barely giving Andy another glance, the billeting officer turned to the next person in the queue. Andy was tempted to stay put and argue the point, but he knew that would only upset the kids more.

Gripping Mark's hand tightly, he made his way across the road to where the official had indicated. It was not long before a lorry with an open back drew up. Everyone in the waiting crowd surged forward; the children were lifted, pushed, shoved and heaved on top of the vehicle.

'Dad!' screeched Mark. 'Don't leave me.'

Andy stood motionless. He felt Evie's wet tears on his neck as she clung to him. He heard Mark's sobs and felt his son's terror.

'Last chance for today,' said the driver, jerking his thumb. 'Your two can squash in there.'

'Where are you taking them?' Andy demanded.

'Norfolk, mate.'

'Norfolk?' Andy repeated in alarm. 'How far's that?'

'Dunno. But I've got to get cracking.'

Andy stared into Mark's eyes, red with tears. How could he let this happen?

Molly's feet had been going round ten to the dozen on the pedals. Every time the bicycle hit a hole in the road, it careered right or left. The store's delivery bike was sturdy enough, but was custom-built for strength, not speed.

At the coach station she dismounted and threaded her way through the busy traffic. There were two coaches parked by a sign saying EVACUEES. One coach was leaving, the other filling up fast. An official wearing a suit and holding some papers seemed to be in charge.

'Have you seen a man with two small children?' she asked.

He rudely ignored her as he called out instructions to the stream of parents. She looked for Evie and Mark at the windows of the coach and when she couldn't see them, pushed her bike back in front of the man.

'I'm looking for a boy of five called Mark and his younger sister Evie,' she repeated loudly.

The man eyed her suspiciously. 'Who are you?'

'A friend of the children's. Have you seen them?'

'I see hundreds of children and can't be expected to remember their names,' he said, turning away.

Molly followed him. 'I must find them,' she called. 'Perhaps you remember their father? A tall dark-haired man with a beard.'

'Oh, him,' the man said, stopping. 'No host family, no details. Unregistered. And most unpleasant. I sent him on over the road to wait for the lorries.'

'What!' Molly gasped. 'You don't mean children are driven in lorries?'

'I most certainly do. They're very lucky to be provided with any sort of motorized transport other than trains.'

Molly watched helplessly as he turned away, obviously annoyed and determined to be unhelpful. She pushed her bike off the pavement and began to cross the road. Several buses and lorries passed by, and even horse-drawn carts. She searched each one of them for the children's faces. Had Andy put them aboard a lorry and gone on his way already?

She wandered along the pavement, looking inside every vehicle, but there was no sign of them. The queues were slowly dispersing, mostly parents, many of them clearly distressed or in tears.

Then she heard a familiar sound. The cry was faint at first and she stood still to listen. Straining her ears through the rumble of traffic, she was certain she could hear something.

Out of the remaining crowd, a small figure emerged. A little girl was running towards her, with long, tangled blonde hair.

Chapter Seven

Molly leaned her bike against a lamp post and lifted Evie into her arms. 'Hello, Curly Top.'

'Where you bin?'

Molly laughed. 'I've been looking for you.'

'Molly?' Andy walked up with Mark trailing beside him. 'What are you doing here?'

'I thought I was too late. The man over there was very unhelpful when I asked after you.'

'He was the last straw,' Andy said grimly. 'I just couldn't put my kids on a lorry and watch them driven off to God knows where.'

'What about your ship?'

He shrugged. 'The coppers will have to catch me first.'

'They could put you in prison. What would the children do then?'

Again Andy lifted his broad shoulders. 'I'll have to take that risk.'

Molly took a deep breath. 'Evie and Mark can stay with me if you like. That is, until your next leave when you could try to find your friends again.'

Andy looked at her with dark, puzzled eyes. 'Why would you do that? You don't know us. Besides, you've got a store to run.'

'Cissy's going to help me,' Molly shrugged. 'I'm sure we'll manage.'

'I still don't understand,' Andy protested, his frown deepening. 'Why should you care? I'm a total stranger.'

'I was a parent once too,' Molly found herself explaining. 'Ted and me had a little girl ... Emily. She died in the flu outbreak five years ago.'

'I'm sorry to hear that,' he said, but once again he looked doubtful. 'You realize taking on two kids will be quite a handful.'

'I'm willing to give it a try – if you are.'

He stood thoughtfully, then knelt down beside his son. 'Mark, you know I have to go back to sea. Molly said she'll look after you while I'm away. How do you feel about that?'

Mark looked forlorn. 'You said we could go to Betty's.'

'You can. On my next leave.'

'When's that?'

'Can't say, yet.'

Molly saw Mark scuff a tear from his cheek with his sleeve. She knew he was trying to be brave.

'Promise you'll come back for us?'

'Promise.' Andy stood up and looked at Evie. 'Be a good girl for Molly, won't you?'

'Where's you goin'?'

'Back to me ship. But not for long.'

'Have you ever ridden a bicycle?' Molly asked Mark, hoping that she could make this parting feel like more of an adventure.

'No.'

'Well, your dad will sit Evie in the basket on the front and you can ride on the saddle. Hold tightly to my shoulders as I push the bike along.'

With Andy's help, Molly soon had the children sitting comfortably.

As they parted, she smiled at the tall, gaunt-looking man with his anxious expression. 'Don't worry, I'll look after them. Good luck.'

'You too, Molly.' He hesitated, smiling back uncertainly. 'I dunno what to say. Just thanks – again.'

He stood and watched as she pushed the bicycle slowly across the road. When she reached the other side, she glanced over her shoulder.

Andy Miller was gone.

The journey home took much longer than Molly thought it would. The bike, fully laden, was heavy and it took all her strength to keep it steady. She tried to avoid the potholes and bumps, but the wheels seemed to find them anyway.

When at last they arrived at Chalk Wharf, Molly stopped to catch her breath. The air was thick with salty brine from the river and smoke from the factories and the breeze washed it freshly against their faces. Boatmen and factory workers strolled along the cobbled paths, taking their lunchtime break, and to Molly's relief the skies overhead, though filled with the ugly shapes of the grey barrage balloons on their long ropes, were empty of aircraft.

'Can I walk now?' Mark asked and she helped him down from the saddle.

'I know you miss your dad,' Molly said touching his shoulder. 'But it won't be long before he's home.'

Mark looked up at her with his dark, sad eyes. 'He ain't coming home. He's gonna get drowned.'

Molly was taken aback. 'Who told you that?'

'Me mum.'

'Why would she say such a thing, Mark?'

'Cos lots of sailors drown. They sink down to the bottom of the sea and the fish eat 'em up.'

Molly was very shocked by this idea that Stella had planted in her son's head. 'Your dad isn't going to drown, Mark. He's got you and Evie to come home for.'

'I'm 'ungry,' said Evie from the basket, rattling its wicker sides.

She looked down at Mark who still seemed very unhappy. 'Do you think you can find the way from here?' she asked. 'If you walk in front of us you can spot all the holes first.'

As they walked slowly on, Molly wondered what kind of mother Stella could have been to instil such a fear into her child. But then, Stella had been killed in such a tragic way, no wonder his thoughts were centred around people dying.

At last they arrived back at the shop and Mark headed round to the back. Molly followed with the bike and, taking Evie from the basket, they made their way inside.

Everyone stood still as they looked round the glory hole. The tins, bottles and packets were once again strewn over the floor.

'Cissy!' Molly exclaimed when she saw her friend sitting on the bottom stair, nursing a bruised eye. 'What happened?'

'I fell over, that's all. Knocked some stuff from the shelves.'

'Here, let me see.' Molly bent down and pulled Cissy's hand from her face. It was quite a shiner and Molly looked at Cissy suspiciously. 'You fell over?'

'Yer, sorry about the stuff.'

Molly turned to the children who were staring at Cissy, their eyes wide and alarmed.

'It's all right,' she told them. 'You can go and play for a few minutes outside. I'll make something to eat once I've bathed Cissy's eye.'

Molly helped Cissy upstairs and sat her down in the kitchen. 'So what really happened?' she said as she ran a rag under the tap.

'Couldn't say in front of the kids. Didn't want to frighten 'em. I found a couple of tearaways nicking your stuff. They clobbered me and ran off.'

'Oh, Cissy, I'm going to get a bobby.'

Cissy snatched the rag from her hand. 'Don't do that, for Gawd's sake.'

'Why not? You've been assaulted.'

'The coppers won't do nothing,' Cissy protested. 'Just ask a lot of nosy questions.'

'This is a nasty injury. Even if I don't call the law I'll have to tell Mr Stokes.' Molly pushed Cissy's tangled hair from her face.

'Why?'

'I'm sure you can give him a description.'

'Not likely,' Cissy said emphatically. 'It was your fault anyway. The back door was open. Anyone could've sneaked in. And they did.'

Molly sighed. 'Yes, you're right, it was my fault. I was in a hurry to get to the bus station.'

'What the bloomin' heck for?'

'I wanted to find Andy and the children to tell him I'd look after them.'

Cissy sneered at her. 'Blimey, you are a soft touch!'

'I wouldn't say that at all.' Molly was put out by this comment. After all, she'd offered Cissy a roof over her head too. Did she consider that a soft touch as well?

Cissy screwed up her eyes. 'Speaking of kids, who's that little girl and the soldier I clocked in the photographs?'

'The man in uniform was my husband, Ted, and the little girl our daughter, Emily,' Molly said as she bathed Cissy's eye. 'She wasn't quite Evie's age when she died of the flu five years ago.'

Cissy gasped. 'Blimey, you've had it rough, gel. Now I can see why you've taken such a shine to these young 'uns. But remember, you're liable to get hurt when their dad comes back home and takes 'em away. None of my business, of course, it's up to you what you do with your life.'

Molly knew there was a grain of truth in what Cissy said. So perhaps she was a soft touch after all?

But she just couldn't help herself . . .

The next few days were very busy as Molly spent time with Mark and Evie, trying to make them feel welcome, while Cissy worked in the shop, cleaning and arranging the shelves and, to Molly's delight, learning the prices very quickly.

One afternoon Molly took the bus to the public telephone at Poplar. She had decided not to postpone the call to her sister any longer. 'Lyn, is that you?' she asked when the pips went and she put her money in.

'Molly?' Lyn's voice was faint. 'I hope you haven't telephoned before. We've only just come back from staying with Oscar's parents in Margate.'

'Did you have a good time?'

'Yes, we were thoroughly spoiled. How about you and Dad?'

'I'm afraid it's not the best of news.' Molly explained about the explosion that resulted in their father being taken to hospital.

'Have you talked to the doctor about his leg?' Lyn asked immediately.

'I haven't yet,' Molly admitted. 'But the nurses are very good and—'

'Molly,' Lyn interrupted patiently, 'we need to have all the medical facts to hand before we make any decisions.'

'What decisions?' Molly asked, feeling inadequate as usual, as though she'd missed something very important.

'Dad's no spring chicken. We need to know where the break is and how quickly it will mend. And that bump to his head could mean he'll require specialized investigation.'

Thereafter followed so many questions that Molly was relieved to hear the pips interrupt their conversation, and as she had no more money with her, she had to ring off. But not before Lyn had told her she would drive down the following week to get the matter settled.

Molly took a slow walk home, thinking about Lyn and how capable her older sister was. At twenty-nine, two years old than herself, Lyn had been born for leadership, whereas Molly's natural inclination was to listen and follow orders. That was the pecking order in their growing up, and when Ted came along, Molly had automatically taken a back seat in their marriage. Ted, like Lyn and Dad, was so good at everything. Molly wouldn't have known how to live any other way.

Well, at least I've got the call over, Molly decided as she finally got back to Roper Street. Whatever Lyn wants to do, she'll have to run it past Dad first, anyway.

At the store, she found Mr Stokes waiting outside. 'I've tried the door but it's locked,' he told her. 'I just came by to tell you I've got a couple of beds for those kids you've got staying with you. And while I was here I was hoping to have a word with your lodger.'

Molly peered through the window. 'She must be out.'

'Never mind, I'll pop by again.'

'Thanks, Mr Stokes.' Molly waited for him to go then went round the back, where she found Cissy hiding in the shadows.

'Has he gone?' she asked, creeping out.

'Yes. But Cissy, why wouldn't you speak to him?'

'I told you, I don't trust uniforms.'

'Mr Stokes is just the warden. He looks out for everyone in the neighbourhood, that's all. Without him calling for help on the night the bomb went off, I'd never have got Dad to hospital on me own.'

'That's as maybe,' Cissy muttered, letting them in the back door. 'But I ain't you.'

Molly heaved a sigh and decided to change the subject. 'Next week we'll go to the market,' she suggested, thinking this might cheer Cissy up. 'You desperately need some clothes. And so do the children.'

'I'm brassic,' Cissy said as they stood in the glory hole.

'Not to worry. You can have an advance from your wages.'

'What wages?' Cissy demanded. 'I don't expect charity.'

'You'll earn your keep,' Molly replied, wondering if all her coaxing was worth the effort. Cissy could be very argumentative when she felt like it. 'Besides, we have to visit the council offices.'

'What for?'

'Mark and Evie and you have to be officially registered with me as temporary residents, and you'll need coupons and new identity papers. You won't be able to do anything without them.'

A remark that sent Cissy scuttling away, rudely muttering under her breath once again.

The following Monday, Molly left the children with Jean and managed with some difficulty to persuade Cissy into going to the market.

Cissy sat on the bus with her chin jutting out and a resentful expression. But Molly was not put off. Cissy needed clothes of her own and couldn't keep borrowing hers. The children also needed jumpers as they had exhausted the supply in the suitcase. It was essential everyone staying at the store was registered with the council but Molly could see it was no use trying to explain to Cissy. The silence on the bus deepened but Molly was resigned to it; she had other concerns on her mind.

What would she say to Lyn, who might call in at the store after she'd visited Dad? What would Lyn be planning in that focused mind of hers? And what was she going to say when she found Cissy and the children living at the flat?

Half an hour later, Molly and Cissy were standing at Cox Street market's second-hand clothes stall. The hustle and bustle was enjoyable and Cissy finally chose a sensible skirt and two warm blouses to wear under her overall. Having bought clothes for the children too, they set off for the council buildings a ten-minute walk away.

'They'll want to know a lot,' Cissy complained. 'What am I gonna tell them?'

'The truth. That you were bombed out, and give them your new address. Tell them you lost everything and need new documents.'

'Where are you going?'

'To the Food Office on the next floor. Mark and Evie need orange juice, cod liver oil and extra milk supplies.'

'What a lot of palaver.'

'Yes, perhaps. But we've got to do it.' Molly marched Cissy right up to the door of the Welfare Department. As she didn't trust her to stay there, she waited until she was seen. Then she made her way upstairs.

Later, as arranged, they met on the steps outside. 'Well, how did you get on?' Molly asked as they walked to the bus stop.

'Grilled me something rotten,' complained Cissy. 'Wanted to know all me private business. Bloody nosy cows.'

'But did you get your new papers?'

'Said they'd send me a letter. Got to check up first.'

'Me too,' Molly replied as they climbed aboard the bus. 'They have to try to keep track of people in wartime.'

'Pity they couldn't keep track of my old man,' Cissy growled as they settled themselves on the seats. 'Never had a tanner off him and I was left with his debts.'

'Oh dear. He does sound like a bad penny.'

'Vince was a penny that managed to roll right under the authorities' noses and into the wide blue yonder.'

Molly didn't reply. She was beginning to see why Cissy acted so moodily and sounded so bitter. Yet there were just a few moments every now and then when the mask dropped and Molly glimpsed the sensitive, almost childlike person behind it.

'So you still want me to work for you?' Cissy demanded

after a while. 'Even though I ain't got no papers or nothing?'

Molly chuckled. 'That was our deal.'

Cissy just gave her that long, chin-out, suspicious look as she burrowed down into the collar of her coat, a trademark expression that Molly was quickly becoming accustomed to.

Chapter Eight

On Friday morning there were a few flakes of snow and, even though it was freezing, Cissy insisted on scrubbing the shop floor. At a few minutes past ten, just after Molly had given the children breakfast, Cissy called up the stairs.

'Someone here for you!'

Molly hurried to see who it was. She immediately recognized the tall figure of Liz Howells and, hurrying across the shop, pulled her into her arms. 'Liz, how are you? I'm so glad you're safe.'

'Nice to see you, gel. I've been over me aunt's gaff at West Ham. What about you?'

'I'm all right, but Dad's in hospital with a broken leg. This is Cissy. She's going to help me in the shop.'

'Pleased to meet yer, Cissy.' Liz smiled, pulling down her shapeless grey hat over her long, thin face. She nodded to the ruins across the road. 'I used to live over there in that pile of ashes.'

Cissy nodded. 'You got my sympathy, love.'

'Sorry to hear about your dad, Molly. You opening up again?'

'Yes, I hope so. Have you any news on Mrs Lockyer?'

'Afraid she didn't make it.'

'Oh, dear.' Molly fell silent. She'd known the elderly lady almost all her life.

'Still, you gotta get on with life. I've found a room in the next road, Garland Street. So I'll be back to spend me coupons with you. And I'll tell everyone I meet to come with me. Swift's is the best general store this side of the water.'

Molly smiled gratefully. 'Thanks, Liz. We'll need all the custom we can get.' She watched her old friend Liz walk away, her tall, stooped figure passing a woman coming the other way. Unlike Liz, the younger female was elegantly dressed and walked with purpose, as she made her way around the hole in the road that was now cordoned off from pedestrians.

Molly gasped, then hurriedly removed her overall and pressed down her crumpled skirt.

'What yer doing that for?' asked Cissy in surprise.

'Because that's my sister Lyn,' Molly answered, while trying to thread her fingers through her tangled hair.

Smelling sweetly of lavender water, Lyn hugged her. 'Molly, I've just come from the hospital. I had to park Oscar's car in the next road because of that dreadful hole!'

'That's where the bomb fell.'

'When are they filling it in?' Lyn said, glancing at Cissy.

'Don't know.' Molly said quickly, 'Lyn, I'd like you to meet my new assistant, Cissy Brown.'

'Assistant?' Lyn repeated, as Cissy decided to squash out her dog-end with the tip of her boot at Lyn's feet. 'What do you need an assistant for?'

Molly took her sister's arm as Cissy stalked off into the glory hole. 'You'd better come upstairs. There's a lot to tell you.' She wheeled her through the shop and up the stairs to the kitchen.

'Sit down and I'll put the kettle on.'

'I can't stay long, the roads in this area are a nightmare. It'll take me hours to get back to Sidcup.'

As Molly made them tea, she explained how she'd met Cissy, Andy and the children on the night their father had been admitted to hospital. And how, as a result of both Andy and Cissy no longer having roofs over their heads, she had offered Cissy a job as well as taken on Mark and Evie until Andy's next leave.

'But ... but ...' spluttered Lyn as she looked up at Molly. 'These people are strangers. You can't just invite them to stay in your home.'

'Well, I have,' Molly said as she sat beside her sister and filled two mugs with tea. 'Cissy will look after the shop and the children when I visit Dad.'

'But, Molly, this is ridiculous. You're talking as though you have a future here in the East End.'

'I do. We do. Dad's leg will get better—'

'I doubt that, my dear. I spoke with the doctor this morning who gave me rather bad news. The fractures may very well leave him with a limp, at best. At worst, he might not be able to use the leg at all.'

Molly put down her mug with a gasp. 'But it's only a break.'

'A complicated one. Which is why you should start planning to leave this – this place.' Lyn looked around her as though she was sitting in some kind of slum.

'Lyn, we grew up here. This has been our home. Me and Ted had plans to build up the business—'

'Ted is gone, Molly,' Lyn said sombrely. 'You're on your own here. And naturally, as your sister, I want what is best for you. Now, please start thinking sensibly. And don't go giving Dad any ideas of returning here. I told him this morning he would come and convalesce with us.'

Molly was shocked. 'What did he say?'

'Not very much, as he's still suffering from the concussion. I told him, tactfully, that this is the right time now for both you and him to move to Sidcup. There's very little bombing compared to what you've had here. It's safe and very picturesque. Oscar will find a nice little cottage for you to rent while you sell the shop.'

Lyn smiled, a satisfied look on her attractive face. In her blue coat, the same shade as her blue eyes, with a slightly paler blue handbag over her arm, Molly thought how elegant and fashionable she looked. She hardly recognized her sister these days.

'Lyn, I don't want to sell our old home and my livelihood.'

'I understand that, Molly, I do. But you must think of Dad now. He'll need your support. And so do I and Oscar.

Besides, Elizabeth and George have hardly had the chance to get to know their aunt over the past few years.' Lyn drank the rest of her tea hurriedly, then, frowning at Molly's anxious face, she said persuasively, 'Think about it, Molly. What have you left to stay for? Oscar thinks this war is going to be long and drawn-out. There's no money coming into this part of the capital and there's bound to be more bombing of the docks. The East End is finished, dear. Surely that's obvious?'

Molly gulped down her shock. She couldn't believe her ears.

Cissy stood in the shadows at the bottom of the staircase and strained to listen to the voices upstairs. She had taken an instant dislike to Molly's sister, and was well aware the feeling was mutual.

What worried Cissy the most was the fact that, according to the snatches of conversation from above, Molly was being pressured into selling the store. Who was this Oscar who seemed to have such a big say in things? And what business was it of anyone else but Molly and her father?

Cissy felt the old feelings of fear creep slowly back. When she'd found those kids in the shop, stealing from Molly, she'd thought it was Ronnie's men, who would have done far more than punch her in the eye. Years ago, she'd believed her old man, Vince, would stick by her, but he'd proved to a be a spineless git and had soon ditched her. She'd been a soft touch after, for that animal Ronnie who'd won her trust and then put her on the game. Fear had followed her like a shadow since then. Ethel had been her last chance of escape. But now the old girl was gone, and Molly, although she was a nice kid, seemed to have no backbone.

Just then she heard the children and she jumped away from the stairs.

'Hello, you lot,' she said a little guiltily as Simon, Susie, Mark and Evie came running in from the yard.

'Mark fell over,' Susie said, showing Cissy her bloody handkerchief. 'His scab's come off.'

Simon stepped forward, his face very red under his freckles. 'We didn't push him or nothing.'

'You gotta have that graze washed, old son,' she told Mark. 'Come on, we'll go upstairs and bathe it.' She lifted him into her arms and followed the others, who bounded up the stairs in front of her.

Cissy smiled to herself. Mark's bleeding knee would make a timely interruption in Molly's conversation with that bossy cow, Lyn.

Chapter Nine

Molly shivered, hugging herself as she came up the stairs and entered the kitchen. On finding herself faced with a room full of noisy kids, her sister had quickly taken her leave.

'Well, that went well,' Cissy observed dryly as she drew a carving knife through the bread and handed a slice to each child now sitting round the kitchen table.

Ignoring the sarcasm, Molly smiled at the children. 'Is your knee better, Mark?'

'S'all right. Cissy put something on it. Who was that lady?'

'She's my sister, Lyn. We grew up together here. Now she's married and has two children, George and Elizabeth, who are five and six.'

'Why didn't they come too?' enquired Susie.

'They're at school where they live in Sidcup.'

'We're going to school on Monday,' said Simon, licking his lips. 'Mark can bring Evie too. She's a bit young, but our teacher won't mind as most of the kids go there till the war's over. Mum said she'll take them. It ain't a proper school cos ours is closed right now. But you still learn plenty of things.'

'I wanna go ter school!' Evie shouted, banging her spoon on the table and poking out her tongue. Everyone laughed, including Cissy.

Molly had watched with some interest the way in which Cissy had made Mark sit on the chair next to Lyn as she unravelled his bloody sock. With Evie climbing onto Lyn's lap in order to get a better view of the minor operation, and putting her grubby hands all over Lyn's clean coat, their discussion had soon come to an end.

'Can we go out and play in the snow again?' asked Mark.

'Yes, but no more falling over.'

Laughing and shouting, the children all jumped up from the table and ran down the stairs.

Molly looked at Cissy, who seemed to be enjoying their company. 'So, now you've met my sister.'

'She's posh, ain't she?'

'Lyn's an East Ender like me and you.'

'Well, she don't sound like one. Are you gonna sell the shop?'

Molly smiled curiously. 'Were you listening?'

'No, course not. Couldn't help but hear a bit. For my money's worth, I don't reckon the East End's finished. Do you?'

'Well, no . . . but—'

'You'll have all your old customers come in on Monday, and like your mate Liz said, the word soon gets around about a good store.' Without another word, Cissy was off down the stairs.

Molly stood thoughtfully in the kitchen. It seemed Cissy, a virtual stranger, had more confidence in restoring the business than Lyn did. But what if Lyn was right about Dad and he could never use his leg again? What hope had she of rebuilding their lives here in Roper Street, if Dad wasn't part of her world?

The hospital, on Sunday afternoon, was busier than ever when Molly arrived. Relatives, friends and casualties from the overnight raids were filling the hospital's corridors. Molly hadn't slept well in the Anderson. She couldn't stop thinking about Lyn's plans for Dad. Should she just agree to them? What about Dad? Did he want to live in Sidcup?

As she walked into the ward, she saw his bed was empty. 'Your father's been transferred to the longer-stay ward,' a nurse informed her, giving directions of how to get there.

'I'm Mrs Swift. How's my father?' Molly asked at the small office which stood adjacent to the new ward.

The sister looked up. 'Have you spoken to the doctor?' she asked.

'No, but my sister did when she visited and was told his injury was more serious than we thought.'

'Yes, I'm afraid so. But with patience and physical therapy he may be able to walk again.'

Molly felt very shocked. Lyn was right. Molly had been hoping that she might have exaggerated in order to get her way. 'Does Dad know?'

'We've explained the situation. But at the moment, because of the concussion and to relieve him of any pain, his medication is helping to ease any worries. And I must warn you, he may not remember immediately who you are.'

The sister took Molly to a small room with only a handful of beds. It was very quiet in here and the visitors at each bed all looked up and smiled. Molly felt grateful for the welcome but found it hard to look at her father, who lay in a bed by the wall, a small figure under the white sheets covering the unsightly cage.

He was asleep and so she sat down on the chair. His cheeks were sunken under the bandage and he was propped into position by pillows.

'Hello, love,' he said, suddenly coming awake.

The tears were very close as she held his hand. 'I'm glad they've found you a nice quiet ward.'

He sighed and dredged up a smile. 'How's tricks with you?'

'You'll be glad to know I'm opening the shop tomorrow.'

Molly decided not to say anything about Lyn's visit unless he spoke about her first. But then he fell asleep again and Molly sat quietly listening to him breathe. After a while, he woke with a start. 'Molly, love! How long have you been sitting there?'

'Not very long, Dad.'

'How do you like my new bed?'

'Much better. It's nice and quiet in this ward.'

'I've met a new pal. He's over there, Charlie – see? He was a docker in his time and knows Roper Street.'

Molly looked over to where a man sat in his bed, propped by pillows and reading a newspaper. 'I'm glad you've made a friend.'

Molly listened to her father as he told her about the doctors and nurses, and the routine of the new ward, which seemed to be all he was concerned about. Deciding not to refer to Lyn or the shop, Molly felt better. It must be as the sister had warned her, she decided: Dad was living in his own little world. So for the rest of the visit she sat and listened, until his eyes closed and he fell back to sleep again.

All too soon it was Monday. The bombing overnight had kept them all awake in the shelter, even the kids, and she had wondered if number one Roper Street would end up like Liz's house, a pile of burning bricks!

But, miraculously, the shop and flat had survived the night unscathed. Leaving Mark and Evie to play in their room, Molly and Cissy went downstairs and turned the sign to OPEN.

'Ready for the rush?' asked Cissy in her usual mocking manner as she put on her overall.

'Well, we should have a delivery today,' Molly replied as she too put on her overall. 'Last week I wrote to the whole-salers, so it should come today. I warned them to send their van up the street the other way, as there's still the big hole in the road.'

'What's on order?' asked Cissy, who Molly saw had washed her dark hair and minus her turban looked very presentable.

'The usual order for our registered customers, bearing in mind that paraffin and kindling are in short supply. It's the paraffin we need the most, as people are using it to stop the red army released from the brick cavities after the bombing. On the food side, I'm hoping for a full quota of Spam, condensed milk and Camp coffee if we're lucky. Oh yes, and bags of flour and some cereals and a little veg.'

'What do we do till we get our first customer?' Cissy asked, prowling the floor.

'Let's practise,' suggested Molly. 'I'll be the customer.' She took several items from the shelves. 'You take my money and ring up the amount in pounds, pence and/or shillings.'

For the rest of the morning, in between stopping to talk to the children, Molly and Cissy continued to practise in the empty shop.

Just as Molly was wondering if the shop door would ever open, the van driver arrived. Most of Molly's order was complete, and as they began to unpack it a customer came in, followed by another and then another. Molly couldn't contain her delight as everyone wished her success – faces old and new, who assured her they would make Swift's their chosen store.

The day had been a success, Molly congratulated herself that night. Lyn had been mistaken. There was still business to be had in the East End, despite the bombing. And Cissy had taken like a duck to water to the running of the shop and serving the customers. When she visited Dad later in the week, Molly would be able to leave the shop and the children in the capable hands of her new assistant.

*

After a very busy Monday, Tuesday was a complete disaster.

There were only a few customers as news came through from the wholesalers of sweeping new price controls from the Food Minister, Lord Woolton. These applied to poultry and preserves, coffee, cocoa, rice, biscuits, custard and jelly, and many more. By the end of the day, with no business, Molly was crestfallen.

'Bloody government,' Cissy complained as she swept the shop floor and Molly turned the sign to CLOSED. 'Always out to make a fast buck.'

'We'll have to struggle on,' Molly said as she cashed up the meagre two pounds and sixpence. 'We can't fall at the first hurdle.'

But by the end of the week Molly was beginning to wonder if Lyn wasn't right and the East End was finished. The number of new customers who had registered with the shop was small so far. Each one complained of the higher prices, which Molly could do nothing about. Fortunately Evie and Mark's ration books had arrived, but Cissy was still waiting for hers and Molly was using her own coupons to meet their needs.

Then on Saturday morning, Liz Howells bustled in as usual, wearing her trademark grey hat. Molly was delighted to see that several neighbours accompanied her.

'Don't worry,' Liz assured Molly and Cissy. 'The new prices was a shock to everyone at first, even the shops up west suffered. But we've all got to eat and we know that Swift's won't rook us.'

More customers followed, and by the end of the day Molly had taken enough money to pay the wholesalers' bill.

The most welcome news came from Jean, who had asked
the school if they would register both Evie and Mark on their
books. The answer was in the affirmative and Molly allowed
herself to hope that perhaps, as from now, life wouldn't pose
such a struggle and all her good intentions would finally bear
fruit.

Chapter Ten

New customers arrived daily as word went round that Swift's General Store was open for business again. Other customers came by word of mouth and registered at Swift's, and Molly always made it worth their while. She knew she was up against the markets and other corner shops, so she offered to make deliveries on her bike. Once again Cissy proved her worth and shared the rounds with Molly.

This was a successful arrangement and many customers who were housebound chose Swift's as their store.

Molly was pleased to see that Cissy spent her hard-earned wage on new clothes rather than on filling her flask. She had taken a fancy to the big wardrobe in Dad's room and whenever she had a spare moment Molly knew she would be upstairs, rummaging around on its shelves.

By the middle of February business was buoyant, but there was no word from Andy. Molly had hoped for a letter, but nothing had come through. Mark missed his dad and was often withdrawn, unlike his sister, who was the centre of everyone's attention with her winning ways. Even the teachers told Molly that she was a most welcome addition to the class.

At the end of the month, on a cold and drizzly winter morning, a stranger walked into the shop. He was tall and slim, his face shaded by a trilby and the turned-up collar of his raincoat. Molly noticed that all her customers left quickly.

'I'd like to speak to Miss Brown,' he told her, looking round with a suspicious expression in his dark eyes.

'She's out on deliveries,' Molly said, frowning. 'What do you want with her?'

'When will she be back?'

'I don't know,' she said, not liking his questioning.

'How long do deliveries usually take?'

Molly straightened her back. 'That's no business of yours,' she said coldly. 'Who are you? And what do you want with Cissy?'

The man looked at her for one long moment then slid his hand inside his raincoat. He showed her his identity card. 'Detective Constable Longman,' he said in an official tone. 'Are you Mrs Swift?'

'Yes, why?'

'Your store was burgled and it wasn't reported. Do you know it's an offence to obstruct the law?'

Molly had known all along it was wrong not to tell the authorities about the looters. Mr Stokes must have passed the information on, as Cissy had gone out of her way to avoid him.

'If you mean those kids pinching a few things,' Molly said, trying to sound as though this was unimportant, 'it was nothing. And it was my fault anyway, as I left the back door open.'

'Trespassing, nevertheless,' said the policeman. 'Witnessed by Miss Brown.'

'Who told you that?'

'I think I'd better ask the questions, don't you? Now, how long has Miss Brown been working for you?'

Molly didn't like this line of questioning at all. It was as if he suspected Cissy of wrongdoing. 'Long enough for me to trust her,' she replied without hesitation. 'If it wasn't for Miss Brown I wouldn't be able to open the store. My dad's in hospital and I have to visit him. Added to which I'm looking after two children whose mother died in the blitz just after Christmas. We've struggled through some very hard times and after losing my husband at Dunkirk last year, I considered giving up the business. But I was lucky enough to find someone I could rely on to help me.' Molly took an indignant breath.

'Did the thieves take any money?' the policeman asked.

'No, there wasn't any to take. Now, are we finished?'

'I'm only trying to do my job here,' the detective replied. 'We have to protect the public from criminals. And the only way we can do that is to track them down, whoever they may be. Stealing is stealing, whether it's a couple of kids or a gang. And don't forget, if those kids are successful once, they're liable to try again.'

Molly felt a little guilty. He seemed a decent sort and of

course he did have a point. Those kids shouldn't have done what they did and getting away with it might have spurred them on to more break-ins. Besides, she was certain they had caused Cissy's black eye, which was her greatest concern. 'Yes, I do understand,' she relented. 'But there's nothing here for you to worry about now. I've had new bolts fitted and don't keep much cash in the till.'

'I'm glad to hear it.' A friendly smile lifted his lips. 'We do seem to have got off on the wrong foot. Do you think we could start again, this time without an interrogation on my part? And may I also say how sorry I am to hear of your loss. Those boys at Dunkirk were very brave lads.'

These sympathetic remarks surprised Molly. He was at last sounding human. 'I realize you have a very difficult job to do,' she admitted cautiously.

'I've only been doing it a month, actually,' he replied. 'Before that I was a uniform on the beat. The thing is, I volunteered for this new unit in the Force. Community Liaison has been set up to deal with looting and burglary during the blitz. There's so much thieving going on now, under cover of the blackout. But it's quite unusual for a shop to be forcefully entered in daylight. Most looters are opportunists and steal quite randomly from the many hundreds of bombed sites.'

Molly could now understand the reason for his questioning. 'Well, I'd like to help you,' she told him truthfully. 'But really, Miss Brown – er, Cissy – didn't see the faces of these kids. She couldn't even describe them to me, let alone give you a description. And that's what you're looking for, isn't it? Some sort of clue as to what they look like?'

'Yes, that's about it.'

'Who told you about the break-in?'

'It was reported by a warden.'

'I thought so. Well, Mr Stokes is well meaning and does a grand job, but this time he's made a fuss about nothing.'

The tall stranger nodded slowly. 'I take your point. But if I could speak to Miss Brown just for a few minutes, at least I could tell my gaffer that I've interviewed her. And that would be the end of that.'

Molly didn't know what to do. Cissy would refuse point-blank as she hated the law. But how could she tell this copper that?

'Perhaps I'll call another day,' he said, sliding his hat on as a customer walked in. 'I won't hold up business. Good afternoon, Mrs Swift.'

Surprised at the turnaround in his attitude, Molly watched him walk out. When the door closed, she quickly served the woman, a younger lady by the name of Mrs Owens.

'Copper, was he?' she asked Molly suspiciously. 'You can tell 'em a mile off.'

'He was very polite.'

'That's how they get their information. A tin of sardines, please, if you've got one. Here's me ration book.'

'Well, it's their job, I suppose,' Molly said, and after serving her with what she wanted, was more than surprised when her customer added that she'd read in the newspaper that twenty cases of looting had been tried at the Old Bailey, of which ten were auxiliary firemen. 'Someone turned 'em in, poor buggers,' Mrs Owens said. 'All the firemen did was help themselves to a few bits and pieces that no one else would've wanted.'

'How do you know that?' Molly asked.

'Because my other half is a volunteer fireman and got the inside gen,' came the caustic reply. 'A man risks his life to keep London safe and what happens? The law comes down on him like a ton of bricks just to make an example of ordinary, decent blokes. I tell you, I wouldn't have come in here, love, if I'd known I breathed the same air as that copper.'

'Hear, hear,' said a voice behind Molly, and she turned to see Cissy standing there, her cheeks glowing red.

'Cissy, I didn't know you were back.'

'Yeah, I'm back all right.'

'Take a tip from me,' said the woman, 'stay away from the rozzers, love, if you want to keep your customers.'

Molly was taken aback when, after Mrs Owens had left, Cissy stared at her angrily. 'I never thought you'd do the dirty on me,' she hissed. 'I never should have trusted you!' Then, turning on her heel, she ran up the stairs.

'Cissy?' Molly called a short while later as she stood outside Cissy's room.

'Door's open.'

When Molly walked in she saw Cissy's clothes piled on the bed. 'What are you doing?'

'I'm leaving. Here, you can have this back.' She threw a herringbone coat towards her.

'Don't be daft! It's yours. I gave it to you.'

'Dunno why you wanted me to stay in the first place.' She

pulled on her shabby old coat, the one that Molly had first seen her wearing at the hospital.

'Are you leaving because of the copper?'

'You told him everything!' Cissy almost spat, her grey eyes narrowing bitterly. 'You've landed me in it.'

'Sit down on the bed and talk to me sensibly.'

'No, I'm leaving.'

'Not without an explanation,' Molly said firmly. 'You owe me that at least.'

Cissy's eyes glittered with defiance, but this time Molly wasn't going to let her get her own way. She pointed to the bed and inclined her head with a jerk. 'Sit down, Cissy. I don't often lose me temper, but you are certainly testing it now.'

'Why should I stay?'

'Because we're friends, or I thought we were.' Molly sat down on her father's bed next to the pile of clothes. She wondered if Cissy was going to walk out on her. Then what would she do? She couldn't physically drag her back. Cissy was behaving like a spoiled child, showing the other side to her very capable nature. But, with a sullen frown and a jut of the chin, Cissy sank down on the bed. She folded her arms over her chest and looked at Molly sullenly.

'Thank you,' Molly said politely. 'Now, you must have overheard the last of my conversation with Mrs Owens, who should have known better than to say what she did. The police have a very difficult job to do—' Molly put up her hand as Cissy was about to interrupt. 'Let me finish, please. I want you to know that I didn't report the break-in to the law – even though I felt I should have. I only told Mr Stokes because I assumed you wouldn't mind having a word with him. He obviously got browned off trying to find you and reported the incident. So, Cissy, if only you had thought it through, we could have avoided this unpleasant situation.'

Cissy still stared at her defiantly, but Molly could see that her anger was now subsiding and so she continued.

'As your friend,' she said quietly, 'I was very upset when I saw your bruised eye. And, after all you've told me about your feelings toward the police and authorities, do you really think I would deliberately "land you in it"?'

Cissy dropped her head, letting her thick dark hair fall over her face as she stared into her lap. 'So what's gonna happen now?'

'Do you mean if you don't run off in a paddy?'

'I can't help me temper.'

'Well, I'll tell you what the policeman told me.' Molly explained all about the newly appointed detective and the Community Liaison set up to protect the public from looters and burglaries. 'All he needs is a few words with you so his boss can close the books.'

'He'll go asking me all sorts of questions,' said Cissy, frowning at Molly. 'And I won't have no answers.'

'I don't think so.'

'Why's that?'

'I've told him I trust you completely and without you I couldn't open the store.'

Cissy's light-grey eyes widened. 'Blimey, what did you say that for?'

'Because it's true. I do trust you and you're a great help. You even seem to be getting on with the children of late.'

Cissy sniffed and tossed back her head. 'They ain't bad kids, I suppose.'

'So will you think about not legging it when the copper comes back to talk to you?'

Cissy sat up, on the alert again. 'When's that?'

'I don't know. Mrs Owens came in and he left.'

'I can't promise nothin'. There's things I ain't gonna tell anyone.'

Molly took a soft breath and nodded. 'Whatever's happened in the past is your affair. It don't make one iota of difference to me.'

Cissy looked at the clothes on the bed. 'S'pose I'd better put them back in the wardrobe again.'

'I suppose you had.' Molly smiled as she left the room. That was probably the closest Cissy would ever come to an apology.

Soon it was March and Molly decided, as there was no word from Andy, that she would search for the Denhams herself. She would begin at the Red Cross depot where Andy said he'd already enquired. But perhaps someone might recognize the names of Betty and Len Denham.

'They could be anywhere by now,' Cissy said, as one Wednesday morning after Molly had walked the children to school with Jean, she told Cissy her plan.

'It's worth a try.'

'Well, good luck. Don't worry about the shop. I'll manage.'

'I won't be long,' Molly promised as she did up her coat and slipped her shopping bag over her arm.

Cissy waved her off into the murky morning and Molly walked to the bus stop in Westferry Road where she caught the number fifty-seven to Poplar. After the night's raids the street cleaners were out in force, as were the Civil Defence and fire brigade. The old Red Cross depot was just off the high street and was undergoing repairs. The depot's volunteers had distinctive red crosses pinned to their clothes as they helped the many displaced families.

How lucky I am not to be homeless, Molly thought gratefully, as she struggled through the crowds and found a woman in a dark-blue uniform and white apron. She was bending down to an old man who sat silently on a wooden box, staring into space.

'Excuse me,' Molly said, tapping the woman's shoulder.

'Yes, what is it?' She looked at Molly with a harassed expression.

'I'm searching for a couple who were bombed out of their home late last December. Betty and Len Denham is the name. They were from the East India Dock Road area.'

'All these people here are recent casualties,' she was told. 'Are they your relatives?'

'No, but the Denhams are members of the Salvation Army.'

'Then you would be better off enquiring at the Mission Hall up the road.'

'I thought perhaps you could tell me if you have any Salvationists working here?'

'Not that I know of. But look around you. There are many who volunteer on a daily basis, then we don't see them again. You could walk around and ask, if you like.'

Molly tried a few people, hearing, as she went, stories of terrible heartbreak. So many had lost everything they owned. Many people were in a state of shock, their eyes vague or full of sadness. Some were still being treated for cuts, bruises and minor wounds. Others, like the old man, were sitting or standing without saying a word. Some talked at a rate of knots, some wept, some were silent. Others tried to cope with humour or complaints.

Eventually Molly gave up. If the Denhams had been brought here on that fateful night in December, no one remembered them now.

Her next call was to the Salvation Army Mission Hall up the road, where a service was in progress. The wooden bench creaked as she sat down. There were nods and smiles from the gathering as a young girl standing at the front began to sing 'All Things Bright and Beautiful'. Dressed in her bonnet and dark uniform, she was accompanied by a brass band.

Molly found her mind drifting back to the hymns she remembered from her own childhood. She'd attended Sunday school with Lyn, while their parents did the ordering and wrote up the accounts of the shop. Sunday was supposed to be a day of rest, but not for Bill and Thelma Keen.

She smiled at the memory of her dad's words as he lay in the hospital. Yes, their lives had revolved around the store. As soon as they'd been old enough to count pence into shillings and shillings into pounds, she and Lyn had been drafted in to help.

'Welcome,' a small voice said, and Molly jumped. She looked around. The service had come to an end and the young girl was smiling down at her. 'Have you come to worship with us?'

Molly felt awkward. 'No. I'm not religious.'

'We're all soldiers of Jesus.'

'I've come to ask about some people I'm trying to find. You see, they were Salvationists and were bombed out of their house last December. I need to find them quite badly.'

'Did they attend this Mission?'

Molly shrugged. 'I'm not sure. Their names are Betty and Len Denham.'

The girl, who looked almost as young as Susie, frowned. 'I'll ask the band sergeant. He's been here a long time.'

'Thank you.' Molly watched her walk away. She went up to a small group of band members who each held an instrument. Molly guessed they were about to practise as they took their seats again.

The girl was talking to a tall man in uniform and Molly's hopes rose as he put down his brass cornet and scribbled some words on a piece of paper. Perhaps it was the Denhams' address?

'Did you find them?' Molly asked hopefully when the girl returned.

'I'm afraid not. But our bandmaster has written down the address of our headquarters in Queen Victoria Street. You could perhaps write first, giving them all the information you have and asking if your friends can be traced. They will be the people who know.'

'Do you think that's possible?'

'Have faith in our Lord Jesus Christ,' said the girl with a big smile. 'He that believeth has witness in himself.'

Molly tucked the note in her shopping bag. 'Thank you.'

She got up and left. As she stood waiting for the bus home, she wished she could have the kind of faith the girl talked about. But since losing Emily and Ted, the faith she had been taught at Sunday school as a child seemed very far away.

By the end of March, Molly hadn't made any more headway with her enquiries. Between the shop and Evie and Mark, all her time was taken up. Then one morning a a familiar figure walked into the shop. This time, Detective Constable Longman had a smile on his face and politely removed his hat. 'Good morning, Mrs Swift.'

'Detective Constable Longman,' Molly nodded. She was aware of the silence from the glory hole where Cissy was weighing out potatoes.

'Is Miss Brown about?'

Molly guessed that he knew she was, as he could have been watching the shop. All the same, she was reluctant to call Cissy, who had been in very good spirits since their last heart-to-heart.

'I'm Cissy Brown,' Cissy said before Molly could answer, walking in and standing at the counter. 'What do you want?'

Molly was very surprised, but also relieved that Cissy hadn't made herself scarce like she had done before. Perhaps, she thought, Cissy had really taken notice of what she had said about friendship and trust.

'Miss – er – Brown.' The detective glanced over Molly's shoulder. 'Is there somewhere we can speak in private?'

'You can say all you've got to say in front of Molly.' Cissy's tone was curt.

'Yes, but this is a place of business. You may have customers walking in.'

'So what? I ain't done nothing.'

'You can go upstairs,' Molly said quickly. 'Cissy will show you the way.'

Just then a customer did come in and Molly attended to what she wanted as Cissy, forced to comply, led the way up to the flat. As Molly filled the woman's shopping basket with her weekly rations, she hoped this time Cissy would remember it was in her interests to finally resolve the problem, and then, with luck, the police wouldn't bother her any more.

When Cissy, some time later, came down followed by the detective, she threw a sour look at Molly, grabbed the broom and disappeared.

'Well, that's all for now,' said the detective to Molly as he put on his hat. 'I'm able to make my report and unless you have anything else to add, I'll take my leave.'

'No, nothing,' Molly assured him.

'Here's my card, just in case.'

Molly glanced at the card on the counter but didn't pick it up. He gave her a long look and hesitated. She hoped he wasn't about to think of something else to ask and so she turned, took a duster from under the counter and began to clean the shelves.

When he closed the door behind him, Molly went to the window and looked out. She saw the policeman pause on the other side of the road. He slipped his hand into his pocket and brought out a packet of cigarettes. Sliding one between his lips, he struck a match. Slowly he looked over at the shop.

Molly stepped away and bumped into Cissy. 'Oh,' she gasped, 'you gave me a fright.'

'Is he still there?'

'Yes.'

'Quite the charmer, ain't he?'

'What do you mean?'

'Well, he was all sweetness and light, trying to get round me. But I knew exactly what he wanted. He was waiting for me to make me first mistake.'

Molly stared at Cissy in astonishment, then laughed. 'Cissy, you've seen too many films.'

'No, I ain't. But I've got a nose for coppers.'

'So you keep telling me.'

'He was all eyes. Looking round your place, seeing what you had. Weighing it up.'

'Well, he is a policeman, after all.'

'At least I ain't been handcuffed and taken off,' said Cissy going to the window and peering through the glass.

'He wouldn't do that.' Molly frowned. 'You were just a witness, that's all.'

'Yeah, but he don't like me.'

'Why would you say that?'

'It's one law for posh people like you. Another for women like me.'

'Cissy, don't say that.'

'Why not? It's true. He could see at a glance what type I am. And when I opened me mouth to speak, that put the tin hat on it.'

Molly shook her head with a big sigh. What had happened in Cissy's past to make her so bitter? What was she hiding? Whatever it was, it was clear she had no intention of putting her trust in authority.

'Oh, and now we've got another visitor. Thank Gawd it's not for me this time.' Cissy turned round with a smirk. 'You're welcome to go upstairs and talk in private,' she mimicked as Molly saw her sister walk up the street, and quickly Molly took the detective's card and slipped it into her pocket.

'Have you seen Dad?' Molly asked a few minutes later as Lyn carefully took off her smart fawn coat and matching gloves, handing them to Molly as she sat down on the settee in the front room.

'Yes. Unfortunately Elizabeth's had a dreadful cold so I haven't been able to go until now. I didn't want to pass any germs on to Dad.'

'Is Elizabeth better?' Molly asked, sitting beside her sister.

'Yes, thanks.'

Molly served her sister with a cup of tea made in the best china. 'Did you talk to the doctor?'

'Dr Neil and I thoroughly discussed Dad's case. He said his leg will need lots of physical therapy and he'll be confined to a wheelchair for a period.'

'A wheelchair?' Molly took in a breath. 'How long for?'

'Who knows?'

'But they must have given you some indication!'

'Molly,' her sister said slowly, as if she was talking to a child, 'this is no ordinary break. It's a fracture of all three leg bones including the hip.'

'Why wasn't I told?'

'Probably because you didn't ask the right questions. You have to sit these medical people down and demand answers. I told him that I wanted a weekly report telephoned to me and that any expense incurred will be paid for by Oscar.' Her smile told Molly that her sister had enjoyed this discussion. 'I also explained,' Lyn continued, 'that after everything possible has been done for him in the hospital, Oscar will send a vehicle to bring him home to us.'

'Lyn, you should have asked me before you decided on that.'

'Why? It's obvious he can't come here.'

Molly put down her cup. 'I'm going to have the glory hole made into a room so he won't have to go upstairs.'

Lyn looked at her blankly. 'Molly, that's not a very good idea. The glory hole is purpose-built for the shop as a store-room. Where would Dad bathe? He'd need a bedpan because he couldn't possibly use the closet in the yard. And with two children and a stranger living on the premises, he'd have no privacy at all.'

'The children won't be here forever,' Molly protested. 'Their father's making other arrangements when he comes back from sea.'

'How do you know he will come back?'

This brought Molly upright in her seat. 'He has to. They've no one else.'

'Precisely. If he perished – quite likely, in his role as a merchant seaman – they'd be orphans. And you, Molly, would be saddled with his family.' Lyn took an impatient breath. 'Besides, what on earth would you do with Dad in a wheelchair during the raids? You couldn't take him into the Turners' shelter. And pushing him along to a public one, together with your other – er, other "responsibilities", well – I'm sorry, my dear, but you must agree that Dad coming back here is out of the question.'

Molly felt close to despair. She'd refused to consider the possibility that Dad might not return. This was his home, the home he had lived in for most of his life, and it was inconceivable that he should live elsewhere.

'I know this is a shock for you,' Lyn said and patted her arm. 'But after you've given the matter some thought you'll see it's all for the best.'

Molly sat, unable to express the feelings that were gripping her. First Emily, then Ted and now Dad. How could fate be so cruel in taking them all away? She was angry and bewildered and hurt. She wanted to shout out against the unfairness of life. Lyn had her lovely family, two growing, healthy children, a husband who loved and protected them and a big, safe house in the country that was in far less danger of being attacked by the Luftwaffe than the East End of London.

But hard on the heels of her turmoil came the voice of reason and the clear knowledge that Lyn, as usual, was right.

'Come along now, darling.' Lyn put her arms around her. 'My advice to you is as it's always been. Leave the shop and flat. Move out to Sidcup with us and Oscar will find you a lovely new home.'

Molly sighed heavily. Was there any use in protesting? 'I'll make us something to eat before you leave,' she said as Lyn patted her arm.

'No, I can't stay, I'm afraid.' Lyn stood up and Molly hurried to fetch her coat and gloves.

Downstairs in the shop, they embraced once more. 'Telephone me soon. And remember, Mum would want us to stick together. She would be very relieved to know that you and Dad were out of harm's way and enjoying your life with us.'

Before Molly could reply, her sister had opened the door and was walking down the street, a tall, stately figure avoiding the barrier around the hole and making her way to her car parked in the next street.

Chapter Eleven

It was the end of March and the nights were becoming lighter, but people were weary of the blitz. Molly read in the newspapers about the deliberate aerial attack on the Queen's residence and, like Roper Street, Buckingham Palace was showered with incendiary bombs. The Palace survived, but after six months of continual attack, Molly was beginning to wonder if the store's luck would eventually run out. Each day there was news of the devastation caused to many British cities, ports and industrial areas. So far, number one Roper Street had withstood the pounding. But for how long could her luck last?

She knew too, that soon the doctor would release her father from hospital, as he was now being taught to use a wheelchair. One afternoon when the weather became warmer, Molly pushed him out to the small garden at the rear of the hospital.

'They wheeled me down to the shelter last night,' her

father complained as Molly sat on a bench beside his wheel-chair. 'Didn't get any kip, what with all them low-level bombing runs the buggers are doing. Being in this thing don't help. I ain't got the hang of pushing meself yet.'

'You will with practice, Dad.'

'So they tell me.'

'You'll have to be patient and keep trying.'

'That's what your mother would say.'

'Well, then, she'd be right.'

He sighed and nodded. 'What about the store, ducks? Are you managing all right? Still got that girl and those two kids with you? Forgotten their names, though.'

Molly smiled, happy to know he remembered Cissy and the children. 'Evie and Mark are doing well at school,' she told him. 'Cissy looks after the shop while I'm here. Dad, it's nice to know your memory's coming back.'

He grinned. 'Maybe. Tomorrow I could be off with the fairies.'

'Have you seen Lyn lately?'

'Yes, but she don't stay long. Has to get back to the kids.' Molly guessed what was coming next. 'Your sister wants me over at her place. I suppose you two have talked about that?'

Molly nodded. 'It does seem the sensible thing to do.'

'Grin and bear it, should I?'

She smiled. 'Just while you get better. It'll be nice for Elizabeth and George to have their grandfather around.'

'Yeah, but I'd like to kick a ball with them. That sort of thing.'

'You can still throw a ball from a wheelchair.'

When Molly left the hospital that day, she felt very down. She knew things had to change. But must they change so soon?

That night in the Anderson Molly got very little sleep. The Luftwaffe was concentrating its efforts on London and the South East, so the Home Service reported. Simon, Susie, Mark and Evie were growing tired of being cooped up in the bunks; the novelty of their camp had finally worn off and Molly had noticed how restless Cissy was. Even Jean was short-tempered.

Her thoughts turned to Andy. She was certain he would never desert his children. But what if, as Lyn had said, he didn't survive? The children would be orphans. And who would take care of them?

If only Ted were here. If only she had his strong shoulder to lean on and he could take over all the important decisions that she found so difficult to make.

Business was brisk over Easter, though stock for the shop was in short supply. Molly was told by the warehouse that goods would be limited while British merchant ships were at the mercy of Germany's U-boat wolf packs. She realized she didn't even know which ship Andy was serving on. Why hadn't she asked him?

On Easter Sunday, Molly decided to take her dad some little brown cakes that she'd made with Evie. They were more cocoa and carrot than flour, but she hoped they would cheer him up.

The nurse looked at her in surprise as she walked into the ward. 'Have you come to see your father?'

'Yes, is he in the garden?'

'No, he was discharged this morning into the care of your sister and brother-in-law. There's a letter in the office for you.'

Molly stared at the young nurse. 'But the doctor didn't tell me he was going.'

'It was all rather quick,' the nurse agreed. 'We're desperately short of beds, you see. Your father was well enough to leave so I believe the doctor telephoned Mrs Highfield.'

'Can I have this letter?'

'Of course.'

Ten minutes later, Molly was sitting on the bench in the hospital garden, where she had sat with her father. The letter wasn't very long. It also looked rather hurriedly written.

Dearest Molly,

Doctor Neil phoned today, Friday, and said Dad was ready to leave on Sunday. Oscar is driving me; we have bought a wheelchair for him already so we won't have to borrow one from the hospital. If you would like to telephone me next week, I can tell you how Dad is settling in. Happy Easter.

Love Lyn

Molly brushed a tear from her eye. She looked at the tall trees in front of her, just coming out in bud. Spring was here. She wanted to put her arms around her dad and wish him a happy Easter.

Why didn't she have a telephone? Why couldn't she afford to buy a wheelchair and drive a large car? Why couldn't she have a nice house where Dad could recover in comfort?

The following week, Molly wrote to the director at the Salvation Army Headquarters in the city. She was now determined to find these Denhams. Having thought things over, she knew that the children must be reunited with this married couple as soon as possible. Andy had said they were trusted friends and had looked after them since they had been very small. Although they were not true family, he looked on them as next of kin. It was only right that Evie and Mark should have a future with them.

On Sunday, having posted the letter, she telephoned Lyn from the call box. It was Oscar she spoke to, as Lyn, she was told, was out with the children.

'Your father is being well looked after,' Oscar explained in his clipped, capable tone of voice. 'You've no need to worry, Molly.'

'Can he come to the phone?'

'He's having his afternoon nap.'

'When shall I phone again, then?'

'Next week,' Oscar decided. 'Mrs James will know more by then.'

'Who is Mrs James?' Molly asked in surprise.

'His physical therapist. She's getting him to take exercise, something he's reluctant to do, I'm afraid.'

'What sort of exercise?' Molly asked in concern.

'You'll have to ask Lyn for the details,' Oscar replied in a brisk tone. 'Now, if you don't mind, I have business to attend to and must go.'

When Molly replaced the receiver, she felt extremely annoyed. Why hadn't Lyn written to her about this Mrs James? Was Dad ready for exercising? He was usually so active and energetic. It seemed uncharacteristic of him not to want to try.

Molly walked slowly back home. There was nothing more she could do until she spoke to Lyn. Resolutely she turned her mind to practical matters. There were deliveries to be made, customers' orders to attend to. Fretting about Dad just wouldn't help.

It was at the beginning of May when a letter plopped on the mat from the Salvation Army Headquarters. Molly opened it eagerly.

> *Dear Mrs Swift,*
>
> *Thank you for your letter concerning Mr and Mrs Denham from the East India Dock district. We shall be able to help you in your search and provide you with a forwarding address. However, this must be done through the proper channels. We can offer you an appointment with our clerk, Mr Grey, on Monday May 12th at midday. Please bring some form of identification with you.*

'Blimey, what a turn-up!' Cissy said when Molly explained what it was. 'They must know where the Denhams are, then?'

Molly was very excited. 'Yes, it seems so.'

'Lucky they ain't snuffed it.' Cissy said bluntly. 'And the kids will finally get moved on.'

Now there was the possibility of a permanent home for the children, Molly found herself in a dilemma. Had she the right to 'move them on', as Cissy said, without Andy's permission? Would the Denhams continue to send them to school? What accommodation would they be given and how far away would they be? Andy would need to travel to wherever they were on his leave.

'So what you gonna do?' asked Cissy as if she was reading her thoughts.

'Keep the appointment, of course.'

'How you gonna get up there?'

'I'll wait till the weather improves then catch a bus to Aldgate. From there I'll get another to the Mansion House and then Queen Victoria Street.'

'They say lots of roads are blocked off after the bombing.'

'I'll just have to take a chance. It might take me all day, though. Jean will keep an eye on the kids after school if you'll look after the shop.'

Cissy shrugged. 'I'll have a chance to gas with the customers without you looking over me shoulder.'

Molly grinned. There was something about Cissy that was very endearing even when she was insulting you.

The night before Molly planned to go to Queen Victoria Street, the Luftwaffe returned. No one got a wink of sleep and when they climbed out of the shelter in the morning, covered in dust from head to toe, it was to discover that part of the Anderson roof had been dislodged.

'I'll have to reinforce it before we can use it again,' Dennis told them as they inspected the damage and shook the debris from their clothes. 'The shop's okay, Molly, but the bicycle factory caught fire. The fire brigade is up there now, checking it over.'

'Leave the children with me,' Jean insisted. 'I'll get them ready for school. You get off to the Sally Army.'

'*If* the buses are running,' Dennis warned. 'There won't be much of a city left to bomb, the way things are going.'

Molly and Cissy walked up the street to the shop and stopped to watch the firemen dousing the blackened bricks of the bicycle factory.

'A close call,' remarked Cissy. 'It was lucky we put the bike in the shop.'

'The shop's van was in there,' Molly sighed. 'Don't think there'll be much left of that to drive when the war is over.'

'Come on,' said Cissy purposefully, seeing her sad expression. 'What the eye don't see, the heart don't grieve over. Thank Gawd it wasn't the shop and flat, so let's open up and then you can catch your bus.'

'Are you sure you'll be safe on your own?'

'Why shouldn't I be?'

As they were talking a figure in a raincoat and trilby walked out of the smoke.

'Blimey, look who it ain't,' said Cissy. 'I'm off.' She hurried down the side path to the back of the store.

'Good morning, Mrs Swift.' Detective Constable Longman tipped his hat.

'What are you doing here?' Molly asked in alarm.

'The overnight reports for this district came in stating the bicycle factory was on fire. Your shop is right next door, so I came to check you were safe.'

'You needn't have troubled.'

'Perhaps you're not aware that last night was one of the worst nights of bombing? St Paul's, the British Museum, the House of Commons and Westminster Hall have all been damaged. Not that London is unique. Liverpool, Clydebank, Portsmouth, Southampton, Plymouth and other towns and cities suffered very badly. You're lucky to have come through unscathed.'

Molly hadn't realized just how bad the bombing had been until now. 'Do you know if the buses are running?'

'I would say that's doubtful until the roads are cleared. Do you have to travel somewhere?'

'Yes, Queen Victoria Street. The headquarters of the Salvation Army.'

'Are you a member?'

'No, but it's an urgent personal matter.'

'I see.' He rubbed his chin. 'Does it have to be today?'

'Yes, my appointment is for twelve.'

'Well ...' He hesitated, checking his watch. 'I have to report into headquarters myself. I can drive you some of the way, if not all.'

Molly was suddenly aware of how she must look after a night in the Anderson. To meet with officials, her dirty face must be washed, her crumpled clothes changed and her hair brushed and pinned.

'I can't go like this,' she said quickly. 'I must clean up first.'

'And I have to speak to the fire officer. If we meet in, say, twenty minutes outside your shop, then I'll drive as close to the city as possible.'

Molly was on the point of refusing, for she didn't care to spend any more time in the inquisitive policeman's company. But what chance did she have of getting to Queen Victoria Street otherwise?

Finally, she nodded and he gave another brief tip of his trilby before hurrying back into the clouds of smoke and soot.

Chapter Twelve

As she expected, Cissy was not pleased when she heard the news. But Molly held her tongue, quickly washed her face and brushed her hair and put on her best coat. With Cissie's protests ringing in her ears, she met Detective Constable Longman in the street and walked with him to where he had parked the car.

He politely opened the door for her and as she made herself comfortable in the front seat, she wondered if he was about to fulfil Cissy's prophecy and begin to interrogate her once more on the break-in at the shop. If so, she would be trapped in the car, unable to escape.

But her concerns came to nothing, as his concentration was focused on the widespread damage to the East End. The roads were chaotic, with many diversions through the blast-damaged landscape. Roofs, walls and pavements were covered in a smoky grey veil through which they could see skeletons of buildings, random piles of rubble and mountains of masonry. The auxiliary firemen were working frenziedly to put out small fires still burning amidst pools of water from the hoses. Molly could see there would have been very few buses today. At least, not from this part of the East End.

After they gained access to the Commercial Road, the way seemed a little clearer and Molly began to relax. 'Is Queen Victoria Street close to your headquarters?' she asked.

He took his gaze from the road briefly. 'Not far away. I drive in each day, as my digs are over at Walthamstow.'

'That's a long way to come.'

'You have to make the effort if you want to be part of the team.'

'Do policemen get special allowances for petrol?'

'It depends what squad you're in.'

Molly thought that remark sounded very much like a policeman.

They resumed their silence again as he navigated the armies of road workers, Civil Defence, firemen and Home Guard.

Molly stared out at the battered and bruised streets of London. Would the capital ever recover? So many towns and cities of Britain had suffered in the same way, but then she had also heard disturbing reports of the bombing raids by the British air force on Germany in retaliation. It was, she felt, tit for tat, with ordinary people like herself involved in warfare over which they had no control.

She blinked hard as the nose of the car turned the corner of Poplar High Street and Cotton Street. This was where she would have caught the bus to Aldgate. Houses and shops had been flattened, while others had buckled or had no doors or windows, with wallpaper stripped away as if torn by a giant hand.

And yet, Molly thought in admiration, people were out and about, scurrying like ants in order to put together the broken city.

Even before they got to Aldgate, Molly was on the edge of her seat, gripping the dashboard of the vehicle he told her was a Wolseley. She had never been in a police car before. Although this one, she was given to understand, had been requisitioned for service, and was not in the best of conditions.

The ride had been bumpy and several times the engine had stalled as the policeman tried to pursue a route over the hole-riddled streets. The air was filled with a thick yellow mist and made their journey even more perilous. The signs they were forced to follow often took them in circles. But it was when they arrived at the foot of Ludgate Hill and the car came to a stop that Molly saw the true extent of the bombing.

Many of the ancient and historic buildings on either side of the road were still on fire. A putrid-smelling fog swirled around the famous dome of St Paul's and its pinnacle. For a while they sat and stared in silence at the scene before them.

Workmen were crawling through the ruins and attempting to clear the roads for traffic. People were evacuating the area, pushing carts, prams, barrows, all loaded with what they could salvage. Their children were tagging along, black-faced and tattered, trailing wearily over the rubble and stones. Noisy sirens and whistles joined with the clunk and rattle of machinery, and barring their way was a sign that warned, DANGER. ROAD CLOSED.

Molly put her hands over her mouth. 'I just can't believe it.'

'Up till now I thought there was a chance we might get through,' said the detective, narrowing his eyes. 'But it's clear we shan't. Wait here while I try to get some information from the road workers over there.'

She watched him climb out and make his way over the rubble to a group of men working near a crane. Molly looked back to the outline of St Paul's and marvelled that it was still standing. It was a miracle!

Detective Constable Longman opened the car door and slid in beside her. 'I have some rather bad news. There are diversions everywhere from Lombard and Fenchurch Street to Mincing Lane. And perhaps the worst news for you is that Queen Victoria Street was hit pretty badly.'

Molly took a breath. 'Did you ask about the Salvation Army headquarters?'

'It seems that the building was one of the casualties.'

Molly sat back, her body draining of energy. The Salvation Army was her very last hope. Now she would never find Betty and Len.

'Mrs Swift, are you feeling well?'

'It's just a shock, that's all.'

'I think I had better find us somewhere to eat and drink.'

'I'd rather you took me home.'

The detective nodded, and starting the engine of the

car, he began to reverse the Wolseley. Very soon they were heading in the other direction and back towards the East End.

Molly's head was spinning. Such a cruel twist of fate! And she had come so close! Tears brimmed on her lashes. She took a shaky breath, trying to force them away.

The policeman glanced at her, then slowly brought the car to a halt once again.

'Why have we stopped?'

'Because I really do think you need a drink. A brandy would be best, but there's a coffee stall over there. Come on, let's get some fresh air.'

Before Molly knew it, he was opening her door and helping her out.

They sat on rough wooden benches with mugs of hot coffee, in the gassy-smelling air. Around them, the evidence of the bombing repeated itself: buildings still burning and sand and water pails stacked every few yards. People were trying to get back to some kind of normality, as they pushed, pulled or drove their belongings away from the flames.

Molly sipped the hot coffee and sighed. 'Thank you,' she said softly. 'That's helped.'

'I think this last raid by the Luftwaffe might have been the enemy's last push over the city for a while.'

'Why do you say that?'

'Keep it under your hat, but our intelligence tells us that Britain has turned out to be a much tougher target than the German High Command supposed. We've calculated they've lost a lot of bombers and there may be a respite for us until the Axis regroups again.'

'Should you be telling me this?'

'No, perhaps not. But you seem very upset.'

Molly looked down at her coffee. 'I am. It was vital I got to Queen Victoria Street. I've been searching for two people, members of the Salvation Army, who would take care of Mark and Evie, the children I'm looking after.'

'Where are their parents?'

'Their mother died in the bombing last year and their father is in the merchant navy.'

The detective nodded thoughtfully. 'So you knew the parents well?'

'No, not at all. I met Andy Miller in the hospital on the night Dad was hurt. He was there to identify his dead wife.'

'And you offered to take care of his children?' he asked in surprise.

'Wouldn't you?' Molly asked, turning her questioning gaze on him. 'This is war, Detective Constable. Look around us. People have no homes now, they're desperate, frightened and confused. I have both my home and my livelihood. So it's up to me to do the very best I can for others.'

He stared at her for some while before raising an eyebrow. 'Very commendable. Is that why you took Cissy Brown in too?'

Molly put down her mug. 'I'd like to leave now.'

He looked startled. 'Please finish your drink. I was just interested.'

'Policemen are always interested,' Molly said bluntly. 'But not always for the right motives.'

'We aren't the enemy, you know. And, if you'll let me, I can demonstrate the fact.'

Molly was suspicious. Had he planned to bring her here and get round to asking questions about Cissy? She said nothing, turning the possibility over in her mind. But she was very surprised when he next spoke.

'If you'd like to give me what information you have on these Salvation Army people, I'll check our records for you. I can't promise anything and it might not be particularly quick, but I might be able to turn something up.'

Once again, Molly found herself torn. What should she do? On the one hand her hopes of finding Betty and Len had vanished today, and on the other, there was this new offer of help. Should she take it?

'I can give you their names: Betty and Len Denham, once of the East India Dock Road. I was to meet a Mr Grey this morning, a clerk who would give me their new address.'

'The name is something to go on. I'll check with our records office and see what I can find.' He smiled. 'I'd like to restore this copper's reputation.'

Molly stood up. 'It's getting late. I must get back.' She didn't want to get too friendly. But she did want to grasp the one last chance she might have of finding the Denhams.

In the coming weeks, Molly often thought about that day at the coffee stall. Had she been too quick to judge the policeman? Perhaps he really could help? Or was he just inquisitive?

It was very strange, however, that he always dropped Cissy's name into the conversation.

As the days passed, her doubts were confirmed when he failed to show up. She knew she had been naive to tell him what she had. Though there was one thing he had told her that had turned out to be right. The nightly invaders had not returned in force, and London was licking its wounds – at least for the time being.

One morning at the end of the month Molly received a short letter from her father. She'd written to him several times but this was his first reply. '*I'm not doing so badly,*' she read aloud to Cissy as they stood in the shop:

> *A woman comes in to make me exercise. Supposed to do me good, they say. I've got my own room and can see out to the garden. There's doors I can get the wheelchair through. But how I miss home! The newspapers say the blitz is over. But the* Hood *went down with many lives lost. What next? Write again soon and tell me all your news.*
>   *Love, Dad*

'Poor sod,' remarked Cissy as they waited for the first customer of the morning. 'Stuck out in the back of beyond.'

'Sidcup's very pretty.'

'Yeah, but it ain't the East End.'

'I'd like to go out and visit him.'

Cissy shrugged. 'You know I'll look after the shop. Jean

can bring the kids back after school and I'll give them tea. You could even stay a night with your sister.'

'I don't know about that.'

Cissy shrugged as the bell over the door tinkled. 'Well, it's up to you.'

Molly smiled at Liz Howells who plonked her shopping bag on the counter. 'Have you heard the news?'

'No, what?' Molly and Cissy said together.

'Our navy's sunk the unsinkable *Bismarck* and took revenge for the *Hood*. Didn't stand a chance. Over a thousand crew gone to the bottom.'

'War is a dreadful thing,' Molly said, thinking of Andy. Was he, too, at the bottom of the ocean? Her stomach tightened as she considered the children's fate. What was to become of them?

'You look a bit peaky, Molly,' Liz said as Cissy served her.

'I'm all right.'

'How are those two kids? Is there any news of their dad?'

Molly shook her head.

'What you gonna do if he don't turn up?' asked Liz as she gave her ration book to Cissy.

'I don't know.' Molly was glad when another customer came in. She hoped the store would be busy today – and then her imagination wouldn't run riot.

Chapter Thirteen

Cissy was serving in the shop, hoping she would find time to have a quick fag and a swig from her flask. She didn't need the drink but it was comforting. Not that Molly would have approved. Still, Molly wasn't likely to be back till after tea-time. At least she hadn't had to bother with trains or coaches. That snotty-nosed Oscar had called to collect her in his posh car. He hadn't even bothered to get out, but kept the engine running as he waited.

'Hello, beautiful,' said a newly registered customer who had been into the shop several times before. 'Lovely weather for June, ain't it?'

'So they tell me.' Cissy placed her hands in a businesslike fashion on the counter. 'Now, what's it to be?'

'Give us a bit of kindling, will you? Me bloody fire keeps going out. It's the nutty slack that does it. Makes a terrible stink.'

'You don't need a fire in June, chum,' Cissy retorted as she went to find a bundle of wood.

'Wait till you're old and decrepit like me. You'll need a fire up your arse every day.'

Cissy laughed at the language and returned to the counter. 'Anything else?' She pushed the wood across the surface.

'What you got to offer?'

'You cheeky bugger. Nothing. At least not what you're thinking about.'

One light-blue eye, slightly lower and almost crossed with the other, twinkled at her. 'How do you know what I'm thinking?'

'It's written all over your ugly mug.'

He laughed loudly and pushed back his navy-blue cap. 'Can't help me good looks, sweetheart. God threw the mould away after he made me.'

Cissy liked a bit of banter and when this customer came in, she got it in full. He was a lot older than her, but not too old. Probably in his mid forties. So there'd be about twelve years or so between them. It was a long time since she'd had a laugh with a bloke who could take insults in his stride. He never bought much, though, and she had a feeling he only called by to give her a bit of aggro. Once or twice he'd had a small dog at his heels, a rough-looking terrier that seemed to be watching her every move.

'Well, cough up,' she demanded. 'I can't waste me time gossiping with you.'

'Here you are,' he said, dropping a shilling on the counter. 'Keep the change.'

'I'll get rich on that, won't I?' Cissy rang it up and threw the pennies back at him. 'Not enough for a pint, even.'

'I could make it enough.' The smiling, blue-eyed cockney tilted his head. 'What about a quick one at the Quarry after you finish?'

Cissy's smile faded. She'd thought he was a bit different. But no, all the chat was just to pull a stroke. 'No, thanks. Now bugger off.'

'What have I said?'

'Too much, that's what.'

'How many more bloody bundles of kindling do I have to buy to get you to come out with me?'

'Save yer breath and yer lolly, chum. Now clear off.'

The man studied her with exasperation. 'You're a hard nut to crack. I thought we was having a laugh.'

'You thought wrong. Now, do I have to walk you to the door?'

Her customer grinned. 'Yes, please.'

Cissy stared angrily at him. Then, marching round the counter and to the door, she tugged it open. 'Out!'

He gave her a lopsided smile. 'Blimey, what an offer!'

Cissy pointed, mouthing the word again. She watched him walk out, tip his cap and bow ceremoniously. She noticed he had thick black curly hair, and though he was several inches shorter than her, he appeared to be a decent shoulder size as he took off his duffel jacket, swung it over his shoulder and strolled off whistling, with the kindling under his arm.

'Bloody men,' Cissy muttered, nevertheless studying the swagger and blushing as he turned back to catch her gaze.

Ten minutes later she was drinking from the flask when

the rear door creaked. She hurriedly pushed the drink into her apron pocket as a tall figure entered the room.

She jumped back, fearful of who it might be.

Then her mouth opened in shocked surprise as a familiar face greeted her.

'Strike a light, I must be seeing things!' Cissy gawped at the man, who she had last seen sporting a full beard and long overdue a haircut. He was now clean-shaven, and his dark hair was cut short to his scalp. His face was lean and his dark eyes looked almost black. But all in all, Andy Miller was still very much alive and kicking.

'Hello, Cissy.' He swung his kit bag to the floor and stood with his hands stuffed in his navy seaman's jacket.

Cissy sniffed loudly. 'So you ain't swimming with the fishes?'

'No. Is that what you thought?'

'What else, mate?' Cissy scoffed. 'Not a bloody word in six months.'

'Where's Molly? Where's the kids?' he asked, ignoring her comment.

'Molly's off seeing her dad at her sister's and won't be back till later. The kids are at school.'

'At school?' He frowned, looking around him. 'When will they be home?'

'Dunno. Jean's giving them tea today.' Cissy put her hands on her hips. 'Why ain't you sent word to Molly?'

'Couldn't,' he shrugged, just as a customer walked in.

'Well, you'd better go up and help yerself to a brew,' Cissy told him off-handedly. 'You look like something the cat dragged in.'

'Thanks, I'll do that.'

'But don't go snooping around while I'm not there.'

To Cissy's surprise, he laughed and said as he turned to go, 'You ain't changed, Cissy, not a bit. Tongue as sharp as me razor. They should put you on the wireless to frighten the enemy.'

For once Cissy was speechless, although she managed to hide her smile as she served her customer.

Molly had just eaten a lavish meal, or so it seemed, as farm-fresh eggs were so scarce – except in Sidcup, so Oscar had said. Lyn had served an omelette, yellow as butter, and fluffy, with a slice of cheese. Molly now felt very guilty. Cissy, Evie and Mark had shared two eggs several weeks ago and thought it the height of luxury.

Now, as she sat with her father, sister and brother-in-law in their newly decorated sitting room, which Lyn explained had suffered with the decorator's use of inferior wartime utility paint, Molly gazed at the comfortable sofa and matching chairs.

The suite was covered in a floral material that cleverly reflected the view of the garden outside, through the large windows. The scattered rugs were placed strategically. Not an inch of rough brown lino could be seen. Her father's room had been similarly decorated, and his bed faced the spacious patio outside where he escaped to smoke his pipe. Smoking was prohibited indoors, he had confided.

'How far can you walk now, Dad?' Molly asked as they drank tea from bone china cups.

'Oh, quite far, love.' He gave a sly wink to Molly which she translated as a slight exaggeration. 'Mrs James likes a circuit of the garden every day.'

Molly remembered that Mrs James was the physical therapist. 'That's very good,' she said encouragingly.

'Though it needs to be stepped up a bit,' Oscar said peering from behind his newspaper as he sat in his armchair. 'We need to have a challenging regime.'

Molly looked at her father who gave her a roll of his eyes.

'Mrs James keeps a diary,' Lyn said, looking elegant in a deep-pink wool suit and high heels. 'She keeps a daily check, doesn't she, Dad?'

Bill Keen sighed. 'Yes, love.'

'I don't know where we'd be without her.' Lyn pushed back her soft blonde hair and smiled. 'She's a treasure.'

'We'll be doing a few country walks very soon,' said Oscar, rustling his newspaper. He narrowed his eyes behind his spectacles and bent his head, showing a neat parting in his wavy light-brown hair. 'George and Elizabeth are singing in the church choir next week. So we hope to go as a family.'

'I'll need me wheelchair,' said Bill, looking alarmed.

Lyn patted her father's arm. 'We'll see, Dad.'

Molly caught her father's desperate glance. 'Would you like me to push you round the garden, Dad, before I go?'

'That'd be nice, ducks. Give us a hand into it, will you?'

There seemed to be a lot of fuss and bother from Lyn as they took their father's arms, and Oscar commented that the short journey should be made easily. But Bill dropped heavily into his wheelchair with an exhausted sigh. He nodded to Molly and she pushed him through the open doors to the garden.

'It's lovely to see you, ducks,' Bill said as they made their way over the green lawn to the trees that stood at the bottom. He looked furtively over his shoulder. 'I'm gasping for me puff. Stop over there where that seat is and I'll get me pipe and baccy out from its hidey-hole. They can't see me from there.'

'Why do you keep it hidden in the wheelchair?' Molly asked as she watched him furtively unravel the newspaper at his side.

'Oscar and Lyn say I should give it up as it gets me coughing.'

'Does it?'

'Only a bit.'

Molly smiled as she sat down on the seat and watched him light up. The familiar odour of pipe tobacco wafted in the air and Molly breathed it in hungrily. 'I've missed that smell so much.'

'Blimey, girl, so have I. Can't do nothing round here without someone nagging.'

'Lyn's only trying her best.'

'Yes, I know. But we've all got our ways.'

'Do you think you'll be able to go to church to hear the children sing?'

'Dunno. Don't mind going. And the kids have got lovely voices.'

'But?'

'I'm showed off, see? Like some sort of bloody trophy.

Meet this, meet them, say hello. All got long names I can't remember. Not my sort.' He puffed fiercely on the pipe. 'When do you think I can come home?'

'I don't know, Dad.'

'Gotta find a way to get up them stairs.'

'Try to be patient. You'll soon get walking again. Especially with Mrs James helping you.'

'She can talk the hind legs off a donkey.'

Molly grinned. 'So can you.'

They laughed together and Molly told him all her news, and how relieved she was that the blitz had stopped. He asked about the children and she explained the reason for her trip to the Salvation Army. He pulled a sympathetic face when she described her fruitless drive up to the city with Detective Constable Longman.

'So you've been out with a copper?'

'He offered to drive me, yes. But the route was impassable. St Paul's was surrounded by devastation. It was a terrible sight. Then came the news that the Salvation Army headquarters, in Queen Victoria Street, had taken a hit. So it was all a useless effort anyway.'

Bill sat in silence puffing. 'These kids mean a lot to you, don't they?'

Molly shrugged. 'It's not their fault, this bloody war.'

'No, it ain't. But listen, girl, set your mind at rest. They can stay as long as they like with us. I mean you.'

'Oh, Dad. That's a lovely thing to say. But they need their father.'

'Well, all's not lost. Men turn up from the fighting every

day. You read about it in the newspapers. Don't give up hope. Now what about that other girl, Missy, or Cissy, was it?'

Molly grinned. 'Cissy. I'm glad to see that your memory seems to be coming back.'

Bill snorted and took a few puffs of his pipe. 'Shock did it. And shock undid it. Coming to live here I've got to have me wits about me. I soon got me brain to work. Now, about this Cissy. Is she pulling her weight?'

'I wouldn't be here today if she wasn't. The customers like her and she likes them.'

'In that case, give the girl a medal.'

They began talking again, as Molly knew that anything to do with the business cheered her father up. He was a shopkeeper through and through, something that Ted had completely understood and was why he encouraged him to keep his hand in at the store. She was surprised, though, when her dad said, 'It's a whole year now, since Ted's passing. There was you and me in the shop when Winnie came on the wireless. Remember it like yesterday. Which is saying something, as I almost lost me marbles after that bomb dropped.'

Molly nodded. 'A year exactly.'

'How are you feeling, love?'

'I take comfort from the fact Ted's with Emily.' Molly didn't want to admit that she hadn't been looking forward to the year's anniversary. She'd put it to the back of her mind and she hoped her dad wasn't going to dwell on it.

'You were too young to lose so much.'

'A lot of people lost much more. Homes, families. The blitz took so many good souls.'

'Nevertheless, you were robbed.'

'Not of me life, Dad. Or yours.' She suddenly saw movement on the patio and was quite relieved to see Oscar waving at them to return. 'I think it's time for me to go. Oscar's driving me back home. He does have a schedule to keep.'

Bill tutted. 'Like a bloody copper he is, missed his vocation there.'

Molly smiled as Bill quickly put out his pipe. 'I'm not sure when I'll be out here again. Will you write to me, Dad?'

'I'll have a go, love. But your mother was the woman of words.'

'Well, just put a few together to let me know how you're doing,' Molly said as she began pushing the chair back to the house.

'I'll give you a rundown on me exercises,' Bill muttered under his breath. 'That's sure to fill up a page or two.'

Molly chuckled to herself. Her father definitely wasn't an easy patient.

Andy looked around the room that was clearly kitted out for his kids. Two beds; a brown, eyeless teddy bear on one, and a small, battered metal car missing three of its four wheels on the other. His heart tightened when he saw a pair of boys' shorts folded over a wooden stool. He walked across the bare floorboards and stood on the patchwork rug, gazing down into the street. There were people now, customers disappearing into the shop below, a bicycle or two weaving past the crater in the road. The two houses opposite no longer smouldered, but were a desolate pile of rubbish. He craned his neck to see if he could see his kids down the road at Jean's. Should he walk there and surprise them?

Suddenly his legs gave way beneath him. He sank onto the bed, resting for a moment as the mist thickened in front of his eyes. He coughed, hearing the rattle in his chest. He knew he had to wait for the spasm to pass. The doctors had told him it was the result of what had happened before he hit the freezing water. But all that seemed like a dream now.

Suddenly he heard voices. Was it Mark and Evie?

He stood waiting, uncertain of his emotions. He was on the edge and he knew it. If he was to see their faces, touch them, smell them ... could he hold it together?

Then there were footsteps, slow at first, until they reached the landing. He waited, breath held.

'Andy?' a soft voice called.

'Molly!' He felt relief and apprehension all at once.

She came into the room. Neither of them spoke and he took a deep breath, hearing the crackling behind his lungs. She looked so – so – what was the word? Beautiful, he supposed. Tall and slender, with a cloud of copper-coloured hair down to her shoulders. Deep-brown, shimmering eyes that seemed to fill her face as she stared at him. She was wearing blue, a colour that reminded him of the sea. A peaceful, friendly sea, unlike the grey wastes of choppy, freezing water that had held him, briefly, a prisoner.

'Andy, I can't believe it's you!'

He managed an ungracious nod. 'It's me, all right.'

'But how – where – what happened?' She came towards him and he wanted to take her in his arms. To hold her, to know that he was still alive and part of this world. But he stood stock still, in spite of his desire, waiting for the power of speech.

'You – you look, well, different. No beard. And no hair.'

He smiled falteringly, clasping his chin. 'About time I had it cut. And the kids never liked me beard scratching their faces—' He stopped, unable to continue.

'Oh, Andy!' She moved hesitantly forward. 'You don't know how glad I am to see you.'

He tried to smile in return, but tears smarted in his eyes. Somehow he didn't feel embarrassed as, seeing his distress, she reached out, sliding her arms around him. They stood, he unable to move as he felt her warmth, her femininity, her comfort and he found his arms linking gently around her waist, his head falling down against her soft hair as he replied, his voice shaky with emotion, 'Likewise, girl. Likewise.'

The moment was only brief as he pulled himself together. He wasn't going to make a fool of himself now, not when he was finally back in Blighty. This thought made him smile and he grasped her arms, gently prising her away from him.

'You look different an' all. Last time I saw you, you was pushing a bike, with me kids somehow attached to it.'

She laughed, straightening her jacket self-consciously. 'Six months, can you believe?'

'I'm sorry I ain't written.'

'What happened, Andy?'

'A lot. Never thought I'd be standing here like this. Never thought I'd see me kids again.'

'Dad?' a voice called and Andy listened to the patter of small feet on the stairs. His son and daughter ran in and he caught them in his arms, hugging them to him, with the tears of joy escaping from his eyes.

That evening, Molly closed the shop early and cooked a pie in celebration of Andy's return. The five of them sat at the kitchen table, enjoying the diced carrots, onions and potatoes mixed with a teaspoonful of porridge to glue the pie together under a scattering of breadcrumbs. Molly smothered the well-browned top with gravy, regretting the fact that she hadn't brought any farm eggs back with her from Lyn's. But the pie went down very well and Evie, as usual, demanded more, as she sat on her father's knee.

'You still haven't lost your appetite, young 'un,' Andy said to his daughter as Molly squeezed out a last tiny portion for the children.

'I can cook now,' Evie said, grinning up at her father. 'Don't I, Molly?'

'Yes, you cook very well.'

'I helps Molly.'

'She certainly does.' Molly met Andy's gaze with a rueful smile.

'An' I goes to school, don't I, Molly?'

At this everyone laughed – even Cissy, Molly noticed, who had come round to being fairly cordial to Andy after he'd explained that he'd been shipwrecked off the coast of Ireland. And, after being rescued, had languished in hospital until three weeks ago.

'Mark,' Molly said as she looked down at the boy's pale face, 'tell your dad how good you are at sums.'

'I can say up to me ten times table.' Mark blushed pink.

'Who taught you?'

'Me teacher. And Molly says 'em with me. But me elevens is too hard.'

Once again Andy met Molly's gaze. 'You've done a treat with the kids, Molly.'

'They're both very bright.'

'Stella was the bright one. Not me. If it hadn't been for the—' He stopped, realizing all eyes and ears were on him. He smiled at his son. 'You get your brains from your mother, Mark.'

'She's dead, ain't she?' Mark said, his face suddenly full of sadness.

'I'm afraid so, son.'

'I thought you was too.'

'No,' Andy replied. 'Not by a long shot.'

'I told you your dad would come back for you,' Molly said as she ladled custard into the bowls. 'Mark's been very worried,' she told Andy.

'If I could have sent word, I would have,' Andy said quietly. 'But you ain't allowed to say where you are or what you're doing, as the convoys we was on were top secret.'

'What's convoys?' asked Mark.

'Ships that sail together with navy escorts. Convoys guard our trade ships as we carry important supplies the nation needs to win the war. But I'm sad to say that me own ship was sunk by a German U-boat. We was about a hundred miles off Ireland at dusk with our destroyer escort when a skirmish broke out on our flanks. The next thing we knew a sub was in the middle of us. We put on our cork life jackets, took our positions and the last thing I remember was firing into the ocean. They must have hit us amidships, as we was going down within minutes. I remember choking, breathing in the smoke, and then the icy water crawling over me.' He paused, stroking his son's head lovingly. 'It was thinking of you kids that kept me going. That and me life jacket and the bit of wood I clung to.'

Molly was silent, imagining the terrible event. She could hear the rattle in Andy's chest as he spoke and she knew that his long spell in hospital hadn't cured him completely.

'Will you get sunk again?' asked Mark.

'Your dad's got nine lives,' Cissy said then, putting down her knife and fork. 'Or he must have seen a black cat. One of them crosses yer path and you're made for life.'

'Did a black cat cross yer path, Dad?' Mark asked.

Molly saw Andy look at Cissy and grin. 'I reckon it did.'

'I wanna cat,' giggled Evie, pushing her sticky fingers over Andy's face and patting his cheeks. 'You gonna buy me one?'

Once again, mischievous Evie relieved the tension and

Molly was pleased to see that, finally, Mark had a smile on his face.

And so did she.

In fact, she felt a little guilty that she was much improved, even though it was just one year ago that Ted had left her.

Chapter Fourteen

In the days that followed Andy's homecoming, Molly arranged for him to sleep on the settee in the front room. Each morning, she watched from the window as he walked Evie and Mark to Jean's where they would join Simon and Susie for school. She would always have this happy picture in her mind: Andy, tall and lanky, ambling his way down the road, holding his children's hands. Then he'd hoist Evie across his shoulders, and kick an old, battered ball to Mark over the debris.

After the children were at school, Molly could rely on him to attend to the jobs that needed doing around the store. He occasionally helped Dennis at nights with the fire-watching duties, though, as the raids were far fewer, he was spending more and more time at home.

'The boards over the window have had their chips,' he told her one wet July day as a large pool of water formed on the floor. 'I'll ask Mr Stokes if he can rustle up any glass down that depot of his.'

Molly knew glass was in very short supply. A great deal of building material had been destroyed during the blitz, so she was very surprised when, at the end of the month, Mr Stokes arrived with his van.

'Keep this under your hat, love,' the warden whispered as, helped by Andy, he removed several panes from its interior. 'Can't do this for everyone, but yer dad is me mate.'

'Thanks a lot,' Andy said when the glass was safely inside. 'I owe you one.'

'A pint down the Quarry will do.' Mr Stokes grinned, thrusting a dirty hand through his iron-grey hair. 'The glass is a bit chipped and scratched. But at least you'll have some sort of window back.'

Molly was delighted when, after Mr Stokes had gone, Dennis appeared, his tool bag in hand. 'I see old Stokesy has come up with the goods.'

'Not bad quality either,' agreed Andy as they examined the panes.

'Blimey, our customers will see every bit of dust now.' Cissy grabbed her duster as, with much banging and cursing, Andy and Dennis removed the old boarding and secured the window.

'Dad really would be heartened to see the shop now,' Molly said wistfully.

'How is the old rogue?' Dennis asked. 'When's he coming home?'

'As soon as he can walk.'

'How long will that be?'

'Don't really know, Den.' Molly thought of Lyn's last letter, saying their father wouldn't cooperate with Mrs James's exercises.

'Like I said before, me and Andy could fix up the glory hole. Then he wouldn't have to go up any stairs. While Andy's at home, we could do the job together.'

Molly wanted more than anything to agree, but what would Lyn say? Would this cause a family feud? That was something her dad could do without right now. 'I'll think about it, Den.'

'Right, now all the hard work's done, I'm off. See you later, Andy.' Dennis grinned, picked up his bag and, after patting Andy on the shoulder, went on his way.

Andy gave her a big smile as he mopped his brow with a rag. 'Like old times, ain't it, with your window back?'

'I just hope it doesn't get blown in again.'

'Not so many raids now. Mostly in daylight. And they seem to have given up on this bit of turf.'

It was then that the shop door opened and in walked Detective Constable Longman.

'Hello.' She hadn't expected to see him again and was very surprised at this visit.

The policeman glanced at Andy, who was putting the finishing touches to the window. 'I'm sorry it's been a while since I've called,' he addressed Molly. 'I was transferred to North London to take on a very serious case. I see you've now got your windows back. Not much glass around these days.'

At this, Molly saw Andy look up. She said quickly, 'Andy,

this is the policeman I told you about. Detective Constable Longman, this is Andy Miller, the children's father.'

Andy's dark eyes narrowed. 'So you're the copper who Molly said could find my pals?'

'I thought I might be able to help Mrs Swift, yes.'

'Had any luck?'

Molly noticed that Andy's stare wasn't friendly. He stood in a tense manner and his fists were clenched.

'As a matter of fact, yes, I have some new information,' said the detective casually.

'You have?' Molly was surprised. 'Why didn't you let me know before?'

'As I said, I've been away. When I came back, I traced your clerk, Mr Grey, with whom you had an appointment in Queen Victoria Street. Sadly, this man perished in the raid, but I was able to locate the whereabouts of the Denhams.' He gave his charming smile to Molly. 'I was about to ask you if you'd like me to follow it up?'

'What do you mean, "follow it up"?' Andy asked suspiciously.

The policeman's smile vanished. 'I was talking to Mrs Swift.'

'It's me who's looking for the Denhams,' replied Andy bluntly. 'If you've got something to say, mate, then you can talk to me.'

Molly's heart sank as the policeman did not reply but took out his notebook and tore off a sheet. He dropped it on the top of the counter. 'Nice to see you again, Mrs Swift. Here's the address. And, er ...' He glanced at the window. 'Good to see you have the store up and running again.' With that, he turned and walked out.

'The more I see of that copper, the less I like him,' Cissy said, making an entrance.

'You heard everything, I suppose?' Molly said, watching Andy as he picked up the piece of paper.

'With a voice like he's got, you'd have to be deaf not to.'

'I can't believe this,' Andy said on a gasp. 'Why didn't I think of it meself?'

'What?' asked Molly and Cissy together.

'Betty and Len are in living in Southend with Betty's sister Gert. Me and Stella and the kids went with the Denhams on a day's outing. A small flat near the sea.'

'Southend is a long way off.'

Andy gave a faint smile. 'Len joked it was the rollercoaster at the Kursaal funfair that got Betty into his arms when nothing else would.' He gave the paper back to Molly and she slipped it in the shop drawer.

'Well, it seems we've come to our journey's end,' he told her. 'I'll go to the coach station and see about booking seats.'

'What if the transport is only for evacuees?' asked Molly.

'That's what the kids are, ain't they?' shrugged Andy. 'Evacuees.'

'Will you write to Betty first?'

'Course. Only proper to ask. But I already know the answer. They love these kids as their own.' Andy went to the window whistling and began hammering again.

Molly found it hard to believe the children were actually leaving; that Andy had finally found the people he'd been searching for. She knew she should be very happy for them.

And she was, wasn't she?

It was a hot day in August when, one morning before the shop opened, Molly found a letter addressed to Andy on the mat. She ran upstairs, softly knocking on the front room door, so she wouldn't wake the household.

'This came for you,' she whispered when Andy greeted her. He stood in his trousers and vest. Molly blushed, as she had never seen him without his shirt. In the short time he had been home, he'd put on a little weight. His arms and chest had added muscle and his black hair had grown, curling softly at his neck. That rattly cough which had plagued him had subsided and his eyes were now clear and bright. 'Is it from the Denhams?' he asked eagerly.

'I think so.'

'Come in and we'll open it.' He shut the door behind her.

'It's from Betty,' he said, his face lighting up with a broad smile. 'She writes to say there'll be no problem with having the kids.'

'That's good news,' said Molly, wondering why she was feeling so strange. She knew that Andy trusted these people and would never leave the children with someone he couldn't rely on.

'They often stepped in to look after the kids,' he said, interrupting her thoughts. 'Christ only knows how I would have coped if they hadn't.'

Molly knew she should be very happy for Andy and his little family.

'The only hurdle now is my medical tomorrow.'

'Do you think you'll pass it?'

'Don't see why not.'

'So when do you think you'll be leaving?'

'The 1st September is Evie's birthday. My plan would be to take them to Southend on the day, as it'll be a real treat for them. After I've settled them with Betty, I'll hitch across country down to Portsmouth, where I'll sign on.'

'So you won't be coming back here?'

Andy shrugged. 'No point. You must have had enough of us by now.'

Molly tried to smile. 'I'll miss the children.'

'Will you?'

'Course. They're lovely kids.'

'Molly, you've done more than your share for us. I ain't very good with words. And thank you don't seem enough.'

'I – you needn't thank me. I just want to see Mark and Evie with a home again.'

'It'll be bloody hard for them leaving you. They've taken a shine to this place, especially Evie. But you've got your own life to get on with.' He pushed the letter in his pocket then reached out to tilt up her chin. 'Don't look so glum. I bet when your dad hears about the new window, and with us gone, he'll be home like a shot.'

Molly nodded, a little shiver going over her. He'd never touched her before and her reaction was a surprise. 'Dad said the children are welcome to stay,' she blurted, 'as long as they need a roof over their heads.'

'And I'm grateful to him for that. But a man's home is his

castle. He won't want to come home to a place full of kids and strangers.'

Molly knew it was in the children's interest for them to be with the Denhams, but she was finding the prospect difficult.

'Will you ever come back to the East End, do you think?' she asked as she looked into his lovely dark eyes. She could smell the soap he had washed with coming from his body and her tummy gave a little skip.

'We'll have to see.'

'Southend is very nice, so I hear.'

'Yes, it ain't bad. The kids will like the sea, and the funfair when it starts running again.'

Molly fell silent, as did he. She knew that the parting of the ways would be as hard for her and Cissy as it would be for the children. Now they were leaving, she realized just how fond of Mark and Evie she had become.

'Molly, we'll all miss you.' His hand slipped slowly from her face and he took her arms, at first in a friendly gesture, but then before she knew what was happening his chest was against her and her lips were parting. His kiss was gentle at first, as though the chemistry between them surprised him as much as it did her. All her senses reacted as every scent that she had grown up with in the docks drifted from his warm body. She shivered and felt him shiver too. And soon their arms were locked passionately around each other, the over-whelming need that had been, up until now, quite hidden, melting from their bodies.

In that passionate embrace Molly knew that this was

nothing – not even remotely – like friendship that they shared, but something of a much deeper kind. Something she hadn't shared with Ted throughout the happy years of their marriage.

It was the Sunday night before the Monday when Andy and the children were to leave. After tea, Molly was in the kitchen packing Andy's kit bag with the children's clothes. But it was hard to stop thinking about the night a week ago when she had found herself in his arms, kissing and wanting more, savouring his touch and enjoying his arms tightly around her.

And then suddenly she had thought of Ted, and guilt had been like a bucket of freezing water thrown over her. Andy had been the first to apologize, almost as embarrassed as she was as he stepped away and allowed her to escape from the room.

'Why's you puttin' stuff in me dad's bag?' Evie enquired, bringing Molly sharply back to the present.

'It's your birthday tomorrow, Curly Top. Your dad's taking you to the seaside.'

'I's four, ain't I?' Evie held up all her ten fingers as she sat on the chair by Molly.

'No, you only need four fingers, like this,' Mark corrected as he joined them in the kitchen.

Evie pulled a face. 'I's as big as you tomorrow.'

'You ain't,' Mark disagreed, throwing himself onto another chair. 'You're just a squirt.' He looked at Molly. 'Are we really going to live at Betty and Len's?'

Molly sat down at the table with them. 'Yes, your dad has fixed it all up.'

'I thought Betty and Len was dead.'

'I know you did.' Molly threaded a hand around his shoulders. 'But didn't I tell you they weren't?'

Mark considered this. 'Will we have a room like we got here?'

'You might.'

'Is you comin' to the seaside?' Evie said, and sliding from her seat pushed her head under Molly's arm.

'Not just yet.' Molly had a lump in her throat.

'You ain't never coming to see us?' Mark asked, his face filling with apprehension.

'Perhaps, one day. But getting about is very difficult, as you well know, Mark.' Molly had grown so fond of this little boy and his sister that, even if she did get to Southend, it would be unbearable to leave them again.

When Andy walked into the kitchen, Molly looked into his eyes and he smiled. They had had very little chance to talk since he'd taken his medical and now, in hindsight, she wondered if he regretted that impetuous embrace. For after all, what could come of it?

Molly didn't sleep that night. She tossed and turned, and finally rose as light broke through the kitchen window. She made carrot fudge for Evie's birthday and before they left Molly gave her the sweets.

'Happy birthday, Curly Top. Don't look inside the parcel until you're on the coach. It's a birthday surprise.'

Evie turned the brown packet in her fingers. 'Ain't you comin'?' she asked once more.

'I've got to open the shop.'

'But it's me birfday.'

'I know. Be a good girl for Betty and Len.'

For a few seconds everyone stood silently.

Then Andy turned to Cissy. 'Thanks for everything,' he told her, slinging his bag over his shoulder.

'Look after yourselves,' Cissy said awkwardly. 'We'll miss you little devils.'

Molly hugged and kissed the children. 'Goodbye, you two. Look after each other.' She looked into Andy's eyes. 'Good luck, Andy.'

'Thanks.'

She hoped that he too was remembering the moment they had shared that night, for now, as they were parting, she realized how much that kiss had meant to her.

In the days to come Molly missed everything about the children: Evie's laughter and mischievous ways and Mark's sombre, soulful expressions. She missed the fun they had on bath nights when they splashed in the old tin bath that was kept in the tall kitchen cupboard. She missed mornings and the school routine and night-times and the stories she read them before they went to sleep. She knew Cissy did too, even though she tried to pretend she didn't.

It was later, in September, when Jean came into the shop and took a long, calculating look at Molly. 'Have you heard from Andy?' she asked, plonking her basket on the counter.

'No. Why should I?'

'Thought he might write.'

'Can't see him doing that. Not if he didn't before.'

Jean looked at her sadly. 'It don't seem the same round here without him and the kids. Den says it's bloody lonely on his fire-watching duties, now there's not so many raids. And Simon and Susie keep asking me if Mark and Evie are coming back.'

Molly opened Jean's bag. 'So what will it be this morning?' she asked quickly.

But Jean only frowned and continued, 'So, after the war, will Andy go back to Southend to live?'

'Who knows what will happen to any of us after the war?'

'You're missing them, ain't you, gel?'

'It's only natural. After all, they were never any trouble.'

'When was the last time you went out and enjoyed yourself?'

Molly shrugged. 'It was with Ted, I suppose. So long ago, I can't remember.'

'Blimey O'Riley,' Jean gasped. 'Listen, now you've not got the kids to look after, why don't you go out on the town?'

Molly grinned. 'What, on me own?'

'No, take Cissy with you. Have a good laugh. *Destry Rides Again* is showing at the Roxy.'

'I don't like cowboys.'

'Well, it's a good film, so I heard.'

'What's that?' Cissy asked as she came downstairs, tying her turban on her head. 'Did I hear the flicks mentioned?'

Jean nodded. 'I'll get Den to borrow the works van and take you up to Aldgate.'

'You're on,' said Cissy, before Molly could answer. 'Tell

your old man not to be late. We don't want to turn up just as the performance is over.'

Molly opened her mouth, then closed it again. Perhaps she should make the effort. A change of scenery might distract her from thinking about Andy and the kids.

Chapter Fifteen

Cissy had dolled herself up to the nines and felt good as they waved cheerio to Dennis. She had bought a new grey costume at the market and slipped her flask discreetly into the jacket pocket. After all, going to the flicks meant a drink and a fag, even if Molly indulged in neither. But what was the point of a night out if you didn't enjoy yourself? A corny cowboy at an Aldgate flea-pit wasn't her cup of tea. But Jean seemed to think they'd enjoy it.

When Dennis had driven off very slowly, avoiding the holes in the road left by the blitz, she and Molly entered the old, shabby cinema that smelled of wet mackintoshes and stale tobacco. As the blackout blinds were all in operation, they were hurried through the dark foyer to pay for their seats at the interior kiosk.

'I s'pose we're lucky this place ain't been bombed,' Cissy said as they followed the usherette, who when safely inside the auditorium shone her torch along the aisles. 'But blimey, it don't half stink in here.'

'Hold your nose,' Molly chuckled as they took their seats. 'Do you want a toffee?'

Cissy grinned. 'No thanks, I've got me mother's ruin.'

'I thought you might.'

'Do you want a fag?'

'No, thanks.'

They turned and smiled at each other as the lights went down. Cissy satisfied her thirst, a little annoyed that two very tall men had come in to sit in front of them. She sat to one side, noting the biggest nose she had ever seen on a man's profile.

Ten minutes later they were watching Pathé News, with the cockerel crowing and all the propaganda that followed. Pictures were shown once more of the ravages of the blitz and the skies full of billowing barrage balloons on their steel tethering cables, forming a hazard for low-flying enemy aircraft. Then there was military music growing louder as film of the British fighters flying home from German occupied territory passed across the screen. Even though there hadn't been a serious raid by the Luftwaffe since May, the newsreel was insistent that an invasion could still happen any day or night.

Cissy pulled out her flask again and sucked noisily. The tall man turned round and stared at her.

She stared back. So what if she enjoyed a bit of a livener?

After the news, there were more warnings about spies, fifth columnists and the black market. Then, eventually, the main feature began.

Cissy sat back, feeling mellow, to watch the opening scenes. The hero was played by Jimmy Stewart, a sheriff in a tough western town. The similarity to someone they knew was obvious. 'Christ, Molly, that's Andy, ain't it? Without his beard, of course.'

Molly seemed transfixed. 'There is a likeness.'

'He's got that same expression as Andy gave your copper friend. A real eyeballer.'

'The copper's not my friend.'

'Oh, no?'

'Cissy, you're missing the film.'

She drank from her flask again, watching with interest how Molly's expression softened as Destry, who started off a bit of a wimp, suddenly turned into this hard-nosed lawman who could be the twin brother to Andy.

After the film was over and they had stood for the national anthem, they made their way to the street outside. Cissy felt pleasantly tipsy and threaded her arm through Molly's. 'Well, what did you think of lover boy?'

'Who do you mean?'

'Jimmy Stewart. That smile of his, it was Andy's.'

'So you keep saying.'

'Come on, don't deny you fancied him a bit.'

'What?' said Molly blushing. 'Jimmy Stewart?'

'No, Andy. I saw the way you looked at each other, right from the start.'

'You've got a real imagination, Cissy Brown.'

'Listen, Molly,' Cissy drawled, enjoying the after-effects of the drink, cigarettes and Destry's understated charm, 'you can't kid a kidder. You and Andy and them kids, well, you all went together like apple pie and jelly.'

'Apple pie and custard.' Molly smirked.

'There, you see. I was right. I knew—' Cissy was about to enlarge when a tall figure pushed roughly past her.

''Ere, watch it, mate!' Cissy snapped, ready to give the stranger a piece of her mind, when she froze where she stood. She was looking directly up at Big Nose, from the Roxy, who was pushing his chest into hers while at the same time his pal had got hold of Molly. Vaguely, she heard Molly scream, as they were bundled into an alley where, to her terror, Cissy felt two big mitts go around her throat and squeeze. Her hands went up to protect herself, trying to tear away the strong fingers that were locked around her neck. But the more she wrestled them, the tighter they squeezed, until her windpipe was crushed. Great gasps came from her mouth and she knew that her eyes were popping out from their sockets. Her legs lost all their strength.

As she was on the verge of unconsciousness, she heard a whisper in her ear. It wasn't much of a whisper, because it was broken suddenly by a high-pitched whistle that had the effect of making the hands drop her painfully to the ground.

Just before she blacked out, a boot smashed into her side, so hard that Cissy was certain her chest had split open.

Molly was shaking like a leaf. The usherette was staring down at her, as the two policemen who had helped her and Cissy back into the foyer of the cinema watched them intently.

Her hands wouldn't stop trembling. Although she wasn't physically hurt, her insides felt as though they had been screwed up into a tight ball and forced up into her throat. She had been made to watch Cissy attacked, a tiny scrap bounced about by that monster, and she had been unable to do anything but struggle in the other man's arms.

He'd held his hand across her mouth, forcing her to be silent and watch Cissy's ordeal. That was, until she managed to thrust the heel of her shoe into his ankle. He roared in pain and the second he relaxed his grip she'd screamed for all she was worth.

Two bobbies had been walking along the high street at that moment. Her scream had alerted them, but not in time to catch their attackers.

'Cissy – Cissy?' Molly managed to croak, as the usherette and manager of the cinema stood by the chair they had propped Cissy on. The two policeman were holding their notebooks, glancing from one to the other. But Cissy kept her head down, refusing to look up.

'So you say you didn't know them?' one of them asked Cissy once more.

Molly looked at Cissy. She was bent over, shivering, her face hidden under her tangled dark hair. There was no doubt she was hurting. But since she had refused to be taken to hospital, and with her outright disdain for the law, there seemed very little any of them could do.

'You say these men jumped on you after you came out of the cinema?' pestered the policeman. 'You have no idea who they were?'

Cissy shook her head stubbornly.

The same question was asked of Molly. 'No, I didn't know

them,' she replied, 'but I think they sat in front of us in the cinema.'

'What were they wearing?'

'Just coats, with hats pulled over their faces.' Molly stood up shakily. 'I think I should get Cissy home.'

'I'd like to go over the details once more,' persisted the other policeman.

But Molly insisted on leaving. 'You've taken our names and address. And what we can remember, which was very little as we didn't see their faces. As we told you, they came up behind us and bundled us into the dark alley.'

'So you think the motive was theft?'

'It could be,' said Molly. 'But you came along, thank goodness.'

'Perhaps it was something else?' hinted the policeman, giving Cissy a long, curious stare.

'I really don't know,' Molly said sharply. 'Thank you for helping us. But I don't think we can tell you any more. Could you call us a taxi? I know they're few and far between, but perhaps you know of a cabbie who could drive us back to the East End?'

The manager nodded. 'I think we can help you there.' He went off and the policemen put their notebooks away.

Molly knew they really didn't want the bother of looking for these thugs, whose description no one seemed to be able to give. Cissy refused to say much more than a mumbled, 'I don't remember.' And Molly herself had very little to report about the unhappy event, except for Cissy being pinned against the wall, thrust to the floor and kicked.

When at last the taxi arrived, the manager and usherette helped Cissy into the back seat. Molly followed, and before the driver set off she thanked them all again. She felt Cissy still shaking, her eyes coming up to peer into the blacked-out and lonely roads.

When they eventually reached Roper Street, Molly breathed a sigh of relief and hurriedly paid the taxi driver.

She helped Cissy out and together they stumbled round to the back yard. It was very dark and quiet and Molly fumbled as she took out the key from her bag to open the back door. She needn't have bothered, as it stood open.

'Christ,' gasped Cissy, clutching Molly tightly. 'They've done us over again.'

Molly felt sick. Fear overwhelmed her. She clung fiercely to Cissy. What were they to do?

'We can't go in,' Cissy groaned. 'They might still be in there.'

Molly suddenly felt very angry. This was her shop. Her livelihood. Her home and all her possessions. How dare they do this again?

Pulling Cissy into the shadows behind the pump, she whispered, 'Stay here.'

'Where are you going?'

'Inside.'

Cissy grabbed her tight. 'You can't. They might—'

'Don't worry. This time I'll be ready for them. I put one of them struts of wood in the lav that Andy took out of the window.'

'Molly, don't do it!'

'Shall I run for the police, then?' demanded Molly, already knowing Cissy's opinion on the law.

'No! Well, not them. Can we get someone else?'

'Who's awake at this time of night?' Molly left Cissy and tiptoed softly across the yard. She opened the lavatory door, which gave a squeak. She stood quite still, glancing back at the store. No one came out. As there was a bright half-moon in a cloudless sky, she knew they must be still inside, or else they had left.

Molly grasped the piece of wood that Andy had stood by the lav. She remembered him saying it was from the old framework, but too good to throw away. Very carefully she got hold of it and edged her way slowly to the back door.

Sweat was running down her back as she pushed it gently. Her heart was beating so fast that the blood rushing in her ears seemed the only noise in the night. She decided then and there that if she found an intruder she would lash out and scream until she was blue in the face.

After all, she'd had plenty of practice tonight.

She took one step inside and felt a touch on her shoulder. She nearly jumped out of her skin, as Cissy whispered, 'I'm right behind you, but I think we're bloody mad.'

Molly closed her eyes and swallowed. She held the piece of wood aloft. As soon as they were inside she put on the light, and what she saw made her gasp. The store had been looted again. Not a packet or jar was left on the shelves.

'Oh no!' breathed Cissy on a sob. 'The buggers.'

Molly went into the shop. They had overturned the till

and scattered all the stock. But what made Molly's blood run cold was the red paint daubed across the blackout blind.

It said, *Send the tart back where she belongs or else you'll be sorry.*

Molly heard a groan from behind her. Cissy had fallen to the floor.

'Cissy, Cissy!' Molly bent down and took the limp shoulders. She shook her gently.

Cissy gave a moan as she lay on the floor among all the packets and tins. 'Wh-what happened?'

'You fainted.' Molly brushed the dust from Cissy's clothes. 'And no wonder, after what you've been through tonight.'

Cissy burst into tears. They were accompanied by sobs that racked her whole body. Molly looked closely at her friend, who wasn't usually given to weeping. A large red mark around her neck was growing brighter and brighter. Molly could make out the clear evidence of fingermarks. That brute of a man who had attacked her had almost managed to end her life. That was why Cissy had kept her head bowed and wouldn't look up at the policemen. She hadn't wanted them to see just how serious the attack had been.

'Oh, Cissy, why would someone want to strangle you?' she breathed. 'You knew them, didn't you?'

'Leave me alone,' Cissy said, pushing her away. 'You don't want to get mixed up with me.'

Molly sat back on her haunches. 'What do you mean?'

'I'm no good. I'll only bring you bad luck.'

'That's ridiculous.'

'No, it ain't. You only know half the story.'

'Well, tell me the other half, then. But not right now, as I've got to get you upstairs.'

'No. I have to go.'

Molly almost laughed. 'Go? Go where, in the middle of the night?'

'Anywhere but here.' Once more the tears ran down Cissy's cheeks. Molly stared at her bedraggled friend, who wasn't making any sense at all. Together with the fact that they had just been attacked by two strangers and returned home to find the shop burgled once again – and that awful paint daubed across the blind – well, it was just unfathomable.

'Hello? Anyone there?'

Molly jumped, and Cissy immediately stopped crying. They stayed quite still, staring at the back door. Molly knew they were both terrified. Had the looters returned?

She grabbed the piece of wood she had dropped and scrambled to her feet. 'Who is it?' she demanded, though her voice sounded very small and faint.

'It's me. Spot.'

Molly frowned, trying to keep calm. 'Spot who?'

'Yer customer. The one that buys kindling. Can I come in?'

'It's all right,' whispered Cissy hoarsely, looking relieved as she sat up. 'He's a geezer who comes in the shop a bit.'

To their surprise a little black-and-white terrier with a curly tail scampered in. He sniffed at Cissy and gave a sharp bark.

'Come 'ere, Nibbles,' called a voice, and a small, stocky man wearing a peaked cap appeared. Molly had seen him once or twice before but it was Cissy who had served him.

'Blimey, missus,' he said to Molly, sweeping his dog up under one arm. 'What you gonna do with that?' He nodded to the wood she was holding.

Molly leaned it against the counter. 'What do you want?' she said ungraciously.

'My dog was having a wee round the back there. You've got your lights showing. You'll have the warden after yer if you're not careful.' He nodded to the stock on the floor. 'What the bleeding heck has been going on here?'

'We've been looted again.'

'Yer, but what's that?' He pointed to the red daubs on the blind.

'Some sick joke,' Molly replied. 'Can you help Cissy up the stairs?'

'Course. I'll just shut the back door.'

'They broke the lock again,' Molly called after him. 'So draw the bolt.'

As he went away, Molly helped Cissy to her feet. She was very unsteady. When the small man came back he took charge of her and gently guided her to the stairs. Molly watched him go very slowly. But for a small man he seemed to be strong, as he lifted Cissy into his arms and carried her up the steep flight.

Molly was about to follow when her eyes caught the horrible red daubs again. Who could have done that? And what for? What did it mean?

None of this made any sense.

Least of all, Cissy's insistence on leaving.

It was the early hours of the morning by the time Molly got Cissy settled in bed. She'd given her two aspirin from the shop's stores, bathed her bruises and the strangle mark and helped her undress, finally putting out the bedroom light after Cissy had fallen asleep. Molly returned to the front room where the small man was sitting on the settee with his little dog at his feet. He stood up immediately she came in.

'Is she all right?' he asked.

'I don't really know.' Molly sank down on the chair. 'I'm sorry, I don't know your name.'

'Me moniker's Spot. This 'ere is Nibbles.' He nodded to the dog.

'Mine's Molly.'

'Yer, all right missus,' he said and sat down again.

Molly was very confused. What was the reason for Cissy's strange behaviour? And that writing on the blind – who had done it? And why? Perhaps she should have taken the policeman's warning more seriously.

'Yer look done in, missus.'

'I am a bit.' Molly blinked, aware that the man called Spot was staring intently at her. He had one bright-blue eye lower than the other, which gave him a rather comical expression. He'd removed his cap to reveal a decent head of dark hair that came to a widow's peak on his forehead. It was a face you had to smile at. Molly suddenly realized she was glad he was here. She would still be very scared if here on her own.

Molly sighed, feeling she should give some kind of explanation. 'We had a dreadful evening. Some blokes attacked us when we came out of the cinema. Poor Cissy was nearly strangled and kicked in her side.'

'The bleeders. What about you?'

'They didn't hurt me, but I was very frightened and upset for Cissy.'

'Did you recognize any of 'em?'

'No. Two bobbies were passing the alley we were dragged into. One blew a whistle when they heard my scream and the men ran off.'

For a while they were both thoughtful until he enquired, 'And when you got back, your gaff was trashed?'

'Yes. It happened before.'

'When was that?'

'This summer. The police came and warned me that if it was hooligans they might chance their arm again. Perhaps they have.'

'Did they take any money?'

'No, but—' She didn't know why she was telling him all this. He was almost a stranger. 'I'm sure they blacked Cissy's eye.'

'The sods. But it don't look like kids tonight.'

'What makes you say that?'

''Ooligans don't write messages. They're in and out quick, taking what they can nab.'

Molly nodded slowly. 'What could that message mean, then?'

'Dunno. Who else lives here?'

'Just me and Cissy. My dad used to, but he was hurt in the blitz and is living with my sister in Sidcup for a while.'

The little man stroked his dog's head thoughtfully, then said very quietly, 'I ain't one to poke me nose in, but that message ain't for you or your dad, is it?'

Molly stared at him. 'What do you mean?'

'Think you'd better have a chat with your mate tomorrow.'

'What, Cissy? But . . .'

'Look, I think I should hang around tonight. I'll take me dog downstairs with me and keep watch till daylight.'

'I can't let you do that. You've helped us enough for one night.'

'Well, it's either me or the rozzers. And I ain't sure you want the law on your doorstep, not till you've spoken to yer girl.'

Molly looked intently at this unusual and perceptive little man. He seemed to be thinking more clearly than she was, and perhaps that wasn't surprising. It had been a very long day and night. Perhaps she should accept his offer?

'If you're sure,' Molly agreed.

'Leave me to it and get yourself off to bed.'

Molly shook her head. 'I'd rather just sit here.'

'Please yerself,' he shrugged. 'But put this blanket over yer biscuits and cheese. Rest assured that me and the dog'll be downstairs keeping an eye out.' He picked up the blanket that Evie often used to wrap herself in and tucked it across Molly's lap.

Molly raised a smile. 'You've been very kind.'

'Trying to impress, that's what.' He grinned and Molly

was surprised at how his wide smile made him look almost handsome.

'What are you trying to impress me for?' she asked as the dog hurtled out of the door and down the stairs.

'You want the honest truth? I'd do anything for that girl of yours.'

'Cissy?' Molly said in surprise.

'She's a cracker. Gives me the cold shoulder every time I open me cakehole. Hard as nails, or so she likes yer to think.'

With a smile, Molly rested her head back on the chair. 'Well, you've certainly got that right, Spot.'

'I know. But she ain't getting rid of me that easy.'

'I'm glad to hear it.'

'Now, close yer peepers and have a kip.' He gave her a cheeky wink, then disappeared from the front room. She heard his light footsteps on the staircase, then the sound of someone sweeping, before her eyelids eventually closed.

When Molly woke, daylight was streaming through the front room windows. She sat up quickly, the events of the night before suddenly rushing back. The clock on the mantel said half past six, and she threw off the blanket, rising unsteadily to her feet.

All was quiet, with no sound from downstairs. Had she and Cissy really been attacked after the cinema and had the shop been looted again? Brushing down her dusty blouse and skirt, she looked in the mirror over the sideboard. All traces of make-up had vanished. Her hair had fallen untidily to her shoulders in a flurry of copper-coloured waves. It was her brown eyes, still sleep-laden, that seemed to fill her face, reflecting the confusion she felt inside.

Doing what she could to restore her appearance, trailing wisps of hair back into the pins that clung upside down from her scalp and pinching her pale cheeks, she went first to Cissy's room. She opened the door very quietly and was relieved to see Cissy still sleeping there. Her insistence last night that she should leave had worried Molly the most. She had believed Cissy was happy. Or at least, content to stay on at the store for the foreseeable future.

Retreating to the passage and making her way downstairs, Molly took in a breath when she reached the glory hole. The shelves were neat and tidy, all their contents restored to order. The back door was bolted securely and light flooded in from the shop, where the till was now replaced on the counter. The shop blinds had been pulled up, hiding the sight of the alarming red daubs. Here, too, the stock had been returned to the shelves and the floor swept. As she gazed around, a small black nose appeared from behind the sack of potatoes.

'Hello, Nibbles.' The little dog wagged his tail.

Spot walked up to her. 'I tidied up for yer.'

'Thanks. Can I cook you some breakfast?'

He took his cap from his pocket and thrust it on his head. 'No, thanks, missus. I need me constitutional. And Nibbles needs a wee.'

'Nibbles is a very nice dog.'

'He's a ratter, see,' explained Spot, pulling hard on the peak of his cap. 'That's me job, I'm the council rat man. Very busy, an' all. There's vermin all over London after the bombing. They come out from the mains half dozy with shock. Nibbles sniffs 'em, nips their throats and I do the rest. He likes a good nibble, see? I spots 'em, he eats 'em.' He laughed.

Molly shivered, but she smiled all the same. This curious little man was very likeable.

'You got someone to mend your lock?'

'Yes, thanks. Dennis Turner down the road.'

'I'll be back tonight with me dog.'

'What for?'

Spot rubbed his nose and the one eye looked at her doubtfully. 'Missus, you got a problem and I can solve it. Anyone tries to get in your place in future they'll have to reckon with me.'

'But you've done enough already.'

'I told you, I'm trying to impress. I gotta get that girl to take me seriously. And if I can be of use along the way, well, that kills two birds with one stone, don't it?'

Molly smiled. 'Well, all right, but just for a short while.'

He grinned at her, tipped his cap yet again, then went to the door. After he'd gone, she drew the bolt again. When she got upstairs, Cissy was standing in the passage. Her dark hair hung in her eyes and she had put on her coat.

'Cissy, where are you going?'

'I told you last night. I'm leaving.'

Molly didn't know what to say. Why was Cissy acting so mysteriously?

'I can't stay here, Molly. They've found me.'

Molly frowned. 'Is this the other half of the story?'

'Don't matter.' Cissy hung her head. 'I told you, I'm bad luck. You're better off without me.'

'You're beginning to sound sorry for yourself.' Molly jerked her head towards the kitchen. 'Let's have some breakfast, and I'll put some ointment on that sore neck of yours and take a look at your side. Then you can tell me why you're running away. If you still want to go after that, I won't stop you.'

Cissy shrugged and walked into the kitchen.

Molly breathed a silent sigh of relief.

Chapter Sixteen

'Dunno where to start,' said Cissy as she put down her spoon, which was still clean. She couldn't eat the porridge Molly had made her. Her throat was very sore, despite the kaolin poultice Molly had applied to her neck and the tight bandage around her bruised ribs.

'Begin at the beginning,' Molly told her as she poured tea. 'When did your troubles start?'

Cissy rolled her eyes. 'The day I was born.'

Molly tutted as she sat beside her. 'Look here, Cissy, you can sound very bitter at times. I'm sure you have your reasons. But I've told you before that I don't care what happened in your past. In the time we've known each other, I've become very fond of you. I couldn't have looked after the kids and gone to see me dad if it wasn't for your help.'

'I don't deserve you saying that,' said Cissy, feeling guilty. 'I thought you'd be tired of me by now and I'd have to move on again.'

'Well, you were wrong.'

Cissy made herself look into Molly's big brown eyes. 'I'm frightened, Molly. I don't want them to hurt you like they hurt Ethel.'

'I thought Ethel died in the ambulance after the bomb dropped on her house?'

'Yer, she did. But not before they scared the living day-lights out of her. Just like they did to you last night.'

Molly looked bewildered. 'You mean those two men from the Roxy? I thought you didn't know them.'

'I know who sent them.' Cissy knew now she had to tell Molly everything. Well, nearly everything. There was no hiding place left for her. She would always be on the run. Unless she went back to Ronnie. 'Those men work for Ronnie Hook, a villain from over the water,' she told Molly. 'I'm sorry to say, he was once me gaffer.' Cissy swallowed. She knew Molly was a nice person, but even nice people had their limits.

'Go on. I'm listening.'

'I'm a brass flute, Molly. A tart. Does that ring any bells?' She watched understanding dawn on Molly's lovely face. The shame Cissy felt was almost unbearable.

'So that message in red paint was about you?'

Cissy nodded. 'It was a warning. Get shot of me or Ronnie will do something terrible. They made Ethel watch as they roughed me up. Tied the poor old girl to a chair while they clobbered me. It was only the Luftwaffe that sent them pack-ing and saved me bacon.'

Molly was silent for a moment, then said quietly, 'How did you meet these people?'

'I ain't never had anyone. So what did I care what I did? I grew up in a kids' home and hated the world. You ain't got a family, then you ain't got a soul. I just did what people wanted to earn a crust.'

'But you did meet someone. You had a husband, you said.'

'Vince was my old man, all right. I was fifteen when I met him. He put a ring on me finger but soon buggered off. My head was in a really bad place. So I decided to end it all one night at Greenwich Reach. No one was gonna miss me. But Ronnie saw me. He was just this bloke walking along by the water and he made a joke. Told me it was too shallow to drown in and all I'd get was a pisspot of dirty water in me belly. I thought he was different, that he liked me. I thought I was special until one day he told me to get out on the street and pay me way. I ended up being just another one of his girls.'

'Oh, Cissy, that's a heartbreaking story.'

'I should have known better. Who'd want me, for Gawd's sake? Even me name ain't mine. I'm really Lena Cole.'

'But your ration book says Cissy Brown.'

'Cissy is dead. Took a direct hit on the night I met you. She lodged with Ethel and didn't have no husband or family. Worked over at the flour factory. I stole the poor cow's identity papers.'

'That's against the law, Cissy.'

'Yeah, but it was a chance for a fresh start.'

'Is that why you don't like the law?'

'They'd put me in clink if they found out.'

Molly sighed and nodded slowly. 'Things begin to make sense now.'

'I really have got a Jonah on me shoulder. First Cissy, then Ethel and very nearly you last night.' She tried to clear the lump in her throat. 'You know what that big lug whispered as he was strangling me? "Ronnie'll get you, Lena. And your friend too."'

'But they didn't get us, did they?' Molly replied, her voice so steady that Cissy wondered if she'd really understood what she'd told her. 'And nor will they,' Molly continued. 'You've had the courage to leave this man and all he represents. Now you must keep to your path.'

Cissy shook her head, laughing scornfully. 'You don't know this bloke. He's a monster. He made me into a monster too. I done terrible things. Things a person should never have to do.'

'We all do things we regret, Cissy. All of us. But that doesn't mean we can't change.'

'Don't reckon you've ever put a foot wrong in your life, gel,' Cissy said forlornly.

'You're wrong there,' Molly said quietly. 'I could have saved my little girl, Emily. I should have called the doctor. Instead, I waited, believing I could get her better; it was just a cold. Within twenty-four hours she developed pneumonia and was dead. I could have saved my husband. If I'd implored Ted not to volunteer for the war, he would have listened to me. His regiment was slaughtered and I could have prevented him from being one of those men, by saying just a few words: "Wait a bit, Ted, till you get your call-up. Do this for me and our future together."' Molly paused, her eyes moist. 'But I didn't say those words. Pride kept me silent. Pride that my husband wanted to do his duty for his country. Every day of my life I think of these things. So you see, we all have our mistakes to live with.'

'Christ, gel, what you did wasn't mistakes. It was just life.'

'And death,' Molly replied. 'Death welcomed in, as easy as you welcomed Ronnie Hook into your life.'

Cissy stared at this woman who had given her shelter and friendship, and what had she offered in return? Certainly not the truth. 'There's something else too,' she forced herself to admit. 'When I met you in the hospital I thought, here's a soft touch. I've got nothing now Ethel's dead. Nowhere to go. Nothing. Perhaps there's something in this for me. I was out for what I could get. A place to hide. Food on the table. And when you paid me a wage, blimey, I couldn't believe me luck. The only fly in the ointment was Andy and his kids. I thought, what if she prefers them to me and she boots me out? Then, well . . .' Cissy dropped her gaze, for admitting to her guilty thoughts was so very painful. 'Well, I realized it wasn't a case of top dog. It was us all together, people who helped each other in times of trouble. Don't matter who or what you are or where you come from.'

Molly smiled. 'It should always be like that.'

'But it ain't. Most blokes I've met are after something, anythin'! Except for Andy. He was all right. His kids got on me nerves at first, then I found I was being a kid with them. Something I ain't done in years. Perhaps ever.' Cissy smiled fondly as she thought of Evie and Mark. 'I could have a giggle with them, eat sweets, tell them stories. They actually seemed to like me for me. And then there was Jean and Den and their kids, even old Stokesy and Liz Howells. Even your posh sister and her old man. People I'd have a run a mile from once. Nice people, too good for me. And the more I saw of 'em, the more I knew the life I'd lived was so bleeding wrong.' She couldn't bring herself to look at Molly. To see the disappointment and reproach in her eyes.

'Thank you,' Molly told her softly.

'What for?'

'For confiding in me. We've shared things today and that's what friends are about. Now, do you still want to leave?'

Cissy shook her head. 'No, course not, but—'

'Good. So you can stop all that nonsense.'

'You mean you want me to stay now you know everything?'

'What do I call you, Lena or Cissy?'

'Don't like Lena.'

'Then Cissy it is.' Molly stood up.

'But what about Ronnie?'

'What about him?'

Cissy felt a wave of panic. 'You read the message.'

'Yes, and the first step is to get rid of it.' Molly smiled at her. 'How is that side of yours?'

'Just a bit sore.'

'Well, take off your coat and you can sit here and do the books for me while I open the shop.'

'But . . .' Cissy began, only to be silenced by the stern look Molly gave her.

'By the way, Spot asked after you this morning,' Molly said

as she reached out for her overall. 'He kept watch in the shop all night with his little dog.'

'He's guessed, ain't he?' Cissy said, going scarlet.

'Guessed what?'

'That the message was about me. The tart.'

Molly shrugged. 'He's coming back tonight to keep watch in the shop.'

'Silly bloody fool. What's a little runt like him think he can do against Ronnie Hook?'

'I don't know,' Molly replied. 'But what I do know is Spot ain't like the Ronnies or Vinces of this world. He thinks highly of you and that's what counts.'

'He don't even know me.'

'Given time, he could. If you let him.'

Cissy remained silent, for although she quite liked Spot – and Molly was one in a million – she wasn't about to trust another human being for a long while yet. Not while Ronnie Hook still lived and breathed.

It was the middle of October when Molly decided to visit her dad again. She was in two minds about going. Was it safe to leave Cissy alone in the shop? They'd had no further trouble, thanks to Spot and Nibbles who kept guard down-stairs each night. Finally she decided to close the shop for the day, warning her customers in advance. Cissy protested, but Molly insisted she spend the day with Jean.

All went according to plan. After lunch at Lyn's, Oscar drove her home at half past three. She was relieved to see Cissy walking up Roper Street with Jean and the children.

'Here's Cissy now,' Molly said as Oscar kept the engine running. 'You're welcome to come in for a cup of tea,' she offered.

'I thought you said your employee was away for the day,' Oscar replied as he peered through his glasses.

'Well, most of the day.' Molly blushed.

'Better get going, thanks all the same. Things to do, you understand.' He revved the engine. 'Don't forget Christmas,' he called as she got out of the car. 'Lyn would be disappointed if you couldn't come.'

While she was out in Lyn's garden with her dad, Bill had warned her that Oscar's parents were invited for the holiday. Molly had met them several times: nice people, but like Oscar, they came from an extremely well-to-do world. The talk was always about big business, and the store wasn't in the same category. As much as she loved her father, two whole days spent in the bosom of Oscar's family was not something Molly wanted to think about right now.

When Oscar had driven off, Cissy, Jean and the children followed Molly into the back yard. All was quiet, and in the daylight Molly wondered why she had been so anxious. The door was still firmly shut with Den's new lock and all was in order inside.

'Will you stop for a cuppa?' Molly asked Jean.

'Yes, then you can tell me about your dad,' Jean said as they went up the stairs.

'Can we play in Mark and Evie's room?' asked Simon and Susie.

'Yes, course.' Molly took off her coat and hat, her heart

doing a little skip as she thought of Evie and Mark. She hadn't heard from Betty and Len. Not that she expected to. But that didn't stop her thinking each day of how the children were, wondering if they were at school and making friends.

'I'll go downstairs and open up,' Cissy said as she took her overall and scarf from the chair. Even after all this time, the red ring on her neck was still faintly visible. 'Might get one or two late customers.'

After Molly had made tea, Jean asked more about Bill. 'Did you tell Bill about the break-in?'

'No, he ain't feeling too bright.'

'Why's that?'

'He likes his pipe and hides it in his wheelchair. Lyn and Oscar ain't partial to the smell, so he pushes himself outside for a quiet smoke. Mrs James says he should be doing without the chair by now, but of course Dad won't hear of it. And then there's Christmas . . .'

'What about Christmas?'

Molly shrugged. 'Oscar's parents are staying. They ain't really his cup of tea.'

'Poor old boy.'

'I know. I should go and stay too, but what with one thing and another—'

'Can't he come home for the holiday?'

'How? He can't get upstairs.'

'He don't need to if Den brings down a bed. You could borrow our paraffin heater and use your saved coupons on the extras. As you won't be opening the shop on Christmas Day and Boxing Day, you'd have time to look after him.'

'Christmas in the glory hole? Lyn will have a fit. And what about using the lav?'

'Old Stokesy will sort you out a commode from that Aladdin's cave of his.'

Molly's spirits lifted. 'Do you think that would work?'

'Why not? It's only for a few days. And I'll bet Bill would love it.'

'What if the burglars came back?'

'You can't live your life thinking that. And anyway, with so many people about they ain't going to try again right now.'

'S'pose not. I wonder if Oscar would agree to driving him over here?'

'Don't see why not.'

Molly grinned. 'I might just suggest it.'

'That's the spirit. Now, I must finish me tea. I've got to get Den's dinner on.'

'Thank you for keeping Cissy company today.'

'She's all right, she is. The more I get to know her the more I like her.' Jean nudged her elbow and lowered her voice. 'How's the romance with the rat man? Is he still in the frame?'

'I don't know. But he deserves a medal for trying.'

Jean winked her approval, then called to the children. When they were gone, Molly thought about Cissy and Spot. Would anything come of it? Cissy had admitted that her opinion of Andy had changed, so perhaps liking Spot was not entirely out of the question.

It was then Molly decided she would try to make this Christmas very special for both her dad and Cissy. She would telephone Lyn soon. Whatever objection her sister came up with, she would think of an answer.

When a letter dropped on the mat early one morning at the end of October, Molly could hardly believe her eyes as she read the name written at the bottom of the single ruled sheet.

'What's up?' asked Cissy as she tipped the coins from the money pouch into the till. 'You look as though you've seen a ghost.'

Molly sank down on the shop stool. 'It's from Andy.'

'Blimey! What does he say?'

'He's worried about the kids.'

'Why?'

'When he left them in Southend, Betty's sister Gert was laid up and Betty was looking after her.'

'I don't like the sound of that. What about the kids?'

'I don't know. He's asked me to write to the Denhams, find out what I can.'

'He should never have left them there if Betty had her hands full.'

'Well, I don't suppose he could bring them back to London.' Molly frowned. 'This letter is dated the 5th of September, nearly two months ago.'

'Bloody post.'

'Andy says he's frustrated not being able to do anything from the middle of the ocean.'

'Poor sod.'

'I'll write to the Denhams tonight.'

'What you gonna say to them?' asked Cissy.

'I'll think of something. I've got their address in the drawer.'

Cissy folded her arms and frowned. 'It's a bit of a tall order getting you to write to them.'

'I don't suppose there's anyone else to ask.' Molly added lightly, 'Besides, Andy could be worrying for nothing. Gert might be better by now.'

After the shop had closed that evening, Molly sat in the kitchen. It took her a long while to compose a satisfactory letter. She didn't want to sound interfering. After all, these were Andy's best friends and they had known the children all their lives. So she said she hoped they were all well and were the children enjoying the seaside? She mentioned that Andy had written and hoped Betty would write back with all their news as she missed the children's company.

Other than asking outright if Gert had recovered, which might make her seem like a busybody, it was, she decided, the best she could do.

That night as she lay in bed, she couldn't stop thinking about Mark and Evie. And how helpless Andy must feel. She was so preoccupied with her thoughts that she jumped when Nibbles barked downstairs.

'Is everything all right?' she called, after throwing on her dressing gown and rushing to stand on the landing.

'Good as gold, missus,' he yelled back. 'Sorry to wake yer.'

'Are you comfy on that old chair?' Molly heard the creak of its rusty springs.

'Yeah, just having a fag.'

Too wakeful to sleep, Molly returned to the kitchen. She sat at the table and reread Andy's letter.

Could he be worrying for nothing? Being on board ship with the constant threat of enemy attack must be terrifying. Perhaps his thoughts were in turmoil; his children meant everything to him. But she was sure he would never have troubled her unless it was important.

Molly slid the letter back into the envelope. She couldn't write to him until she'd heard from Betty.

She hoped Betty would reply very soon with better news. Then she could set Andy's mind – and her own – at rest.

It was a misty November morning a week later when Detective Constable Longman walked into the shop. As usual, he was dressed in his unmistakable policeman's uniform, a trilby pulled down over his eyes and a belted raincoat. She hadn't seen him since the summer when he had stopped by to give her Betty and Len's address.

'Hello, Mrs Swift.'

'Detective Constable.' She was glad Cissy had just left on the bicycle to make the deliveries.

'Did you have any success with that address?'

'Yes, thank you. It was a long time ago now.'

'July, or thereabouts. You know, I would have helped you to find these people, but I guessed I wasn't welcome.'

Molly blushed. 'It was a very difficult time for Andy. But he eventually found the Denhams, who took the children before he went back to his ship.'

'I see. And ...' He peered over her shoulder. 'Is Miss Brown here?'

'No, Cissy's on deliveries.'

The policeman brought out his notebook. 'We had a report that you and Miss Brown were attacked outside the Roxy cinema in September.'

Molly felt her insides tighten. 'It was nothing. A couple of chancers.'

'Like those who broke into your shop?'

Molly knew she was being questioned. 'What's this all about?' she demanded. 'We didn't do anything wrong.'

'I didn't say you did. But you see, after the report was made by the constables, it went through our vetting channels. We do this to help us identify possible threats to public safety in wartime. And in this case we eventually identified some inconsistencies.'

Molly half laughed. 'What inconsistencies?'

'Did you know Miss Brown has been in prison? That she has a history of petty thieving and prostitution?'

Molly had a sinking sensation. She tried to think how to reply, as the bobby studied her carefully for her reaction. 'I know,' Molly replied, refusing to drop her stare.

'You do?'

'Cissy told me all about her past. But I believe in giving people another chance.'

'I hope your faith is justified.'

Molly straightened her spine. 'That's my business.'

'I'm only trying to help.'

'I don't need any, thank you.'

'I must ask you once more,' he said in a threatening manner. 'Do you know the identity of these attackers?'

'And the answer is the same.' Molly walked past him to the shop door and opened it. 'Goodbye, Detective Constable.'

He came slowly towards her. His eyes seemed to bore right into her head. 'Mrs Swift, you've taken someone into your life who lives off their wits. Please don't let yourself be fooled. You and your store could be at risk. I know you are a good-hearted and law-abiding person. I am trying to protect you. You have my number. Please call me if you need me.' He kept his gaze locked with hers, then just as Molly thought she could bear it no longer, he left.

She watched as his tall figure disappeared into the mist, then gave out a long-withheld sigh that made her head swim with relief.

It was almost unbelievable! By taking a false identity, Cissy was in much more trouble than if she had kept her own name.

That night, Molly broke the news to Cissy. 'He's found Cissy Brown's records,' she explained as they sat in the front room by the fire. 'She'd been to prison and has been in trouble with the law for petty thieving and prostitution.'

'Oh, Gawd, I thought she worked at the flour factory.' Cissy closed her eyes. 'I'll bet he came to arrest her – I mean me.'

'No, I don't think so,' Molly said thoughtfully. 'She might have had a record, but he didn't try to hang around. If he wanted to arrest her, he'd have been back here by now.'

Cissy groaned loudly. 'I knew I should have scarpered.'

'Then they'd definitely think you were guilty of something. As it is, you're turning over a new leaf. Just as I told them.'

'They won't believe that.'

'Why not?'

'Because cons don't break the habit of a lifetime.'

Molly looked into Cissy's fearful gaze. 'You ain't a con, Cissy.'

'I worked for Ronnie Hook though.'

'You've left him and now you are you.'

Cissy put her face in her hands. 'He'll be back, I know it.'

'You must keep your nerve.'

Cissy slowly looked up at her, despair on her face. 'I don't know if I can.'

'I've got Christmas all planned, Cissy,' Molly said, frantic-ally searching for a reason to make Cissy stay. 'I want to have Dad home and I'm relying on you to help me. I'll never be able to do it on my own. You can't let me down now. Not after all I've done for you.' Molly was afraid that Cissy would disappear into the night, never to be seen again.

'I suppose I'll have to stay, then,' agreed Cissy morosely.

'Thank you.' Molly said no more, but she was secretly ashamed to have resorted to a kind of emotional blackmail. But Cissy knew how very important it was to her that Bill should come home for Christmas.

Chapter Seventeen

It was the beginning of December when at last a letter arrived from Betty. And it was not what Molly expected to hear.

Molly,

My dear sister Gert passed away just before your letter arrived. She's not been too good, you see. Then one day she was gone. It was a rotten shock. Now me and Len are moving out tomorrow, as we can't afford the rent. I'm not the the ticket myself and me legs are up like balloons. What with one thing and another, it's been a bit difficult. Looks like we'll have to evacuate again. The Army are taking us as far as the London Road, Romford, where we're told we'll be sent up country. Don't know about the kids yet. They might have to go somewhere else. Sorry I can't tell you more.

Regards, Betty Denham

'Gert's dead?' Cissy asked after reading the letter. 'They're on the move again?'

Molly nodded. 'She doesn't know what's going to happen to the kids. What am I gonna do?'

Cissy was quiet, then slapped her hands on her hips. 'You'll have to get 'em back.'

'But how?'

'Romford ain't as far as Southend. Go there and sort 'em out.'

'But this letter was written nearly two weeks ago. What if they've all been moved on from Romford?'

'You'll have to take the chance.'

Molly put the envelope on the counter. 'I don't even know if there's any buses. So many are out of commission.'

'What about asking Den to drive you in that van of his?'

'He's not allowed to use it any more, so Jean said. As the raids have slowed down, the ARP have tightened up on petrol.'

'Well, it looks like a bus, then.'

'I haven't even got a proper address in Romford. Just the London Road.'

'You can't go far wrong if you ask for the Sally Army.' Cissy came over, wiping her hands on her apron. 'You know you've got to do it. Or else Andy is going to lose them kids.'

'I can't bear to think of that.'

'Listen, why don't you go tomorrow?'

'Tomorrow?' Molly repeated.

'I'll ask Spot if he'll stay with me Saturday. Then you won't fret I'm on me own. Let's face it, as well intentioned as Betty might be, she's having enough trouble looking after herself and Len, let alone the kids.'

'What if something happens? What if I can't get back tomorrow night? What if I can't even find them?'

'I know there's a lot of ifs and buts and neither of us know how it'll turn out. But at least you'll have tried.'

Molly knew Cissy was right. She had to act fast. But would she find a bus going to Romford? She had to leave some cash in the till for Cissy. Would there be enough spare for the fare for the journey? It was expensive to travel. Even if there were sufficient funds, the Denhams and Evie and Mark might have already left Romford.

Molly paused for a few seconds, then hurried off to the kitchen. She lifted the floorboard and took three pounds for her purse. She didn't like borrowing from her dad's savings again.

But this was an emergency.

Early on Saturday morning, Molly set off for Poplar and the bus depot. The street vendors were out, and a little traffic, and one or two buses emerged from the temporary shelter. She called at the evacuation point first, recalling the day she had taken the children from Andy before he went back to sea. Now she was searching for them again – only this time, the area was deserted.

How would she get to Romford if there was no transport? And even if she did, she had no proper address.

Molly sat down on the bench by the bus stop, undoing the two top buttons of her coat. Her warm breath funnelled white into the cold morning air. Would Cissy be safe in her absence? Could Spot be relied upon? What could one man do if Ronnie Hook's men appeared?

Just then a coach pulled up on the other side of the road and she watched the driver climb out, talking to the conductor who was enjoying a smoke.

Molly hurried over to them.

'Hello, love,' one of them said. 'You're an early bird.'

'Are you going anywhere near Romford?'

'Why's that?'

'I need to go there today.'

'Well, you're out of luck with us,' said the driver, adjusting his peaked cap. 'We're going west.'

'Where's that?'

'In the opposite direction to where you want to go.'

'Do you know if I can catch another bus or coach? It's very important I get there.'

The driver looked at the conductor. 'In about half an hour there's some Specials arriving. Dunno if one of them's going near Romford.'

'There's one going to the Dagenham factories,' the conductor nodded. 'You could catch that, then change for Rush Green.'

'How long will it take?'

'How long's a piece of string? With holes in the roads and diversions, could be all day.'

'Where do I wait for this Special?'

'Behind the cafe. I should get yerself a drink an' all. Could be a long wait.'

It was a long wait. Molly had drunk two cups of tea at the temporary hut used as a cafe and had paced the pavement until she felt she had worn a hole in the stones. When the bus arrived, marked SPECIAL and underneath, the word DAGENHAM, she boarded along with a lot of other people who were talking about their work at the factories.

She sat on the back seat and paid her fare, grateful that she had brought Dad's money in case of emergencies. What those emergencies might be, she didn't know. But if she had to catch a train or even a taxi for part of the journey, then she could at least pay her way.

The bus started up and chugged along through the streets of the East End to join the Newham Way leading out of London. She gazed out of the filthy window. This journey could be a wild goose chase. Meanwhile, Cissy and the shop were exposed and vulnerable. There was Spot, of course, but what if—?

Molly shook her head. She mustn't let her imagination run riot. As the bus trundled on, the slow swaying soothed her. The countryside looked misty but green. The little houses and villages were so pretty in comparison to the smoky East End terraces. An occasional tractor squeezed through the narrow roads, but there was very little traffic because of the government's restriction on petrol. She must have fallen asleep when an enormous roar made her jump.

The silence of the countryside was shattered. Everyone looked out of the windows. The driver pulled to a sharp halt. A low drone sounded menacingly in the sky. The driver shot out of his seat and, together with the conductor, shouted at the passengers to evacuate the bus.

Suddenly two low-flying aircraft zoomed down across the fields and seemed almost to touch the top of the bus. A woman screamed and there was panic as everyone tried to disembark. Molly heard the familiar rattle of machine-gun fire. There were more screams and, together with everyone else, she ran towards a long, thick hedge at the side of the road. Before they could take cover, two more aircraft flew over – but this time she saw the familiar rings painted on the sides of the Spitfires.

Heart in mouth, she was half dragged along by the driver, who was shouting at her to keep low. Molly eventually found herself in the field, flattened to the muddy ground.

'Messerschmitts,' yelled one man, who raised his fist. 'Our boys are giving chase.'

The driver pushed him down. Then he almost fell into the hedge himself as the enemy aircraft engaged their guns. Bullets tore up the turf and sent grass and mud in all directions. The dogfight intensified and the noise of the planes' engines roared above them. Molly thought of the blitz and the long nights in Jean's Anderson shelter. She tried to burrow herself into the cold, damp earth. Perhaps the hedge would provide cover.

Folding her coat collar over her ears, she tried not to listen as the ground vibrated with bullets. Why did people want to kill each other, when life was so precious?

'You all right, love?'

Molly opened her eyes and met the concerned gaze of the driver.

'Y-yes, thanks.'

'The Spits chased 'em off. You can let go of that bush now.'

Molly was helped up. Her knees rattled together. Her coat was dirty and her shoes were muddy.

'Let's get you all back on board,' the driver yelled and Molly joined the line of bedraggled, frightened passengers. They were all subdued, taking their places again as the driver started the engine.

'Well, that was a close one,' the conductor said as he looked down the aisle. 'Is everyone all present and correct?'

Molly, along with everyone else, nodded.

'Now, I'm going to show you something,' said the conductor. 'Take a butcher's at this.' He held his ticket machine aloft. 'I chucked it on the ground as we all did a runner.' He pointed to a neat round hole in the metal. 'Could have been me,' he said with a grin. 'Or any one of us, come to that. But the buggers missed. We should count ourselves lucky they had such rotten aims.'

Molly and everyone else gasped. Then suddenly, as if they all realized how close a call it had been, and just how lucky they were, everyone clapped and cheered.

Molly joined in, the fear slowly ebbing away, until she found herself near to tears of relief.

'You dopey sod,' Cissy called reprovingly, 'shovel the spuds in her bag, don't try to wrap 'em.' She tutted, watching Spot as he made their two lady customers roar with laughter by trying to contain the filthy potatoes in a single sheet of newspaper.

Cissy found herself smiling against her will. Spot was a right joker and he knew it. The customers who'd come in today had found him as entertaining as any comic, and were appreciative of his little dog sitting on its hind legs and barking as he whistled 'Pack Up Your Troubles'. They were cards, the pair of them.

Begrudgingly, she had to admit she liked his company. He might be a small man who rarely took off his cap and who winked with his good eye at nearly every other sentence he uttered as if letting you into a big secret, but he refused to lose that grin of his, no matter how fiercely she yelled at him.

When the shop was empty, Cissy took the broom and began to sweep up the evidence of the busy morning. Dog-ends, cabbage leaves, pieces of rubble that always seemed to arrive on the floor of the shop from outside no matter how many times she swept it. Just as she was trying to reach the knots of dust and dirt in the far corner, a hand came out and relieved her of the broom.

'Hey! What did you do that for?' she demanded, swinging around to face Spot.

'With 'ands like yours, all dainty and smooth, you should give 'em a rest.'

'I can take care of me own hands, thank you very much.' She grabbed the broom handle and began to pull. Spot grinned and held onto it.

'You've got the strength of a vestal virgin,' he said, wrinkling his eyebrows.

'I ain't no virgin and you bloody know it,' said Cissy, offended.

'I couldn't care less what you are,' he replied as she ineffectually tried to loosen his hold. 'You're the tastiest peach I've seen since me mum's golden syrup pudding.'

'Will you shut up?' Cissy pushed back her turban and tried to hide her embarrassment.

'Don't you enjoy a bit of intelligent conversation once in a while?'

'If you're intelligent, I'm Mata Hari.'

'Now you're talking. Not only was Mata Hari a cracker, but bright as a button too.'

'Yeah, she was a spy an' all. Now, are you gonna give me that broom?'

Spot held it out to her. 'Take it. I dare you.'

Cissy folded her arms and rolled her eyes. 'Listen, I've had enough of you for one day, you'd better clear off.'

'What, and leave you at the mercy of Ronnie Hook?'

Cissy froze. Her arms fell by her sides. 'How do you know about Ronnie? Did Molly say?'

Spot tapped the side of his nose. 'You told me. You said you was from the other side of the water. And it wasn't fairies as done this place over. I read that muck on the blackout blind—'

'And you put two and two together to make five.'

'I'm close though, ain't I?' Spot insisted. 'Ronnie's a big name in the rackets on the south side. I took an uneducated guess.'

'Then what are you doing here?' Cissy demanded, trying to put on a show of defiance to cover the fact she'd been found out. 'A little squirt like you ain't no match for him.'

'You'd be surprised.'

'I would at that. Your dog's got a better chance of seeing off the enemy than you.'

Spot nodded slowly, then handed Cissy the broom. 'Here you are then, gel. If you don't want me services, we'll be off.' He gave a whistle and called to his dog, who sprang from behind the counter. Stuffing his hands in his pockets Spot strolled to the shop door and yanked it open.

Cissy could have bitten out her tongue. What did she have to upset him for? He was better than nothing and she would be bloody alone too, if he deserted her. It would be just her luck for some of Ronnie's men to turn up out of the blue and do her – and the place – over.

'You got a real thin skin for someone who boasts being a minder,' Cissy called, sinking her pride. 'Thought you could take a joke.'

At this, the small, sturdy figure stopped just outside the shop and turned to grin at her. 'Christ, girl, you got a tongue sharper than a stevedore's 'ook.'

'Well, what you waiting for, then? The floor still needs sweeping.' She held out the broom as a peace offering.

Cissy watched him stride in, with a swagger that infuriated her. He grabbed it from her hand, winking with his good eye, and before she could dodge he planted a kiss on her cheek.

'Give over!' she cried, clapping her hand to her face.

'Couldn't resist.'

'I'm in the kitchen, making a brew,' she threw over her shoulder as she bolted for the stairs.

'Good on you, girl, keep the troops happy,' she heard him call. 'The quickest way to a man's heart is through his gut.'

Cissy stood in the kitchen, trying to regain her composure. The cheeky sod was infuriating, cocky and never short of a reply. She would love to bring him down a peg or two. But unfortunately he was the only insurance she possessed against Ronnie Hook. And, as he had guessed her secret, but not made her squirm into the bargain, there was a redeeming factor to his character.

She slowly filled the kettle and put it on the gas. Just let him say one more word to annoy her though, and – well, he'd have his marching orders!

Satisfied with her decision, she glanced in Molly's small mirror behind the door. Sliding off her turban, she let her hair fall softly down to her shoulders, inclining her head to gaze into the soft, silvery eyes staring back at her.

She wasn't blushing, not at all. Lena Cole hadn't blushed in years.

There were queues of people snaking out from the bus stop on the outskirts of Dagenham. All the passengers followed, like long lines of sheep, making their way to the factories that had managed to survive after being targeted during the blitz.

Molly joined them, hoping there would be a connecting bus to Rush Green or Romford, but she couldn't see any. Many of the houses on the outskirts of town had suffered damage. As with The Isle of Dogs, there was evidence of the bombing everywhere: holed and broken roads, diversion signs and military traffic. Since she didn't know the area, she had no idea what times the buses, if any, would run.

She was still feeling shaken up. Those bullets had come very close as she'd sheltered by the hedge. They had reminded her of the blitz, with the ack-ack firing up at the bombers revealed by the searchlights in the night sky. At least it was daylight now. And even though she had been very scared, her concern for the children was greater.

Molly soon found herself alone. She looked up and down the road, to the big factory buildings on one side and the fields on the other. It was cold and with a hint of rain in the air. She didn't even have her umbrella.

'Where d'you want, love?' a voice called as an open-backed lorry drew up. The driver was an older man, with untidy grey hair and a cigarette dangling from his lips. 'Town centre?'

'No. I want to get to Romford or even Rush Green.'

'I think I can oblige. I've dropped off all me regulars and am on me way back to the London Road.'

Molly almost jumped for joy and hurried over to the open window. 'That's where I want to go!'

'What part?' he yelled above the noise of the old engine.

'Wherever the Salvation Army have a mission.'

He rubbed his chin. 'There ain't no Army mission, ducks.'

'There must be. Some people I know said they'd be there.'

'We got the Catholics, the Methodists and the Baptists. The Crown Hotel and the Golden Mile and a damn fine dog track. Then there's the market, and a bloody good one at that. Sheep, cows, pigs, any fowl you can name, and we've got a Corn Exchange too.'

'Well, that's very nice, but I want the Salvation Army.'

'You better hop in and I'll drop you off at the Crown. And keep yer eyes skinned, as Jerry paid us a visit earlier. Bomb Alley they call us here, as the buggers fly over this way to the city. Give us a bang on the window if you see anything.'

With this warning ringing in her ears, Molly made her way round to the back of the lorry. She climbed onto the rusty step and grabbed the steel struts of the canvas arch. She was soon sitting with her back to the cab, her eyes fixed on the sky. The moment she saw a movement in the clouds, she wasn't going to hesitate in letting the driver know.

Chapter Eighteen

It must have been late morning by the time the lorry stopped at the Crown, as Molly saw people going into the pub.

'Here you are, love, just ask inside,' said the driver as he helped her out from the back of the lorry.

'How much do I owe you?' Molly asked and was greeted with a firm shake of the head.

'I'm paid for driving the factory workers and was on me way home anyway.'

'Are you sure?'

'Course. Good luck finding your friends.'

Molly watched him jump in the cab and drive off. She looked up at the three-storey tavern, with a parapet and several large chimneys. All around its walls were sandbags and buckets. The old-fashioned glass windows were covered inside with criss-cross tape. The bar smelled of tobacco and ale as she walked in and the tables and chairs were filling up quickly with Saturday trade. She went to the bar and asked the young girl serving behind it if she knew where the Salvation Army church or mission was.

'No, love, I don't,' said the girl. 'But there's a Sally Army bloke who lives down the road. He might be able to tell you.' Listening carefully to the directions, Molly thanked her and walked out.

The rain had started in earnest. By the time she got to the small cottage, she was soaked to the skin. The door was open slightly and she could hear the sound of someone crying.

Molly pushed the door gently. She looked inside and saw an older woman sitting in a chair, mopping her eyes with a handkerchief. She looked up and met Molly's gaze. 'Y-yes?' she said falteringly.

'I'm Molly Swift. I'm looking for Betty and Len Denham, and two children, Mark and Evie Miller.'

With that, the woman burst into tears again, rose unsteadily to her feet and threw her arms around Molly.

Molly held her gently until the tears subsided and she was able to talk.

'Oh, Molly, I'm so pleased to see yer, gel.'

'Betty? Is it you?'

'The very same, love.'

'Where are the children?'

'They've just taken 'em. That's why I'm upset.'

Molly released her gently. 'Who's taken them and where?'

'They've been billeted up north and me and Len are being sent to Wales. The captain and Len just took 'em.'

Molly's heart hammered against her ribs. 'Where?'

'Poor little souls,' sobbed Betty, as if she hadn't heard

Molly. 'It was such a wrench to see them go. Bawlin' their eyes out, they were.'

'Go where – *exactly*?' Molly asked more firmly.

'As it was raining the captain drove them in his car to the Crown. They're being collected by the coach to go to Yorkshire and—'

Before Betty could say more Molly hurtled out of the cottage door. It was raining so hard that the big drops splashed painfully against her cheeks and in seconds she was drenched once again.

She began to run, making her way back along the path she had just followed. Her shoes were waterlogged and she could barely see through the sheets of rain. She had come so far to find the children. Surely it couldn't all end like this?

She pressed on, through the muddy puddles and small lakes, all the while saying a frantic prayer – that she wouldn't be too late to find them.

Molly burst in through the pub doors and pushed her way to the bar. 'Have you seen the Salvation Army captain you told me about a while ago?' she enquired of the young girl, who was serving a customer. 'There's another man with him, Len Denham. They're meeting an evacuation coach here – or are supposed to be.'

'No.' The barmaid shrugged. 'But you could try the back yard. A lot of vehicles pull in there.'

Molly searched the room. It was full of country folk – farmers and field workers, she guessed. There wasn't a Sally Army uniform in sight.

The men all turned to stare at her as she pushed her way through the small groups who were drinking and talking, until she reached the door. When she was outside once again, the rain filled her eyes and beat against her face. Her stomach was tied in a knot that she thought might never undo.

The yard behind the pub was deserted except for a very old car parked beside a small hut. Then from the hut a man appeared. He was wearing a shiny mackintosh and stood in the rain, his collar pulled up to his ears. Another man joined him, an older, grey-haired man who was only wearing an old jacket and, like her, was drenched.

She followed their gaze and suddenly saw a large vehicle drive out from behind the hut. Molly tried to wipe the wet from her eyes. One minute she could see the coach, the next she couldn't.

Her heart leaping fiercely, she stepped into the vehicle's path, waving her hands and yelling at it to stop, as the rain ran in streams down her hair and face.

The coach still drove towards her. Molly could see the driver behind the windscreen wipers. His face was full of alarm. She kept waving and refused to move. He had to stop!

'You bloody fool!' the driver cried as he leaped from the coach after a dramatic swerve and squeal of brakes. 'I could have killed you. My brakes ain't the best in this foul weather!'

Molly had thought for a split second the big vehicle wouldn't stop. She had been frozen with fright. But then, a few feet away, it had splashed to a muddy halt in the middle of a puddle.

'Sorry,' apologized Molly, dragging her wet hair from her face. 'But I had to stop you. Are you the evacuation coach taking people to Yorkshire?'

'Yeah. But I ain't got any room left.'

'I want two of your passengers. Mark and Evie Miller.'

'Well, you can't have 'em, you bloody lunatic!'

Molly went to push past him but he grabbed hold of her. They were struggling like this when the two men she had seen appeared.

'What's this? What's going on?' the man in the mackintosh asked.

Choking back her frustrated cries, Molly shrugged herself free. 'My name is Molly Swift,' she gasped. 'I'm a friend of Andy Miller's. I've come from the East End to take his two children back with me.'

'Molly?' the grey-haired man said, stepping forward. 'I can't believe it's you!'

'Len?'

He nodded. And before she knew what she was doing, Molly was hugging him for dear life.

Then there seemed to be chaos as Molly saw Evie and Mark, their little faces pressed up to the wet coach window. Some of the passengers were trying to restore order as the children banged their palms on the glass, clearly distressed.

The driver turned his attention to the panic inside the vehicle and jumped up through the open door. Molly pushed herself away from Len and followed. There was bedlam as she moved down the aisle and Mark and Evie saw her.

The driver was calling out for calm, and when Molly at last reached the children, she fell to her knees and held them tightly.

'Oh, my darlings,' she gulped, pressing their tear-streaked faces against her cheeks. 'I've found you. I've found you! Everything's going to be all right now.'

Evie couldn't speak for her deep sobs. She held on to Molly, refusing to let go.

'It's all right, Evie,' Molly comforted, lifting her into her arms and away from danger. Then, taking Mark's hand, she looked into his anguished face. 'Come with me, Mark. We're going home.'

He needed no more explanation and squeezed Molly's hand, following her along the seats past the astonished faces of the passengers.

The driver barred Molly's way as he stood by the open door. 'You ain't going nowhere with those kids,' he told her, looking very red under his peaked cap. 'They're on my list to go to Yorkshire.'

'They're going with me,' Molly argued, 'and if you try to stop us, then I'll ask for the police to be called to sort all this out. And then you'll never get to Yorkshire.'

'It's all right,' called the man in the mackintosh outside. He looked up at them, mopping his wet brow and the rain from his eyes. 'I'll take responsibility. You can let them pass.'

'Bugger me,' the driver responded. 'It's usually people trying to get on me coach, not leave it. But if you say so, squire, then I suppose they can go.' He jerked his head at Molly and stood aside.

Molly jumped down with the children, and Len and the man hurried them to the old car parked a few yards away. When safely seated in the back with the children either side of her, Molly hugged them, trying to disguise her emotion.

How close she had come to losing them!

'And so you see, love, the fates were against us,' explained Betty that evening as she hung all the wet coats on the fire-guard in front of the blazing fire. 'With Gert gone, the rent going up and nowhere else to go, we didn't have no choice.'

'I was very sorry to hear about your sister.' Molly was sitting on the captain's old leather sofa, pushed so close to the hearth that their cheeks glowed scarlet. Evie and Mark had curled up to her, one on either side. They had both fallen asleep after devouring the soup and thick slices of bread that were prepared for them.

'Please call me Roger,' the captain said, and explained that his cottage acted as a halfway house for Salvation Army evacuees. Molly liked him immediately. A tall, rather stern-looking man in his early fifties, he had heard about her from the Denhams.

'But why didn't you ask me to take the children?' Molly asked Betty.

'We should have,' Betty acknowledged as she sat down beside Len.

'We talked about it,' Len broke in, a worried expression on his sombre face. 'But Andy told us you have a shop to run and a dad what's ill. Well, if that ain't enough to cope with in wartime, I don't know what is.'

'Len has a point,' Roger interrupted. 'How do you propose to look after two young children as well as carry on with your business and look after your father?'

'Dad's staying with my sister, Lyn, until he's better,' Molly explained. 'The children were never any trouble.'

'You're very kind-hearted,' Roger told her. 'But what if something happened to Mr Miller? Or to your home, since the East End has been a prime target of the Luftwaffe. Who's to say the raids won't start again?'

'If they do, then we'll manage like we did before,' Molly said firmly. 'I've very good friends to help me and the children were happy. Although they did miss Betty and Len – and, of course, Stella.'

'Oh, don't worry about that, she wasn't with 'em half the time,' said Betty disparagingly. 'Used to palm them off whenever she could. Not that we minded. They was like our own, which was why we were so upset to see them taken off to Yorkshire.'

'You can come and visit any time,' Molly said generously. 'We'd make you very welcome.'

Roger dropped his hands on his knees and stretched his back. He stood up and looked at the clock. 'You can't think of leaving now. It's dark and still raining. Besides, there won't be a bus to London until the morning.'

'Stay the night, ducks,' said Betty, glancing at the captain. 'She can kip on the sofa, can't she, Roger?'

'Of course. I have plenty of blankets.'

Molly glanced out of the cottage window. She had forgotten how quickly it got dark in December. And how, with the blackout in force, there would be no hope of getting back to the island today. Would Cissy be worried about her? At least Spot would be there to keep her company.

'I'm sorry,' she said regretfully. 'I seem to be putting you to a lot of trouble. Without you and Len helping me to get the children off the coach I don't think the driver would have cooperated.'

'You gave him quite a fright.' Roger quirked an eyebrow. 'And me too.'

Molly blushed. 'I was desperate to stop him.'

'Evidently.'

'Our Andy thought very highly of you,' said Len with a grin. 'You did him a kindness and gave him back a bit of faith in – well, in other people.'

Roger went to the cupboard and opened it. 'You'll find all the linen you need in here. Betty and Len and the children sleep upstairs in the front room. I'm at the back. It's only a small cottage but it's seen many heads pass under its roof.'

'You do wonderful work,' Molly said appreciatively.

'We simply have faith in our Lord Jesus Christ,' he replied with a dismissive shrug, reminding Molly of what the young Salvation Army girl had said to her at the Mission Hall.

Molly looked down at the two tiny heads burrowed under her arms and thought of how close she had come to losing them. She'd said a prayer as she'd been running in the rain to the Crown. A prayer she hadn't even really known she was saying. And miraculously, tomorrow they would all be on their way home.

*

At first light, Molly was woken by the tall figure of Roger dressed smartly in his navy-blue uniform, standing over her holding a cup of tea. 'Good morning, Molly. I hope you slept well.'

Molly nodded, sitting up slowly on the sofa. She was still fully dressed, but dry now, and there was the pleasant smell of woodsmoke lingering in the small room. The embers in the grate, she noticed, had been fanned with the bellows, reviving the tired fire.

'Yes, I did, thank you.' She took the cup and saucer. 'Is everyone up? Have I slept late?'

'Not at all.'

'Is it raining?'

'Yes, I'm afraid so.

Molly's heart sank. The poor children would get soaked unless she could borrow an umbrella.

Roger went back to the hearth and knelt beside it. He poked the burning logs and drew a bright cloud of spitting orange flames. 'When we've had breakfast, I'll drive you back to the Isle of Dogs.'

Molly put her feet to the floor. 'But what about petrol?'

'I have an allowance for evacuees.'

'Yes, but not for us.'

'I'm sure we can squeeze you into our quota.'

Molly shook her head. 'I don't know how to thank you.'

'Our founder, General William Booth, told us that God loves with a great love those whose hearts are courageous. And, my dear Molly, I think you have won that accolade as a widow, having suffered the tragic loss of your daughter and then your husband, as I am given to understand by Betty.'

'I don't know that I have courage,' she said uncertainly. 'I'm just living from day to day. When Dad was injured, I was frightened he'd die. Just like Ted, and Emily our daughter. And then, in the midst of it all, I met Andy and the children and another woman who had no home. We were all frightened – frightened of something . . .' Molly swallowed. 'It was then my thoughts began to change.'

'By the grace of God,' Roger nodded.

'I'm not a spiritual person,' Molly admitted. 'But I would like to be.'

Roger's eyes creased at the corners. 'I'm sure our Maker will have something to say about that.'

Just as he spoke, two small faces appeared at the door. Mark and Evie ran into her arms. She hauled them up on the sofa beside her.

Mark looked up and yawned. 'Are we going home now?'

Molly nodded. She felt a wonderful pleasure at the word 'home'. Molly brought her gaze up to meet the captain's. He too was smiling, his expression telling her that everything had worked out all right in the end.

Chapter Nineteen

Cissy was worried. Molly had been away all Saturday and hadn't turned up last night. Spot had assured her Molly could take care of herself. But what if she'd been jumped by a gang? Even worse, what if Ronnie's men had somehow got hold of her?

And then there was the letter that had plopped onto the mat yesterday after Molly had left. It was postmarked Sidcup. Was it good news or bad from headquarters, as Cissy had privately named Lyn and Oscar's place of residence? Molly had been waiting on tenterhooks for the answer to her request that the old boy come home for Christmas.

Cissy was so distracted she couldn't concentrate on the egg she was frying for Spot. He had stayed overnight, faithfully keeping watch downstairs. Nibbles had barked several times, but she was accustomed to the racket now. She even liked the noise, in a funny kind of way.

The egg spat fiercely and Cissy removed the frying pan

from the gas. Spot appeared at the kitchen door and Nibbles trotted in and sat at her feet.

'I can smell something tasty,' said Spot, keeping his distance.

'It's one of the eggs you probably nicked,' Cissy replied without turning round. She slipped the juicy egg between two slices of bread and placed the meal on a plate.

Spot laughed, licking his lips. 'Can I come in and eat it, then?'

'Are your hands clean?'

'Just washed 'em under the pump.'

'Has the ratter had a wee?'

'His bladder is as empty as me old granny's purse.'

'Here you are, then. And there's an extra bit of bread to give to the dog.'

Spot bounced forward and took a seat at the table. By the time Cissy had made a strong brew and was filling two mugs to the brim, he'd finished.

'Blimey, you must have cast-iron guts.' Cissy watched him plunge the remainder of bread in the yolk stain and feed it to the waiting animal. Then he leaned back and clouted his chest, expelling a ripple of wind.

'Never 'ad such a flavoursome start to me day.'

Cissy glanced at the mantel clock. It was almost eleven. 'Do you reckon Molly's all right? Do you think she found them kids?'

'The answer to both is yes.'

'Why's that?'

'Gut feeling.' He tapped his nose.

Cissy spluttered laughter. 'You and your stomach.'

'Well, it's in prime condition this morning after being fed so well.'

She sighed, for even Spot's teasing was failing to distract her. The more she considered the threatening possibilities for Molly, the more she brooded.

'Don't worry,' Spot advised her, letting his hand creep across the table until it reached hers. 'Like you, your mate's got chutzpah.'

Spot's fingers inched over hers. Cissy wanted to drag her hand away, but she didn't.

'Why don't you let me try standing up for you once in a while?' he asked. 'All you got to do is say the word.'

'What word is that?'

'I ain't half taken with you, Cissy. You must know that. Let's make it official.'

'What!' Cissy snatched back her hand. Her eyes bulged out of their sockets. 'Not in a million years, sonny boy.'

'I'll wait, then.'

'I ain't having you hanging around me that long!' She jumped to her feet, almost spilling her tea.

Spot stood up and faced her, pushing his hand thoughtfully around his unshaven jaw. Nibbles barked as she took hold of the greasy frying pan.

'Don't you try anything on, you dirty bugger!' she yelled at Spot. 'I thought you was after something!'

'Tell me what I'm after?' asked Spot holding out his arms innocently. 'It ain't yer money, sweetheart. And it ain't yer tender nature. But I like what I see. You're a real eyeful with a bundle of spirit. You've captured me heart. I reckon we could make a go of it.'

Slowly Cissy lowered the frying pan. She felt all choked up for some reason. Perhaps she was more worried about Molly than she thought, to bring on this sudden emotion?

'Listen, let's tie the knot,' Spot said reasonably. 'I won't let you down. I'll make you happy.'

'How do you propose doing that?' Cissy demanded.

'I've got a good job and rooms over Narrow Street what me mum and dad left me, Gawd rest their souls.'

'Limehouse?' Cissy questioned. 'That's all Chinese.'

'Well, I agree it ain't Pall Mall, but I've got the deeds. And me old folks never had no bother.'

'I don't know if I can trust your credentials,' Cissy huffed. 'You might be making it all up.'

Spot slapped his hand on his chest. 'I'm as kosher as the King, I swear it.'

'I don't know nothing about your past.'

Spot pulled himself up to his full height. 'I've never been in the jug. Don't owe a penny. And I'm in robust health, although I failed me medical to get into the army. The trouble is me eyes, one looking left, the other right. The doctors was afraid I might shoot our own troops.'

Cissy resisted the urge to smile. 'So you're giving me to understand you've got potential?'

'Me only liability is him,' Spot said, nodding down at the dog. 'The bugger needs feeding and costs a fortune in leftovers.'

Cissy was torn between laughter and tears. This funny

little man had somehow got under her skin. In comparison to Vince and his philandering and Ronnie and his violence, he probably was lily white. But doubt still tugged at her insides. She hadn't known a bloke who didn't want her for her services. So was this little squirt just trying to trick her into bed?

'Here's the deal,' he continued in a serious tone. 'You gotta be better off when you slide me ring on your finger, cos I'll write out a letter for the beak, stating if ever you're displeased with the goods, it's you who take me gaff and all that's in it. And after you give me the boot, you won't ever set eyes on me again.'

'What you going on about?' laughed Cissy, astounded.

'I'm telling you, I want to marry yer and it'll be signed and sealed in your favour.'

All the bravado went out of Cissy. She was weakening in her resolve against men – one in particular – and she didn't like herself for it.

She stared belligerently into his lopsided eyes, although now they were up close she could see they were attractive in their own way, and his generous lips, perhaps his best feature, were pursed. They were coming closer, and she wanted to retreat, but she didn't. For some reason she couldn't explain to herself, her eyes were closing. And when they'd closed, she felt his hands lightly touch her arms and his mouth cover hers. To her further surprise she enjoyed the taste and the feel of the kiss. From being a reluctant kisser, she turned into an eager one, her heart leaping about inside her chest as if it too wanted to be loved.

They were cuddling quite strongly when suddenly the back door rumbled open downstairs. Nibbles shot off barking and Cissy nearly died of shock, as the two kids came running up the stairs and into the kitchen to fling their arms around her.

'I'll just pay my respects,' Roger said, sweeping off his Army cap and tucking it under his arm as Molly led the way from the back door and up the stairs. 'I mustn't dally, for as you know, Betty and Len are leaving tomorrow for Wales.'

Molly nodded, remembering with fondness the Denhams' last tearful goodbyes at the cottage. 'They're good people. I hope they get a decent billet and don't miss the kids too much.'

'The Army will do what we can to help.'

'So you've decided to turn up again!' Cissy exclaimed, one arm around Mark and the other Evie, when she saw Molly and the captain walk into the kitchen.

'I thought you might be worried.'

'Why should I be?'

Molly guessed by the look of relief on Cissy's face that she was hiding her concern. 'Cor blimey, you two have grown!' Cissy said as she sat on a chair, hugging Mark and Evie against her. 'You both must be at least two foot taller than when you went away.'

Molly was pleased to see that children's faces were wreathed in smiles. It had been upsetting for them to leave Betty and Len.

'I's hungry,' giggled Evie, glancing at the yellow stains of egg on Spot's plate. 'You got eggs for us 'n' all?'

Cissy looked at Spot. 'You'll have to ask him.'

Spot jumped to attention. 'Give us a tick and I'll nip away for some.' He walked over to Molly. 'Nice to see yer back, gel.'

'And it's nice to be home.'

Spot grinned at the tall figure of the Salvation Army officer. 'Mornin', squire.'

'This is Roger,' Molly introduced. 'He was kind enough to put me up for the night and drive us back from Romford.'

'Well, I told her you'd be all right,' said Spot, nodding at Cissy. 'She's bitten her fingernails down to the quick with worry.' With that, he hurried out of the kitchen.

'Roger, this is my friend Cissy,' Molly said after he'd gone.

'Glad to meet you, Cissy.'

Cissy nodded. 'You an' all.'

Roger smiled at Molly. 'It's been a pleasure, Molly. God bless you and your little tribe.' He put on his cap, said goodbye to the children and dashed down the stairs.

'Well, isn't this wonderful,' Molly said as she joined everyone at the table. 'Here we are, all together again. We missed you two when you were in Southend.'

Evie climbed on her lap. Her blonde curls dangled over the coat that Molly had given her from Emily's suitcase. 'Gert clipped me round me ear and said a rude word.'

'That's because you cheeked her,' admonished Mark, frowning at his sister.

Molly and Cissy hid their smiles.

'We didn't have no bed,' continued Mark as Cissy straightened the collar of his dirty shirt. 'So we had to sleep on the floor.'

'Never mind,' said Molly. 'You don't look any the worse for wear.'

'Gert died,' said Evie, still eyeing Spot's empty plate. 'And we didn't have nowhere to go. Nuffink to eat either.'

'Well, now,' Molly said gently, 'this is your home and will always be for as long as you want to stay here.'

'Can we have our room back?' asked Mark.

'Course you can.'

'Can we go down to Simon and Susie's?'

'What, now, this very moment?'

Both children nodded.

'All right. But Spot's coming back with your eggs, don't forget.'

Mark grabbed his sister's hand. They ran from the kitchen and Molly smiled as she heard their footsteps on the stairs.

'It's nice to have 'em home,' Cissy said when the back door slammed. 'The poor little buggers have been through the mill again.'

'I didn't think you liked kids.'

'I don't. But these two ain't bad. Now tell me what happened to keep you away all night.'

'So you were worried, then?'

'I knew you could take care of yourself.'

Molly grinned. It was nice to be worried about, even

though Cissy wouldn't admit to it. 'By the time I reached Romford it was pouring,' she explained. 'I found Roger's cottage and Betty told me that Roger and Len had taken the children up to the pub I'd just left, where they were to get a coach bound for Yorkshire. I was just in time to run back and stop it.'

'That's what I call cutting it fine.'

'It was getting dark, so Roger said I could sleep on the sofa and in the morning he'd drive us home. Being a captain in the Sally Army, he had an allowance for petrol.'

'What's happened to Betty and Len?'

'They're evacuating to Wales tomorrow. The Army is going to help them.'

'Well, that's the good news; now you'd better prepare for the bad.'

Molly sat up in alarm. 'Did Ronnie's men show up?'

'No, but a letter from your sister did. What's the betting she won't let your dad come for Christmas?' She nodded to the mantel and the envelope stuck behind the clock.

Molly went to open it. Lyn's note, as usual, was brief and to the point. She read the few lines over once and then once more, and a third time for good measure. Folding the letter back into the envelope and replacing it behind the clock, she returned to her seat.

Cissy stared at her expectantly. 'Well? What excuse did she use this time?'

'I wish I had taken you up on that bet.' Molly kept a straight face.

Cissy's grey eyes flashed. 'Why?'

'Dad will be here on the night of the 24th. Oscar's driving him.'

Cissy screamed her surprise. 'Never! You sure you read it right?'

Molly nodded.

'How long can he stay?'

'They want him back for New Year. The church have got a special blessing for invalids.'

The two women stared at each other, then burst into laughter. Molly couldn't believe what she'd read, but it was true! Now they would have a very special family Christmas with her dad and the children and Cissy, just as she had hoped.

At last, things were beginning to go her way.

Wearing her dressing gown and slippers, Molly pulled back the curtains in the front room and looked out across the many chimneys of the Isle of Dogs. It was 25 December 1941 and just getting light. There was a bank of low cloud over the docks, bringing a fine but dirty rain that spattered lightly on the glass. Not very seasonal, but the weather didn't matter. Her dad was home and that was what counted!

She went to the kitchen and made two cups of tea, using the best china. Then she crept downstairs with the tray to the glory hole, which was now completely transformed. Red and green paper chains that Evie and Mark had made at school were pinned from wall to wall. The scrubbed floor on which the bed stood, and in which her dad lay snoring, was covered with the rugs from the front room.

All the furniture was on loan from Mr Stokes and installed by Dennis and Spot. For the next six days this was to be the heart of the household.

Molly put the cup and saucer on the small bedside cabinet and gently shook her father's shoulder.

'Wakey, wakey, Dad.'

One eye opened slowly under a bushy grey eyebrow. 'Molly!' He slowly sat up in his striped pyjamas, looking around him.

'Well, bless my soul,' he said, as if seeing the room for the first time.

Molly lit the paraffin heater she had borrowed from Jean, then drew up one of the wooden chairs from the front room. 'Happy Christmas, Dad.' She kissed his cheek and he sighed as he gazed around him.

'Happy Christmas, love. I can't believe I'm home.' He rubbed his eyes and looked around again as if he couldn't take in what he saw. 'Whoever would believe this? Where's all the stock gone?'

'Most of it we put on the new shelves Spot fitted in the shop. The remainder we've stored outside in the shed of the bicycle factory.'

'Won't it get nicked?'

'Dennis put a lock on the door.'

Bill grinned. 'You've gone to a lot of trouble. I wish your sister could see it.'

'I hope Lyn and the kids won't miss you too much.'

'Doubt it. They've got enough family and friends to keep them occupied.'

'Even so, I never thought you'd be here on Christmas Day.'

Her thoughts went to last night and Oscar's big car arriving outside the shop. He'd seemed very gloomy when they'd both helped Bill out, who was, not very effectively, trying to use a walking stick. Her brother-in-law paused only to give Molly the packages Lyn had sent, leaving swiftly with the comment that it was a great disappointment they couldn't all be together on the most important day of the year.

'Look, you've even got Mum's photo on the shelf!' exclaimed Bill.

'Yes, and Cissy's put all your personal effects over there by the commode.'

'Where did you get that from? Buckingham Palace? It looks like a bloody throne!'

Molly laughed. 'We borrowed it from Mr Stokes's supplies.'

'Does the whole neighbourhood know I'm home?'

'The customers will all be in to see you after Boxing Day.'

'Oh, Molly, life is back to normal again. Why, you've even got a whopping big table over there with your mother's chenille cloth and all them little decorations with our names on.'

'Evie and Mark insisted on doing the drawings for you.'

'They're lovely kids, Molly. Gave me a right royal welcome. And that Cissy, well, she's salt of the earth. Said she's keeping me bed warm upstairs for me, the cheeky maid.'

Molly sighed contentedly. They'd enjoyed a wonderful evening together last night before Bill had retired to bed. As

Molly had anticipated, Bill and Cissy and the children had got on like a house on fire.

'Ah, you don't know how I've longed to be back,' Bill confided as he drank his tea. 'I miss the Smoke something rotten.'

'As soon as you can get up those stairs, there won't be nothing stopping you from coming home.'

'It's me hip plays me up, now.'

'Can it be put right?'

Bill gave her a long, wistful look. 'We'll see, love.'

In the early light of the Christmas morning they sat in contentment; neither of them knew what the future held but Molly thought how special it was to enjoy this moment together.

'What do you think of the new shop window?' Molly asked eventually.

'It's better than it was before that bloody bomb dropped,' Bill said ruefully. 'But when are they going to fill in the hole in the road?'

Molly shrugged. 'There's so many repairs to be done all over the East End. I suppose they'll wait till the war's over.'

'Could be a few years yet.'

'Oh, Dad, do you think so?'

'Well, at least we've got a bit of muscle with the Yanks coming in after the Japs bombed Pearl Harbor.' He took another long and satisfying gulp of tea. 'Now tell me, have you heard from that young man of yours?'

'Dad, he's not my young man.' Molly blushed.

'Well, have it your way. Is he still on the merchant ships?'

She explained how Andy had been shipwrecked and

rescued and how he'd taken the children to Southend. Her dad listened without comment until a smile slowly parted his lips when she told him about her journey to Romford and meeting Roger.

'You're quite a girl, Molly. The spit of your mother.'

'I wish she was here, Dad.'

'So do I, love. So do I. But I tell you one thing. She'd be the first to take those kids under her wing and help you out. And there'd be no question about their future while their dad was away.'

'I'm so glad you said that,' Molly replied, feeling relieved. She had taken on a big responsibility in removing them from Len and Betty and Roger's care. She only hoped that Andy would prefer them to be with her rather than evacuated to strangers.

'Does Andy know his kids are safe?' her father asked.

'I've written and told him. Though when he'll get the letter I don't know.'

Bill nodded thoughtfully. 'Level with me, girl, this lad means a deal to you, don't he?'

Molly couldn't lie or even pretend. Her dad would see through her straight away. 'I'm trying to work it out in my head, Dad,' she told him quietly. 'I loved Ted dearly, but in a different way. I can't explain this attachment I have to Andy and his family, even to meself. I don't know if he'll survive the war. What will I do then? Lyn says the children need to be found homes – proper homes – by the authorities. But as evacuees they'll be just two names, sent to people who don't know them and who might not really care.'

'When this gammy leg of mine is back to normal and I can get up those bleedin' stairs, I'll be home like a shot to help you.'

'Can't wait for the day,' Molly said, wondering if that day would ever come.

Christmas was exactly how Molly had imagined it would be. The one exception was that Andy was absent – not that she had held out any hope he would be home for Christmas. But with Evie and Mark there wasn't a dull moment. Though they didn't have a tree, as they were so scarce and very expensive, their presents were placed on the table, ready to be opened after Bill was presentable.

The morning was filled with laughter and excitement, especially when Spot arrived with the chicken, stuffed and ready to be cooked in the oven.

'I suppose it stuffed itself before popping its clogs?' was Cissy's wry comment as they all inspected the plump white bird.

'It's from me cousin's cousin who's in the trade,' replied Spot, tapping the side of his nose.

Molly thought how smart he looked without his cap for once. His wiry dark hair was newly trimmed and neatly combed, showing his widow's peak to its best advantage. Wearing a white shirt and trousers, complete with a striped waistcoat, he'd even tucked a red handkerchief in his top pocket. He'd brought bottles of ale too, once again provided by the cousin's cousin, and enjoyed them with Bill while the women and children went upstairs to cook dinner.

'Can we open our presents now?' asked Mark as they watched Molly peel the potatoes and scrape the carrots.

'Not till the bird's in the oven.'

'Where's its head gorn?' said Evie, kneeling on the chair and poking her finger into the parson's nose.

'Watch it don't bite,' laughed Cissy as Molly opened a bottle of cheap sherry and poured two glasses full to the brim.

'Happy Christmas, Cissy,' said Molly, 'and it is a very happy one for me.'

'I'll second that. Chin, chin.'

While the meal was cooking, everyone sat with Bill in the glory hole, with continual refilling of the glasses, and the air became thick from the smoke of Woodbines and the familiar smell of her father's Three Nuns tobacco.

'Where did you pinch this lot?' asked Cissy, admiring the presents Spot had brought for them: nylons for her, a powder compact for Molly, a tin of Empire Shag for Bill and a game of snap for Mark and Evie.

'I traded with the GIs,' Spot shrugged innocently. 'They had a bit of trouble with vermin at their base, so me and Nibbles solved their problem.'

Molly had heard her customers' tales of trade between the British and the American GIs at the base just outside the city. It appeared to be true.

'Can we open these?' asked Mark, gazing at the brown paper parcel on the table with his name written on the top.

Molly nodded. 'There's a surprise for you too, Evie.'

She watched with pleasure as Mark unwrapped a small red metal fire engine. The paint was a little faded but it had only cost twopence at the market. She knew Mark loved his little car, which he had kept safe all the time he'd been away. Evie, as usual, brought a smile to everyone's lips, as she shared her chocolate toffee with Nibbles.

When the Turners arrived, the children went upstairs to play and the serious business of making merry got under way.

It was while Spot was singing 'Danny Boy' that someone knocked on the back door. Thinking it might be Mr Stokes or Liz, Molly was very surprised to find the policeman standing there.

'A merry Christmas,' Detective Constable Longman said. He looked quite different in a smart dark-blue suit and cheerful tie. 'The constabulary are distributing these this year to help relations with the community.' He handed her a white envelope.

Inside Molly found a cartoon of a snowy policeman, reminding the public that their safety was a matter of the utmost importance, even during the Christmas holidays. 'Thank you,' she said politely, 'but the law don't need to worry about my safety. As you can hear, I've people staying with me and we're having a family party.'

He looked over her shoulder curiously.

'Is there anything else you want?' Molly kept the door closed behind her.

'Yes, as a matter of fact there is.'

I knew it! thought Molly, immediately on the defensive. He was after something and had expected to catch her off guard on Christmas Day.

'I thought perhaps you would like to know,' he said in a

smooth tone, 'that we have apprehended a number of criminals during a West End burglary. One of them is Ronnie Hook, a man we believe was connected to the attack on you and Miss Brown.'

Molly stared at him. 'Why should you think that? I've no idea who this man is.'

'One of his gang said that Ronnie Hook knew Miss Brown and was after her, and forced him to rough her up.'

Molly managed to look surprised. But inside she felt like jelly. What did this mean for Cissy?

'Hook and his men have been arrested and charged,' the detective continued, 'for running illicit gaming houses and a string of brothels.'

Molly met the policeman's stare. Was he trying to trap her? 'So why should either Cissy or I be interested in this?'

'I just thought you should know.'

'Well, I'm glad to see that justice has been done,' Molly said, trying to keep her voice steady. 'And if this Hook is put away, he's one less criminal for you to have to catch.'

'That's one way of looking at it, I suppose.'

She stepped back and opened the door a little. The noise of laughter echoed out. 'I must go now as I'm about to dish up dinner.'

'Is your seafaring friend celebrating with you?'

'Why should you want to know?'

'Just asking, that's all.'

Molly stepped back inside. 'Goodbye,' she said, without wishing him a happy Christmas. He was still in the yard, snooping around, when Molly closed the door.

'Who was that?' Cissy asked when Molly walked back in.

'Come upstairs and I'll tell you.'

In the kitchen, Molly showed Cissy the card. 'I forgot to show you this. The copper left it in the shop.'

'That bluebottle? The slimy bugger!'

'Yes, but listen to this. He told me Ronnie's been arrested for running a string of brothels and bookies.'

'What!' Cissy's grey eyes flashed in alarm.

'One of Ronnie's men confessed to attacking us at the cinema.'

'So I'm rumbled, am I?' Cissy could only splutter.

Molly shook her head. 'Quite the opposite. Think about it carefully, Cissy. They've got a loose connection to Cissy Brown, not you – Lena Cole. Ronnie didn't spill the beans. He couldn't, unless he wanted to incriminate himself.'

'But Cissy was a pro too.'

'But can the copper prove it? Not on the word of a thug. He'd have arrested you without delay if that was so.'

'Oh, Gawd, so Ronnie's going down?'

'Yes, we have nothing more to worry about, Cissy. We're in the clear.'

Cissy's eyes filled with tears. She mumbled something then fell into Molly's arms. Together they jumped up and down until the children heard them and came in to see what the noise was.

'What you two doin'?' demanded Evie, her mouth covered in chocolate.

Molly stopped, breathless, and swept her up into her arms.

'We're celebrating, that's what we're doing!' she exclaimed. And together with Cissy, Mark, Simon and Susie, they all began to sing 'We Wish You a Merry Christmas', as they danced round the kitchen in hokey-cokey style.

Molly was so very happy. She knew she would never forget Christmas Day 1941.

BOOK TWO

Chapter Twenty

Eight months later, August 1942

It was a hot August day late in the month and the warning siren had just sounded. All Molly's customers had scuttled from the shop, cursing the Luftwaffe for its untimely appearance once again. The Baedeker raids in the spring, so called because the enemy had vowed to bomb every historic building in Britain marked with three stars in the Baedeker travel guide, were still fresh in everyone's mind.

Molly turned the sign to CLOSED and hurriedly locked the doors. She and Cissy chose to remain at home now, rather than go to Jean's Anderson. Mr Stokes had installed a Morrison shelter upstairs in the front room. Not that they'd used it much. Neither of them liked being squashed flat in the long, narrow wire-mesh cage with the reinforced steel top.

'Hurry up,' called Cissy as Molly bolted the back door. 'I've made us a cuppa. Let's drink it before those swines fly over.'

Molly hurried up the stairs. Infrequent daylight raids had

disrupted life again and the wireless reports were still frightening to listen to: repeated warnings that there could be more intensified attacks on the East End.

'Can't hear any planes yet,' Cissy said as Molly entered the kitchen. 'Should we go down and fetch the kids from Jean's?'

'No. They'll all be in the Anderson. Safer there than here.'

'Let's drink our tea, then. I've got something to tell you.'

Molly sat at the kitchen table. On it were two mugs, filled with steaming brew, and in the middle of the table was a pre-war shoebox in which all the letters were kept. Two were from Andy and very short. He wrote that he was safe but didn't hold out much hope of having any shore leave as he was so far away. He'd received Molly's letters and said how relieved he was the children were in her care. That was all, so Molly assumed that some of his letters had been censored. Another letter was from the Denhams giving an address in Cardiff. Several more were from Bill and Lyn.

As the post was so infrequent, Molly kept them all in the shoebox just to remind them how lucky they were that there was still a postal service, however irregular.

'So, what is it?' Molly said as she sat anxiously listening for the ominous drone in the sky. She didn't like being separated from the kids when the sirens went. In term time, the school took them into the underground shelter, but hopefully this was a false alarm, when the bombers flew in another direction.

'Have you noticed anything lately?' Cissy said, with a faint blush on her cheeks.

'Like what?' Molly asked.

'I dunno. Just anything.' Cissy wore an impatient expression.

'Well . . .' Molly hesitated, her thoughts still on the children. 'Mark is growing so fast, he'll be up to my shoulder soon. Simon's cast-offs don't fit him any more. I really should get him new clothes for school next week. I thought about going to the market—'

'It's not about Mark,' Cissy interrupted sharply.

'Well, Evie is still tiny—'

'It's not about Evie, either.'

Molly frowned. 'What is it, then?'

'I'll give you a clue. You're looking right at it.'

Just then, the noise everyone dreaded, of approaching aircraft, sounded in the distance: a faint rumble turning very quickly into thunder. Both women glanced up and, abandoning their tea, made a dash to the front room.

Sweeping the green chenille tablecloth from the solid steel top of the Morrison shelter, Molly and Cissy climbed inside. They lay next to each other, listening to the roar of the Luftwaffe's engines and the fire of the British guns beneath. There were distant explosions, all vibrating through the wire mesh of the cage.

Molly thought about the children in the Anderson and wished she had run down to Jean's to be with them. It seemed their lives were constantly ruled by the warning siren and the threat of bombardment.

As the fleet of planes passed over they lay as still as possible, every nerve tensed as the ground trembled and shook. Cissy let out a stifled groan.

'What's up?' Molly asked in concern.

'Dunno.' Cissy squirmed and wriggled and eventually snatched at the wire mesh, trying to get out of the shelter.

Molly called after the disappearing rear end. But all she saw was a pair of flat lace-ups running towards the door. She knew her friend hated the Morrison, but to deliberately leave it during a raid was reckless.

Scrambling out of the cage, Molly hurried along the passage to Cissy's bedroom. Her friend was on her knees hanging her head over a pail. She retched and heaved, then looked up at Molly.

'Pass me that towel, will you?'

'Are you ill?' Molly was bewildered.

Cissy rolled her watery eyes. 'Here's another clue, I'm busting out of all me clothes.'

Molly's eyes dropped to where Cissy's overall was straining across her stomach. It was true, she had put on weight recently.

Cissy wiped her mouth with the towel and raised her heavy dark eyebrows questioningly. 'Well, it must have sunk in by now.'

Molly swallowed. 'You're not—'

'I am.'

'Oh, Cissy!'

'You know who the culprit is, of course.'

Molly nodded slowly. 'Spot.'

'The bastard.'

'Why? Doesn't he want the baby?'

Cissy leaned over the pail again. It was some while before

she was able to turn her attention back to Molly. 'He wants it, too bloody true he does.'

'Then what's the problem?'

'He took me unawares.'

Molly began to laugh. Very soon Cissy was laughing too. And despite the roar of low-flying aircraft and the shuddering of the whole building, they both had tears of joy in their eyes.

'I ain't living over no pukka-poo den,' Cissy declared as she burst in through the shop door a fortnight later.

Molly was serving Liz and they both turned to look at Cissy and Spot.

'There's no gambling at Narrow Street, love. The Chinese are very hard-working.'

'Limehouse don't get its reputation for nothing.'

'Everywhere's got good and bad,' Spot protested. 'Just come and have a look.'

Liz heaved her shopping bag onto the counter. 'Hello, Cissy, gel. Spot. What's all the fuss?'

There was a look of desperation on Spot's face as Cissy folded her arms over her full chest. Molly noticed that at six months, having added a good few pounds, her bump was showing noticeably under her coat.

'Hello, love,' Spot said politely, and glancing at Molly he raised his eyebrows. 'I was telling Cissy about me rooms in Narrow Street. I lived there as a kid and me mum and dad never had a moment's bother. They used to take in seafarers, made a nice living an' all. There's five big rooms, a kitchen and—'

'A dosshouse on the other two floors,' Cissy interrupted with a frown.

'Cissy,' returned Spot patiently, 'it's a boarding house. People rent the rooms, decent folk with families and so forth.'

'Does this mean you're tying the knot?' Liz asked, interrupting their quarrel.

Spot nodded. 'That we are, ducks.'

'When's the big day?'

'Tuesday, 10 November. It was the quickest we could be fitted in.'

'What about the new arrival?' Liz looked at Cissy's stomach.

'What about it?' Cissy demanded offendedly.

'Just wondered, that's all.' Liz looked uncomfortable. 'Well, congratulations to you both. And the little'n. Have you got a ring yet, gel?'

Spot nodded, nudging Cissy's arm. 'Go on, Cissy, give her a butcher's,' he urged.

Molly had seen the engagement ring already. It was lovely: a tasteful diamond set in a cluster of coloured stones.

Reluctantly Cissy stretched out her hand. The ring glimmered on her finger and Liz gasped.

'Oh, bless you, it's a beauty.' She leaned forward and hugged Cissy, then Spot. 'And now you've got your first tiff over, you can enjoy the making up.'

'Humph,' muttered Cissy, snatching back her hand.

'Ain't she lovely?' Spot chuckled, sliding a hand around his fiancée's thick waist. 'I'm a very lucky man.'

With that, Cissy stalked off upstairs, leaving Spot looking dejected.

'Never you mind,' Liz said to Spot as he held the door open for her to go out. 'Remember what they say: the course of true love never runs smooth.'

When they were alone, Spot said in a quiet voice to Molly, 'Could you have a word with me girl? She takes notice of you. Sort of speak on my behalf?'

Molly agreed, but it wasn't until after the shop was closed that night and the children were in bed that she had the chance to sit down beside Cissy in the front room and ask why she was so upset.

'I don't want to live anywhere iffy,' Cissy explained as her fingers played nervously in her lap. 'I've kipped in slums and dives all me life. I want better for my kid.'

'What's wrong with Narrow Street?' Molly said in surprise. 'Spot says there's never been any trouble there. And it's a nice large flat.'

'Yeah, but they all speak double Dutch in Limehouse.'

'Don't you mean Chinese?' Molly giggled.

This brought a reluctant smile to Cissy's face. 'What am I gonna do if I don't understand their lingo?'

'You understand Spot and he says he grew up there.'

'Yeah, but is he spinning a yarn?'

'What would he do that for?'

'I dunno.'

'Cissy, it's not as if he's dragging you off to the other side of the world.'

'Wouldn't mind Australia. They speak the King's English.'

'Well, you've got Limehouse instead. And it's not so far from here. I'll easily be able to come and visit you.'

Cissy looked under her long eyelashes. 'Would you?'

'Course I will! Me and the kids will be over on the bus the day you move in.'

Cissy nodded sadly and looked around the room. 'The thing is, I like being with you all, as though I was one of the family.'

'Oh, Cissy, you are.'

'I know I can't stay here forever.'

'I've told you a hundred times, this is your home for as long as you want it. You'll always have a roof over your head.'

Cissy's eyes grew misty. 'I'm scared, Molly. What if it don't work out with me and him? And I've got another bun in the oven?'

'Do you really love Spot, Cissy?'

'I – well, I ain't sure what love is.'

'It's what Spot feels for you.'

Cissy quickly wiped away a tear. 'Would you come with us and see his gaff on Sunday?'

'Yes, course.'

'I'll ask Spot to bring the ratter's cart, then the kids can come too.'

'I didn't know Spot had a cart.'

'It's the council's. They use it when they ditch the dead rats. But don't worry, he cleans it out regular.'

Molly smiled. As usual, Cissy's down-to-earth attitude was very endearing.

And when Sunday arrived, Cissy and Molly took their place on the top of the ratter's cart pulled by an elderly black horse. Mark and Evie, dressed in their best clothes, sat in the rear of the cart with their boots dangling over the tailboard.

As it was a warm September's day Molly wore a light jacket with a black velvet collar and scooped her long chestnut waves into a plait at the back of her head. Cissy had put on a well-ironed blouse and full skirt to camouflage the baby and added a straw hat to her newly washed hair. Though she showed little enthusiasm to Spot, Molly could see the excitement brewing in her eyes.

When Spot pulled the cart into Narrow Street, groups of people came out of their front doors and surrounded them. Spot jumped down and shook their hands. Some men, with moustaches and pigtails, even made a bow. Others, who came with their wives and families, apart from their oriental looks were dressed like any other East Enders.

'I told you so,' whispered Cissy. 'There ain't no English in sight.'

'As good as,' corrected Spot, overhearing her as he returned to help them down. 'These people have lived here most of their lives. And many were born in these streets, just like I was.'

'Christ, you never told me you was Chinese,' spluttered Cissy.

'I ain't,' admitted Spot with a grin. 'But me gran was. Half, anyway.'

Cissy gawped. 'Was this your gran's place, then?'

'Yes, handed down to Mum and Dad. But when they popped their clogs, I moved to the island. Wasn't the same without them. I let the place idle, I'm afraid. But it could easy be done up.'

Molly smiled at all the nodding heads. The men, women and children followed them to a door next to a small restaurant with little golden lanterns hanging in the dark window.

'Follow me,' said Spot, turning the key in the door.

Molly half expected the curious crowd to accompany them, but by the time they had climbed two flights of stairs they were on their own and Cissy was puffing.

Spot unlocked another door. Nibbles ran out, barking loudly around their feet. 'Come here,' Spot said to Cissy and lifted her into his arms. 'I'm carrying you and me heir over the threshold a bit early, but it don't matter.'

Molly laughed at Cissy's embarrassed expression.

When they were inside Molly and Cissy inspected the dirty but extremely spacious rooms. They all had a faint smell of cooking from the restaurant below. The ceilings were hung with cobwebs and the bare boards needed mending. Evie and Mark raced ahead of them with Nibbles, inquisitive to know what came next as they tested the old chairs and searched the cupboards. Spot took them all to a large window on a landing overlooking the back yards.

'You can just see the water,' he said proudly. 'Imagine looking out on the river every morning. The gateway to London in all its glory, and the tugs and little ships. You'd be hard pressed to find a better view than this.'

Molly cast her eyes back to the room they were standing in: dusty, dark, but extremely large and accommodating. She could see Cissy and her child here, and when she looked at her friend, whose gaze was centred on the gleam of dazzling water reflected off the docks, she knew Cissy could see the same vision too.

'Well, it ain't bad, I suppose,' Cissy agreed. 'But I'll have to think about it.'

'You do that,' said Spot, plonking a kiss on her cheek. 'You're my lovely thinker.'

Just then, Mark and Evie ran in. 'Can we go down and play with them kids in the street?' asked Mark.

'No, cos you won't understand 'em,' retorted Cissy.

'I fink I will,' said Evie. 'Cos I can pull me eyes back same as them.' She pushed up the corners of her eyes with her grubby fingers.

Everyone laughed so much that Molly made no objection when, together with the dog, they bolted off down the stairs to a babble of welcoming voices beneath.

The days leading up to the wedding were filled with excitement. Molly, the children and the Turners were invited. All were to have new outfits.

As Cissy was getting rather large and her back ached continually, she couldn't stand for very long, so Liz came into the shop and helped out.

It was the first Monday in November when the arrangement took effect. After leaving the children at Jean's, Molly and Cissy caught the bus to Cox Street market.

Cissy purchased a second-hand coat in dark-blue wool and a matching blue hat. The parcels were left with the stallholder for Spot to collect. The coat was as large as a tent, but disguised Cissy's bump. She also bought a pair of patent shoes, low courts in size seven that hadn't been worn down to the heel.

'You know what,' Cissy said, as they walked arm in arm through the crowds, 'I wish Andy was home. If he was, I'd ask him to give me away.'

'That's a very nice thought,' Molly said, wishing Andy was home too. Their shared kiss seemed so distant that sometimes she wondered if it had happened. Had their kiss meant anything to him? Or was it all just in her imagination? His letters had been grateful that she was looking after the children, but other than that, she couldn't read anything intimate into his words.

Yet her thoughts were often with him. A day didn't go by without the children talking about their dad. They believed so confidently that he would return safely – even Mark, who was once plagued by doubts about his father's welfare – that it kept them all going. And Cissy saying that she would like Andy to give her away made him feel closer, even though he was hundreds, perhaps thousands, of miles distant.

'This bloody war puts the mockers on everything,' Cissy continued as they paused by the bric-a-brac stall.

Molly agreed. 'It's certainly changed the course of our lives. I once thought Ted and me would grow old together. And look what happened.'

'But now you've got a new life,' Cissy said as she picked up a little half-moon brooch attached to a blue ribbon. 'All I hope is Andy don't get torpedoed again.'

Molly's heart dropped. Cissy's bluntness was always disarming. She quickly changed the subject. 'I'll buy that for your wedding present.' She took the brooch from Cissy's grasp. 'You've got to have something borrowed and something blue on your wedding day, to bring you luck.' Molly paid the sixpence and then pinned the little half-moon and its ribbon on Cissy's collar. 'Now we can buy a few bits and pieces here for your bottom drawer. P'raps a sheet and a pillowcase over on the bedding stall, and then—'

'Molly, I'll have to sit down.'

'Is it your back?'

'No, me stomach.'

Molly froze as Cissy bent over, wincing. She put her arm around her and guided her to the benches outside the stall selling hot drinks.

They sat down and she felt a dart of fear. Cissy was looking grey. Molly glanced anxiously around. Cissy had insisted on catching the bus here, but it was out of the question when it came to the return journey.

'What's the matter, love?' yelled the man wearing a peaked cap and white apron, serving teas.

Molly left Cissy and hurried up to the counter. 'My friend's expecting and she's not feeling very well.'

'When's it due?'

'January.'

'I'll see what I can do.' He came down the steps. 'Leave it to me.'

Half an hour later a large saloon car pulled up, with its rear end cut out and a big red cross painted on the back. A young woman driver climbed out wearing blue overalls and, with the aid of several traders, Cissy was hoisted into the back.

Molly squeezed in and the woman rolled down the canvas flap.

'My name's Mary,' she said, bending over Cissy. 'I'm just the driver but I work with the ARP ambulance service. I'm afraid we're short of volunteers at the moment, as after the blitz many drivers and first-aiders were called back to their trades.'

'I'm Molly and this is Cissy,' Molly hurriedly explained, as Cissy writhed on the mattress covered by a ground sheet. 'My friend's due in the new year, but she started having pains as we walked round the market.'

'Have your waters broken?' asked Mary, pulling up Cissy's coat and skirt and feeling round her stomach.

'No, course they bleeding haven't,' Cissy shouted as Molly held her hand.

'Well, unless you sat in a puddle, I think you're well on your way.'

'It can't come,' protested Cissy. 'I ain't married yet.'

'Are you sure of your dates?'

Cissy squealed and pulled up her knees.

'I'm no expert but this baby feels very low, as if the head was engaged. When did you last see the doctor?'

'A couple of months back,' Cissy lied. 'He ain't no bloody good anyway. The last time I went he said I'd got me dates wrong.'

'Well, he may have been right.'

'Oh, my Gawd!' screamed Cissy. 'I don't want to drop it here!'

'The new East End Maternity Hospital's not far away. I'll drive as quickly as I can.'

Once more Cissy let out a howl and Molly tried to take a deep breath, but she could barely think straight. Could Cissy be wrong on her dates? Even so, if it arrived now, the baby would be very early.

Cissy opened her eyes and looked around. She'd been fast asleep, exhausted from the events of the last twenty-four hours. She couldn't see much, as the nurses had pulled the screens around her. But she could hear voices. Then she remembered yesterday, the trip to the market and the acute labour pains that had come on without warning. Mary, the ambulance driver, had been right. Her waters had broken and the baby was struggling to come. Cissy sniffed at the thought. The pain that had gripped her as she swung in and out of consciousness had been agonizing. But just in time, the doctors had saved her child's life.

The thrill of holding this tiny mite against her had been worth all the pain.

She closed her eyes, wanting to feed him again and feel him close. He had weighed just over five pounds. He was so small that she had doubted he was even breathing. And yet, please God, they said he was perfectly formed.

She was jarred from her thoughts by the sound of a familiar voice. She tried to sit up, but she was still very sore. Tears were on her lashes as the screen moved and Spot appeared.

In seconds he was comforting her, and choking back his own tears. She felt his deep emotion and for a moment ran her fingers through his thick, wiry hair.

'That's enough now,' she croaked, pushing him away. 'Or you'll get me going as well.'

'Cissy, gel, I've missed you.'

'I ain't been gone long.'

'Are you all right?'

'Yeah, the poor little bugger had a rough passage. But they tell me he's going to be all right.'

'Thank Gawd for that.' He nodded over his shoulder. 'Molly's outside.'

'Why ain't she come in?'

'They won't let her, cos of the germs.'

'Tell them Cissy will kick up a stink if the poor cow ain't allowed in.'

Spot chuckled and went out. Cissy quickly wiped away her tears, and by the time Spot reappeared with Molly, she had composed herself.

'Oh, Cissy!' was all Molly kept saying as she bent to embrace her. 'Oh, Cissy!'

'Give over,' she mumbled eventually. 'I've only had a baby, not died. Sit down, both of you.'

She smiled as they meekly sat on the chairs provided, one either side of the bed.

'Well, what's our son like?' Spot asked after a while, leaning forward to take her hand.

'A cracker, though I say it myself.'

'The nurse said he's small,' said Molly, her brown eyes wide in concern. 'Did you get your dates wrong?'

'Must have,' Cissy said, grinning at Spot. 'Trust the little bugger to come when I was out enjoying myself. I thought that driver, Mary, was off her rocker when she asked me if my waters had broke. Then I realized me knickers was drenched!'

'I've brought a change with me and your nightdress too,' said Molly. 'The nurse took them.'

'Thanks.'

'What about you? I hated leaving but they wouldn't let me stay. Spot and me have been up all night pacing the floor.'

Cissy giggled. 'I must have screamed blue murder. The doctor said the the baby was in distress. Had I known that, I'd have screamed even louder. But when they finally got him out and cleared off the mess, he didn't half yell too. All I saw was these big blue-grey eyes under all the wrinkled red skin. And you should see his hair. It ain't really hair, just bumfluff.'

'Like his dad's,' said Spot with a smirk as he drew his hand over his thick head of hair.

'Have you fed him?' Molly enquired.

'Once the nurse gets him on, he don't have no trouble in sucking. And there's plenty of milk there. I'm as bloated as a pregnant sow,' complained Cissy, looking down at her swollen breasts.

'What we gonna call him?' asked Spot. 'As long as it ain't Horace, I ain't fussy.'

'Who's Horace?' said Molly in surprise.

'Horace Fryer, to give me full moniker,' said Spot, looking embarrassed.

Molly grinned. 'I didn't know that.'

'Well, you wouldn't boast of a name like Horace, would you?'

Cissy quite liked Horace. It could be shortened to Harry.

Just think. She wouldn't be Cissy Brown or Lena Cole, but Mrs Fryer. 'Christ, Spot, we're meant to be getting married in a week.'

'We'll still manage it.'

'How? I've got to stay in here for ten days at least cos of the baby.'

'They'll let you out for an hour, won't they?' Spot squeezed her hand encouragingly. 'I'll hire a cab. You won't have to walk far, just up the steps to the registry office. I'll get the Registrar to make it quick while the cab waits.'

'Blimey, and here was I thinking, this man is going to marry me in style.'

'And style it will be,' Spot assured her. 'But that particular knees-up will have to come later.'

'I'll bring your new coat and shoes in to the hospital,' said Molly. 'And I'll help you wash your hair at visiting time the day before.'

Cissy felt the long-held sobs erupt from her chest. She didn't know why she was so emotional and could do nothing to stop the big, salty tears from cascading down her cheeks. 'I dunno why I'm being so daft,' she spluttered. 'I can't seem to help meself.'

'I was tearful too after Emily,' Molly said, sitting back on the chair. 'I just couldn't take it all in.'

Cissy felt ashamed of herself. Here she was shedding tears, when Molly didn't have Emily to go home to. And never would have.

'How are the kids?' she asked instead.

'Wanting to see the baby you've bought.'

'Bought?' Cissy laughed. 'Is that what they think?'

'I promised we'd buy a lively one,' said Spot. 'Give him a few days and he'll be out in the street playing with 'em.'

Just then, in walked the nurse. She held a tiny package in her arms, wrapped in a hospital shawl.

'Meet your son, Mr Fryer. But only for a few minutes.' She slowly lowered him into Spot's arms. Cissy felt a kind of breeze flow over her body, sweeping up the hairs on her head and whirling into the pit of her stomach. This was her very own child and this was her husband-to-be. She had a family of her own. Once she'd had nothing. Not even a proper name to call herself by.

'He's beautiful,' Molly said, echoing Cissy's thoughts.

Spot nodded. 'He's got Cissy's good looks and my brains. Well, coming from a long line of Fryers he might even be a genius. Here you are, love, have a cuddle.'

Cissy took her little boy and marvelled at the human being in miniature: his wrinkled forehead and tiny closed lids, the sucking red lips squashed above a dimpled chin, and two tiny fists barely the size of a sixpence.

'Time's up, I'm afraid,' the nurse told them and wafted the baby away.

'Better go,' said Spot, bending to kiss her cheek. 'Keep yer pecker up, gorgeous.'

'Bye, Cissy. Get your rest, now.' Molly waved.

Cissy swallowed on the hard lump in her throat. She gazed at the people whom she loved and who loved her. She would never have thought when she was on the run from Ronnie that she would end up like this. Her life had been turned round. Gone was fear and bitter loneliness, to be replaced by peace and motherhood.

If it hadn't been for Molly and her kindness where would she be today? Not on this earth, came the answer. For after Ethel had died, the only living soul who'd cared about her, she had intended to end it all. As she'd never swum a stroke in her life, it would not have taken much effort to throw herself from the nearest wharf and slip below the murky waters of the Thames.

No one would have missed her. Except Ronnie, perhaps. But for all the wrong reasons.

29 December 1940 was the day her life should have ended. Two years later and at the age of thirty-four, she had just produced the miracle of her lifetime.

In eight days, if Spot was to be believed, she would become Mrs Cissy Fryer, wife to Horace and mother of Harry Junior, of Narrow Street, Limehouse.

Chapter Twenty-One

It was a grey and sunless November morning when the day came for Spot and Cissy to be married. Molly had arranged to meet the happy couple at the Mile End registry office, since Spot had given their address as Narrow Street even though they were planning to stay at Molly's until the decorating had been carried out.

Everyone was very nervous as they gathered at the shop, where parked out in the yard was an old Morris that Dennis had managed to borrow for the morning. Petrol coupons had been pooled, and all the guests were dressed to the nines, the women smelling of Phul-Nana face powder and scent, and wearing brand-new nylons, all provided by one of the customers whose daughter was walking out with a GI.

Molly wore a cream coat and a tiny white veiled cap that closed around her auburn hair pinned up behind her head. Jean had chosen a market bargain, a brown striped two-piece with a muffler. The four children, Simon, Susie, Evie and

Mark, were all wearing coats from the school's swap shop. They also had new socks and brown lace-up shoes polished until they shone. All six passengers squeezed in the car, driven by Dennis, who for the first time since the onset of war was dressed in a pinstriped suit and waistcoat. Molly had asked Liz to open the shop at nine and had given her a key.

So by the time the Morris pulled in to the kerb outside the Mile End council building, Molly's expectations that the event would go off as planned were high.

But as soon as a cab pulled up and Spot jumped out, she knew something was amiss. His face was drawn and tense and as he hurried round to open the other door for Cissy, he barely acknowledged them.

'Christ, what's happened now?' Jean whispered to Molly as they stood waiting on the pavement.

'I visited Cissy the day before yesterday and helped her wash her hair. She was a bit quiet, I'll admit. But I put that down to pre-wedding nerves.'

'Perhaps she don't like leaving the baby.'

'Yes, perhaps.'

They all gathered at the entrance as Spot took Cissy's arm and led her inside. Cissy smiled weakly, and although she looked very smart in the coat she had bought at the market, she leaned against Spot as they all filed into a small annexe.

The registrar nodded and when they were seated gave a short address. The children sat quietly and attentively, Molly was relieved to see, even Evie whose tiny feet in her polished shoes dangled inches above the floor as she sat on the chair beside Susie.

Within a few minutes Spot and Cissy had exchanged vows. Molly expected the service to be short and sweet under the circumstances, and when Spot drew Cissy towards him and kissed her, everyone cheered.

Molly got out of her seat and went up to Cissy, who was still being assisted by Spot.

'Congratulations, Mr and Mrs Fryer,' she said excitedly, but Cissy's face was tense.

'Thanks. But we can't stop.'

'Are you all right?'

Cissy nodded, her eyes dark-rimmed and tired under her heavy eyebrows. 'Can you do me a favour and fill in the papers, Molly?' she asked. 'The baby's not feeding. I tried all night and he flatly refused. He's lost four ounces in weight in just a few days.'

'He'll put them back on, love,' consoled Spot who looked very anxious too, despite his smart dark suit and checked tie.

'Take me back,' Cissy insisted. 'I've got to see me baby.'

'Course, off you go.' Molly knew Cissy was very upset.

Leaning on Spot's arm, she shuffled slowly out of the room, leaving everyone staring after them. The four children gathered round.

'Ain't she stopping to talk to us?' asked Mark.

'No, she has to feed the baby.'

'When can we play with it?' said Evie, tossing back her golden curls.

'As soon as Cissy brings him home.'

Simon and Susie were silent and Jean took them to one side as Molly went to speak with the registrar.

For a day that had been planned to be Cissy's happiest, it was all a bit of a disappointment.

After the ceremony, they went back to Jean's. Molly thanked Dennis again for the loan of the car and stayed a short while to chat to Jean. But they were both preoccupied, thinking about Cissy and little Harry. Was Cissy overreacting, Molly wondered – yet if Emily, as a baby, had stopped feeding, she would have felt just as troubled.

Late that night, Spot called round with more disturbing news.

'They don't know what's wrong with Harry,' he told her as he sat at the kitchen table. 'She's frantic.'

'Perhaps he doesn't know how to feed just yet,' Molly suggested. 'After all, he was early and very small.'

'He's smaller still now.'

'What are they going to do?'

Spot shrugged. 'Dunno. I'm going back there now.'

'Have you eaten?'

'Don't fancy any grub just yet.'

'Where's Nibbles?'

'A mate's looking after him. Reckon I'll be at the hospital a fair bit.' He stood up, and to Molly looked quite unlike the robust little man she knew, with his tie undone and a worried expression. She felt very sorry for this usually happy-go-lucky character.

'Is there anything I can do?' Molly asked as she followed him down the stairs to the door.

'I'll let you know. They ain't letting visitors in at the moment.'

'That's understandable.'

'Don't seem like we got married today.' Spot turned and sighed. 'Say one for the baby, won't you?'

Molly nodded. She watched him walk off into the dark night. As she locked the door she recalled how Spot had loyally kept watch over the shop with Nibbles at his feet. She wished that now she could do something for Spot in return. She knew the suffering Cissy must be going through, as she had travelled that very same path herself when Emily was taken ill.

Molly couldn't sleep that night, and eventually the dawn broke. A pale November sun glowed through between the white clouds.

She stood at Cissy's bedroom door where the wooden crib rested beside the big bed which was to have been occupied by Cissy and Spot until Narrow Street was put in order.

Quickly she walked to the kitchen and, as usual, made her first cup of tea, the answer to all life's many problems.

'You heard any news yet?' Jean asked Molly at the weekend. It was a busy Saturday, and in between customers they had time to discuss the only topic that really concerned them.

Molly shook her head. 'Spot's not been by.'

'That's unusual.'

'I thought about going up to the hospital.'

'Will they let you in to see her?'

'I suppose not.'

'If you ain't heard anything by tonight, shall we go

tomorrow? Being Sunday, Dennis will keep an eye on the kids. What harm can it do? The nurses can only turn us away.'

Molly had a deep sense of unease. So to keep herself from worrying she went about the day's business of serving in the shop, ordering from the wholesalers and looking after Mark and Evie.

On Sunday, Molly took Mark and Evie down to Jean's. The children all went out to play in the street while Dennis worked in his shed.

Molly suggested that she and Jean take the bus and, even though it wasn't quite visiting time, they went to the maternity ward and waited at the doors until a nurse arrived.

'We're friends of Mr and Mrs Fryer,' Molly said. 'Is there any news of the baby?'

The nurse looked at them. 'Are you family?'

'Not exactly,' said Molly. 'Just good friends.'

'In that case, I'm afraid I can't give you any information,' the nurse replied, and with that she went through the door to the ward.

As they were staring after her, a shout came from the corridor.

Molly was shocked at Spot's appearance. He was wearing his old coat and trousers and his black hair stuck up in untidy tufts as though he hadn't run a comb through it in days. The growth on his chin was dark and bristly, and there were hollowed shadows beneath his crossed eyes.

'Blimey,' said Jean as he neared, 'he looks a bit rough.'

'Spot? What's happened?' Molly asked as he came breathlessly to a full stop.

'Dunno,' he said, blinking at them tiredly. 'I'm on me way in to see Cissy.'

'How is she?' Molly and Jean asked together.

'It's been touch and go with the baby.' He stood agitatedly, glancing over their shoulders. 'He's been very sick.'

'Oh, Gawd.' Jean put a hand to her mouth.

'He's got what they said is a complication of the blood. Cissy's been trying to feed him every couple of hours. She ain't slept and don't want no grub, but forces it down, as they tell her she's got to eat for the baby's sake.'

'She must be exhausted.'

'I have to wear this cap and gown and look through a glass window at them. The nurses tried to keep me away but Cissy created a stink. I'm afraid to leave in case something happens. So I kip out here, anywhere I can find a chair.'

'How awful for you both.' Molly touched his shoulder.

'She's bloody brave,' Spot told them, his haggard face showing the distress he was in. 'Never shed a tear since we found out he's got something wrong. But I don't like the look of her. She's taking it all inwards. And as we can't speak through this bloody partition, it must be like being in the jug for her.'

'Will you let her know we came?' Molly asked.

'Course. I better go now.'

'Take care of yourselves,' Jean said, but Spot was gone before she finished her sentence.

'Poor Cissy,' Molly said as they left the hospital. 'She was so happy and then all this.'

'What do you think's wrong with the baby?'

'Don't know. But it doesn't sound good.'

'Oh, well,' sighed Jean as they waited for the bus, 'there ain't nothing more we can do for the time being, I suppose.'

When they were seated on the bus, Jean said pensively, 'Cissy and Spot's troubles must bring back rotten memories for you, gel.'

Molly nodded. 'I've had Emily on my mind a lot lately. One day she was a fit little toddler, the next a very sick child.'

'I don't know what I'd be like if Simon or Susie was that ill,' Jean admitted. 'I think I'd go to pieces. I dunno how you and Ted managed to carry on.'

'Dad sold us the shop and that was a lifesaver.'

'Do you think losing your Emily was the reason why you never had any more kids?'

As Molly thought over this very personal question, she shook her head slowly. 'I don't think so, Jean. Another baby just didn't come along.'

'Perhaps you didn't want it to after such a tragic experience,' Jean said perceptively. 'Going through what you did was devastating. You'd never want it to happen again. If it was me I think I'd try to cut meself off from any more pain.'

Molly suddenly realized just how right Jean was. Both she and Ted had thrown themselves into the shop, spending all God's hours at work, to build up the business. It was as if they'd looked on the store as their child, a replacement for Emily, a focus to keep them both sane. And as she thought this, another clear understanding came to her as though the clouds in her mind parted to let the blue sky through. She could see now that the store, for Ted, hadn't been enough to counteract the void left by Emily. He must have realized that, which was why he volunteered in 1939, when war broke out. Courageously and without hesitation he'd gone to enlist, as though it was his fate to do so. And, with this in mind, she understood now why she'd never tried to stop him: Ted had to fulfil his destiny, as she must hers.

'Penny for your thoughts,' said Jean as the bus rocked from side to side.

'I was thinking about Ted,' she replied on a deep sigh. 'I'm beginning to understand things now that have been a mystery.'

'Like what?'

'You can't live someone else's life for them.' She looked at Jean. 'No matter how much you love them. We all have our paths to tread.'

'Funny,' said Jean with a faint smile, 'I was thinking that just the other day.' She put her hand over Molly's. 'Not in those same words, but as near as damn it. I used to worry meself sick over Dennis. When those bloody bombers came over and he was out all times of the night I thought, that's it, one day it'll be a copper at the door and I won't want to hear what he says.'

'So you don't worry about him now?'

Jean smiled. 'When I get that thought in my head, I say to meself, come on now, girl, what's a better thing to think? After all, nothing's happened, has it? It's just the thought, like a splinter, that irritates until you believe it. So what flamin' use is that? Torture, it is. When you could be thinking something nice, like, when we get into bed tonight, I'm gonna warm me hands on his lovely bum. Cos if there's one thing I've always fancied about my old man, it's his arse.'

Jean looked seriously at Molly, until she threw back her head and burst into laughter. Molly did too. Both she and Jean knew that laughter was the antidote they needed at times like this.

The first frost of the year came on the last day of November, and with it a change in the baby's condition.

It was Spot who called at the shop on Monday, one of his few brief visits over the last two weeks. He told Molly that two nights previously, when they had almost given up on little Harry, he'd taken to Cissy's breast and drawn out the life-giving milk.

'Honest, Molly, we thought we'd lost him,' Spot said as he stood in the shop, leaning heavily on the counter. 'But all of a sudden I see Cissy looking at me as she holds the baby against her. And she's got this big smile on her face. I almost broke in the glass to cuddle her.' For the first time in weeks, Molly witnessed a happy Spot.

'Have they weighed him?'

'Five pounds, six ounces. But he ain't lost no more.'

'Early days yet.'

'They said he's not out of danger.'

'Is he still as yellow?'

Spot grinned again. 'She reckons 'e's got me old granny's blood. But the doctor said it's jaundice that didn't clear up like it should have. And with him being a bit early and not getting the dates right . . .' He pushed his hands over his thick stubble and scratched his jaw. 'I'm gonna have a good shave. Spruce meself up a bit and go back this afternoon.'

'Tell her we miss her.'

She watched Spot hurry out, a spring in his step once more. Then she turned the sign to CLOSED and put on her raincoat. She would run down to Jean's and tell her Spot's news.

Outside, the street was busy. Everyone had got used to the hole in the road and walked round it. Molly was pre-occupied as she thought of little Harry. Was this really good news or was Spot jumping the gun? The doctor had warned him Harry wasn't yet out of danger. What did that mean? And then she remembered Jean's words and how she found it helped to change her thoughts for the better. Well, she would try, only it wasn't easy!

She was concentrating so intently that as she made her way down the street, she didn't see a tall figure standing at the end of it. Her head was bowed, so that when she did look up, it was several seconds before she recognized the clean-shaven face and deeply set dark eyes staring in her direction.

Andy Miller paused as he stood in Roper Street, carefully inhaling the crisp November air, and with it his memories of London's docklands; this street in particular that had been torn apart during the blitz and was now, like a battered old brig after a refit, revitalized and seaworthy again.

Not that the raids were over. Molly had written of the Luftwaffe's unwanted attention still focused on the cities and ports. Many of his pals had lost family and friends in the attacks on the coastal areas and historic towns targeted by the enemy.

But in the year he had been away, the East End had shaken itself alive again, come up for round two, surviving the damage of high-velocity bombing and incendiary raids that had almost broken its back.

Andy swept the woollen cap from his head and narrowed his eyes at the Turners' house, wondering if Dennis and Jean were at home; he was tempted to knock before walking on up to the store.

But then a slim figure caught his eye. She was at the far end of the street, occasionally hidden by idling shoppers, casual pedestrians, a couple of cyclists and women pushing prams around the hole in the road which had got neither wider nor deeper in his absence.

His heart lifted, or rather jerked to attention as he braced himself. He found his gaze pinned to the slender young woman wearing a dark, belted raincoat and ankle boots. She walked thoughtfully, gracefully, head bowed, as she man-oeuvred her way past the banked rubble.

He stood still, then forced his legs into motion, swinging his kit bag over his shoulder, placing his steps in alignment with hers.

As he drew closer, a fist at the bottom of his stomach clenched. He sucked in a calming breath, though not entirely with success. For at that very moment she looked up and their gazes met.

Her hair was just as he remembered: a thick rope of

auburn plaited around her head. Her heart-shaped face was solemn but unchanged from a year ago.

Slowly her full lips parted and she stopped, her hands coming out of her pockets as she recognized him.

He had to prevent himself rushing forward as he felt the prickle of sweat under his thick navy roll-neck service jumper, which now seemed a size too small. The excitement, the hope and the disbelief were swelling inside him and telling him he was home. On dry land. In England. On Roper Street, where one particular dwelling had become a sanctuary for him and his kids – against all the odds.

And then he found himself breaking into a run. As though a force had taken him over, driving him forward. Choking down the throb inside his chest, he called her name, and called it once more.

And then she began running too. Her breath fanned up into the clear winter's air. As energetically as a five-year-old he leaped the obstructions along the path.

Finally they met, he unable to do more than gasp her name. And she, doing much the same, until they were in each other's arms and holding on so tight that it was then he really knew he was home.

Chapter Twenty-Two

Molly could neither laugh nor cry; even to speak was challenge enough as the world went on around them. The earth neither opened up nor did the sky fall in, though with the shock of seeing Andy she wouldn't have been surprised at anything. He was here, in the flesh, and she looked up into his face in disbelief.

'Molly, Molly,' he said, and holding her at arm's length, he gave that almost shy smile – Cissy's Jimmy Stewart smile – a slow parting of the lips and the sight of even white teeth; and the smell of him! Oh, the smell! Of the ocean, the wind and the waves embedded in his skin and hair. It took her to a place that she remembered when he'd kissed her that day before they parted.

'Andy – I can't believe me eyes!'

The smile widened then and he nodded. 'Me too. There you was. In the street. Walking towards me.'

Molly felt the tickle of laughter in her chest. 'Are you on leave? Why didn't you write?'

'I sent you a letter three weeks ago.'

'It's not come yet. But the surprise is better. Much better.' She wanted to hold him again, to sink into his arms. And she knew he wanted that too, as his grasp on her was strong and possessive.

They both let laughter loose then, awkwardly standing apart and conscious of the people in the street.

'You've had a good shave,' she said, and he nodded, rubbing his smooth chin.

'Docked at Portsmouth last night and stayed at the hostel. Had a good scrub. Caught the train this morning. And, well, here I am.'

'The kids are at school.'

'Funny, I thought they might be over at the Turners'. I was about to knock.' He cleared his throat. 'How are they?'

'Never better.'

'I dunno how to thank you for what you did at Romford.'

'You don't have to thank me. Listen, why don't we go over to Jean's? I've got something to tell them and I'd like you to hear it too.'

He lifted his kit bag to the other shoulder. 'We'll talk after, right?'

She nodded and together they made their way down to the Turners', her steps light as they walked arm in arm.

'Come here and give us a hug, stranger.' Jean threw herself at Andy and Molly smiled as they embraced. Dennis took his hand and shook it and the two men slapped each other's shoulders. During the multitude of questions Molly absorbed the changed appearance of the tall, broad-shouldered figure who hadn't seemed quite real. As he'd stood in Roper Street, he had seemed so tall and upright, his bearing much improved from the sick man who had once been shipwrecked at sea and almost drowned.

His thick, dark hair was trimmed short and his sea-whipped skin was glowing and healthy. He'd filled out considerably. The close-fitting naval jumper showed a proud, broad chest squared off by strong shoulders. As he gazed at each of them, trying to answer their enquiries, he made light of what Molly knew must have been a dangerous year at sea. He described the battles of the Atlantic and the perilous convoys of merchant ships to and from Russia that were notorious in every headline of the newspapers.

But every so often his gaze caught hers, a light in his eyes that told her how relieved he was to be home. Sitting at the table in the Turners' kitchen as Jean made tea, Molly was amused at Dennis, who thought of every excuse not to go out to work, as he listened enthralled.

The conversation then turned to all that had happened in his absence. Molly watched Andy's face fill with pride as he learned how well Mark and Evie were doing at school. How they had made friends and had settled back into East End life after leaving Southend and saying goodbye to Len and Betty.

But his expression saddened as he learned of Cissy and Spot's troubles, and Molly, not wanting to spoil his home-coming, quickly added that Spot had brought better news today.

'Harry's gonna make it,' declared Dennis confidently. 'With parents like Cissy and Spot, he's got fighting blood in his veins.'

After yet more tea and gossip that could have gone on all day, Molly stood up. 'The store won't run itself, much as I'd like it to.'

'You'll both have a couple of hours to catch up before the kids get home,' Jean said, giving Molly a sly wink. 'And give us another hug, Andy. I want to make up for lost time.'

Everyone had a smile on their face as Molly and Andy left, walking slowly hand in hand up Roper Street, skirting the hole and the debris and passing the bicycle factory to amble up the little path at the back of the shop. But before Molly could push her key into the lock, he took her in his arms and, gazing into her eyes, whispered, 'I've dreamed of this moment, Molly. Though I didn't think it would ever come to pass. I wondered if that kiss we shared was just a figment of my imagination.'

'I did too,' she admitted, feeling the warmth of his body close to hers and realizing they were completely alone and unobserved. 'You never said any more in your letters.'

'Didn't know if you felt the same.' He lifted her chin. 'Do you feel like me, Molly? I know how much you loved Ted. He was a good man and died for his country. I'll never be able to fill his shoes.'

'It ain't about dying, Andy. I've learned that life is all about living. Yes, Ted was a loving and loyal husband and that part of me life has treasured memories. But I'm still here, and I have so much to be thankful for. Including you and the kids.'

He said no more, but this time sought out her lips with a fierce passion and she responded, knowing that from this moment onwards there was not only a future to look forward to, but most importantly, she understood the value of every precious moment.

Leading him upstairs and into her bedroom, she closed the door. 'The shop can wait. I can't.' She drew him close. 'The children won't be home for a while.'

'Molly, I've thought of you every day. Probably every hour.' He bent his dark head and kissed her passionately. She felt as though she was spinning above the clouds as desire overwhelmed her and very soon they lay in bed, locked in each other's arms.

Much later, they dressed and sat together at the kitchen table holding hands. They were hungry but decided to wait for Mark and Evie and share their first meal together.

'I'd better go down and open up before they come home,' Molly decided.

'Thank you,' he whispered, kissing her again. 'That was wonderful.'

Molly thought so too and wished they could sit here together for the rest of the day. Instead she put on her overall and went down to the shop. As she served her customers she wondered if any of them could see the change in her. But no one mentioned the flush on her cheeks or her distracted manner. And when the rush was over, Andy appeared and pulled her into the glory hole. 'I can't wait till tonight,' he told her. 'Now I've started kissing you, I can't stop.' He ran his fingers through her hair and kissed her cheeks.

They giggled like children as someone walked in the shop door and the bell tinkled. Molly served her customer, and found Andy beside her once more.

'Don't worry, I'll behave myself.'

'It's not you I'm worried about, it's me.' She smiled and pushed back her hair self-consciously. 'I'm so glad you're home.'

He looked at her longingly, then with hands in pockets, he reclined against the counter and studied her. 'Tell me about Romford,' he said quietly. 'You made light of it in your letter, by but God, Molly, I'd have gone crazy if you hadn't found them.'

She explained how she'd located Roger's cottage and managed to prevent Mark and Evie from being evacuated on the coach. And how Roger had put her up for the night and driven them back to London the next day.

'I don't know what I would have done without you,' he said, only to be interrupted by yet another customer. Molly saw how easily he spoke to the women and how warmly they welcomed him. The talk, though, always returned to war and their menfolk, who, like Andy, were serving on ships in the freezing cold north, or toiling in the deserts of North Africa. There were those, too, whose men had been taken prisoner or perished in Burma and Japan, and in Europe there were stories of the merciless atrocities in Jewish ghettos.

It was late in the afternoon when the shop door opened to reveal two young faces, both unaware of the surprise awaiting them.

It took Evie only a few seconds to fly into her father's arms, and then Mark, close on her heels. After the initial surprise came the questions, and breathless delight when Andy opened his kit bag to give them each a small gift.

'I made these for you,' he said, his voice breaking slightly, 'a little souvenir for both of you.'

Molly smiled as Evie examined the raffia horse made by her father and Mark the carved wooden submarine that Andy had sculpted from driftwood.

'Has you got something for Molly?' Evie asked and Andy nodded, presenting Molly with a small square box. Inside was a little silver anchor on a chain.

'It's beautiful,' Molly said as Andy clipped it around her neck.

'She's a sailor now, ain't she?' said Evie, and Andy roared with laughter. Lifting Mark and Evie, one under each arm, to squeals of laughter, he grinned at Molly. 'Reckon it's time we got out of your way.'

'I'm putting you two in charge of showing your father what's for dinner,' she told the children. 'There's yesterday's mash and veg for bubble and squeak. And cold custard and apple pie for afters.'

'Are you coming?' Mark asked Molly as Andy lowered him to the floor.

'I'll close the shop first.' She met Andy's eyes as she fingered the anchor around her neck.

His smile told her he was thinking the same; they couldn't wait to be in each other's arms once more.

When the children were asleep that night, they sat together in the front room holding hands. They had shared so much happiness in the last few hours that Molly had almost forgotten Cissy and Harry. Now, as Andy's fingers stroked lightly across hers, she almost felt guilty for that happiness and she suddenly wondered about the Denhams. 'I hope you won't worry about Betty and Len,' she said softly. 'I'm sure Roger would have found them a decent billet in Wales.'

'Molly, it's not the Denhams that worries me. It's that copper who was hanging around you.'

'Who? Detective Constable Longman?' she said in surprise.

'Has he been round?'

Molly's cheeks flushed. Ted had never been the jealous type and she had never given him cause to be. But she could see by the look in Andy's eyes that he was a different kind of man. 'Only at Christmas to tell us that Ronnie Hook went to jail.'

'Christmas ain't the time to be calling on folk. Did he make a nuisance of himself?'

'I didn't give him a chance to. It was the day Dad stayed and the Turners and Cissy and Spot were here. I was polite but sent him on his way.'

'I wish I had been here,' he growled, pulling Molly to him. 'He would have got a very different reception.'

'Andy, he's just a nosy copper.'

'Don't care if he's nosy. Got nothing to hide. But I don't want him pestering you.'

Molly laughed and held his face between her hands. 'This is a very funny feeling.'

'What is?'

She put her lips close to his. 'Knowing that someone cares enough to say that.'

'I care all right,' he whispered. 'You'd be shocked to know just how much.'

Molly silenced him with a long and tender kiss, then, leaning back against the settee, he said very slowly, 'I want us to be together always. Do you?'

'I think you know the answer to that.'

'Then there's something important I have to say.' He looked down at their joined hands then slowly brought his gaze up. 'Before the war, I took a course in signals. Was going to make something of meself as a signalman. But when I married Stella, me dreams all went out of the window. Until now, when it wouldn't take too long to get myself up to scratch again – or so I'm told. The good thing is, I'd be in England for a while, at a signals training camp.'

'Oh, Andy, that's wonderful news.'

'I might not pass the course.'

'You will, I'm sure.'

'I ain't never had anyone show any faith in me before.'

She nodded slowly. 'I have all the faith that's needed.'

'So you're up for it?' he asked uncertainly.

'Of course I am. It must be safer than being on the guns.'

For a moment he looked away, but soon he was telling

her what might be involved. 'The story goes that our British boffins have broken the German naval code. For a while our Atlantic convoys have been getting through, a few losses but not as many as there were. Then in February, something must have happened. Ships started sinking again. So the code breakers went back to the drawing board. Meanwhile, we're relying on flag signals or wireless telegraphy. And that's where I come in.'

'Do you have a choice in this, Andy?'

'Because of my previous experience I've been asked to volunteer.'

Molly was silent as her ribs seemed to squeeze painfully together. Ted was a volunteer and now Andy was.

'I'll be on destroyers.' He paused, letting this sink in. 'If you was against it, I'd turn them down. This is all about us now, not just me.'

Molly's thoughts were in a whirl. History was repeating itself. Her fear was that the same thing might happen to Andy as it did to Ted.

'The decision's not mine to make,' she answered, recalling her conversation with Jean on the bus. And although it wasn't easy, she nodded. 'If it's what you want I won't stop you. There are no guarantees to anything in life, Andy. I've learned that.'

'I can guarantee you one thing,' he told her, a little choke in his voice. 'Wherever I am, whatever I'm doing, and as long as I draw breath, you'll be in my heart. I love you, Molly Swift. One day, when all this is over, I'll marry you.'

He kissed her with a fierce hunger that she knew matched

hers in every way, no matter what problems were posed in the future. Then, raising his eyebrows, he whispered, 'Will you wait for me?'

Molly smiled, her brown eyes full of love. 'I'll wait, you know that. And I'll take good care of Mark and Evie. Wherever you are, our thoughts will be with you.'

His eyes closed in momentary relief but as he was about to kiss her again, a noise disturbed them.

'I's 'ungry,' said a small voice and they broke apart, turning to stare at Evie's tiny figure standing in the doorway. Her nightie billowed out as she hugged her raffia horse and padded barefoot across the room to her father's lap.

Andy kissed the wheat-coloured curls framing his daughter's innocent face and soon there were some very wide yawns, until Evie held out her arms to Molly.

'Hello, Curly Top, are you still awake?' she said as Evie nestled against her chest.

'I's 'ungry,' Evie mumbled again, promptly falling asleep. With the warmth of Evie's body against her, Molly looked silently into Andy's eyes.

No other words were needed.

Chapter Twenty-Three

With so very little time until Christmas, and wanting to spend every free moment with Andy, Molly decided to postpone her visit to Sidcup. Concerning her, too, was little Harry, who although he was now breastfeeding, was still too small to leave hospital.

Cissy had no choice but to be with him and so Spot told Molly he would prepare the Narrow Street rooms ready for when Cissy and Harry were discharged.

Andy looked every morning for the all-important letter of approval to the Signals Corps training camp. He and Molly had very little time alone together as the children's school holiday had begun and Mark and Evie loved having their dad home.

There was no end of bus rides and long walks, and a day out to the Tower of London. Meanwhile, Molly asked Liz to work in the shop on the days she spent with Cissy at the hospital.

And so it was on a chill winter's Friday close to Christmas that Molly arrived with news that was to surprise even Cissy.

'A telegram came this morning,' Molly told her friend as they sat in the hospital canteen. 'Andy has to report to Glenholt on Sunday 20th.'

'But that's the day after tomorrow,' gasped Cissy. 'He won't be home for Christmas!'

'No, seems he won't.' Molly could barely raise a smile as she tried to hide her disappointment. She had thought that, as he hadn't been notified this late in the year, it would be January before a letter came.

'Will you be going to your sister's instead?'

'Too late now,' said Molly. 'She'll have her Christmas all arranged.'

'What about your dad?'

'I wrote and asked him if he'd like to come and stay like last year. But he said he felt he had to be with George and Elizabeth this time.'

'They've got him all year round.'

'Yes, but they are his grandchildren.'

Cissy stuck out her chin. 'Well, you've got kids an' all.'

'Yes, but they ain't mine.'

'You and the kids can come and keep me company, in that case,' Cissy grinned. 'Not that spending your Christmas in hospital will be very much fun. But we can have a few laughs.' Her grey eyes looked bruised with purple shadows, after days and nights of worry and upset over Harry. Although she was allowed to wear her ordinary clothes now,

Cissy still complained of the cap and gown she was made to wear when she fed her baby.

'But will Mark and Evie be able to come?' Molly asked doubtfully.

'I'll fix it up with the canteen manageress. I've got to know her quite well. Spot will bung the staff a few quid and we can all enjoy our Christmas dinner in here.'

Molly looked round at the rows of square tables where the nurses, porters and hospital workers gathered, hugging their mugs of tea. It wasn't an unpleasant atmosphere; cooking smells laced with a faint aroma of disinfectant. But the noise of the big, shiny, bubbling urns of tea was somehow comforting and reminded her of home.

'Sorry it's not much of an offer,' said Cissy, giving her old, edgy expression.

'We'd like to, thanks,' Molly said quickly. She didn't want to upset Cissy, as she was only just now on the brink of returning to her old self again with the thought that in the new year she might be discharged with Harry.

But it wasn't how Molly had hoped Christmas might be. She'd planned to cook a chicken or even a rabbit if she could find a decent one at the butcher's. Jean and Dennis had invited them for Christmas Eve and afterwards she and Andy would come home to hang the children's stockings from the mantel. She'd dreamed of how, later into the night, when she and Andy were together, they would make love with all the desire and fervour that they tried to hide from the children.

Cissy's voice broke into her thoughts. 'Where's this place your Andy's going to?'

'Somewhere near Plymouth, I think.'

'So he'll have to catch the early train?'

Molly sighed. 'I s'pose so.'

'Bloody war,' Cissy growled and gulped her tea. 'Do the kids ever talk about Betty and Len?'

'Not much. Mark went through that troubling time, thinking everyone he loved got killed. Sometimes he says he still has bad dreams about being taken away.'

'Poor little bugger.'

'I think it has to do with being trapped on that coach.'

'Well, all I can say is they're lucky you got to them in time. What you read about in the papers and evacuee kids going missing is enough to turn you grey.'

Molly quickly finished her tea. She didn't want to think of what might have happened if she'd been just a few minutes later in trying to stop that coach. 'I've got to get back for Liz. She's leaving the shop early to go to her aunt's at West Ham. What can we bring on Christmas Day?'

Cissy rolled her eyes, and with a straight face, pretended to consider the offer. 'A packet of fags would be nice, and a drop of the other. Do you think you could smuggle 'em in until I get home and can really let me hair down?'

Molly stared at her. 'You told me you'd given up for the baby's sake.'

Cissy began to laugh. 'You should see your face. I'm only kidding.'

Molly sighed in relief, glad that Cissy was teasing. The nurse had warned her friend that alcohol in large quantities might affect her breast milk.

Molly stood up, unable to resist a smile. The new leaf Cissy had turned over was a precarious one. Old habits died hard. She didn't want to encourage Cissy in any way. She was so very close to leaving the hospital with Harry after being cooped up here for what seemed like an eternity.

On Sunday morning, in the very early hours, Andy was ready to leave. He'd shaved and washed in the kitchen and put on the only service gear he had: his navy-blue roll-neck jumper and canvas trousers, with his old duffel packed along with a bite to eat wrapped in newspaper.

He and Molly had hardly slept a wink. If he wedged a rug under the bedroom door, they were alerted to Evie's nocturnal visits, increasingly frequent since he'd been home. She liked to climb into bed with them for a cuddle, which seemed quite natural to her.

When it was time, he took Molly in his arms and held her close. 'We won't wake the kids. I said all my goodbyes last night. I'll write soon, but don't forget my letters will be censored.'

'Will you be able to write how long your training will last?'

'Don't see why not.' He hugged her again. 'You can't imagine how much I'll miss you.'

He felt a physical ache; being parted from Molly and the kids was unbearable. He wanted to be with them. Now he had found the girl of his dreams, his life at sea would be very different from before. 'I'll have my money sent through to you. Don't know how long before you'll get it though. Will you be able to manage?'

Molly placed her hands on his shoulders. 'Listen, Andrew Miller, the shop will provide, so don't go worrying on that score. Just look after yourself. That's the most important thing.'

'I'll make it all up to you after the war, and that's a promise.'

'Do you think there will be an *after*?'

'Course I do,' he said in surprise. 'The whole world wants an *after*. It ain't just us, the Allies, but ordinary people everywhere who have got swept up in this thing we call war.'

'Why don't our governments put a stop to it, then?'

He took her hands between his and sighed heavily. 'Big characters, egos, money, territory – greed and pride. That's how it starts. And it takes a war to end it. But it's a sobering sight when you see the reality: poor buggers just like me in the freezing water, screaming out for help. Whoever they are, they're trying to stay alive to get back to their loved ones. Just as I'll be doing.'

They were both shivering in the frosty December morning and he blew lightly on her fingers to warm them. She stared into his eyes and for the umpteenth time he thought how beautiful she was. Her pale skin was almost transparent in the gloomy morning light and it reminded him of fine bone china as he lifted a finger and trailed it over her cheek. 'I love you so much, Molly.'

'I love you too,' she whispered.

Their kiss sent the blood draining from his legs for the desire of her. To think that one day she would be his wife was almost unbelievable. And it was this that would keep him going in the days and months ahead.

'Your train won't wait,' she said and he nodded, yet still they couldn't tear themselves apart. Just one more kiss, he thought, and then drawing on all his reserves he hugged her so tightly that he felt her bones would crack if he squeezed any harder.

Then before they could say or do more, he found the strength to pull the door open and step out into cold, crisp air that instantly sobered him up. One brief glance over his shoulder told him she was watching and that felt good, even though it was the hardest thing he had ever done. It wasn't in him to walk away from the loves of his life and the future they had just talked about. But neither was it in any man, not if peace reigned in this world instead of conflict.

It was Christmas Day and, true to her word, Cissy arranged dinner at the hospital. Molly wore a smart black astrakhan coat, freshly out of mothballs for the occasion. With her auburn hair pinned up elegantly at the back of her head, she made her way along the draughty corridors of the hospital, proud of Evie and Mark as they walked beside her. Evie's hair shone like spun gold and Mark's was combed flat with a neat parting. They were both well shod and wore their Sunday-best clothes. Molly thought of their father and knew he would be proud of them too. She hoped he had settled into camp life and that he was enjoying Christmas, despite being away from them.

The children missed him terribly but had enjoyed last night at the Turners'. Molly smiled as she thought of the games they'd played until quite late: blind man's buff, find the sixpence and charades.

Dennis had seen them home safely, and by the time the kids woke this morning she'd hung their stockings from the mantelpiece. They were just old woollen socks, but inside she had squeezed toffee apples, oranges, and some nougat that Andy had bought and broken up with a hammer. There was also a comic for Mark and a tiny red velvet purse with a strap for Evie.

As soon as they walked through the big doors into the canteen, the smell of cooking made Molly's mouth water. She knew they were very lucky to be able to spend the day in such a festive atmosphere with an abundance of free food. All the nurses and staff on duty wore paper hats and had been forewarned that guests would be arriving this year.

As Spot made his way through the busy diners to greet them, there were smiles and waves from the assembled hospital staff. Spot opened his arms and lifted Evie up high, making her giggle. He did the same to Mark, who after his first embarrassment at so many people patting him on the head, began to lose his shyness.

'Over here,' Spot said, escorting them to a long table which was actually two benches pushed together and covered with a hospital cloth. 'Cissy's just giving the baby a feed. She'll be along soon. Now, you sit here at the top, Mark, next to me. We'll put the women down the other end so they can have a jaw.' It was so noisy in the echoey canteen that Spot was having to shout.

They took their places and Evie clapped her hands in

delight at the prospect of food. Large knives, forks and spoons were set out before them. There were little sprigs of holly that Spot had brought to decorate the table, and a candle in the middle.

When Cissy appeared a few minutes later, there was loud applause from all the other tables. Molly knew that Cissy was a very popular character at the hospital. Everyone admired how hard she had fought for little Harry's life.

'Happy Christmas, Molly.' Cissy threw her arms around her, then embraced the children. 'Thanks for coming.'

Molly watched as Spot brought the plates over from the table on which they were piled. The hot food was ready to be served and Molly's mouth watered even more at the thought of the roast chicken that was such a delicacy throughout the war years. She only hoped Andy was faring as well.

Very soon their plates were filled with generous portions of meat covered in thick brown gravy, accompanied by huge roast potatoes, batter pudding and carrots.

'I'm 'ungry!' Evie yelled, and was the first to shovel a huge forkful into her mouth.

As the meal was eaten they were served with lemonades, as no alcohol was allowed in the hospital.

When the Christmas dinner was over, Mark and Evie, wearing their paper hats, ran round all the tables. They were the centre of everyone's attention and loved it. When all the merrymaking was over, Spot stood up and cleared his throat. He began to sing 'Silent Night' in his deep, rich voice. Everyone joined in. Afterwards there was a deep hush, for they were all thinking of their families, friends and loved ones.

Molly thought it was a perfect end to Christmas Day. The words of the carol were full of peace and goodwill, and told of a time that everyone longed to return to.

Chapter Twenty-Four

In Molly's household 1943 arrived quietly and the children went back to school in the first week. A light sprinkling of snow fell later in the month, the very same day that Andy's letter arrived. She was so excited at the prospect of opening it, she kept it in her overall pocket until after the first flurry of customers had left.

Unlike all his letters at sea, this one gave her more information. She guessed he was stationed near Plymouth still as he said nothing to the contrary. 'The course is divided into three parts,' he wrote. 'Eleven weeks to begin with and then our first exam. If I pass, I'll go on to the next part. In all, I'll have made twenty weeks and should be guaranteed a long leave, once I've done my finals in May.'

Molly was both delighted and anxious. How hard were these exams to pass? Andy went on to talk about the men he shared his hut with. He liked them all and had made friends. He asked about the children and home, and this time, he ended the letter with 'Love from Andy. XX'.

It was an improvement, she decided, on those impersonal letters he'd written last year. But she knew she had to accept that he wasn't a man to wear his heart on his sleeve. Perhaps he was worried about the censors, or still unsure of her feelings? Or maybe he'd written to Stella over the years and never received a response.

Molly decided to write back immediately. She told him she couldn't wait to see him as soon as his training was over. He would be home in May, which seemed an awfully long time to wait. But at least she had a date. May was a beautiful month: springtime.

She folded the letter and put it in her pocket. Tomorrow, when Liz came in, she would go to see Cissy and tell her the good news.

The following day, as the feathery coating of snowy flakes turned a mucky brown in the gutters, she walked to school with Jean and the children.

'So he'll be home in May?' Jean asked as Molly explained. 'Have you told the kids?'

'No. I'll leave it until I know he's passed his exams.'

'What's he going to do then?'

Molly shrugged as they stood at the gates of the school, a flat-roofed building with a tiny annexe for the teachers. 'That's the bit I don't like.'

'But he won't be on the guns.'

'No. I just hope these signals ain't more dangerous.' She couldn't help but remember that evasive look in his eye when she'd first enquired about it.

'At least you'll have him home for a bit.'

After leaving the children at school and saying goodbye to Jean, Molly made her way back to the shop and Liz. Since there were not too many customers in the cold and slushy weather, Molly decided to go straight to the hospital.

She caught the bus in West Ferry Road but it hadn't gone very far before the bus conductor opened the doors and looked into the sky.

'Everyone take cover,' he shouted. 'There's a shelter across the road.'

'The warning ain't gorn,' an annoyed passenger shouted.

'No, but me ears ain't gone deaf either.'

Molly's heart leaped. Was this a false alarm? There had been so many over the last few months. Would the children be safe? There was no time to go back to the school now. Reluctantly, she went with all the others, crammed into the small brick-built shelter, where everyone listened to the noise and chaos outside.

'Can you hear the Luftwaffe?' someone asked.

'They ain't over us yet.'

The low drone was distant. Molly prayed it would stay that way. She knew it was selfish to think that, for other poor souls would be suffering.

Soon there were loud reports from the ack-ack guns and the clear drone of the approaching planes.

Molly sat squeezed on a bench and tried not to listen to the pandemonium outside in the streets. The teachers always took the children to safety. But why hadn't the sirens gone off?

Some time later, an ARP warden came in through the

reinforced door. He looked very shocked and, removing his helmet, he sank down on the edge of a bench.

'What's up, cocker?' a man asked. 'What's going on? Who's bought it this time?'

The warden took out a dirty rag, wiped his forehead and blew his nose. For a few minutes he was silent. Then, when he was more composed, he spoke very quietly.

'We was telephoned at the post. It was a tip-and-run raid. Retaliation for our boys bombing Berlin three days ago.'

Everyone spoke at once, wanting to know where exactly the bombs had been dropped. They all had families and loved ones. Panic began to set in.

Finally the harassed warden put up his hand. 'Can't tell you much. Think the other side of the river got it worst.'

'Oh, Christ! I'm from Deptford.' A young woman jumped to her feet. And another. Until there was so much chaos in the small shelter that when the all-clear sounded, everyone pushed to get out.

Molly caught the warden's sleeve as he went to follow. 'Was it just south of the river? Why wouldn't they come over the docks?' she asked.

He couldn't look in her eyes. 'There's talk of Greenwich getting it, and a school—'

This was enough for Molly. The only thing separating Greenwich from the island was a strip of water. She didn't wait to hear any more and ran after the crowd.

Molly ran all the way back to the island. The word 'school' blazed in her mind as if she could see the flames and black smoke rising up right before her. Though she couldn't see any sign of burning or bombed buildings there were policemen, firemen, ambulances and ARP out on the streets.

The panic seemed to be catching and people were running in different directions. Her heart was racing and her mouth was dry, as the cold winter air rushed in icily to the back of her throat.

She stopped one of the policemen, who seemed as bewildered as she was. No one knew what had happened.

By the time she got to the school she had imagined so many terrible things that when she actually saw the flat roof intact, with parents and children milling around in the playground, she found it impossible to believe her eyes.

The teachers had assembled the pupils in neat lines and she could see Mark and Evie standing together. Jean was already there with Simon and Susie. As Molly stopped to regain her breath, she realized tears of relief were sliding down her cheeks. A huge sob was lodged in her chest and she fought for enough breath to let it out. Eventually the eruption came, while her body shook and her legs, previously fuelled with fearful energy, now gave way to weakness.

'Molly, gel, are you all right?' She looked up into Dennis's concerned face.

She managed to nod, but when he slipped his arm around her shoulders she gave way to her feelings.

'Hey, your two are as good as gold, love,' Dennis soothed her. 'You've no need to worry.'

Molly took out her handkerchief and quickly wiped her eyes. 'I-I was on the bus going to the hospital,' she stammered, 'but we didn't know if it was a raid or not. And the conductor told us to go to the shelter and—'

'Hey, they're safe,' Dennis assured her once more, taking her shoulders and giving her a little shake. 'Watch me lips. Everything's fine.'

Staring into his eyes, Molly nodded. 'I must pull meself together.'

Dennis gave her a wink. Then taking her arm he marched her across the playground. Evie and Mark saw her, and threw themselves into her arms.

It was then she realized how much she cared. Mark and Evie were not her blood, but she had begun to love them as her own.

The following day, the local schools were closed. This was as a mark of respect to the many children and staff who had perished in a Catford school, south of the river.

'Why didn't the warning go?' Molly asked Dennis, who had spoken to Mr Stokes earlier that morning.

'It did, but too late. Some bloody hiccup in the works.'

'So what was the death toll?' asked Jean as they stood in her kitchen, watching the four children playing in the back yard.

'They reckon over thirty kids and any number of staff. Still digging them out of the rubble.'

Both Jean and Molly put their hands to their mouths. 'Oh, Dennis, them poor parents.'

'There was a lady in the shelter from Deptford,' Molly said, her mind returning to the moment the warden had told them about the raid.

'The bombers also destroyed Lewisham's barrage balloon sites and the Deptford power station took three direct hits,' Dennis continued. 'The President's House over at the Royal Naval College got clobbered too.'

'But bricks and mortar are nothing, compared to those little lives,' Molly sighed, her eyes lingering on Evie's tiny figure, her blonde curls hanging over her scarf as she played with Susie. 'How will people ever recover from such a loss?'

'Here and in Germany,' Jean added as she looked at Dennis. 'After all, we've flattened their towns and cities. There must be mothers and fathers in Berlin just like us.'

Molly knew Jean was right and her heart ached for all those in the world who had loved and lost children. It was bad enough when an adult was a casualty, but children should play no part in the conflict of war.

'I'd better get back to the shop,' Molly said then. 'I'll come for Mark and Evie at dinner time.'

'I won't let 'em in the street today,' Jean nodded.

Molly knew they were both very anxious about the children being out of their sight now – even though Dennis warned them the kids wouldn't thank them for restricting their freedom.

It was a week before Molly found the courage to take the children to school again. And Jean was of the same mind. Neither of them could wait until they met them from school. It was only when all four children noisily complained that they preferred coming home on their own that finally the old routine was reinstated.

*

It was the first week of February when Cissy and Harry were discharged from hospital and Spot took them home to Narrow Street. Molly asked Spot if they could call during half term as all the children wanted to see the baby.

And so it was on the last day of half term when Molly and Jean and the children went to visit the Fryers. Molly was not surprised to see Cissy and Spot's neighbours in the street as they got off the bus. Somehow the word had got round, and once again a welcoming committee had formed. Hands were shaken and the children admired as they stood waiting for Spot to open the door.

When at last Spot came to the rescue, a small black-and-white terrier came rushing out, nipping at people's heels, barking loudly.

Spot laughed as he watched Nibbles attack and retreat, then disappear as quickly inside again.

'He's on guard for the baby, see?' Spot explained as he herded them up the stairs. 'Just in case he catches a bloody big rat.'

The children ran ahead. Molly felt very excited. She could hardly contain herself and when she saw the difference Spot had made to the dull and dowdy rooms that she had visited, her mouth dropped open in surprise. This flat was a palace, compared to what it had been before.

The walls of Spot and Cissy's vast flat were distempered in a soft creamy colour, shedding light into all the dark corners. Spot prided himself on the job lot of paint from the council, despite Cissy's request for wallpaper.

After greeting them all, Cissy led the way. 'Me lace

curtains are from Mrs Wong upstairs,' she explained. 'And Li from the restaurant below gave us the china and chopsticks.'

'Do you use them?' asked Molly in surprise.

'They look nice on the dresser,' Cissy said with a grin.

Molly had to smile, as Cissy showed off an oriental silk cover across the settee: a dragon breathing gold, green and red flames. The pattern was very beautiful, but not what she'd expected Cissy to like. There was a large black china cat standing on the mantelpiece.

'It's lucky,' said Cissy, tapping its bouncing head. 'Couldn't refuse that from the Chengs.'

'You're speaking Chinese already, Auntie Cissy,' said Simon.

'Yes, my love. And a right caper it is too.'

Molly grinned as Cissy displayed more treasures: two little figurines with jet-black hair, pinned with a slim needle-like stick. The girls were dressed in traditional oriental robes, their faces white with red-spotted cheeks and their hands hidden in their wide sleeves.

'These were Spot's mum's,' Cissy announced as she showed them a pair of Victorian vases decorated with gilded roses. 'And this is them, Mr and Mrs Fryer. Note the family resemblance.'

Molly and Jean stared at the oak-framed picture. Mr Fryer had a decidedly pronounced widow's peak with a slash of grey in his hair, while Mrs Fryer was not looking quite straight at the lens of the photographer.

Molly resisted a smile as Cissy conducted the grand tour. The floorboards, she noted, had been painted a shiny chocolate brown, and rugs of every description scattered over them: a combination of traditional Chinese patterns and English country gardens.

When Cissy displayed their bedroom, there was a united 'Ahhh!' Beside the monstrous iron bedstead with its brass furnishings stood the baby's cot.

Everyone tiptoed around it.

'Crikey, he's adorable,' said Jean as they all stared in wonder at the sleeping pink face, surrounded by a white bonnet.

'Can't see,' complained Evie, the smallest of the four children, and Molly lifted her into her arms.

'Don't wake him,' Jean whispered to Simon and Susie. 'Just look.'

All were silent as they studied the baby, until Cissy led the way from the room.

'Can I 'old him?' asked Evie.

'When he's a bit older,' said Molly.

'We don't want him to get our germs,' said her brother in a grown-up fashion.

'I ain't got any,' disagreed Evie and there was laughter all round.

As the children scooted off with Nibbles, Jean turned to Cissy with admiring eyes. 'You've a lovely family, gel. And a lovely home. And you deserve them both.'

'I second that,' said Molly.

Cissy bit back her tears. 'Do I? Dunno about that.'

'Now, now,' said Jean sliding an arm around Cissy's shoulders. 'What's all the tears for?'

'Dunno,' spluttered Cissy. 'Thank you for being me mates.'

At which there wasn't a dry eye left between them as, standing together in the long passage with the smell of fresh distemper and the food drifting up from the restaurant, they hugged each other tightly.

Chapter Twenty-Five

Molly looked back on that day with great fondness. It seemed to her that many bridges had been crossed. Not just for Cissy, but for herself and Jean, who, as they rode back on the bus with the children, talked of what they, too, would want in the future. But for Molly, the school incident had worried her; there wasn't a day that went by without her thinking about the raids. They seemed more ominous and threatening than they had done before and Jean gave her opinion as to why.

'Mark and Evie have become as important to you as Emily, ducks. And why not?'

'Trouble is, I worry more now.'

'That's motherhood, I'm afraid.'

'Do you think it's wise to send the kids to school?'

'They've got to be taught, ain't they?' posed Jean. 'And the only other option is what you and me don't want. Evacuation.'

Molly nodded. 'No, I wouldn't want that.' But there was a niggle in her mind all the same. The war wasn't over by a long shot. There would be more raids, and who knew what the enemy would do next? Lyn's offer to her had not included Mark and Evie. But what if she was to accept on the provision that the children went with her to Sidcup? This was not a happy thought for Molly, but she felt that, with a little persuasion, Lyn would agree. They could rent a house or rooms for the time being. With the savings she had accrued and Andy's money coming through, there would be enough to survive on.

But could she bring herself to leave the East End? It was a radical decision. And she didn't want to make it. Yet she knew that one day, in an uncertain future, she might have to.

It was a rainy Wednesday morning in early March when the letter fell onto the shop floor and Molly, recognizing the writing, tore it open immediately.

There were no customers in sight, so she sat down on the stool behind the counter. Reading Andy's words, she felt a rush of pride as he told her that, due to his satisfactory examination results, he had been accepted for the rest of his Signals training. And that, if he were to pass his finals, he would be given the opportunity of – after a year's service – being promoted to a commissioned rank.

'What's commissions?' Mark asked when he came home from school and Molly read the letter out loud.

'Your dad will have the chance to become an officer.'

'What's that?' asked Evie as she climbed on the kitchen chair to eat her supper.

'It's something special in the navy.'

'Can I go in the navy when I'm old enough?' asked Mark, joining his sister.

'If you like.'

'Can I?' asked Evie, squeezing a hefty slice of bread and dripping into her mouth.

'Yes, but it's mostly for boys. There's other things for girls.'

'I'm as big as 'im,' said Evie with a full mouth and glaring at her brother.

'You ain't,' replied Mark. 'And anyway, you're a gel.'

Molly was about to interrupt this familiar argument when suddenly the warning went. They'd had two false alarms recently and though the noise sent a shiver of fear down her spine, she remained seated at the table. The siren continued to wail and from the street she could hear shouting. She told the children to stay where they were and turned off the light. When she peeped out of the window from behind the blackout blind, she could see the shapes of people running below in the gloomy evening dusk.

To Evie's dismay Molly swept the dishes from the table. Then, bending to snatch open the door of the Morrison shelter, which was disguised as the table, she bundled them inside.

Five minutes later they were all huddled together, listening again to the siren that heralded the return of the Luftwaffe.

It was early next morning when Molly woke, surprised to find that she had fallen soundly asleep during the night. Her arm was numb, wound over the children as they lay curled together.

Slowly stretching and easing herself out of the Morrison,

she made her way to the passage, unhooked her coat and drew it round her shoulders.

The morning light crept under the blinds in the front room and she hurried down the stairs, anxious to discover if there was any damage to the shop.

All was secure; the jars, bottles, packets and tins were still on the shelves and she peeked under the blind to the window which was now letting in the dawn light.

It was a damp morning outside. The roofs of the houses were glazed with dew and there were dirty puddles in the road. An hour or so later, after the children were up, they all rushed downstairs to see who was banging at the back door.

'Are you all right?' Jean asked in concern as she stood with Simon and Susie.

'We slept through it all in the Morrison. What happened in the night?'

'Dunno. I've asked everyone in Roper Street and other than the racket of the siren, like us they didn't see or hear anything. Dennis is still out with the fire brigade, so somewhere must have bought it.'

'The kids are ready for school, but I wasn't sure about sending them.'

Jean shrugged. 'Might as well. No sense in keeping them home if the coast's clear.'

Molly called to Mark and Evie and after Liz arrived to open the shop, she and Jean and the children set off for school.

Once again Molly gave thanks it wasn't their part of London that had been attacked. But how long would that last?

*

It was just before midday when Liz left the shop, much earlier than usual as she had to help her housebound aunt in West Ham. Molly was told this was a temporary measure, but she missed the easy-going hours they had once enjoyed.

So Molly was alone when Dennis and Jean walked into the shop looking pale and sombre. At once Molly's mind went to the children.

Guessing her thoughts, Jean said quickly, 'It's nothing to do with the kids.'

'Thank God for that.' Molly relaxed, until Dennis spoke.

'You ain't listened to the wireless, then?'

'No. Why?'

'They've just put out a bulletin. Last night there weren't no raid.'

'But there was! I heard the warning. We all did.'

'Our ARP batteries heard the sound of gunfire too. That set off the alert. They dunno quite what happened, but everyone made for the Bethnal Green tube, as it was the nearest shelter to the sound of the ack-ack.'

'So the bombers did fly over?'

'Not a bleeding sign of them.' Dennis swallowed and wiped his dirty face with even dirtier hands. 'According to the official government statement put out this morning, someone tripped on the tube stairs and fell. There ain't no handrail and there's about nineteen steps what lead down from the street. It was dark and wet and no one could see where they were going. They fell one on top of each other, piling up like bloody dominoes.'

Molly took a horrified breath. 'Were there many

casualties?' Expecting Dennis to say there were a few, she felt sick when he answered.

'By the time we arrived with the fire engines and ambulances, they was laying them out in the street. Over a hundred at the first count, and by the time we left in the early hours, we'd counted another fifty.'

Molly and Jean stared at each other. It was too terrible to think of, and they looked at Dennis who had witnessed the tragedy at first hand. His eyes were red-rimmed and swollen. Molly realized he must have shed many tears throughout the night.

'Dennis, I don't know what to say,' she whispered hoarsely.

'I never seen nothing like it.'

'Do you know what the gunfire was about?'

'Someone said a new kind of bomb was being dropped.'

'Was it?' asked Jean, searching her husband's face.

'Dunno. There's rumours flying everywhere. People say foreign agents infiltrated and planned it all. Whatever it was, I'll never forget them bodies and dragging 'em out from the stairwell.'

Molly saw that Dennis was in no state to talk. His hands were shaking and Jean took his arm and said softly, 'Come on, Den, let's go home.'

He didn't seem to hear her and gazed into space; Molly knew he couldn't forget what he'd witnessed.

Accompanying her friends to the door, she watched them leave the shop and walk slowly down the street.

Once again, the thought in her mind was: this was what war did to people. There were no rules or regulations to prevent tragedy happening and in cases like this, when there hadn't been one German bomber seen overhead, people were saying it must be spies.

What could possibly come next?

For days after, the East End buried their dead once again. Molly listened in sympathy to her frightened customers. Some had relatives or friends who had been in Bethnal Green on that rainy night when mysterious gunfire had set off the stampede in the tube stairwell.

No one had an answer. It was all suggestion and suspicion. There was an endless array of propaganda posters, pamphlets, booklets and leaflets issued to the general public. Molly refused to put up any in the shop and was immediately reproached by Mr Stokes.

'Come along, Molly,' he told her, waving the poster in the air. 'You've got a space in your window. It's only fair to give people warning.'

'I've got enough trouble,' she argued, 'with Evie and Mark listening what the kids say at school. Like "Careless Talk Costs Lives" and "War Spies – Keep it Under Your Hat". It frightens the kids.'

'This poster's not bad,' cajoled Mr Stokes. '"Loose Lips Sink Ships".' He waved it in front of Molly.

'Yes, and immediately Mark would think of his dad at sea. I'm sorry, but the answer's no.'

Molly was relieved when the prime minister finally decided to soothe the nation's unrest. His long-awaited statement to the general public was, at last, positive:

'We have reached the conclusion that existing orders can now be relaxed and the church bells can be rung on Sundays and other special days to summon worshippers to church.'

It wasn't much, Molly thought to herself, but it had the desired effect.

Church bells rang all over London at the weekend, and when Andy's letter plopped on the mat the following week, it was hard for Molly to contain her delight at his news. Passing his finals with flying colours had earned him an unbelievable ten days' leave!

The date they could expect him home was set for Sunday, 23 May. He would catch the early train to London and arrive in time for dinner.

Molly was over the moon!

Chapter Twenty-Six

May arrived with a warm rush of spring air, a little light rain and a burst of high temperature. Molly was in a whirl of excitement. As she had a room spare now and Andy would have her father's bed to sleep in, she bought a pair of good second-hand pillowcases from the market and a navy-blue feather eiderdown that just needed a little darning. She also invested a shilling in a pair of men's slippers. They were almost new and looked about Andy's size.

'Why don't we have a party?' Jean suggested one day. 'A sort of congratulations and welcome home all in one.'

'Where would I hold it? Upstairs might be too small and we ain't got a yard.'

'We have though,' offered Jean. 'If the weather's good as this, we could put up a bit of bunting. Lay the food out on the ARP trestles. And have some booze indoors for the blokes.'

'That's a nice thought, Jean, but what about Dennis? He ain't been himself lately.'

'A knees-up will do him good. It'll be just like old times. Harry's old enough now to come out with Cissy and Spot, and why don't you ask Lyn and your dad to visit? I mean, it would be the perfect time to get them together with Andy and the kids.'

At first Molly was uncertain. Would Lyn consider the offer? They hadn't seen each other since the day she last came to the shop. But the more she thought about it, the better she liked Jean's suggestion.

So she wrote and asked her father and sister if they could come to a family party in celebration of Andy passing his finals. To her surprise, the answer came very quickly. 'It's about time the family got together,' Lyn wrote. 'You'll be pleased to see how well Dad's keeping. The country air seems to suit him. I really do think it would suit you too. I miss you, dear, and hope you'll consider a relocation.'

Molly sighed as she read the letter. It was typical of Lyn to miss the point of Andy's success and mention her own agenda of persuading Molly to move to Sidcup.

Oh well, she thought, I'll be proud to show Andy and the kids off. They were her family now and the sooner Lyn accepted that, the better.

The day came and Molly was both nervous and excited. The weather had held and it was a beautiful May day. She was up with the lark, cooking, baking and trying to calm her nerves. Dennis had come out of himself a little in order to help with the party. He'd organized the kids, mustering them to hang the paper flags they'd made around the back yard and over his shed roof. The small patch of brown grass had been trimmed and the tables laid out.

At eleven o'clock, an hour before Andy was expected, they ferried the food Molly had cooked down to Jean's. Molly gave the four children baskets and bags full of cakes, pies, pastries, pickles and preserves, while Jean's old pram was used for the knives, forks, plates and tumblers that were to be set on the table in the Turners' kitchen.

At a few minutes past the hour a noisy green van came spluttering up the road and parked outside the Turners'. Molly saw it from Jean's window and called to everyone that Spot and Cissy and the baby had arrived.

There were gasps of delight as Spot whispered he'd managed to procure a van for the day and in the rear was enough beer to last for the duration.

No one asked any questions. And when Cissy climbed out, handing the child in her arms to Spot, everyone gathered round.

'Ain't he a charmer?' said Spot as he bounced Harry in his arms.

'He's enormous!' Jean squealed as she tickled Harry's plump chin. 'And such a bonny little boy.'

Molly agreed, but was most happy to see that Cissy looked radiant in a smart white tailored jacket and skirt with her thick and glossy dark hair pinned up in an elegant roll at the back of her head.

'Dunno where he gets his good looks from,' Cissy laughed as they all paraded into the house and out into the yard. 'Reckon he got left on the doorstep.'

Everyone gathered again round Harry, the focus of attention. Molly could hardly believe he was that same struggling infant whose life had hung in the balance almost five months ago.

With a head of straight dark hair and dimples in both cheeks, Harry's skin was a healthy pink. His large deep-grey eyes, like his mother's, went intently over the faces in front of him. A glistening strand of drool spun from his mouth and there were roars of laughter when he smacked his lips together and sucked them in with a burp.

Leaving the Fryers surrounded, Molly and Jean put out the rest of the food and Dennis, together with Mr Stokes, enjoyed a first beer with compliments from the large brewery crate hurried in from the back of the van.

When all was ready, Molly went up to Jean's bedroom and changed from her overall into a cool summer blouse and short skirt. She was putting the finishing touches to her appearance, brushing her auburn waves into place over her shoulders, when there was a knock at the door. Her heart was in her mouth as she ran downstairs to open it.

Expecting to see Andy, instead she found her sister and two very tall, thin children whom she barely recognized. They were all standing stiffly on the doorstep, dressed as if they had stepped this very moment from one of Selfridges' shop windows.

'Sorry we're late,' Lyn apologized from under a large white linen hat that neatly covered her bobbed fair hair. 'We started off early but the roads were congested with service vehicles. All Americans, of course. They think they own our roads.'

'Where's Dad?' Molly asked anxiously as she peered out to Oscar's car parked in the road.

'He's on his way.'

'Can he walk?'

'Slowly, with his stick. But he's so very much better than when you last saw him, thanks to our wonderful Mrs James.'

'Does she still treat him?'

'Only once every two weeks now. He'd be a wreck still if it wasn't for the physical therapy. Expensive, of course, but nothing is too much for Oscar.' Lyn gestured to her children. 'Now, Elizabeth, George, say hello to your aunt. You haven't seen her for ages.'

'Hello, Aunt Molly,' they both said at once in cut-glass accents.

'It's so good to see you.' Molly kissed her nephew and niece. They smiled politely but looked very nervous at the sound of raucous shouting echoing in from the back yard. 'My word, you're both almost as tall as your mother.'

Dark-haired, brown-eyed Elizabeth smiled, standing awkwardly in her navy-blue school blazer and green-striped summer dress. George, a year younger at eight, was coppery-haired and blue-eyed. He wore his school uniform too and Molly noted that the motto on his breast pocket was written in Latin, which she took to be a clue that he was now at the private school Lyn and Oscar had chosen for the children.

Just then, Jean appeared and embraced all three with a warm East End welcome. 'It's ages since I've seen you lot,' Jean laughed. 'Blimey, what are you feeding these kids on,

Lyn? Whatever it is, I'll have some of it for Simon and Susie! Now, I can see Bill's on his way with your husband, so let me take you outside to meet everyone. The kids are dying to see you.'

Molly watched Jean take Lyn's arm and propel her along the passage. George and Elizabeth dutifully followed and very soon drinks were being poured by Dennis, and everyone was herded out into the yard where the old gramophone with its HMV recordings had been placed for the afternoon.

Molly thought how regal Lyn looked in a pink summer coat and white gloves. Though she was an East Ender born and bred, after meeting Oscar she had certainly changed her lifestyle. Good for you, Molly thought; Lyn's was a success story, and Molly felt a wave of pride in her sister.

'Molly, girl, is that you?' a croaky voice called from the street.

Looking back, Molly saw Oscar bending to brush an invisible speck of dust from the wing of his car, careful not to dirty his grey blazer and white flannels. A few yards away was her father, limping slowly towards her, leaning heavily on his walking stick. He was stooped and puffing a little, but he looked wonderfully smart in a sports jacket and tweed cloth cap. Even his walking stick was decorated with a gleaming brass trim. Molly could see Lyn's personal touches to this East End shopkeeper who had been transformed into a country gent.

He stood very still and smiled his lovely smile, reminding her that this was the father she loved and missed so much.

*

Andy made his way down Roper Street, as he had many times before. He was running late, well over an hour, as there had been delays on the line, and though every instinct told him to veer towards the shop, he passed it with a cursory glance.

Skirting the crater in the road, he listened for the sound of children, for Molly had said she and the kids would meet him at Jean's. Since it was a Sunday she had said the youngsters would all be playing together; it would fill in the time for them as they excitedly awaited his arrival.

He was grateful for this, for the friendship and support this little family had given his kith and kin. And he looked on Dennis as his best mate, a bloke he could truly rely on.

He was thinking about what Molly had written, of the impact of the Bethnal Green tragedy, when he was startled out of his thoughts. There in the road was the biggest car he'd ever seen, with a shine on it to equal his boots on parade morning.

There was no one around. He paused to study its magnificence, straightening his shoulders under his navy-issue duffel jacket. Then, as the Turners' front door opened, a slim, auburn-haired woman appeared, dressed in a white short-sleeved blouse and short dark skirt. His heart did a loop-the-loop. Molly's hair reminded him of English chestnuts in an autumn wood as it flowed over her shoulders. In the next breath she was running towards him and he to her.

'Oh, darling, darling,' she whispered as she threw herself into his arms.

Andy held her close. 'Molly, my God, Molly. I'm not dreaming this, am I?'

She laughed then, her brown eyes seeming to be alight. 'If you are, we're in the same dream together. Welcome home.'

Grinning, he looked over her shoulder. 'I want to kiss you and not stop but I suppose I'd better wait.'

'Maybe. The house is full of kids.'

'Is the mayor visiting?'

'No. That's Oscar's car.'

He shook his head slowly. 'It's a wonder it ain't got the Union Jack on the front.'

'I don't think that's Oscar's style.'

He pushed back a lock of her hair, feeling its softness. Oh, how he'd longed just to do that. 'Are Mark and Evie okay?'

'They will be, when they see you.'

'The train was delayed. Nothing I could do but count the minutes till I got here.' A soft trickle of music floated in the air. 'Has Dennis got hold of a brass band?'

'You've got a surprise waiting.'

'Is it one I'm gonna like?'

'I think so.' She took hold of his arm and marched him to the Turners' front door. 'Wait there.'

He held his breath, watching her hurry down the hall, his eyes unable to leave her slim and graceful shape. Suddenly Vera Lynn's 'White Cliffs of Dover' was interrupted and all went quiet. When she returned she put her hands over his eyes. 'Keep them closed. And don't peep.'

He did as he was told, absorbing the warm and homely

smells as she pulled him along; the tantalizing aromas of cooking, floating on the air like an invisible streamer.

Then she stopped, her hand dropping away. 'You can open them now,' she whispered and he did, dragging in a gasp of surprise as the world and his wife appeared before him, clapping and cheering as Mark and Evie ran forward and threw themselves into his arms.

'Hello, son, congratulations,' Molly heard her father say, as after all the welcome pats on the back, Andy took a seat beside Bill. 'Molly told us you'd passed them examinations. You should be proud of yourself.'

'Thank you, Mr Keen.'

'Not so much of the Mr Keen. It's Bill. I've heard a lot about you. All good, I'm pleased to say.'

'I'm relieved to hear that.' Andy looked at Molly, a slight flush on his face. Then he turned back to Bill and the two men fell into conversation.

Molly hovered uncertainly; Lyn and Oscar were talking to Mr Stokes who had brought his wife, Elaine, a small but boisterous lady who was an active member of the WVS.

Molly knew Andy and Bill would hit it off but she guessed that Lyn and Oscar would have their reservations. For after all, Andy was not about to impress with either an educated accent or a life story that would hold their attention. She could already see that Lyn was watching George and Elizabeth, who were clearly enjoying the loud music with Simon, Susie, Mark and Evie.

Just then, Lyn turned and met Molly's gaze. She nudged

Oscar, and they left the Stokeses and made their way towards her.

Molly decided to get the introductions over quickly. 'Lyn, Oscar, this is Andy Miller. Andy, my sister and her husband.'

Andy shot to his feet and put out his hand. 'Pleased to meet you,' he said and added quickly, 'Molly's often spoken about you.'

'Has she?' Lyn said frostily, quickly shaking hands.

'Andy's home for ten days,' Molly continued. 'As I wrote, he's passed all his exams.'

'For what?' Oscar asked, a frown stretching across his high forehead and accentuating his large ears.

'Signals,' said Andy simply. 'I was in the merch and decided to volunteer.'

'Not the Royal, then?' Oscar dismissed.

'No, I'm afraid not.'

'Now let the boy alone,' Bill intervened, raising his walking stick an inch or two. 'Sit down, Andy, and tell us how you're doing.'

Molly saw Andy sit down, but this time he looked uncomfortable as Bill tried to extend the conversation.

Lyn looked at Molly and said a little too loudly, 'Have you given any thought to moving out of London as we discussed?'

'No,' Molly replied, catching Andy's eye. 'I haven't.'

'You can see how much better Dad is now,' Lyn said in a high, polished tone. 'That bomb was a blessing in disguise. You could rent the shop out or close it altogether before you move to Sidcup.'

Molly felt very embarrassed. She hadn't mentioned to Andy Lyn's attempts at persuading her to leave Roper Street, and his expression was shocked.

'I don't think we should talk about that now,' Molly said, and looking at Oscar she asked, 'Can I get you another drink?'

But her sister was not to be put off. 'No time like the present,' Lyn interrupted. 'For after all, it might be a while before Oscar can get matters arranged.'

'That's enough now, girls,' said Bill, looking upset. 'We're here today to celebrate this young man's success. That's what this party is for.'

Molly managed to smile. She knew how much he hated hearing them bicker. 'Yes, that's right,' she agreed and looked into Andy's eyes. 'It's not often we get a chance to celebrate.'

Lyn was about to interrupt again when Cissy and Spot with Harry made a timely appearance. Even my sister can't fail to be won over by Harry's charms, Molly thought in panic.

But Lyn paid little attention to the baby and caught hold of Molly's arm. 'We must talk,' she said in a firm voice. 'In the house, perhaps?'

Molly nodded and together with Lyn she made her way indoors.

'This room will do,' Lyn said, pushing open the front-room door and shutting it after Molly.

'Lyn, that was rather rude,' Molly said abruptly.

'Not at all,' declared Lyn. 'This is the one opportunity I have to get your cooperation.'

'Lyn, I'm not moving. When will you accept that?'

'Dad is perfectly happy with us,' he sister assured her. 'He won't be coming back here, you know.'

'Has he told you so?' Molly asked.

'He doesn't need to. It's obvious those stairs are impractical. Besides, he likes being part of our family. And you should too. I can introduce you to new people when you live close by. You'll make new friends. Perhaps even meet someone special. After all, you're not getting any younger.'

Molly burst out laughing. She stared at her sister's pale, discreetly made-up face under the white hat.

'What's so funny?' Lyn asked in surprise.

'You are.' Molly shook her head in wonder. 'Hasn't it sunk in, Lyn? I *have* met someone special. Andy.'

'I meant someone to take care of you. And not the other way round.'

Now Molly felt very angry. 'Lyn, I won't be moving to Sidcup. I've no plans to sell the shop. And those two little children you saw, Mark and Evie, who you hardly acknowledged, I look on as my own. Their father and I hope to be married after the war. We want to spend the rest of our lives, together, God willing. It's not just about taking care of, although you may disagree. It's about love. And I've found it.'

Her sister looked at her as though she was speaking a foreign language. She took a handkerchief from her bag and carefully dabbed either cheek. Replacing it slowly, she blinked and pushed back an invisible strand of hair under her hat. Very slowly she stood up. 'This conversation is getting us nowhere. We'll talk again when you finally come round to seeing the sense in leaving the East End after it has been razed to the ground.' Her tone was so bitter that Molly hardly recognized her sister.

'I think it's time we went,' Lyn continued. 'One never knows what roads are open and what are closed. And Oscar has a committee meeting early tomorrow morning.'

Molly quickly grasped her sister's gloved hand. 'Lyn, please try to understand. You may not agree with my choices, but that doesn't make any difference to us, does it? You have a wonderful family and Dad is part of it. I'm happy for you. But I have a family too. And I hope you'll welcome Andy and Evie and Mark into your lives. It would mean a great deal to us if you did.'

Molly watched her sister's expression, hoping against hope Lyn would accept that her little sister had finally found a voice.

But that was not to be. Lyn turned, holding her head high in the white hat, and opened the door of the front room to the laughter of the children outside.

Chapter Twenty-Seven

After the big car had driven away, Molly returned wearily to the party. Harry's warmth and affection helped to distract her from the sinking sensation inside; why was it so impossible to win Lyn's approval? There seemed to be no answer to this. And though Andy hadn't mentioned the embarrassing scene, she could see that he had been hurt by her sister ignoring him.

'Well, ladies,' said Spot, emerging from the shed where the men had been ensconced, drinking beer, 'time to take me other halves home.'

'Come over and see us soon,' Cissy said as she walked with Molly to the elderly green van. 'And chin up, girl. Your sister will come round.'

'Do you think so?'

'She's got to. Or else she's the one who'll lose out.'

At these words Molly hugged her friend, who more than anyone, except Jean, knew just how much she sought Lyn's approval.

They all stood in the evening sunshine waving as the noisy vehicle trundled off. When at last it was out of sight, Molly found herself standing in the street alone with Andy.

'I enjoyed my surprise,' he whispered as he slipped an arm around her waist. 'But what was all that about moving to Sidcup?'

'I'm so sorry Lyn was rude.'

'Didn't take no notice.'

'I'm sure you did. I was hoping this could be a real family affair. But Lyn's always had her own ideas on what she thinks is best for me.'

'I gathered that. But you're a big girl now.'

'Yes. It's hard to convince her. Ever since we were small she's been the leader and I've followed. It's not so odd for the pecking order in a family. And Lyn has been so success-ful. She was clever at school and when she left she picked a wealthy husband with a high-ranking job. My world with Ted seemed to be very small in comparison.'

'But you loved Ted,' Andy said gently. 'You had something that Lyn hasn't, a real husband and a real life going on that wasn't fabricated.'

'What do you mean?' Molly asked curiously.

'Oscar's afraid to be himself. He didn't even want to drink until your dad got to him to partake. When we got him a little tipsy and told a few jokes, the man really came out of himself.'

Molly nodded thoughtfully. She had always hoped that Oscar wasn't really the stuffed shirt he portrayed himself to be. 'That was nice of you, to make him feel comfortable enough to relax.'

'I think Oscar and me will rub along.'

Molly shivered from top to toe. Andy was talking so positively and it made her feel wonderful inside. She wanted him to kiss her and she wanted to kiss him back but, smiling at each other, they walked slowly indoors.

As she helped Jean to wash the dishes, Molly was preoccupied. She had never really given Oscar much consideration over the years, but Andy had broken down the barriers in just one meeting. She loved him for this, for it had given her a new outlook on her sister's marriage and the reasons why Lyn seemed to have changed so much from the East Ender she used to be. Wealth and prosperity had forced both Lyn and Oscar to adopt roles in life that made them seem remote, even arrogant at times.

'Don't worry about it, gel,' said Jean as she tidied away the china.

'Worry about what?'

'I've been gassing for the last ten minutes and you ain't noticed.'

'Oh dear. Sorry.'

'Listen,' said Jean knowingly, 'it's you and Andy that matters. No one else.'

Molly smiled. 'Thanks. Is it that obvious?'

'Only to those who can read you.' Jean nudged her elbow and winked. 'Enjoy yourself while you've got the chance, that's my motto.'

That evening, as they left the Turners', she and Andy walked home arm in arm, while Mark and Evie scampered happily ahead. The sun was low in the sky and a crimson sunset cast a fire over the roofs of the houses, reflecting its image in all the windows. Jean was right. It was too beautiful an evening to think about anything other than how happy she was to have Andy safe beside her.

That night, after the children were in bed, Andy took her in his arms. As if by magic all her worries disappeared. She could only think of how much she loved him, and of how they would be together when the war was over.

When the war was over. The words were like a mantra in her mind. Words she could cling to that gave her all the reassurance she needed in a world that felt, at times, so alien.

Although Molly still had to open the shop that week, Andy took Mark and Evie to school and was there to meet them in the afternoons. They would call for Molly on their return and she would join them for a walk to the park, or a picnic in Island Gardens, or a game of football on the nearby pitch.

When Saturday arrived and Liz looked after the store, they all caught the bus to the city. Mark and Evie were so excited they couldn't sit still, jumping up and down to see the sights.

Molly was very proud of them. Mark wore a new pair of short trousers and a clean white shirt. Andy had run a comb under the cold-water tap, threaded it though his son's dark hair and drawn a neat parting at the side. Molly had brushed Evie's hair until it shone in gold ringlets and dressed her in a blue-and-white gingham frock. Andy had been unable to take his eyes from his growing family.

Since there had been no daylight raids in the past week, the roads were clear. It was an uninterrupted drive to Covent

Garden where they dismounted, bought sticky nougat under the great pillared entrance, and toured the many stalls.

As Mark and Evie ran around the busy area, Andy slipped his arm round Molly's waist.

'Happy?' he asked her and she nodded.

'Are you?'

'Very.'

'Do you think they know?' Molly asked as they watched the children playing.

'About us? Course they do.'

'They're special kids. Really lovely. They always make me feel liked.'

'Why shouldn't they?'

'I'm not Stella. I can't replace their mother.'

'They don't want that. They want you, Molly, the person who, next to me, loves 'em most in all the world.'

At this Molly smiled. She still had her doubts about the role she was taking on, for no one could replace a parent. But she wanted the children to know that they were safe with her and she would never let them down.

It was later, as they stood outside the imposing gates of Buckingham Palace, and Andy showed Mark the many troops guarding the home of the King and his family, that Evie began to tire.

Molly lifted her into her arms and felt two skinny legs curl tightly around her waist.

''As the King got a princess in there?' she whispered tiredly, her head dropping to Molly's shoulder.

'He has – two, in fact.'

'Can we see 'em?'

'Sometimes they stand on a balcony.'

'They ain't standing there today.'

No answer was needed as Evie fell soundly asleep, her breath warm on Molly's neck.

'Enough sightseeing,' Andy said in Molly's ear as he returned with Mark. 'Let's find somewhere to eat.'

The bus took them to a British Restaurant canteen, and for under a shilling, they ate as much as they possibly could. Molly was surprised to find the food piping hot: mashed potato spread over minced meat with carrots and green peas. For afters there was stodgy pudding stuffed with real raisins.

'Dead flies, ain't they?' decided Evie. 'But I like 'em anyway.'

Even Mark laughed at this and failed to argue the point.

By the time they reached home, the children were ready for bed. As had become their routine, Andy told them a story about camp life and the friends he had made there. There were a few yawned questions, but soon they were asleep.

When Andy returned to the front room, Molly was waiting, flushed and content. He took her in his arms and held her gently.

'Molly, let's go to bed too.'

In reply, Molly kissed him passionately, her body longing for his love. He took her hand and they tiptoed along the passage, pausing briefly to listen to the soft snores inside the children's bedroom.

Like thieves in the night they crept into Molly's bedroom and soon they were in bed, bodies entwined.

'This is the best part,' Andy told her as they lay there. 'Knowing we've got all night and waking up to find you there in the morning.'

'Where else would I be?'

He gave a deep sigh and kissed her mouth with such sweetness that Molly wished she could keep the taste of his lips on hers forever.

'I love you, Andy,' she told him, her fingers folding over the muscle of his arm. 'I need you and the strength you give me.'

'I want to protect you, Molly,' he replied, pressing her so closely she thought they felt like one. 'I don't want to go to war and leave you and the kids. Look what you've gone through already to keep them safe. But as I have no choice in the matter, I'd like to take these memories with me. It's the closest I'm going to get to the vows we'll make when it's all over. Does that make sense?'

'Perfectly,' Molly whispered, and their kiss was the seal on their tryst.

If Molly had thought that guilt would creep into her thoughts, she was wrong; guilt that Ted was gone and she was loving another man in his place, when their lives had once been bound together so intensely in marriage and by their love for Emily.

What she felt for Andy was an entirely different emotion; it was a kind of arriving 'home' after the wilderness years. She could leave behind that void of darkness and desperation she had felt after losing her daughter, the chasm that had never been bridged for either Ted or herself. Ted had gone to war – his calling, and his redemption, despite his tragic death. But she had been left, wondering why she had survived to handle the pain alone, her only comforts the shop and Dad.

And then Dad had gone. A loved one removed once again from her life, and she'd had to face the fact she was alone, having to come to terms with loss thrice over. Yet fate had been kind to her. She had stumbled somehow into Andy and the children's lives and found a different kind of loving.

As Andy lay beside her, exploring her body and bringing her such exquisite joy, Molly gave thanks. She wasn't sure who to, for she wasn't a religious person, though she had sometimes uttered a prayer in those dark times of the blitz.

Now her thanks were combined with a knowledge of herself that she had never had before. She was prepared to give herself completely and take the chance. For who knew what was to happen in the future?

For now, she took what she could: his kisses, his ragged words of desire, his beautiful naked body and the uninhibited pleasure he gave her beyond all physical expectation.

But mostly, the love. Unconditional. Yet committed. Loving her as she loved him. For however much longer they had together.

Over the coming weeks and months, after Andy had returned to camp, Molly was to think many times of his lovemaking. The unpleasantness with Lyn paled into insignificance, as she recalled the whispered words that she and Andy had shared.

And when in August he wrote to her that, as a commissioned signalman and Morse code operator, should he still be land-based, he was putting in for leave at Christmas. He couldn't say more, he wrote, but told her not to discount the possibility.

Liz was the one, however, to burst her bubble. One morning she brought in the daily newspaper and, opening it wide on the counter, read an extract from one of the country's best-informed war correspondents.

'"Although Britain's engagement in the Atlantic has been highly successful over the summer and the threat to our Allied ships from the German U-boat fleets has been countered, the theatre of war in Russia and its latest offensive is of such importance that the whole war may depend on the outcome."'

'So what does that mean for us?' Molly asked in confusion.

'Well, if our navy has done the trick in the Atlantic, where are our sailors gonna be sent next?'

Molly's heart leaped. 'I don't know. Does it say anything else?'

Liz read on. '"The American and British armies and navy are pushing forward in Sicily and Italy. Allied warships have been sent to shell the coasts, and bombers are on full assault along the length of the Italian coastline."' Liz looked at Molly and nervously adjusted her brown beret. 'Looks to me like it's all hands on deck in the Mediterranean. I reckon your Andy is likely to be drafted down there.'

'Do you really think so?'

'Dunno, love. But the papers say this is a bloody big push in Europe. Don't want to worry you, but I shouldn't count on him being home for Christmas.'

Molly knew that Liz studied the papers intently and that her friend spent many hours discussing the current situation with their customers. Was she right about this? Was the war in Europe escalating? What did that mean for Andy?

Restless thoughts whirled around in her head and for the rest of the day she couldn't relax. War was so cruel. It disrupted so many lives and often extinguished the smallest of hopes.

Her answer came in late September, when a very brief letter arrived from Andy. It bore no English postmark. By the way it read, she could tell it had been heavily censored from overseas. He told her he loved her and the children. That he missed them dreadfully and would always treasure the memories of his last leave, which would sustain him in the months to come.

Unlike his other letters from camp, this one had an ominous undertone and since no mention was made of Christmas, Molly feared that Liz was right.

As the daily wireless bulletins increased in number and Molly listened with the customers in the shop, it was clear to one and all that the war in Europe was reaching a climax.

Which way would it go, everyone questioned? When the conquered Italy decided to declare war on Germany, its once ally, all the customers cheered. But when the sickening news came through of the Nazi capture of a Benedictine monastery at Monte Cassino, transforming it into an impenetrable fortress, everyone stood still, shocked by the reports of the slaughter that was taking place on such holy ground.

Molly felt as though she was living in a surreal world. Daily, the shop became a meeting place for people to come and absorb the latest triumphs and failures of the Allies and Russia, who had fought so long and so hard in the merciless freezing conditions against the German army.

Many customers were still waiting for news of their men scattered not only in Europe but in far-flung places like South-East Asia, Burma, New Guinea and all across the Pacific. Like Molly, none of them had any confirmation of where they were or when they would see them again.

Letters became few and far between. The postal service was erratic. Everyone dreaded the arrival of a telegram.

Molly broke it to the children in December that they were not likely to see their father at Christmas.

'Me dad's on a big ship, ain't he?' Evie said, at once accepting the fact. 'He's gonna teach us to swim when he comes 'ome. Then I can be a sailor too, like 'im.'

Molly expected Mark to correct his sister, as was their usual routine. But this time, at a very grown-up eight years old, he gave no response.

The little boy was becoming a man too early, keenly aware now that the war machine rolled steadily onward, influencing not only his own life and his sister's, but the life of the father he adored.

BOOK THREE

Chapter Twenty-Eight

Six months later, June 1944

Molly was serving her customers in the shop but her thoughts were on the day, exactly four years ago, when Ted had perished in the bloodied waters of Dunkirk. He was just one of the many thousands of men who had failed to reach the escape provided by the gallant armada of 'little boats' from Britain.

But today the nation waited for news, as the long-anticipated D-Day landings were to be confirmed, though no place details were to be given; nothing, said Churchill, that would assist the enemy.

Molly felt it was as if the whole of Britain was holding its breath. Had the Allies successfully stormed the shores of France? Headscarves had even been removed from heads to let their wearers catch every word that was delivered from the old wireless on the shop counter.

After a loud crackle and buzzing, Molly managed to tune in to the station. A terse, low-key voice began to speak.

'The King and prime minister together with General Smuts, the South African prime minister, have coordinated with supreme commander General Eisenhower at his head-quarters. Allied naval forces, supported by strong air forces, have begun landing Allied armies on the northern coast of France. The invasion of Europe has begun.'

There was a united gasp in the shop. Eyes went wide as saucers, then to a chorus of *shush!* and *quiet!* the voice informed them that no further information would be given until further notice. But the country should be aware that, on this day, a unique history was in the making.

'What bloody use is that?' one voice piped up as yet another series of crackles erupted from the wireless. 'We want to know if we're going to win. How our boys are doing. And that it's not going to be another fiasco like '40.'

''Ere, watch what you're saying,' someone else returned. 'Our Molly's Ted copped it then.'

'Aw, sorry, Molly, gel, don't mean no harm.'

Molly shrugged her indifference and a babble of excited voices all began to talk at once. The consensus of opinion was that the Allies, joined with the United States of America, were determined first to liberate France, the stepping stone to Europe.

That night, after the shop was closed, Molly reread the last letter she had received from Andy almost three months ago. It was a letter that went to her heart: shaky handwriting on crumpled blue paper and words that spoke both of his cour-age, and also his desperation.

There was no mention of the Christmas that had passed

without him. Nor was there any clue as to his fortunes. He repeated several times how much he loved her and the children and would forever, no matter what happened in the next few months. This had been too much for Molly and she'd shed many tears, knowing their love had sustained him but also that he now feared more than ever losing a future that was their shared dream.

Later, before Molly checked on the children, she went downstairs to the shop and turned on the wireless. She listened with both relief and trepidation to the late-night bulletin broadcast to reach the whole country.

'The prime minister, Mr Churchill,' the voice said solemnly, 'told members of parliament tonight that our Allied forces, despite sustaining losses, have penetrated several miles inland on the French coast after enemy batteries have been weakened by bombing from our naval ships and air force.'

As Molly stood still, staring at the blackout blind and the pale shaft of moonlight creeping in under the shop door, she suddenly knew that Andy was there, in the midst of battle in France.

It was a feeling like no other. A certainty. An instinct.

She reached out to switch off the wireless and the room spun. Andy was in the very same place where Ted had perished. She didn't need anyone to tell her that fate could be as cruel as it was kind.

History was repeating itself, she thought, clutching the counter tightly as she went hot and cold, a clammy sweat breaking over her forehead.

All she could do was hope – and pray. And that night, she did both.

'Get this out, old man, and right away. There's no time to lose. The bulkhead's been breached.'

'Badly?' Andy enquired.

'There'll be no repairs, let's put it like that.'

'Are we losing power?' Andy managed to blurt as he stared up at the sweating senior officer.

'As soon as the engine rooms are flooded, we'll have no generator. So get along with it, lad. We have to let the rest of the division know where we've—' He paused, tipping back his peaked cap, and swept his wet forehead with the back of his hand. 'Where we are,' he corrected himself, managing a brave grin. 'And Andy, kit yourself up for the water, right? Don't leave it too long.'

Andy just stared at the dirtied, round and amiable face of Bruce Jefferson, an officer who had taken him under his wing since he'd boarded in December. Bruce understood that Andy had had to live down the insult of being a part of the Wavy Navy; the contempt for volunteers was widespread – something Andy hadn't reckoned on.

But he'd turned a deaf ear to the insults and Bruce had advised him always to look every bastard in the eye; he was as good as the next man every time.

Andy admired him for that. But as he looked Bruce in the eye now, he knew their time together was up. He grabbed a strip of paper and scribbled an address. Tearing it from the pad, he handed it to Bruce. 'If – if anything happens, do me a last favour? Tell her. Face to face. Tell her I love her. And the kids. I love them all.'

Bruce took the paper and stuffed it in his pocket. 'I'll do my best.'

Andy could see on the officer's face the same gut-wrenching fear he felt in his belly, and he guessed at this moment it was imprinted on every face aboard HMS *Avenge*. It didn't matter about rank, or creed, or colour. The sea was master of all.

'Good luck, old son,' Bruce said quietly, and then he was gone.

Andy felt the roll and sway of the sinking battleship, and the loneliness of his situation engulfed him. He thought of those days at camp when he'd had such high hopes of bettering himself and making Molly and the kids proud. Of how every night he'd planned a future: a little boarding house, maybe, or even another shop if Molly was of a mind. And maybe – just maybe – in the years to come, a brother or sister for Mark and Evie.

Their names flew around in his thoughts and his eyes filled with desperate tears. But as another forceful listing of the vessel caused him to hold on to his desk, he felt a cold calm come over him.

Regaining his position at a lopsided angle, he tapped a last message on the knob of the key. He had already developed a 'glass arm' from hours of sending signals, but that was before – before—

Andy pulled himself together and adjusted his headphones; the tap, tap, tapping fading and then returned with a frightening force.

He glanced once again at the tactical signal passed to him and knew it was imperative to deliver the coded message before the end.

He was fiercely attempting to report the situation, when he felt the first cold fingers of seawater at his ankles.

Another sharp listing, creaking and an almighty surge of water in the corridor outside. He completed his last message, tried to stand and was sucked down in one huge gulp by a filthy whirlpool, too much of a weight to resist.

He bobbed up and gasped for air. Catching hold of a metal bar, he tried to wade forward. Then he realized he was at an acute angle in the upside-down ship. His ears were deafened with the sounds of tearing metal, and his strength began to ebb away in the swirling waters.

Two weeks after D-Day, Molly and the children were back in the Turners' Anderson once more. They were listening for spluttering engine sounds, the noise of the enemy's new 'miracle weapon': a pilotless flying bomb that dropped from out of the sky like a stone.

'That bloody Goebbels,' Jean said, referring to the German propaganda minister, as they cowered on the benches. 'Telling us we were all doomed. He put the fear of God into everyone.'

'Our boys have got their work cut out on the ack-ack,' Dennis said, as he rechecked the security of the steel door once again. 'Just listen to 'em. Giving them buzz bombs hell.'

'But why ain't they stopped them at the coast?' Jean asked

in a whisper as a lethal drone passed overhead and continued on its way.

'It ain't for the want of trying,' Dennis answered as he drew Susie and Simon onto each knee. 'They've got the Spits and Mustangs and Tempests out too, trying to pick them off in the air, but there's so many of them they still reach us.'

'It's when their engines cut out, that's what scares me,' Molly said quietly, waiting for the next rattle in the sky. 'And the silence afterwards.'

Jean nodded, retying her headscarf and picking up the thermos to pour another cup of tea. 'It's any time of the day or night as well. Here, Molly, you'll have to come and stay with us if this carries on. That steel cage you've got ain't no bloody use. You and the kids can sleep in our front room.'

Molly knew that Jean was right. The V-1 bombs were extremely destructive, causing widespread devastation; they also set off a huge blast wave, bringing down everything in the near vicinity. Even this Anderson was really of little use.

'I've shut the shop so many times now,' Molly said anxiously, 'that I'm beginning to wonder if I should just close down for the time being.'

'God only knows how long this is going to carry on,' said Dennis. 'Our only hope is that our forces will find where they're being launched from. It's gotta be near the coast somewhere.'

Just then, a thud and a rippling vibration went through the shelter. They all fell to the floor, covering their heads. Molly flung herself over Mark and Evie. She knew that her body would be no protection, but it was a reflex action.

As she lay there, the corrugated ceiling rained down dust and dirt and the mechanical noise in the sky grew louder. It was a horrible spluttering and grinding and as they all waited for it to pass over, Molly made a vow that she wasn't going to let the children out of her sight. School was over for them while these monster bombs were active.

She heard Evie whimper and felt Mark shaking. Jean was kind to offer her accommodation – but against such a powerful weapon, no house or shelter had any defence. Tomorrow, she would shut the shop and go down the tube, for at least there was a chance of survival down there.

Despite the Allies' success on D-Day, people never knew when the V-1s were going to fly over. Molly decided that her plan to use the tube wasn't practical. She would never get to the nearest underground in time, and being caught out in the open would be terrifying for the children. The school had shut its doors and so Molly wrote on the sign on the shop door, *Closed until further notice.*

She had put by some money for a rainy day and hid it under the floorboard together with Dad's savings. She would use this while there was no business and hope that her nest egg would last until she could reopen.

It was Dennis who solved the problem of shelter, for he remembered that the shed next to the burned-out bicycle factory had been built with a cellar.

They opened the creaky trapdoor, navigated the stone steps and cleaned the cellar below. To make it more cheerful, some of the contents from the Anderson were taken down

into the freezing cold room. But even in June the air temperature was so low, they could see their breath.

The children hated it. Molly and Jean did too, but Dennis
gave them a lecture that as a member of the Heavy Rescue
Squad, he would not be on hand to protect them when the
buzz bombs flew over.

So Molly brought down the duckboards from the flat and
they furnished the cellar with two old chairs that had lost
their stuffing and were to be thrown out from Mr Stokes's
hoard.

The trapdoor above was heavy and shut out all light, so
tilley lamps were installed, but they ate up the oxygen and
caused the children to cough.

A month passed with constant bombings, and the terror
of V-1s became widespread. Mark and Evie had continual
coughs from the cellar's dank and dusty atmosphere; no one
wanted to go down there, even for short periods.

On a beautiful day in late August, Molly noticed that
people were venturing out on the streets. When Liz, with a
beaming smile, knocked on the shop window, Molly knew
it was good news at last.

'They reckon our lads have found and destroyed the V-1
launch sites in France!' Liz declared as Molly opened the shop
door.

'Really?' Molly sighed in relief. 'Thank goodness for that.
We hate that bloody cellar.'

'No wonder. You'll all catch your death down there.'

'Like it or not, it's the best place to be when those buzz
bombs appear.'

'Who's this coming up the road?' Liz said, tugging down her grey hat and squinting into the distance. 'Blimey, it's a uniform. It ain't Andy, is it?'

All thoughts of the lethal missiles went from her head as Molly stood very still, her heart thudding with anticipation. She suddenly felt as though she could brave any enemy there was; the cellar didn't matter, nor did the buzz bombs. Andy was home!

She hurried past Liz and out into the street. But then, as her eyes focused on the tall figure in naval uniform, making his way past the hole in the road, her heart sank.

It wasn't Andy at all, but a stranger. A man pausing every so often as if searching for the street numbers.

A few feet away, the naval officer removed his cap, tucking it under his arm. His hair had been cut so short she could see peculiar patches of brown on his scalp.

Molly knew then, as he stood before her and said in a low, grim tone, 'Mrs Swift? I'm Bruce Jefferson. I served with Andrew Miller aboard HMS *Avenge*,' that Andy wouldn't be coming home.

'Sit down,' Molly said, standing very still in the front room, as though if she didn't move, the moment when the senior Royal Naval officer approached her in the street would disappear. As if he had been an illusion.

'I'm very sorry to have brought you such distressing news, Mrs Swift,' said Bruce Jefferson, cap under his arm as he chose the armchair by the mantel, folding his long legs and sitting stiff-backed to watch Molly eventually sink down on the settee.

'What happened?' Molly asked, her voice so distant it was like a whisper. 'Do you know?'

'The last I saw of Andy, he was in the signals room, messaging the fleet that we had sustained a direct hit and giving them the coordinates of the enemy.'

Molly wanted to ask if there had been time – if he'd – if there was a chance he might have survived … but she couldn't find the courage. If she didn't ask the questions and Bruce Jefferson was not offering any answers then there might still be hope.

It was then the tears crept through like sharp shards of glass through her eyes. Tears that were every bit as agonizing as those she'd shed for her daughter and husband. More so, perhaps, for this time there was a finality written in the officer's eyes along with the pity.

'He did say –' Bruce Jefferson began hesitantly – 'he asked me to tell you that he loved you and the children. There was no time for more, I'm afraid. It was a case of doing our very best in what limited time we had.' He bent his head and Molly saw that the patches of brown on his scalp were injuries of some kind that had just begun to heal.

'He was a good man,' continued the officer. 'He was a brave man. And I count myself fortunate to have served with him.'

Molly quickly wiped the dampness from her cheeks with her handkerchief. She didn't need telling; she knew all that Andy Miller comprised, down to his very core. They had become one, a very special completeness, a once in a lifetime experience that they had both believed – no! *knew* – would last forever.

'Did you find him? Did they find his—'

Before she could finish the officer shook his head slowly. 'I'm sorry, I have no more information. You will of course receive notification from the War Office. Is there any way I can help? This must come as a dreadful shock to you.'

Molly looked into his face and wondered if Andy had suffered. Then, shaking her head slowly, she said, 'My friend follows the conflict very carefully and guessed that Andy might be part of the assault on the French coast. But I think I knew it anyway. I don't know how; the feeling was just there.'

'A lot of brave men perished that day. But for a great cause, though that of course can be of very little comfort.'

'How did you find me?' Molly asked. 'After all, I'm not a relative.'

'I found Andy an amiable but very private man,' Bruce Jefferson replied. 'But the one part of his life I knew something about was his intention to return to his family: Mark, Evie and Molly. Before we parted he wrote down your address and asked me to find you should it be necessary.' Once more he looked down at his cap. 'I was fortunate. Though I sustained injuries, they were superficial. I was discharged from hospital yesterday and came straight here.'

'Thank you,' Molly said quietly. 'I'm grateful.'

'Have you a family member or friend who can be here with you?'

Molly nodded. Cissy had taken the children down to Jean's for the morning and she was to join them later. But for now, she wanted to be on her own. To absorb this loss which seemed so unreal, and so unjust. She stood up slowly and Bruce Jefferson did the same.

He took an envelope from his pocket. 'Inside you will find my address. I live just outside London. If you need me in the next week or so I can be here in a very short time. The Allies, after the successful invasion, are driving south in Europe and so I shall be recalled very soon to duty. But you have my telephone number there – just in case.'

Molly bit back the emotion that was filling her and put out her hand. 'Thank you again for coming in person.'

He looked into her eyes and for a moment she was afraid he might not leave, so great was his concern for her. But she needed desperately to be alone and release the grief inside before seeing Jean and the children. He must have sensed her discomfort, as he bade her goodbye and saw himself down the stairs.

She heard the back door go and stood very still, gazing down at the white envelope in her hands, waiting for the tears to come.

Chapter Twenty-Nine

And so there was another new world in which Molly found herself. Another beginning that seemed too much like an end. This time she had in her care two orphaned children; Mark and Evie had only her to rely on. If she hadn't met Andy and his family, she wondered as the days passed, what would she have done with herself? Moved out to Sidcup? Or stayed in the East End, living through the bombing with only herself to worry about?

But that other life hadn't happened. Nothing could ever make her regret falling in love with Andy and sharing what little time they'd been spared together.

'Get the shop open again, gel,' advised Cissy a fortnight later as they sat in Cissy's large and airy kitchen while Harry enjoyed his midday nap. He was almost two now and as energetic as a spring lamb. 'There ain't been any buzz bombs for a while and it looks like we're getting the upper hand on the enemy. So in my humble opinion work is the answer for you,

Molly. It always has been. Get your teeth into something challenging.'

'I've Mark and Evie to think of,' she answered, unable to find any enthusiasm whatsover to reopen the shop. As she listened to Mark and Evie's voices drifting up from the road where they were playing with the other children, she found it hard to muster any energy at all. 'They've not got a mum or dad now, Cissy. They come first.'

'Have you told them about Andy?'

Molly shook her head. 'They just seem so happy to be out of that bloody cellar and playing in the fresh air again. Every day we do something, a walk or a bus ride somewhere. I'll have to break it to them one day as time goes on, of course.'

'Has there been a letter from the War Office?'

'No. Nothing.'

'No news is good news.'

'Bruce Jefferson didn't hold out any hope. At least, if he did, he didn't tell me.'

'Well, love, as you are always reminding me, keep your pecker up.'

Molly gave a wistful sigh. 'Don't worry, I know I'm lucky compared to some. The news of those awful death camps in Poland is heartbreaking. And although it seems Brussels will be liberated and the French Resistance is joining with the Allies to liberate Paris, there is a wake of destruction left behind. What will happen when we have to rebuild the world afterwards—?'

Just then, Mark and Evie ran into the kitchen with

their friends, stopping Molly in mid flow. She couldn't tell how many children there were, but the many faces were a mixture of oriental, white and black. They were all so excited and yelling at once that Molly stood up to quieten them.

'What's going on?' she asked. 'You'll wake Harry. Now, one at a time.'

'It's the coppers,' gasped Mark, his dirty face full of concern. 'They're coming up here!'

'What! No! Why?' Cissy screeched, and all the children started jumping up and down. Little black pigtails flew this way and that as Molly tried to calm them. She moved towards the door to see for herself, but it burst open before her eyes. In charged a group of policemen, wooden truncheons in their hands, and pushing her aside they immediately spread out over the flat.

'Come back here!' cried Molly. 'Stop this at once!'

She knew Cissy would be having kittens, and the children, in an absolute panic, flew past her and ran down the stairs. All except Mark and Evie, who grabbed hold of her hands as a tall figure entered.

Dressed in his usual uniform of dark raincoat and trilby, Detective Constable Longman strode up to her.

'You!' Molly gasped. 'What do you want?'

'Still defending the guilty, Mrs Swift?'

'What on earth do you mean?' Molly demanded, her shock quickly forgotten, to be replaced by anger. 'Get out of here! You're trespassing!'

His smile was surly and full of contempt. 'I have a search

warrant,' he barked, 'and am authorized to search these premises.'

'What in God's name for?' Molly shrieked. 'There's nothing here you'd be interested in.'

'That's where you're wrong,' he muttered, glancing over her shoulder. Molly turned and saw Cissy with Harry in her arms, her face as white as chalk. 'Good morning, *Miss Brown*,' he said sarcastically. 'Or should it be Mrs Fryer now?'

Cissy hurried to where Molly and the children were standing. Molly could see that even the ends of her dark hair were shaking.

'What do you want in my home?' Cissy asked, hugging Harry tightly. 'Whatever it is, you won't find it here.'

The detective's light-coloured eyes narrowed as his men made noisy thumps and bumps that Molly guessed were the furniture going over. 'Is it just women and children here?' he demanded as he strode along the passage and they followed him.

'My husband's not here,' Cissy replied defensively. 'He's at work, doing his job for the council, catching rats that are a lot better-mannered than you.'

It was this insult that brought the policeman turning sharply on his heel. Pushing his face into Cissy's, he taunted, 'I couldn't give a damn about your husband, although I would like to see his face when he hears about his new wife's criminal past. For I'm sure he's going to find out when Ronnie Hook turns up on your doorstep.'

Molly heard Cissy's gasp. 'But Ronnie's in the nick!'

The policeman pulled back his shoulders and smiled

unpleasantly. It was with a look of contempt in his eyes that he replied, 'Wrong again. You see, Ronnie Hook and three others killed a guard before escaping from prison today.'

Molly managed to pretend she wasn't upset to hear this dreadful news, but she could sense Cissy's deep distress. 'So why should we be interested?' she asked.

'We apprehended the third man, who made a full confession.' He stared straight at Cissy. 'We have reason to believe that Hook and his cohort intend to find you and recover the money that you stole from him.'

'I never stole any money,' Cissy declared. 'And you can't prove it.'

'We'll see about that.' The cold light in the man's eyes had now turned to one of threat. He nodded to the policeman beside him, who came to stand before Cissy. 'Perhaps you'll feel a little more like helping us with our enquiries at the station. Resist, and we'll have to use handcuffs.'

There was silence before Cissy turned to Molly. Her chin jutted out and there was a steely look in her eyes. 'Look after Harry for me. And don't worry. There's nothing to tell them, but all the same, when Spot comes home, tell him I don't fancy a night in the jug.'

Molly watched in dismay as Cissy was marched out of the flat, a tiny figure in the midst of all the burly policemen.

Spot was on his way home, giving Nibbles enough time to cock his leg on the street corner after a long day ratting. The evening breeze had stilled, and with its disappearance a cold chill now threatened. He was eager to get home, take off his working gear and wash, so that he could play with Harry.

His lovely wife insisted on cleanliness around the kid; she might as well have inspected every inch of him with a magnifying glass, for she was terrified of catching germs.

He smiled as he strolled, hands in pockets under the lamp-light, thinking of how he'd first tease her into a cuddle and then, half naked from his ablutions, he'd chase her around the flat until he caught her. Having a cuddle depended entirely on Harry: if he was awake or kipping. And on whether or not the dinner was cooked!

Spot licked his lips. Who would have thought he'd be such a fortunate man? A beautiful, clever wife and a healthy toddler and a job that he'd managed to hold down throughout all the bombing. Nobody had a good word for those bloody V-1s that dropped like dead weights from the sky and left so much damage. The only good thing he could think of himself was the fact that they blew up the widespread colonies of rats that infested the city.

Nibbles sniffed out the escapees with no effort at all; the vermin were so disorientated. Stank to high heaven though, and were riddled with lice and ticks. Daren't tell Cissy – she'd have him bathing in carbolic!

As he opened the street door, he was stopped by the voices of Li and Cheng, who were peering out from the restaurant.

'Plenty trouble, Spot,' they both said together, looking identical in their small embroidered silk caps worn over plaited dark hair. 'Coppers come today.'

Spot stared at them bewilderedly. 'What for?'

'To take missus away.'

'What! Whose missus?' Spot demanded.

'Spot's missus.' Both heads nodded simultaneously.

'Christ almighty! You on the level?'

The heads nodded again. 'Take her down nick. Friend got Harry upstairs—'

Spot didn't wait to hear more. Heart in mouth, he leaped up the staircase and saw the front door ajar. Bursting in, he ran along the passage. The first thing he clocked was Molly holding Harry in her arms and the two kids sitting beside her on the settee. Every other article, picture and piece of furniture had been turned over.

Molly tried to keep her composure as she explained the catastrophe to Spot; how the policemen had plundered each room then taken Cissy away for questioning. But she was still shaking and upset.

'It's not Ronnie Hook but the money they're after,' Spot replied, his fury showing on his usually mild face. 'Did the copper think we'd keep a stash hidden here in our drum? He's off his rocker. Cissy didn't have a penny when I met her.' He looked with his strangely focused eyes at Molly. 'As only you and I know, Cissy ain't Cissy Brown, but Lena Cole. The real Cissy must have turned Hook over. That's why she was on the run and lied that she worked at the flour factory.'

'Oh, Spot, what a muddle,' Molly sighed, as she tried to comfort Harry who had begun to grizzle loudly. 'That detective's got it all wrong, but to explain what happened—'

'Would be a wrong move,' Spot finished for her as he took Harry in his arms and rocked him. 'All he's after is the loot.'

'But what do we do about Cissy?'

'Get her away from him, that's what,' Spot said under his breath. 'Then I'll make the bugger pay.'

'Spot, don't do anything daft.'

'They've got my wife.'

'I know. But try to think calmly.'

Spot ruffled his son's hair and returned him to Molly. He gave a little pat to Mark and Evie's shoulders as they looked up at him anxiously. 'Listen, you two, I'm sorry the coppers frightened you. But old Spot's gonna sort things out.'

'I wanna go home,' Mark said solemnly.

'I do as well,' mumbled Evie.

'Right you are, then this is our plan. I'll get you all back to Roper Street, but first I'll have Li downstairs give you a good feed. How's that sound? I'll just give him the nudge.'

Molly watched him rush out and heard his footsteps on the stairs. When he returned five minutes later he was back to his old, smiling self.

'Right you are, me loves, follow me. Li and Cheng have got a nice, comfy seat ready for you in their gaff and you can eat till you can't eat no more. By the time you're finished, I'll be back with the ratting cart to take you all home.'

Molly didn't ask more as, leaving Nibbles to guard the flat, they trailed after Spot down the stairs and into the darkened restaurant below. The golden lanterns were just being lit and a delicious smell wafted from the kitchens.

'Don't worry, gel, I'll take care of everything.' He winked at Molly then bolted out of the door.

'You eat good,' said Li, urging her forwards with many bows as he folded his hands into his long sleeves. 'Please sit here, kids.'

Molly lowered Harry onto the cushion that Li had supplied, one for each of the children so they could reach the table.

'Spot back soon,' said Cheng, appearing from the shadows. He had a long, thin moustache that drooped down below his pointed chin. 'Now, what you like?'

Molly shrugged and looked at Mark and Evie who sat with Harry in between them.

'I'm 'ungry,' said Evie, picking up the spoon.

'We'll have what you give us,' Molly decided. 'Have you something soft for Harry to chew on?'

Both men smiled. 'We got good grub for kids.'

Mark had a deep frown on his face as they waited for their meal. 'Our teacher said they eat snails.'

'It's the French who eat snails,' Molly explained with a smile. At least the Chinese restaurant was a distraction, she thought, as Harry began to blow bubbles and Mark and Evie burst into laughter at his antics.

Very soon Cheng and Li returned with small china dishes of hot food accompanied by chopsticks exactly like the ones that Cissy kept upstairs.

Well, this will keep us occupied, Molly thought as the children sucked in their long, slippery noodles and fried rice with the aid of spoons that were hidden under the cloth napkins. But to think of her friend being questioned by that bully detective was almost more than she could bear.

She felt a little better, however, when at the end of the meal she opened her fortune cookie and read that good luck was to be with her today.

Spot remained stubbornly where he stood, feet planted apart, in front of the desk sergeant. 'I ain't moving from here, old son, until I see your gaffer. At least, the man at the top.'

'I've told you, Detective Inspector Richards is on leave.' The sergeant officiously folded his arms across his chest.

'All right,' said Spot, adjusting the peak of his cap, 'the copper that's got my missus, then.'

'Who's your missus?'

'You know bloody well who it is.' Spot placed both his elbows on the desk, which was high and almost above his reach, but he made it. Pleating his fingers together and staring the man in the eye, he said quietly, 'One day you'll need my services, cocker. There ain't a street I don't visit to clean up. Rats can be a rotten curse, running all over the place, up people's legs and biting their private parts. I've seen the arse of a bigger man than you scoot down the road holding his crotch.' Spot smiled in a friendly fashion. 'Just tell the geezer I've got some information on the absconded criminal, Ronnie Hook.'

The sergeant gave a grimace, but Spot could see that he had won his attention, and after a few seconds' deliberation, the man went away.

It was not long before the man that Spot recognized from Molly's description as Longman came into view.

'You have information about Ronnie Hook?' said the copper suspiciously.

'No, but I thought it was a good opener to our conversation.'

'Wasting my time, eh?' growled the detective. 'So that's your game, is it?'

'No, chum, it's no game. Are you arresting my wife? And if so, what for?'

'That's not for you to know.'

'Oh yes it is, handsome. You've had Cissy in your custody all afternoon. For a pregnant woman who had a very difficult first childbirth and is unaccompanied by a legal beagle, I'd say you've stretched your authority a bit far.'

'I'm entitled to question her for longer if I so wish.'

'Well, have the midwife ready, then,' said Spot, patting the desk gently. 'Stress like this can bring the kid on.' He looked the moron up and down. 'And if it all went tits up, then the newspapers might get hold of the story. Now we all know how hard your bosses are trying to win Joe Public's confidence at this moment in time. So demoralizing headlines about an East End constabulary ain't really in line with your gaffer at the top's policies.'

'Are you threatening me?' the detective demanded, but by the sudden glimmer of alarm in the man's eyes, Spot sussed he was on to a winner. He had an ace up his sleeve and he was going to play it.

'Threats, no!' he exclaimed innocently. 'I'm one hundred per cent aware good old Lily Law don't take kindly to threats.

Count this as a bit of good advice, pal. Just between you and me.'

The policeman hesitated. 'Just who do you think you are?'

Spot's face darkened to its strangest. 'Just an ordinary bloke, that's who I am. Now, knowing my rights as I do, I'd like to see that warrant you've got for turning my place over. The one that Detective Inspector Richards must've signed this morning.'

The look he received back was one of barely contained fury, but also fear. Raising a bushy black eyebrow, Spot tilted his head to add, 'Unless, of course, you've had your fill for the day and want to get down the boozer with your mates. In which case, we'll forget the minor details and me and the missus will be on our way.'

Spot was barely able to hide his satisfaction as, departing like a thundercloud over the horizon, the policeman stormed off, leaving Spot with a genuine smile on his face as he awaited Cissy.

'Cissy, oh Cissy!' Molly threw her ams around her friend as they stood in the gloom of the restaurant. 'I've been so worried about you.'

'I was a bit worried meself,' admitted Cissy, shivering as she lifted Harry into her arms and hugged him. 'But I wasn't going to let them see that. They kept on asking about Ronnie but I never offered a word. Just kept shtum, with me arms folded over me belly.'

'What did Spot say to get you out?'

'He told them I was having another kid.'

'You're not, are you?'

'No, course not. But my other half thought it was a good tactic. He said if I dropped it then they was to blame as I was so delicate. And, oh yes, the important part. My husband used his noddle and took a gamble that they didn't have no search warrant.'

'What?' said Molly in surprise.

'That idiot copper took it on himself to plough in with his heavies on a bluff. He wants the money that Cissy stole.'

'But there is no money!' protested Molly. 'You're Lena Cole, not Cissy.'

Cissy nodded. 'But Longman doesn't know that. Only Ronnie does.'

'So why would Ronnie think you had Cissy's money?'

'Because I was mates with Cissy, I suppose.'

Spot interrupted their conversation. 'The rozzers are out the front, keeping watch. I've brought the cart round the back so we can all go back to Roper Street. We ain't gonna hang around here like sitting ducks.'

Spot gave a little bow to Cheng and Li before beckoning Molly, Cissy and the children to follow him through the steamy kitchens.

A cool breeze met them as they stood outside by the cart. 'I managed to nip upstairs to get the dog,' Spot whispered. 'There's nice warm bales of hay in the back and some blankets. Make yourselves comfortable.'

Soon they were all aboard and joined Nibbles in the sweet-smelling hay that hid them all from view. As Spot drove the horse and cart into the darkened alleys of

Limehouse, all was silent, with only the starry sky above for company.

Every nerve in Molly's body was on the alert as the wagon rolled gently over the damp cobbles.

Ronnie Hook was on the loose again.

When would he strike?

Chapter Thirty

The next day Molly woke in her own bed, but still with the same sense of alarm. She hurried to find Cissy and Harry, and was relieved to find them both asleep in Cissy's old bed. When she opened the door of Evie and Mark's room, she saw two small heads nestled under the covers.

Blinking the sleep from her eyes, she dressed quickly and went to the kitchen to put on the kettle. But no sooner had her hand touched the handle when she heard the creak of the back door. Opening the table drawer, she took out the rolling pin. Footsteps came slowly up the stairs. What use would a rolling pin be if Ronnie and his accomplices had broken in?

When a man and a small dog appeared, she closed her eyes in relief. 'Oh, Spot, thank goodness, it's you.'

'Sorry to give you a fright.'

'I forgot you kept watch last night.'

'Don't worry, you can put that roller away. The coast is clear.'

'I'll cook you some breakfast.'

'As much as I'd like that, I'd better get the old nag and cart back to the council's yard. I'll be back as soon as I can get away from work. Now, don't get the wind up, but I suggest you open the shop as per normal.'

'But Ronnie might come here if he escapes the coppers,' Molly replied anxiously. 'He knows Cissy lived with me before she was married.'

'Can't see him turning up here in broad daylight. Two cons would stick out like a sore thumb. But just in case, keep Cissy and Harry upstairs. Bolt the back door after me. The dog will see off anyone he hears in the yard. Have a good chinwag with your customers so there's always someone in the shop with you. I'll be back soon as I can.'

Molly followed Spot downstairs. As he instructed her, after he'd gone, she drew the two heavy bolts top and bottom, leaving Nibbles to stand guard.

Upstairs, she sat in the kitchen and tried not to let her thoughts wander, but this was an impossible task. So she prepared breakfast for the household and then, when the sound of voices outside in the street caused her to hurry to the window, she peered suspiciously out from behind the lace curtain.

It was a great relief to see Jean walking towards the shop with Susie and Simon. She had forgotten entirely that the kids were due back at school. She ran downstairs again to draw the bolts and let them in.

It turned out a very long day for Molly. After she explained to Jean all that had happened, Jean coaxed her into letting the children go to school.

'They'll drive you nuts cooped up in the flat. They'll be safe at school and I'll bring them home at teatime.'

'P'raps you're right,' Molly agreed, but after Mark and Evie had left with Jean, Cissy sat miserably in the front room with Harry. 'I don't know how long I can bring meself to hide away like this,' she said dismally as she brushed Harry's dark hair into a parting. 'My lovely home has been turned upside down. Spot is well-meaning, but I'd rather face my enemy. I'm sick of running, Molly. I thought it was all over when Ronnie was nicked. Now I'm back to square one again.'

'No, you're not,' said Molly firmly. 'You have a husband and lovely son who care for you. You're a family now, with responsibilities to each other. Try to be patient and do as Spot says.'

But Molly could tell by the look on Cissy's face she was taking this turn of events very hard. Her old defiant expression returned, and she stuck out her chin as she scooped Harry up and took him into the bedroom.

Molly herself felt no better. She jumped every time the shop bell tinkled. When strangers passed by she found herself scrutinizing them, wondering who they were. And despite all the care she had taken to follow Spot's orders, the feeling that had started last night in the ride on the cart to Roper Street only deepened. By late afternoon, she felt exhausted and decided to close up.

The last customer left and Molly drew the blackout blinds securely, then locked and bolted the shop door. But glass was easy to smash! It was as she stood considering this that someone hammered on the back door. Her heart seemed to leap out of her chest. It wasn't until Nibbles yapped that she managed to make herself move.

'Spot, is that you?' she asked before drawing the bolts.

'It's me,' he confirmed. But Molly was shaking as her fingers touched the cold metal.

'Is that my old man?' a voice said, as Cissy, with Harry in her arms, thundered down the stairs.

Spot swiped off his cap as he made his entrance. 'Everything all right?'

'Thank Gawd for that,' Cissy exploded at Spot. 'You're home at last.'

'Blimey,' Spot said with a broad grin. 'What a welcome!'

'It's not you I'm relieved to see,' Cissy muttered as she passed Harry to his father. 'It's that lav in the yard. I've had to use the pisspot all day.'

Molly found herself smiling, the tension broken for a short while, as Cissy flew across the yard to the closet.

After the three children had been fed that evening, Molly, Cissy and Spot sat at the kitchen table, which had been restored to its rightful place after the Morrison had been removed to the cellar of the bicycle factory. Everyone hated the contraption – almost as much as they hated the cold, damp cellar.

'So this is what I found out from Cheng and Li,' Spot said, in a low voice so the children wouldn't hear. 'The law is staked out in Narrow Street. Two bloody great goons done up to look like dockers, reading newspapers and prowling around like scalded cats. Ronnie Hook must be having a laugh if he's clocked them.'

'Did they see you?' asked Cissy anxiously.

'Not likely. Went in through Cheng's back door.'

'Is there any chance the law will catch Hook?' asked Molly.

'With those two nitwits stuck outside, the most they're gonna catch is a cold.'

'But we can't stay locked up like this all the time,' Cissy complained irritably.

'Listen, love, you've got to be patient,' admonished Spot. 'What would you do if you was Ronnie?'

Cissy shrugged disinterestedly. 'Dunno.'

'I'll tell you what he'll do. He'll lay low until the blue-bottles get fed up and leave.'

'And when will that be?'

'Our detective friend will realize he's on to a loser when he sees the flat is empty. He can't afford to waste time. If he hasn't found Hook, his gaffer will be after him for results.'

'I still don't see how that helps us,' Cissy said morosely.

'Cheng's going to give me the nudge when the stake-out's over. We'll move back in then. For now, I'll be here to keep you girls company, just in case.'

Molly felt a little better, though she still wasn't certain that Spot was any real match for these villains should they decide to pay the shop a visit.

'So what about Molly when we do go home?' Cissy asked, reading Molly's thoughts.

'If Hook ain't been nabbed by then, Molly and the kids come with us.'

'But I've got the shop to think of,' protested Molly. 'There's been enough interruptions to business with the bombing. And there's school. The children will wonder why they're not attending.'

'Let's take it a day at a time,' Spot said as he rubbed his chin. 'The law might nab Hook soon, if we're lucky.'

'What if we're not?' Cissy demanded. 'Ronnie Hook is a—'

Just then a low, deep thud shook the walls briefly. A shower of dust fell down from the ceiling. The vibration continued for a few seconds and then there was a long, eerie silence.

'What was that?' breathed Molly as they looked at one another. 'The Luftwaffe? The siren hasn't gone.'

'No. But they've been wrong before.'

No one knew quite what to do. Cissy hurried to the children and Spot went downstairs.

Molly listened for every sound. She could only hear Cissy and the children, and Nibbles yapping downstairs. After a few minutes, her thudding heart began to settle. If it was a V-1 then the newspapers must be mistaken. The launch sites of the deadly bombs were still in action.

The minutes ticked slowly by and another faint thunder roll shook the air. The hours passed with noises in the distance that no one could identify. When Molly went to bed she lay awake, listening to the sounds of the night. Not only was Ronnie Hook out there, but there was something else too. Could it be a resumption of the V-1s? The prospect depressed her almost as much as the thought of Ronnie Hook.

'Oh, Andy,' she whispered as she turned her face into the pillow. 'I wish you were here.'

It was Liz, the following morning, who brought news with her that took everyone's mind off their troubles.

'Staveley Road in Chiswick was bombed last night,' she gasped breathlessly. 'And it wasn't a V-1.'

'What was it?' Molly, Cissy and Spot all asked in unison.

'It was something out of the sky like a rocket. There was another one in Epping Forest and another not far off.'

'But how can this be?' Molly said bewilderedly. 'The siren didn't go.'

'Whatever it was made a tearing sound like an express train. And people was killed and injured.'

'How do you know that?'

'I met old Stokesy on me way here. The city's going frantic. The wardens have been told to say it's gas explosions, but everyone knows it's not.'

'So where do these things come from?' Spot asked. 'I thought after Normandy we were supposed to be winning the war.'

'Stokesy reckons the Allies miscalculated and there was more launch sites than they found.'

'You mean more bombs?' asked Cissy. 'Like the V-1s?'

'Worse,' stated Liz knowledgeably. 'Ones that are so lethal the top brass want it kept secret.'

'Well, I ain't going down in that bloody cellar again,' Cissy said emphatically. 'Bombs or no bombs.'

After Liz had gone the neighbourhood was very quiet, but then the rumours began to spread. A new and more deadly weapon had been fired at London. So deadly, the authorities were trying to cover it up to prevent any panic.

Over the next few days, there were more explosions and terrifying stories of blast waves caused by this new weapon. Molly thought that at least the fear of Ronnie Hook had taken second place to the slowly growing terror of what people were now calling the threat of the V-2.

All the same, Molly was relieved to have Spot around, and the customers took up their old habit of congregating in the shop to discuss the secret weapon that was waging war on London.

'My sister, who lives over the water in South London,' said one customer in a hushed tone, 'has seen the effects of the V-2 rocket first hand. It was like an earthquake and the crater it left was deep, but the blast wave shook buildings for miles around, even cracked people's washbasins.'

'Yes, we heard the noises from here,' Molly said dismally. 'But how many more are to come?'

The answer to this came over the next week, when the rockets spread terror throughout London. The raids weren't as frequent as the V-1s, but the damage done to the sites of impact was much worse.

It was almost two weeks after that first night when Staveley Road became the first V-2 victim that Spot returned one afternoon after a visit to Narrow Street. 'The law has gone,' he told Molly and Cissy, as he burst in at the shop door. 'Cheng said they left one uniformed copper to walk up and down for a couple of days, then slung their hook. Cheng and Li and a couple of our neighbours went upstairs to the flat yesterday and let themselves in with the key I gave them. They've had a good clear-up, love,' he said, pulling Cissy into his arms and plonking a big kiss on her lips. 'The old manor is back in shape again, so we can go home.'

'Thank Gawd for that,' Cissy sighed, and Molly smiled as she gave a rare display of affection and returned Spot's kiss. 'This is the last time I'm gonna let anyone frighten me out of my own home.'

'I take it Cheng and Li haven't seen Ronnie?' Molly asked as she locked the shop door.

'No – and they've all kept a watch. Not a shadow, not a whisper.'

Molly smiled. 'Cissy, are you sure you want to go home?'

Cissy nodded. 'As much as I love it here, Molly, I've got to start living me life again. You and the kids could come too, but I know you feel the same as me. We ain't gonna be ruled by fear.' She walked over to Molly and put her arms around her. 'You've been such a good pal, Molly. Thanks, love.'

There were tears in Molly's eyes as they stood there.

'Don't worry about us, Molly, half the neighbourhood is on the watch. I'd like to see Ronnie and his mate turn up unannounced.'

It was a happy, almost normal meal they all shared that evening, and Molly assured herself that Cissy going home was all for the best. But she was worried nevertheless, for if Ronnie Hook hadn't shown up at the shop, nor challenged the police watch kept at Narrow Street, where was he? Still watching from somewhere in the shadows? Would he find out that Cissy had returned home and might be vulnerable again? Or, as they were all hoping and praying, had he fled the East End at last, putting his freedom before his greed?

Spot sat in the darkened shop with Nibbles at his feet, drawing the smoke of his roll-up deeply and satisfyingly into his lungs.

As he watched, a chink of starlight broke in at the side of the blackout blind. He congratulated himself on having brought the Ronnie Hook issue to a satisfying close. There was a chance – a small one – that Hook would try again at Narrow Street. He wasn't mug enough to discount the possibility. But he had set everything in motion; now the law was gone, he could operate under his own steam. The twenty-four-hour watch on their home would not be attempted by rookie amateurs, but by his pals of the neighbourhood, like Cheng and Li.

The Chinese were a private and independent lot, but dead loyal to their mates. Thank God his old gran had left him with a dowry: the sense to know who his real friends were and to cultivate them. That was true wisdom, that was. Spot had no intention of wasting another day fretting over

Hook; he would drive the cart over tomorrow. They'd be given a right royal welcome when they got home. And Cissy deserved it for all she'd been through.

He rested back on the wooden chair and propped his feet on a sack of spuds. In the darkness, he took out his tobacco and rolled himself another. He blew rings and chuckled to himself and ground the dog-end out under his boot.

Every now and then his hand dropped to soothe the furrowed silky brow of the animal at his side. For the first time in weeks, he felt drowsy and content. He swept on his cap and tugged it down over his eyes to enjoy forty winks.

Then in the distance came a rolling thunder that shook the ground. The chair trembled and the walls shuddered. He felt a shower of dust on his face. The vibration seemed to go on forever and he jumped to his feet, listening to the peculiar echo.

'That bugger was close,' he said aloud and hurried to the back door and slipped the bolts. The first thing he looked for in the night sky was a glow. If a V-2 had fallen south of the river again, it was closer than ever before. Were the rockets heading this way?

Just as his eyes adjusted to the darkness, Nibbles gave a roar of a bark. Spot turned on his heel as the screeching and snapping of teeth alerted him to the shapes in the shadows. One was coming straight for him. The other, almost invisible and yet far larger, was poised by the closet.

When the first blow fell, Spot took it hard on the right side of his face. He rolled back and fell against the wall and just managed to stay on his feet. The second and third blows came in quick succession. And that was when the other shape moved forward.

Spot swallowed the blood that had filled his mouth and barely gasped as something hard and forceful hit the back of his knees.

It was an old trick, he knew, to fell the enemy. And he found to his dismay that the crippling pain in his calves took away any strength he had left in his legs. Protecting himself on the ground was almost impossible. One steel-tipped boot after another sliced into his chest.

The beating went on, while Nibbles did his best to intervene. The growling and hissing was almost uncanny from the depth of his little dog's belly.

Until a boot found its mark and, as Spot sprawled there, his vision clouded by agony, he heard the pitiful screech of his tiny protector.

'You scum,' growled a voice close to him. 'Where's the money?'

Spot rasped in a breath as two large hands grabbed his coat lapels. He could smell the evil on the man's breath and his stomach revolted.

'Don't know what you mean,' he gagged as he fought for breath, the knuckles closing around his throat.

'Last chance,' spat Ronnie Hook, and Spot felt the spittle land on his face. 'Or am I gonna kick it out of you? Or maybe I should find the bitch first and do the same with her as I done to the dog?'

Spot stared into the outline of the face a few inches away

from him. He nodded and gulped. 'All right, I'll tell you. Come closer.'

The man laughed and breathed foulness over Spot's face. Although it was agony, Spot lifted his head as if to whisper his answer, but instead he used every ounce of strength in his short, strong neck.

Chapter Thirty-One

Molly woke with a start. She stayed very still, afraid to move as the now distant – but not too distant – familiar explosion pulsated through the whole building. Where had the V-2 landed this time? Closer, certainly. And the aftershock seemed to be rumbling on, as if it might reach Roper Street. She knew the thought was ludicrous, but even so, she was riveted to the bed.

There were other noises too. What were they? Was it Mr Stokes, rousing everyone in the neighbourhood, alerting them to danger?

She still hadn't managed to climb out of bed when Cissy appeared, standing in her nightdress at the open door that Molly left ajar for the children.

'Molly! Did you hear that?'

Molly pushed back the covers. 'A V-2? Where did it land, I wonder?' she breathed as she put on her dressing gown and slippers.

'This side of the river, I think,' Cissy whispered. 'Close enough to rattle the knobs on the end of me bed.'

'Is Harry asleep?'

'Yes, so are Mark and Evie. They seem to sleep through anything these days.'

'They've had enough practice.' Molly went to the window and peeped out from behind the blinds. 'It's too dark to see anything. Let's go down for Spot.'

'Wait for me, I'll get my coat on.'

A few minutes later, Molly and Cissy were standing at the top of the staircase. Just as Molly took the first step down, there was another noise. Not a rumble or thud, or anything like the tremor that had woken her, but another noise, indistinct and alien.

'Spot?' she called. 'Are you down there?'

Nothing came back, only an unbroken silence.

'Spot!' Cissy cried, squeezing Molly's arm. 'Where are you?'

They waited, listening, the only sound their breathing, until Molly stepped back onto the landing. 'Why isn't he answering?'

'Dunno,' Cissy whispered. 'He might have gone to the lav.'

They waited, staring down the staircase into the pitch-black darkness of the glory hole. After some minutes, Molly declared, 'Something's wrong.'

'Oh, God,' Cissy breathed. 'I can't hear Nibbles either.'

'We'll have to go down and see.'

'But what if it's—'

Molly pushed Cissy towards the kitchen. Silently she went to the drawer. She slid out the rolling pin and, after a moment's careful thought, the carving knife.

'Which one do you want?' she asked Cissy.

Cissy gave a groan. 'Dunno. I've only ever used a knife to cut bread.'

'Me too. But I'd rather have something in me hand than nothing.' She gave the rolling pin to Cissy.

'Do you think it's Ronnie down there,' Cissy said, her voice breaking, 'waiting for us? And what has he done to Spot?' She let out a choked sob.

'Do you want to stay here to find out?' Molly asked in an urgent tone.

'No,' Cissy replied. 'My old fella might need me. Go on, I'll be right behind you.'

Stealing forward, Molly led the way to the landing. She looked quickly over her shoulder and could see Cissy's white, tense face in the darkness. Gripping the carving knife tightly, she gave a nod.

Every stair seemed to creak.

The well of the glory hole was just a black void in front of them. She stopped again, narrowing her eyes and slowing her breath. They shuffled into the shop and looked at Spot's empty chair.

'He ain't here,' Cissy whispered over Molly's shoulder. And then a cold breeze wafted in and Molly's stomach lurched.

'The back door's open.'

'Oh, lord,' said Cissy. 'What we going to do?'

'Look,' said Molly, as her knees went weak as water.

Together they moved stealthily forward, inching carefully towards the yard door. A few feet away, Molly could feel the cool current of air slipping around her bare ankles. There was no sound anywhere; in the dead of night even the river traffic slept. She paused and saw a few inches of gloom stealing in.

'We going out there?' Cissy asked in a faint voice.

'You stay here,' Molly answered. 'If I don't come back, run in and lock the door.'

'You've got to be joking!' Cissy spluttered. 'Where you go, I go.'

They stood again listening until, stepping forward very slowly, they entered the yard. Molly didn't know what she was expecting: perhaps an attack like the ones at the cinema? Would it have been wiser to hide upstairs? But what then? And what had happened to Spot and Nibbles?

Her unspoken thoughts were answered by a choked groan.

'Spot, is that you?' she called, her voice threaded with alarm.

'Spot!' Cissy called and clutched Molly's arm tightly. 'Spot, where are you?'

The unsettling sound was repeated and Molly stepped towards it, her ears and eyes alert to the other noises now: a shuffling and dragging and, perhaps, a stifled sob.

Cissy saw Spot first. Dropping the rolling pin so that it clattered noisily away, she threw herself on him as he rocked to and fro on the ground.

Molly could see very little under the star-filled sky, but

what she could discern was the drooping shoulders and bent head of her friend and protector. In his arms, a glint of white came from the still form he cradled.

'Spot, oh Spot! What happened? Who done this?' Cissy wailed in the darkness.

Molly knelt by her friends. She couldn't see much, but what she could see alarmed her. Spot's face was swollen and ugly, his thick, dark, wiry hair almost standing on end. In his arms was the shaking form of Nibbles, the whites of his tiny eyes wide in fright.

'They done us over,' groaned Spot. 'Was waiting for me.'

'What made you come out here?' shrieked Cissy. 'You've told us enough times not to open the door!'

Spot shook his head silently, a sob escaping as he rocked the tiny dog. 'Poor little bugger. He didn't stand a chance.'

'Is he dead?' asked Cissy breathlessly.

'As good as,' Spot rasped.

Molly looked around. Was anyone lurking in the shadows? 'Spot, we must go in,' she said urgently. With painful slowness, Molly and Cissy helped him to his feet and linked their arms around his waist.

Every time they paused, Molly peered into the darkness. Was someone about to pounce? The knife was in her dressing gown pocket. Would she have time to use it?

At last they entered the glory hole. Molly quickly shut the door and drew the bolts.

'Don't think I'll make them stairs,' Spot said weakly. He sagged against them.

'Course you will,' Cissy insisted. 'You've got a lot of strength in them short legs of yours. Best foot forward, my love.'

It was with many stumbles and much pushing and prodding that they climbed the steep staircase, until with a last effort they dragged Spot onto the landing. Here he collapsed and Molly prised the little dog from his arms.

'Oh, Gawd!' exclaimed Cissy as she turned on the light and the injuries to Spot became clear. He lay prostrate on the floor, out cold. His lips were bloody, and both eyes had sunk under purple, fleshy flaps of skin. But perhaps worst of all, thought Molly, as she comforted a quivering Nibbles, was the blood that saturated his clothes, staining his white shirt crimson and drying into spikes in the matted muddle of his frizzy hair.

The morning light blinded him and there were pains in every joint. Thick and salty blood oozed from the gap in his front teeth.

'It's all right, handsome, one less tooth in your gob only adds to your good looks. Can you sit up?'

Spot opened his sore eyes fully to the sight of four children and his wife all gazing down at him. He tried to smile but both his mouth and his ribcage hurt like the blazes.

'Blimey,' he managed. 'At long last I've got an audience.'

'Did you fight them all off, Uncle Spot?' asked Mark, his dark eyes wide in admiration.

'How many was there?' said Simon from under his thatch of red hair.

'Shut up, you two,' said Susie, pushing the boys aside, and taking Evie's hand, she said severely, 'He might want to go back to sleep again.'

'Don't think so,' returned Spot as Cissy leaned forward to help him sit up. 'How long have I been out?'

'Two days, on and off,' Cissy said with a smile. 'Now, kids, go down to Molly and tell her that Sleeping Beauty has woken.'

'I reckon it was that last kiss you give me,' Spot said when they were alone, and he tried to make himself comfortable in Cissy's large bed. 'What's this on me head?'

'A bandage. And it's got to stay there till you get up.'

'Who says so?'

'I do.'

'In which case, I won't argue.' He grinned through the pain. Then suddenly, as everything flooded back, he asked hoarsely, 'Nibbles?'

'I'm glad to say the little perisher is on the mend.' She drew up a chair and smiled. 'Though I think his ratting days are over.'

'I thought he'd copped it.'

'So did we. But yesterday he perked up. The kids fed him and now he's asleep on the bed with Harry.'

Spot was unable to speak from relief. Suddenly tears filled his eyes. It was painful even to weep.

Cissy leaned forward and thrust her arms around him. 'Oh, my little darling,' she whispered. 'I love you.'

Spot inhaled a short breath, trying to stop his embarrassing emotions. 'Say that again, will you?' he tried to joke. 'I'll write it down and get you to sign it.'

Cissy looked him in his swollen eyes then placed a tender kiss on his bruised mouth. 'That's it,' she said plonking herself back on the chair, 'you've had your five minutes of glory. Now you can tell me what happened.'

Just then, Molly came in. She put her hands to her mouth and stared at him. 'Oh, Spot, you've had us so worried.'

'I'd have woken up quicker if I'd known I was going to get all this fuss,' he said, and Molly smiled sadly.

'How do you feel?'

'I've had better days.'

'What possessed you to go outside in the middle of the night?' Cissy demanded.

'I wanted to see where the V-2 had fallen, but Hook and his mate were waiting,' Spot explained remorsefully. 'I calculated he would try at Narrow Street again, not here. I had it all set up with Cheng and Li. We was gonna take it in turns watching – the whole neighbourhood was in on it.'

'You're sure it was Ronnie Hook?' Molly asked.

Spot nodded. 'I'm sure.' He didn't want to frighten them by telling them what Hook had threatened.

'So there's no doubt?' Molly said and glanced at Cissy. 'No doubt at all?'

Spot stared at them the best he could through his puffy eyes. 'It was Hook and his mate all right.'

'Do you remember what happened?' Cissy asked with a frown. 'I mean, what made them stop bashing the daylights out of you?'

Spot had never admitted his long-kept secret to anyone, and he wasn't about to do so now. Not if he could help it. If Cissy knew where he'd picked up his bad habit, she was certain to think less of him. He wasn't proud of his misspent youth. Certainly not of the gang he'd got mixed up with before going straight. But if he hadn't learned a few tricks of the trade then Hook wouldn't have left any of them alive.

'Dunno,' Spot lied. He put up a hand to his bandage. 'Me head's hurting. P'raps I will have forty winks more.'

'You can kip when you've told us the truth,' Cissy insisted, and nodding to Molly she added, 'Show him the evidence.'

Molly reached into her overall pocket and brought out a brown paper bag. Spot was trying to get his brains together as she carefully opened it. He had a bad feeling. When she came to stand beside him and showed him the contents, he knew it was all over.

He stared at his bloodied cap, now dyed a deep crimson red, and the blood-spattered, viciously sharp points of the razors sewn into the peak. 'Ah,' he said and sank back against the pillow.

'Is that all you've got to say for yourself?' demanded Cissy.

Spot hung his head. Even that movement was painful. 'I didn't have no choice,' he murmured.

'Do you realize what damage you could do to a person – or persons – with them razors?'

Spot daren't look at his wife.

'Well,' said Molly, 'you'd better read this.'

Once again he watched as she put down the brown bag and reached into the other pocket. She took out a rolled newspaper. With deliberately slow strokes, she placed it on the bedcover in front of him. 'Can you read it or shall I do the honours?' asked Cissy.

Spot's eyes went straight to the headline: NOTORIOUS ESCAPEE MURDERER ARRESTED BY STEPNEY POLICE. He looked up at Cissy, his jaw falling painfully open.

'"Ronnie Hook, a south London gangster and murderer of a prison guard, together with another escapee from prison,"' read Cissy, swiping the newspaper from the bed, '"were found in a warehouse last night, a trail of blood leading the police to their hideout. Hook had been seriously injured and was taken to hospital, while the other man was returned to custody. It is thought Hook fell foul of another gang member who used the unprincipled slasher method to fell his opponent. This practice is frowned on as a vicious form of fighting by street thugs and gangs. Hook was blinded in the fracas. A detective constable working on the case was also detained on charges of collusion with criminal elements in order to profit from stolen goods."' Cissy put down the newspaper. 'That was Longman. I always knew he was up to no good.'

'You were right all along, Cissy,' Molly agreed. 'I should have listened to you in the beginning.'

'So, what have you to say for yourself, Horace Fryer?' Cissy demanded.

'I didn't mean to blind him. I'm sorry, but it was him or us.'

Cissy jumped from her seat and once again threw her arms around her husband. 'Oh, Spot. We'd have all been up a gum tree if it wasn't for you.' He was smothered in kisses and declarations of love once more.

Molly took his hand and said with a rueful smile, 'Spot, you are a dark horse.'

He grinned – also painfully. 'I'm just a little squirt, I have to have something up me sleeve. A razor headbutt was me only defence.'

'In your cap, you mean,' said Cissy, taking his face between her hands. 'I'm so proud of you.'

'Are you?' he asked bewilderedly. 'Even though I'm one of them vicious thugs they write about?'

'Yes,' teased Cissy, 'and you should have told me you what you were before I married you. But seeing as you're now my hero, I ain't complaining.'

Spot felt the salty tears run down his cheeks. As Cissy kissed them away, he looked up into Molly's soft, sweet face. He hoped she didn't think badly of him. But his chequered past was a long time ago, when he was just an ignorant kid.

He'd changed now and had only worn the razor cap at nights when he kept watch in the shop. Though with the news today, it did look as though he might never have cause to wear it again.

BOOK FOUR

Chapter Thirty-Two

Sidcup, a month later

It was a cold but clear October morning when Molly sat in Lyn's garden with her father. There was no wheelchair this time. Bill was using his stick and had triumphed in the pipe war, Molly realized, as he puffed away in the clear morning air.

Each day for the past week they had followed a pattern: breakfast with the family and then a short walk down the pretty lane that ran beside the house; Bill's exercise for the day. Then a rest in the garden before lunch, while the four children, Mark, Evie, George and Elizabeth, went to play in what was still called a nursery, but was in fact the upper floor of Lyn's vast attic room, furnished with just about every conceivable toy, books, paints, crayons and board games.

This morning Molly and her father were both wrapped up in scarves, gloves and hats, despite the bright winter sunshine. Molly had been pleasantly surprised over her stay: Lyn and Oscar had made welcoming hosts and had not brought any pressure to bear on her regarding Mark and Evie. It was as if, with the end of the war in sight, so too had come a truce between Molly and her sister.

'And what about you, Molly?' Bill asked, as Molly inhaled the familiar pipe tobacco that seemed to blend perfectly with the woodsmoke of the local neighbourhood chimneys. 'You've been rather quiet. Everything all right with you and your sister?'

Molly smiled wistfully. 'We seem good now, Dad. I think Lyn understands that Mark and Evie are in my life for keeps.'

He nodded slowly. 'Think she wanted you all here for a bit to make things up. When you wrote about Andy, it came as a shock.'

'It shouldn't have,' Molly said quickly. 'Lyn was always going on about what would happen if he—' She stopped and looked down at her woollen mittens, pulling a thread absently. 'If he didn't come home.'

'Mostly out of concern for you, love.'

'I know that. But she was right, in a way.'

'You ain't having second thoughts, are you?' he asked in surprise. 'You don't want to farm those kids out?'

Molly shook her head firmly. 'Absolutely not, Dad. I just meant – well, I'm a bit at twos and threes. For once in my life it's not the business – the store – that I'm thinking of. It's Mark and Evie. Lyn said they would be a responsibility if – if they were orphaned –' she raised her hands in a gesture of confusion – 'and that's true. But much more than I ever thought. I feel – well, that's the trouble – I *feel* almost too much. It's as if I've come to a mental roadblock. I can't make any decisions. Does that make sense?'

Bill took the pipe from his mouth. 'You mean, love, that something is clouding your judgement?'

'I suppose, yes.'

'You are a bit new at this family lark.'

Molly searched her father's gaze. 'But I've had the children for almost four years! We've been through thick and thin, and now, just when peace is within reach, except for these blessed V–2s, I feel at a complete loss as to what to do for the best.'

For a moment all was quiet, until Bill put his hand on hers. 'You know there's a home here for you in Sidcup, don't you? Your sister would jump at the chance to have you close. Matter of fact, so would I.'

'Does that mean you've decided not to come back to the store, Dad?' Molly felt the quickening of her pulse. If her father said he was eager to come home, she'd move heaven and earth to make it happen. And all decisions would be made for her. She could reopen the shop, begin life again as she had many times before – this time with the children to care for and her father back to the life that he loved in the East End. But as she met his gaze, something in his eyes told her this was not to be.

'Molly, love, one reason I wanted to talk to you, face to face like. You see, I'm getting older now. Nearly seventy. And me leg and hip, they ain't never going to be any better. I'm not likely to be trotting up steep flights of stairs like I did in the old days. Or chasing about serving customers. It was just a dream, I think – me going back to Roper Street. A dream I got you to dream too, to make it seem real.'

Molly felt the tears rush to her eyes. She understood that her beloved father was no longer the bouncy, active, business-minded man who had been at her side since she was little. He had crossed the bridge to retirement, to a comfortable, even luxurious existence, and who could blame him? Lyn had been right again. The country life had been healing and he had accepted its advantages with grace and patience. Now she must accept her own changing role with the same fortitude and bravery.

'I'm glad we had this talk, Dad. Thanks for being up front.'

'You'll never be on your own, girl. I'll be with you and them kids in thought, wherever you go. Whatever you do.'

'I know that.' She leaned across and kissed him.

A voice from the house called their names and Bill raised a shaggy grey eyebrow under his woollen hat. 'Lunch is ready. Cold meat and savouries today, I'll bet.'

Molly laughed. 'Savouries, eh? Something like bubble and squeak?'

Her father chuckled as she helped him to his feet. 'Something like that. With brass knobs on.'

Together they walked slowly across the green lawn scattered with a few rusty leaves. The delicious smell of cooking wafted from the dining room and Lyn stood at the opened glass doors of the elegant country house. Molly smiled and waved.

The tall, blonde, fashionably dressed woman wearing high heels waved back. Molly was glad she had spent this time with her family; she had a clearer understanding of herself and of them, and most importantly of the life that she wanted to pursue with Mark and Evie.

She would enjoy the next few days in Sidcup. But she couldn't wait to be home now. For home, she thought warmly, really is where the heart is.

'Is that an 'orse?' Evie asked as she pressed her nose against the coach window. Her golden curls fell over her shoulders as she pointed excitedly to every farm animal she saw in the fields.

'No, silly, it's a bull, cos it's got horns,' Mark told his sister, sitting on the edge of the seat beside her. Molly felt proud of the children, who had won the affection of everyone they had met at Lyn's. George and Elizabeth had remembered the fun they had had at Jean's on the day Andy had come home, and their friendship had deepened throughout the recent half-term holiday.

Now they were on their way back to Poplar and Molly was pleased she had refused Oscar's offer to drive them home. Privately, she had wanted to enjoy the peace of the countryside without having to make polite conversation with her brother-in-law. As conscientious a host as Oscar had been, Molly was eager to breathe freedom once again. Lyn's house was delightful and they had been spoiled throughout their stay, but now that she had talked to her dad, she felt she could start to think more clearly about the future.

'Are we gonna live in the country?' Evie asked, turning to Molly who sat on the next seat.

'Would you like to?' Molly enquired.

'Don't know,' said Evie thoughtfully. 'Could Simon and Susie come too?'

'Course not,' interrupted Mark. 'They live in Roper Street like us.'

'Will Uncle Dennis be at the coach station to meet us?' Evie wanted to know. 'We ain't got to walk all the way home, have we?'

Molly laughed as she ran her fingers through Evie's silky hair. 'Yes, he'll be there. I told him in my letter the coach arrives at half past two.'

'I wish it was our dad meeting us,' Mark said solemnly. 'He's been away a long time, ain't he?'

Molly nodded. 'Yes, he has, Mark.'

Molly knew the day would come when she had to tell them the truth. But that day wasn't here yet, not yet. She prayed she would find the right words, for they were bright and perceptive children. Like all the East End youngsters, they were uniquely aware of war and the effect it had on their lives. Mark, at nine, was tall and dark like his father; Evie at just over seven must take after Stella, with her long blonde curls and blue eyes. Molly often wondered what went on in their little heads.

For the rest of the journey, Molly continued to enjoy the countryside, pointing out the shapes of the wooded hills in the distance, the small robins and sparrows that sang in the hedgerows and rabbits eating in the fields. Once Mark caught sight of a bushy-tailed red dog and Molly explained it was a fox. There were so many things the children hadn't seen before: small villages with thatched cottages and front gardens full of roses still blooming in winter. Handwritten signs that offered dairy milk, cheese and fresh farm eggs for sale. There was little sign of destruction, either. On every corner in the East End, houses had been demolished or bricked up. Huge craters had been left by the V-1s and V-2s.

Here there were no such sights as the coach bore them down the narrow lanes, in and out of sprawling green meadows, past quaint hamlets and tranquil farms. Farmers drove tractors carrying baled hay and dogs ran freely in their mucky yards. Apart from Nibbles, Evie and Mark had never really been introduced to dogs or even cats throughout their childhood, Molly reflected, for pets were not approved of in war-torn London.

Molly was reminded of her journey to Romford and she thought then of the kind captain, Roger, and of the Denhams, and wondered how they all were. She hadn't written in months and had received no word from either. If only Andy had survived to make that trip to Wales . . .

Molly sighed and, with an effort, returned her attention to the present as the scenery began to change. The fields grew fewer and instead there were houses and factories. Large estates were traversed by busy lorries, cars and bicycles.

Eventually, the suburbs of London swallowed them. To Molly's delight the children grew even more excited. They had been brought up by the river, in the smoke and the noise and clatter. This was their home, familiar and safe, despite the evidence of war in almost every street.

At last the coach pulled into Poplar and their journey was

at an end. Molly took the children's hands and they filed off the big vehicle and stood, Molly thought achingly, on the very spot where she had stood with Andy, that day he'd left to join his ship.

Their lives, it seemed to her as she stood in the cold day, had been a series of opening and closing doors. And now she was entering – or was she passing through? – another.

'Molly! Molly!' Dennis was hurrying towards them. Evie and Mark ran into his arms. Molly joined them and laughed as Mark and Evie tried to tell him every last detail of their holiday in Sidcup.

'Listen, kids,' he said as he recovered Molly's small suitcase from the driver, 'I've borrowed Mr Stokes's van for the day. Petrol's a bit easier to get now. But I've something to tell you before we go home.'

Molly looked into Dennis's concerned face. His ginger hair was thinner now and his eyes a little more serious. As he stood there, he said quietly. 'No other way to say it. A V-2 dropped in the next road. It took out half the houses and I'm afraid the blast caught the store.'

Chapter Thirty-Three

And so began their journey back to Roper Street in Mr Stokes's small van. Mark and Evie sat in the back and Molly, beside Dennis, was trying to recover from the shock. The store had been caught in the V-2 blast wave, were the words going through her mind. Dennis had not elaborated, except to say that he was sorry to be the bearer of bad news and that Mr Stokes was waiting to meet them.

Molly couldn't bring herself to voice the only question she wanted to ask. Could she still call number one Roper Street home?

When Dennis turned the van into West Ferry Road, Molly's stomach turned over. She felt quite sick and light-headed and, seeming to sense this, Dennis took his hand from the gearstick and put it fleetingly over hers.

'Chin up, love,' he said with a encouraging smile. 'What's to be will be, remember that.'

Molly nodded, but the tears were very close. She already

knew inside that the very worst must have happened, or Dennis would have said more. With the certainty of this thought came a quiet calm. *The very worst hadn't happened.* If she hadn't accepted Lyn's invitation to stay at Sidcup, she and the children might very well have been at home when the V-2 fell. Instead, they were all alive and well.

Dennis slowly drew the van to a halt. 'We'll have to walk through the alley. Roper Street's blocked off.'

Molly held the children's hands tightly as Dennis led the way along the narrow lane, still cluttered with debris. Over the top of the high brick wall, Molly could just see the outline of the roofs of the houses in Howeth Street. Some were like blackened skeletons, rafters poking up to the sky. Thin trails of black smoke wound between them and that awful smell of cordite had returned. Even the gulls were keeping their distance. Dust particles flew everywhere. She could hear the noise of machinery and guessed the demolition work had begun.

They passed beside the bicycle factory, which was already a victim to previous raids. To Molly's surprise, the shed that covered the cellar they all hated so much was still standing. But when they came to Roper Street and turned left, they all stopped.

Mr Stokes was standing outside what was left of Swift's General Stores, his tin helmet pushed back from his forehead as he talked to another man. They were looking at the blackened shop window, which, incredibly, was still intact. Around it, Molly saw three large timber supports, all driven into the brickwork to keep the structure safe. The shop sign had been removed to reveal a large crack in the brickwork that wound its way like a snake through the rest of the building. Her eyes slowly lifted to the roof, most of which was missing. Every so often black smoke rose in tiny drifts from the shattered interior.

Dennis took her arm. 'You all right, love?'

She nodded and tried to swallow. 'When did it happen?'

'Two nights ago. We was all thrown out of bed. It was the biggest blast I've ever heard. Seemed to go on forever.'

'Have you any damage?' Molly asked, realizing that the store might not have been the only building to suffer.

'Quite a few tiles off the roof and the chimney's gone for a burton. Lucky, really. But Jean's been right off colour thinking of you. Didn't know whether to phone your sister or wait till you got home.'

Molly stared at the blackened bricks that stood like a sentry, as if Swift's Store had stood there for so long, it refused to give up.

'That's the town surveyor,' Dennis told her. 'Just seeing if anything can be done.'

Molly watched the man in a suit talking to Mr Stokes. Their expressions told her that, of course, very little could be done. Other than to demolish what remained of their home.

After a few minutes Mr Stokes walked over. 'I'm so sorry, Molly, gel. I thought Swift's Stores was invincible. You got through most of this bloody war and just when it's almost over, one of them buggers landed in the next street.'

'Were there many casualties?' Molly asked, managing to find her voice.

'No mortalities,' Mr Stokes explained. 'Most of them houses had been evacuated because of the damage done to them after Christmas last year. Good job too, as when one of those V-2s lands you ain't got much chance. Lucky you was away, ducks.'

'Still, everything we owned was in there. Everything!'

'I'll see if I can salvage anything when the barriers are removed,' Dennis said after Mr Stokes had rejoined the surveyor. 'There wasn't a bloody thing we could do except watch the firemen put out the fires. The place was swimming in water and thick mud. So I don't hold out much hope, love.'

Molly looked down at the children, who had been too frightened to speak. Mark was close to tears. 'Come here, my loves,' she comforted, bending down and holding them tight. 'Mr Stokes said how lucky we are not to have been in there when the bomb dropped.'

'Will the firemen put it together again?' Mark looked at her with his big, sombre dark eyes.

'We'll have to see.'

'Where we gonna live?' Evie croaked, pushing her face into Molly's shoulder.

'With your old pals the Turners,' said Dennis chirpily, lifting her into his arms. 'I've got something tucked away that might bring a smile to your faces. Count yer blessings, that's what I say.'

Molly slid her hand around Mark's shoulders as they walked slowly round the hole in the road that had been the very first of many hundreds of holes scattered about the East

End. She had managed to hide the tears that smarted at the corners of her eyes. Dennis meant well and was trying to help, but she knew it was going to be very difficult to count those blessings, as most of them had seemed wrapped up in the life they had led at number one Roper Street.

Jean hugged Molly tightly. 'Oh, ducks, I'm so sorry. Your lovely shop and home, all gone up in smoke.'

Molly nodded as she was embraced tightly. She didn't trust herself to speak and stood in the hall silently as Jean, with many fond hugs and kisses, ushered the children into the front room where Susie and Simon were playing. When she returned, once again she held Molly close.

'We didn't know how to break it to you,' she said softly as she looked into Molly's tense face. 'Thought it best not to phone Lyn's as there wasn't nothing you could do. And you deserved a good holiday, love, after all you've been through.'

Molly managed a trembling smile. 'Dennis said to count my blessings and I'm trying to. But oh, Jean, what am I going to do? We haven't a stitch of clothing between us.'

'That's easily remedied. You can borrow from us till we go to the market and kit you all out. Did you take your ration books and identity papers with you?'

'Yes,' Molly replied. 'They're safe in our suitcase.'

'And cash? Did you have any in the till?'

Molly closed her eyes in dismay. 'No, but there was a bit put away upstairs under the floorboards. Some of it was Dad's savings and a few extra pounds. I was going to give it back to him when he came home.' She gave a little choke. 'But he's decided to stay at Lyn's – and thank God he has after what's happened.'

'Well, things might not be as bad as you think,' said Jean, taking her coat. 'Your dad's obviously settled and this might be a new start for you and the kids.'

'But we've got nowhere to live.'

'Yes, you have, you're staying here with us. We'll go down the council on Monday and put in for a relocation. You'll qualify immediately as you have the children, and they're making special allowances for businesses, I heard.'

'They can't give me back my stock, though.'

'No, I'm afraid not,' said Jean sympathetically. 'But you will have a roof over your head and the children's, and though it might not be exactly what you want at first, it'll be a stepping stone in the right direction.'

'Jean, you're always a breath of fresh air. And I should do what Dennis told me, count my blessings.'

'That's easier said than done when your whole life has been uprooted overnight.'

Molly felt a shudder inside her and at last the tears escaped from her eyes. She heard the laughter of the children playing in the front room and smiled despite her distress. 'They sound happy enough,' she mumbled, wiping her wet cheeks. 'I should follow their example, big softie that I am.'

'You spent all your life at the store,' Jean commiserated, patting her arm. 'And then you and Ted took over the business. No wonder you're upset.'

Molly gulped down a sob. 'It was just the shock of seeing—'

'I know. Are you ready for another?'

Molly blew her nose and grinned. 'After today, I hope it ain't a bad one. I don't want to end up bawling my eyes out.'

'You might, it depends. Follow me.'

Molly heaved a sigh, her mind spinning around in a daze. What kind of home would she and the children be allowed? Would it be far from the East End? How would they settle in a new district? A new school? Did she have enough strength to make all these enormous changes and, most of all, see to it that Mark and Evie were happy? After all they had been through, the responsibility of their care now seemed even more daunting.

'Right, here we are,' Jean said, taking her hand and drawing her to the kitchen window. 'There's your surprise. I hope you like it.'

Molly blinked the wetness from her eyes. There were three figures standing in a group just beyond the patch of scrubby grass in the yard. Dennis was lighting the cigarettes of the other two, cupping the match in his hand. The tall, thin man with a short haircut, wearing a dark-blue uniform, bent towards his outstretched arm and sucked in a breath, causing a brief red glow at the end of the cigarette. Molly gasped in confusion. 'Bruce?' she murmured incredulously. 'That's Bruce Jefferson, isn't it?'

Jean nodded, her red lipstick emphasizing her wide smile and twinkling eyes. 'And of course, the man standing with his back to us is someone a little more familiar.'

Molly squinted her eyes, moving closer to the window. When the answer came to her, she felt as though she was dreaming, or perhaps it was the after-effects of seeing the ravaged store. 'But it can't be,' she whispered, gripping the sink to steady herself. 'It's impossible!'

'No,' Jean said quietly, 'not impossible.'

'But the *Avenge* went down – Bruce said—'

'It sank all right,' interrupted Jean, sliding her arm around Molly's waist. 'But Andy survived and was washed up on the beach. He was picked up by German snipers who carted him all the way across the countryside as a prisoner of war. They were heading for Nancy, a town on the Siegfried Line, but unknown to them, the town was liberated. In September an American combat unit found them.'

Molly couldn't take her eyes from the shape of the man she knew so well. Thinner and just a little stooped, Andy slowly moved to light his cigarette. Like Bruce he wore his naval uniform, and also like Bruce, his dark hair was cropped, though nothing could change the essence of the man she had fallen in love with and thought she had lost.

'Simon and Susie have instructions to keep your two occupied for a bit. Give you a chance to—' Jean began to laugh slowly. 'Just look at you! Yes, it is him, love. It is your Andy. Now go on, get out of that kitchen door. And give him the homecoming he deserves.'

Molly felt Jean push her gently forward. Her legs were ready to fold at the knees and her heart – it might easily jump right out of her body if there wasn't muscle and bone to prevent it. But when she took a step into the yard and

Andy turned round to look at her, she had wings on her heels.

Wings that flew her into the arms of the man she loved and where home truly was. The only home she had ever really needed.

Chapter Thirty-Four

It was Christmas Day 1944, and Molly, dressed in a pale-lilac suit she had bought from the market, looked around the gaily furnished room that she and Cissy had decorated with the children last week. Chinese lanterns hung side by side with handmade paper chains; gold, red and green drapes bearing fiery dragons hung from the windows adorned with sprigs of holly, overlooking Narrow Street.

The Christmas tree, the first the children had ever enjoyed, was centre stage in the vast room, with presents wrapped beneath it for the after-dinner celebrations. Attempting one last addition to the green branches, Andy, his tall frame attired in a pressed white shirt and tie and casual dark trousers, tied a red ribbon to a small glass tree light. Beside him Mark, Evie and Harry, in their dressing gowns, pressed close to the gifts, eager to see inside. Nibbles sat watching, his nose wet and twitching, regarding the proceedings with a tolerant air.

'What's this one say, Dad?' Mark asked his father. 'Can't read all them funny squiggles.'

Andy grinned as he ruffled his son's thick dark hair. 'You'll have to ask Uncle Spot. Ain't got me diploma in Chinese yet.'

'Where's mine, Dad?' demanded Evie, pushing her brother aside and stabbing a finger into her father's thigh. 'What's in that one?'

'You'll have to wait and see,' Andy laughed, swinging her up in the air and back down again.

Harry lifted his arms and Andy repeated the movement, landing him carefully on his small feet. For a fraction of a second, Molly's eyes travelled to meet the dark, glimmering gaze turned towards her. As usual, her heart raced and a wonderful feeling of closeness without words filled her. Her handsome, dark-haired Andy, and bright-eyed Mark and golden-haired Evie, her family, the people she loved most in all the world, here together at Christmas only six weeks after Andy had been repatriated.

Her own Christmas miracle. For who would have thought, that day when she had returned to discover the shop in ruins, that life could present her and the children with a gift far more precious than bricks and mortar?

The fact that they didn't have a home, and had been staying with Cissy and Spot for the last few weeks, didn't seem to be of any significance now. To have friends like Jean and Dennis who had looked after them all so well for the first fortnight after Andy's return, and Cissy and Spot who had made them so welcome at the Narrow Street flat until the council found them a house, was more precious than gold.

And though Molly missed the store and the rooms above, she had her memories to treasure.

It was, she understood, the presence of loved ones, healthy and happy, in her life, that brought completeness. She had said her goodbyes to Ted and Emily the day they left Roper Street, as nature must have intended.

And she had not looked back since. Why should she? The love that filled her would take her on to unknown horizons, something she had never had the courage for before. Her dad would be happy with Lyn, for he too had his family around him and was living the life he so richly deserved.

'My old gran used to make a new lantern for every Christmas.' Spot broke into her thoughts as he placed tiny lights on the expansive table, already laid with paper flowers that the children had made. Looking fitter than ever and sporting a multicoloured waistcoat and red bow tie, he continued, 'Then she'd string them up at the Chinese New Year, sometime between January and February, and make us all duck and dumplings, like Cissy's cooking today.'

'I don't think I've ever tasted duck,' Molly said, smiling. 'It smells delicious.'

'You don't see 'em around much, but a cousin's cousin managed to coax a couple into his garden.' He looked at Molly with his crossed eyes and straight face. Suddenly they burst into laughter.

'Oh, Spot, this is a wonderful Christmas!'

'Course it is, your other half is home.'

'I still can't believe it.'

'Here, have one of these to celebrate.' He crooked his finger and led her over to the sideboard. An oriental jug and tiny glasses were placed on a gilded tin tray. 'Knock it back slowly,' he warned.

Molly sipped and gasped. 'What is it?'

'Rice wine.'

'Also made by your gran?'

Spot grinned. 'How did you guess? Here, take a glass to the wandering hero and send the kids over to me. I've got a nice bottle of fizz in the kitchen for them.'

'Tell Cissy I'll be in to help her.' Molly took the two glasses and walked slowly across the room.

'Is that for me?' Evie asked, licking her lips.

'No, Curly Top, for your dad. There's fizzy in the kitchen for you.'

In the blink of an eye the three children were gone and Molly gave Andy the miniature glass. 'Happy Christmas, darling.'

He drew her close and whispered, 'I love you.' Kissing her softly, he raised an eyebrow. 'What's this you're giving me?'

'Spot says it's his gran's rice wine.'

Andy laughed, his white teeth gleaming in his lovely smile. 'I know what to expect, then.'

They lifted their glass and drank, and Molly felt the world whirl around her. She was in the arms of the man she adored, and this strange and wonderful sort of Christmas made up of Cissy's world, a mixture of cultures and colours and home-spun hospitality, felt like heaven.

They kissed again, listening to the laughter echoing from

the kitchen and drifting out onto Narrow Street through the open window.

Molly knew there would be many more Christmases ahead, full of the wonders of this new, brave world that was just around the corner. A war almost over, nations ready to pick up the pieces after the futility of conflict, returning the prospect of peace to all their lives once more.

And her family ... the best Christmas gift of all.

CAROL RIVERS

A PROMISE
BETWEEN FRIENDS

1953: Pretty, ambitious, 19-year-old Ruby Payne
and her lifelong friend Kath Rigler are eager
to enjoy their post-war independence.

Moving away from home to a flat in the East End of
London is a chance to break free for them both: Kath
from her abusive family and Ruby from the unhappy
memories of her brother's suicide two years before.

Ruby finds work immediately at a fashionable new dog
grooming parlour close to the city. Kath isn't quite so
lucky and has to make do with her tough factory job,
leaning more and more on Ruby for emotional support.

But then Ruby meets handsome, charming Nick
Brandon – and ignores the warnings from those around
her that he is trouble. Ruby wants a glamorous life –
but it will come at a high cost for her and Kath.

AVAILABLE NOW IN PAPERBACK AND EBOOK

**SIMON &
SCHUSTER**

CAROL RIVERS

A WARTIME CHRISTMAS

Can love find a way this Christmas?

Christmas 1941, Isle of Dogs. The little community on Slater Street has fought valiantly to keep their spirits up through the long nights of the Blitz. Though her husband, Alan, has been called up to serve his country, Kay Lewis is determined to give her young son as merry a Christmas as any other.

But when a strange woman and her son arrive on her doorstep, making terrible accusations, Kay's world is shaken to the core. Could Alan really have been leading a double life without her realising?

When Alan is reported missing in action, Kay has no way of discovering the truth. She will have some difficult decisions to make if she is to protect her family and keep her faith in the man she thought she knew.

AVAILABLE NOW IN PAPERBACK AND EBOOK

**SIMON &
SCHUSTER**